'I really don't think this is a good idea, Elena.'

'Too bad, then, that I do.' She stood on her tiptoes and brushed a kiss across his mouth. 'That's only the second kiss I've ever had,' she whispered against his lips. 'The first was two nights ago, when you held me in your arms.'

He closed his eyes. He was the only man who had ever kissed her? Didn't she realise how much she was giving him, offering him freely? Didn't she know how hurt she might be afterwards? No matter what she said or promised now. She was young. Inexperienced. Innocent.

He forced his eyes open, wrapped his hands around hers and attempted to draw them away for her. 'I don't want to hurt you, Elena.'

'You won't.'

'You don't know that. You *can't* know that. Because you've never done this before.'

'And when am I going to get a chance to do it, Khalil?' she asked, her honest gaze clashing with his. 'I was going to give myself to a man I barely knew for the sake of my country. That possibility has been taken away from me now. *You've* taken it away from me, and I think it's only fair you offer me something in return. You owe me a wedding night.'

RIVALS TO THE CROWN OF KADAR

Ruthless in battle, ruthless in love...

Two powerful men locked in a struggle
to rule the country of their birth...

One a desert prince, once banished and shamed,
the other a royal playboy, cutting a swathe
through the beautiful women of Europe.

Tortured by their memories of the past, these
bitter enemies will use any means necessary to win...
But neither expects the women who will
change the course of their revenge!

Read Khalil's story in
CAPTURED BY THE SHEIKH
September 2014

Read Aziz's story in
COMMANDED BY THE SHEIKH
October 2014

CAPTURED
BY THE SHEIKH

BY
KATE HEWITT

Published in Great Britain 2014
by Mills & Boon, an imprint of Harlequin (UK) Limited,
Eton House, 18-24 Paradise Road, Richmond, Surrey, TW9 1SR

© 2014 Kate Hewitt

ISBN: 978-0-263-24994-1

Harlequin (UK) Limited's policy is to use papers that are natural, renewable and recyclable products and made from wood grown in sustainable forests. The logging and manufacturing processes conform to the legal environmental regulations of the country of origin.

Printed and bound in Spain
by Blackprint CPI, Barcelona

Kate Hewitt discovered her first Mills & Boon® romance on a trip to England when she was thirteen, and she's continued to read them ever since. She wrote her first story at the age of five, simply because her older brother had written one and she thought she could do it too. That story was one sentence long—fortunately they've become a bit more detailed as she's grown older. She has written plays, short stories and magazine serials for many years, but writing romance remains her first love. Besides writing, she enjoys reading, travelling and learning to knit.

After marrying the man of her dreams—her older brother's childhood friend—she lived in England for six years, and now resides in Connecticut with her husband, her three young children, and the possibility of one day getting a dog.

Kate loves to hear from readers—you can contact her through her website: www.kate-hewitt.com

Recent titles by the same author:

A QUEEN FOR THE TAKING?
  (The Diomedi Heirs)
THE PRINCE SHE NEVER KNEW
  (The Diomedi Heirs)
HIS BRAND OF PASSION
  (The Bryants: Powerful & Proud)
IN THE HEAT OF THE SPOTLIGHT
  (The Bryants: Powerful & Proud)

**Did you know these are also available as eBooks?
Visit www.millsandboon.co.uk**

CHAPTER ONE

'Something's wrong—'

Elena Karras, Queen of Thallia, had barely registered the voice of the royal steward behind her when a man in a dark suit, his face harsh-looking and his expression inscrutable, met her at the bottom of the steps that led from the royal jet to this bleak stretch of desert.

'Queen Elena. Welcome to Kadar.'

'Thank you.'

He bowed and then indicated one of three armoured SUVs waiting by the airstrip. 'Please accompany us to our destination,' he said, his voice clipped yet courteous. He stepped aside so she could move forward, and Elena threw back her shoulders and lifted her chin as she walked towards the waiting cars.

She hadn't expected fanfare upon her arrival to marry Sheikh Aziz al Bakir, but she supposed she'd thought she'd have a little more than a few security guards and blacked-out cars.

Then she reminded herself that Sheikh Aziz wanted to keep her arrival quiet, because of the instability within Kadar. Ever since he'd taken the throne just over a month ago there had been, according to Aziz, some minor insurgent activity. At their last meeting, he'd assured her it was taken care of, but she supposed a few security measures were a necessary precaution.

Just like the Sheikh, she needed this marriage to succeed. She barely knew the man, had only met him a few times, but she needed a husband just as he needed a wife.

Desperately.

'This way, Your Highness.'

The man who'd first greeted her had been walking beside her from the airstrip to the SUV, the desert endlessly dark all around them, the night-time air possessing a decided chill. He opened the door of the vehicle and Elena tipped her head up to the inky sky, gazing at the countless stars glittering so coldly above them.

'*Queen Elena.*'

She stiffened at the sound of the panicked voice, recognising it as that of the steward from the Kadaran royal jet. The man's earlier words belatedly registered: *something's wrong.*

She started to turn and felt a hand press into the small of her back, staying her.

'Get in the car, Your Highness.'

An icy sweat broke out between her shoulder blades. The man's voice was low and grim with purpose—not the way he'd sounded earlier, with his clipped yet courteous welcome. And she knew, with a sickening certainty, that she did not want to get in that car.

'Just a moment,' she murmured, and reached down to adjust her shoe, buy a few seconds. Her mind buzzed with panic, static she silenced by sheer force of will. She needed to *think.* Somehow something had gone wrong. Aziz's people hadn't met her as expected. This stranger had and, whoever he was, she knew she needed to get away from him. To plan an escape—and in the next few seconds.

She felt a cold sense of purpose come over her, clearing her mind even as she fought a feeling of unreality. *This was happening. Again, the worst was happening.*

She knew all about dangerous situations. She knew what it felt like to stare death in the face—and survive.

And she knew, if she got in the car, escape would become no more than a remote possibility.

She fiddled with her shoe, her mind racing. If she kicked off her heels she could sprint back to the jet. The steward was obviously loyal to Aziz; if they managed to close the door before this man came after her...

It was a better option than running into the dark desert. It was her only option.

'Your Highness.' Impatience sharpened the man's voice. His hand pressed insistently against her back. Taking a deep breath, Elena kicked off her heels and ran.

The wind streamed past her and whipped sand into her face as she streaked towards the jet. She heard a sound behind her and then a firm hand came round her waist, lifting her clear off the ground.

Even then she fought. She kicked at the solid form behind her; the man's body now felt like a stone wall. She bent forward, baring her teeth, trying to find some exposed skin to bite, anything to gain her freedom.

Her heel connected with the man's kneecap and she kicked again, harder, then hooked her leg around his and kicked the back of his knee so the man's leg buckled. They both fell to the ground.

The fall winded her but she was up within seconds, scrambling on the sand. The man sprang forward and covered her with his body, effectively trapping her under him.

'I admire your courage, Your Highness,' he said in her ear, his voice a husky murmur. 'As well as your tenacity. But I'm afraid both are misplaced.'

Elena blinked through the sand that stung her eyes and clung to her cheeks. The jet was still a hundred yards away. How far had she managed to run? Ten feet? Twenty?

The man flipped her over so she was on her back, his arms braced on either side of her head. She gazed up at him, her heart thudding against her ribs, her breath coming in little pants. He was poised above her like a panther, his eyes the bewitching amber of a cat's, his face all chiselled planes and harsh angles. Elena could feel his heat, sense his strength. This man radiated power. Authority. *Danger*.

'You would never have made it back to the plane,' he told her, his voice treacherously soft. 'And, even if you had, the men on it are loyal to me.'

'My guards—'

'Bribed.'

'The steward—'

'Powerless.'

She stared at him, trying to force down her fear. 'Who *are* you?' she choked.

He bared his teeth in a feral smile. 'I'm the future ruler of Kadar.'

In one fluid movement he rolled off her, pulling her up by a hand that had closed around her wrist like a manacle. Still holding her arm, he led her back to the cars, where two other men waited, dark-suited and blank-faced. One of them opened the rear door and with mocking courtesy her arrogant captor, whoever he really was, sketched an elaborate bow.

'After you, Your Highness.'

Elena stared at the yawning darkness of the SUV's interior. She *couldn't* get in that car. As soon as she did the doors would lock and she'd be this man's prisoner.

But she already was his prisoner, she acknowledged sickly, and she'd just blown her best bid for freedom. Perhaps if she pretended compliance now, or even fear, she'd find another opportunity for escape. She wouldn't even have to pretend all that much; terror had begun to claw at her senses.

She looked at the man who was watching her with cold amusement, as if he'd already guessed the nature of her thoughts.

'Tell me who you really are.'

'I already did, Your Highness, and you are trying my

patience. Now, get in the car.' He spoke politely enough, but Elena still felt the threat. The danger. She saw that cold, knowing amusement in the man's amber eyes, but no pity, no spark of compassion at all, and she knew she was out of options.

Swallowing hard, she got in the car.

The man slid in beside her and the doors closed, the automated lock a loud click in the taut silence. He tossed her shoes onto her lap.

'You might want those.' His voice was low, unaccented, and yet he was clearly Arabic. Kadaran. His skin was a deep bronze, his hair as dark as ink. The edge of his cheekbone looked as sharp as a blade.

Swallowing again, the taste of fear metallic on her tongue, Elena slipped them on. Her hair was a mess, one knee was scraped and the skirt of her staid navy blue suit was torn.

Taking a deep breath, she tucked her hair behind her ears and wiped the traces of sand from her face. She looked out of the window, trying to find some clue as to where they were going, but she could barely see out of the tinted glass. What she could see was nothing more than the jagged black shapes of rocks in the darkness, Kadar's infamously bleak desert terrain. It was a small country nestled on the Arabian Peninsula, its borders containing both magnificent coastline and deadly rock-strewn desert.

She sneaked a sideways glance at her captor. He sat with his hands resting lightly on his thighs, looking relaxed and assured, yet also alert. Who was he? Why had he kidnapped her?

And how was she going to get free?

Think, she told herself. Rational thought was the antidote to panic. The man must be one of the rebel insurgents Aziz had mentioned. He'd said he was the future ruler of Kadar, which meant he wanted Aziz's throne. He must have kidnapped her to prevent their marriage—unless he wasn't aware of the stipulations set out in Aziz's father's will?

Elena had only learned of them when she'd met Aziz a few weeks ago at a diplomatic function. His father, Sheikh Hashem, had just died and Aziz had made some sardonic joke about now needing a wife. Elena hadn't been sure whether to take him seriously or not, but then she'd seen a bleakness in his eyes. She'd felt it in herself.

Her Head of Council, Andreas Markos, was determined to depose her. He claimed a young, inexperienced woman such as herself was unfit to rule, and had threatened to call for a vote to abolish the monarchy at the next convening of the Thallian Council. But if she were married by then... if she had a husband and Prince Consort...then Markos couldn't argue she was unfit to rule.

And the people loved a wedding, wanted a royal marriage. She was popular with the Thallian people; it was why Markos hadn't already tried to depose her in the four turbulent years of her reign. Adding to that popularity with a royal wedding would make her position even stronger.

It was a desperate solution, but Elena had felt desperate. She loved her country, her people, and she wanted to remain their queen—for their sake, and for her father's sake, who had given his life so she could be monarch.

The next morning Elena had sent a letter to Aziz, suggesting they meet. He'd agreed and, with a candour borne of urgency, they'd laid out their respective positions. Elena needed a husband to satisfy her Council; Aziz needed to marry within six weeks of his father's death or he forfeited his title. They'd agreed to wed. They'd agreed to a convenient and loveless union that would give them the spouses they needed and children as heirs, one for Kadar, one for Thallia.

It was a mercenary approach to both marriage and parenthood and, if she'd been an ordinary woman, or even an ordinary queen, she would have wanted something different for her life. But she was a queen hanging onto her kingdom by a mere thread, and marriage to Aziz al Bakir had felt like the only way to keep clinging.

But for that to happen, she had to get married. And to get married, she had to escape.

She couldn't get out of the car, so she needed to wait. Watch. Learn her enemy.

'What is your name?' she asked. The man didn't even look at her.

'My name is Khalil.'

'Why have you taken me?'

He slid her a single, fathomless glance. 'We're almost at our destination, Your Highness. Your questions will be answered there, after we are both refreshed.'

Fine. She'd wait. She'd stay calm and in control and look for the next opportunity to gain her freedom. Even so terror caught her by the throat and held on. She'd felt this terrible, numbing fear before, as if the world were sliding by in slow motion, everything slipping away from her as she waited, frozen, disbelieving that this was actually happening…

No, this was not the same as before. She wouldn't let it be. She was queen of a country, even if her throne was all too shaky a seat. She was resourceful, courageous, *strong*.

She would get out of this. Somehow. She refused to let some rebel insurgent wreck her marriage…or end her reign as queen.

Khalil al Bakir glanced again at the woman by his side. She sat straight and tall, her chin lifted proudly, her pupils dilated with fear.

Admiration for the young queen flickered reluctantly through him. Her attempt at escape had been reckless and laughable, but also brave, and he felt an unexpected sympathy for her. He knew what it was like to feel both trapped and defiant. Hadn't he, as a boy, tried to escape from his captor, Abdul-Hafiz, as often as he could, even though he'd known how fruitless such attempts would be? Deep in the desert, there had been no place for a young boy to run or hide. Yet still he'd tried, because to try was to fight, and to fight was to remind yourself you were alive and had something to fight for. The scars on his back were testament to his many failed attempts.

Queen Elena would have no such scars. He would not be accused of ill-treating his guest, no matter what the frightened monarch might think. He intended to keep her for only four days, until the six weeks had passed and Aziz would be forced to relinquish his claim to the throne and call a national referendum to decide who the next sheikh would be.

Khalil intended to be that man.

Until that moment, when the vote had been called and he sat on the throne that was rightfully his, he would not rest easy. But then, he'd never rested easy, not since the day when he'd been all of seven years old and his father had dragged him out of his lesson with his tutor, thrown him onto the sharp stones in front of the Kadaran palace and spat in his face.

'*You are not my son.*'

It was the last time he'd ever seen him, his mother, or his home.

Khalil closed his eyes against the memories that still made his fists clench and bile rise in his throat. He would not think of those dark days now. He would not remember the look of disgust and even hatred on the face of the father he'd adored, or the anguished cries of his mother as she'd been dragged away, only to die just a few months later from a simple case of the flu because she'd been denied adequate medical care. He wouldn't think of the terror he'd felt when he'd been shoved in the back of a van and driven to a bleak desert outpost, or the look of cruel satisfaction on Abdul-Hafiz's face when he'd been thrown at his feet like a sack of rubbish.

No, he wouldn't think of any of that. He'd think of the

future, the very promising future, when he, the son his father had rejected in favour of his mistress's bastard, would sit on the throne of the kingdom he'd been born to rule.

Next to him, he felt Queen Elena tremble.

Twenty taut minutes later the SUV pulled up at the makeshift camp Khalil had called home for the last six months, ever since he'd returned to Kadar. He opened the door and turned to Elena, who glared at him in challenge.

'Where have you taken me?'

He gave her a cold smile. 'Why don't you come out and see for yourself?' Without waiting for an answer, he took hold of her wrist. Her skin was soft and cold and she let out a muffled gasp as he drew her from the car.

She stumbled on a stone as she came to her feet, and as he righted her he felt her breasts brush his chest. It had been a long time since he'd felt the soft touch of a woman, and his body responded with base instinct, his loins tightening as desire flared deep inside. Her hair, so close to his face, smelled of lemons.

Firmly Khalil moved her away from him. He had no time for lust and certainly not with this woman.

His right-hand man, Assad, emerged from another vehicle. 'Your Highness.' Elena turned automatically, and Khalil smiled in grim satisfaction. Assad had been addressing him, not the unruly queen. Even though he had not officially claimed his title, those loyal to him still addressed him as if he had.

He'd been surprised and gratified at how many were loyal to him, when they had only remembered a touslehaired boy who'd been dragged crying and gibbering from the palace. Until six months ago, he had not been in Kadar since he'd been ten years old. But people remembered.

The desert tribes, bound more by tradition than the people of Siyad, had always resented Sheikh Hashem's rash decision to discard one wife for a mistress no one had liked, and a son he'd already publicly declared illegitimate.

When Khalil had returned, they'd named him sheikh of his mother's tribe and had rallied around him as the true ruling Sheikh of Kadar.

Even so, Khalil trusted no one. Loyalties could change on a whim. Love was capricious. He'd learned those lessons all too painfully well. The only person he trusted now was himself.

'Queen Elena and I would like some refreshment,' he told Assad in Arabic. 'Is there a tent prepared?'

'Yes, Your Highness.'

'You can debrief me later. For now, I'll deal with the Queen.' He turned to Elena, whose panicked gaze was darting in every direction, her body poised for flight.

'If you are thinking of running away,' he told her calmly, switching to English as the language they both knew, 'don't bother. The desert stretches for hundreds of miles in every direction, and the nearest oasis is over a day's ride by camel. Even if you managed to leave the camp, you would die of thirst, if not a snake or scorpion bite.'

Queen Elena glared at him and said nothing. Khalil gestured her forward. 'Come, have some refreshment, and I will answer your questions as I promised.'

Elena hesitated and then, clearly knowing she had no choice, she nodded and followed him across the camp.

Elena took stock of her surroundings as she walked behind Khalil. A few tents formed a rough semi-circle; she could see some horses and camels tethered to a post under a lean-to. The wind blew sand into her face and her hair into her mouth.

She held her hands up to her face, tried to blink the grit out of her eyes. Khalil pushed back the folds of the tent and ushered her inside.

Elena took a steadying breath, trying to compose herself. The only thing she could do now was learn as much as she could, and choose her moment well.

Khalil moved to the other side of the tent, gesturing to an elegant teakwood table and low chairs with embroidered cushions. The outside of the tent had been basic, but the interior, Elena saw as her gaze darted around, was luxurious, with silk and satin furnishings and carpets.

'Please, sit down.'

'I want answers to my questions.'

Khalil turned to face her. A small smile curved his mouth but his eyes were cold. 'Your defiance is admirable, Your Highness, but only to a certain extent. Sit.'

She knew she needed to pick her battles. Elena sat. 'Where is Sheikh Aziz?'

Irritation flashed across his chiselled features and then he gave a little shrug. 'Aziz is presumably in Siyad, waiting for you.'

'He'll be expecting me—'

'Yes,' Khalil cut her off smoothly. 'Tomorrow.'

'*Tomorrow*?'

'He received a message that you were delayed.' Khalil spread his hands, his eyes glittering with what felt like mockery. 'No one is looking for you, Your Highness. And, by the time they are, it will be too late.'

The implication was obvious, and it made her breathless with shock, her vision blurring so she reached out and grabbed the edge of the table to steady herself. *Calm*. She needed to stay calm.

She heard Khalil swear softly. 'I did not mean what you obviously think I meant.'

She looked up, her vision clearing as she gazed up at him. Even scowling he was breathtaking; everything about him was lean and graceful. Predatory. 'You mean you aren't going to kill me,' she stated flatly.

'I am neither a terrorist nor a thug.'

'Yet you kidnap a queen.'

He inclined his head. 'A necessary evil, I'm afraid.'

'I don't believe any evil is necessary,' Elena shot back.

She took another steadying breath. 'So what are you going to do with me?'

It was a question she wasn't sure she wanted answered, yet she knew ignorance was dangerous. Better to know the danger, the enemy. *Know your enemies and know yourself, and you will not be imperilled in a hundred battles.*

'I'm not going to do anything with you,' Khalil answered calmly. 'Except keep you here in, I hope, moderate comfort.'

One of the guards came with a tray of food. Elena glanced at the platter of dates and figs, the flat bread and the bowls of creamy dips, and then looked away again. She had no appetite, and in any case she would not eat with her enemy.

'Thank you, Assad,' Khalil said, and the man bowed and left.

Khalil crouched on his haunches in front of the low table where Assad had set the tray. He glanced up at Elena, those amber eyes seeming almost to glow. They really were the most extraordinary colour. With his dark hair and tawny eyes, that lean, predatory elegance, he was like a leopard, or perhaps a panther—something beautiful and terrifying. 'You must be hungry, Queen Elena.'

'I am not.'

'Then thirsty, at least. It is dangerous not to drink in the desert.'

'It is dangerous,' Elena countered, 'to drink in the presence of your enemies.'

A tiny smile tugged at the corner of his mouth and he inclined his head in acknowledgement. 'Very well, then. I shall drink first.'

She watched as he poured what looked like some kind of fruit juice from an earthen pitcher into two tall tumblers. He picked up the first and drank deeply from it, the sinuous muscles of his throat working as he swallowed.

He met her gaze over the rim of his glass, his eyes glinting in challenge.

'Satisfied?' he murmured as he lowered his glass.

Elena's throat ached with thirst and was scratchy from the sand. She needed to stay hydrated if she was going to plan an escape, so she nodded and held out her hand.

Khalil handed her the glass and she sipped the juice; it was both tart and sweet, and deliciously cool.

'Guava,' he told her. 'Have you had it before?'

'No.' Elena put the glass back down on the table. 'Now I am refreshed.' She took a deep breath. 'So you intend to keep me here in the desert—for how long?'

'A little less than a week. Four days, to be precise.'

Four days. Elena's stomach knotted. In four days the six weeks Aziz had been given to marry would be up. He would lose his right to his title, and Khalil must know that. He must be waiting for a chance to seize power.

'And then?' she asked. 'What will you do?'

'That is not your concern.'

'What will you do with me?' Elena rephrased, and Khalil sat down in a low-slung chair richly patterned with wool, regarding her with a rather sleepy consideration over the tips of his steepled fingers. Elena felt her frayed nerves start to snap.

'Let you go, of course.'

'Just like that?' She shook her head, too suspicious to feel remotely relieved. 'You'll be prosecuted.'

'I don't think so.'

'You can't just kidnap a head of state.'

'And yet I have.' He took a sip of juice, his gaze resting thoughtfully on her. 'You intrigue me, Queen Elena. I must confess, I've wondered what kind of woman Aziz would choose as his bride.'

'And are you satisfied?' she snapped. *Stupid*. Where was her calm, her control? She'd been teetering on a tightrope for her entire reign; was she really going to fall off now?

But maybe she already had.

Khalil smiled faintly. 'I am not remotely satisfied.'

His gaze held her and she saw a sudden gleam of masculine intent and awareness flicker in his eyes. To her surprise and shame, she felt an answering thrill of terror—and something else. Something that wasn't fear, but rather… anticipation. Yet, of what? She wanted nothing from this man but her freedom.

'And I won't be satisfied,' Khalil continued, 'until Aziz is no longer on the throne of Kadar and I am.'

'So you are one of the rebel insurgents Aziz mentioned.'

For a second Khalil's gaze blazed fury but then he merely inclined his head. 'So it would seem.'

'Why should you be on the throne?'

'Why should Aziz?'

'Because he is the heir.'

Khalil glanced away, his expression veiled once more. 'Do you know the history of Kadar, Your Highness?'

'I've read something of it,' she answered, although the truth was her knowledge of Kadaran history was sketchy at best. There hadn't been time for more than a crash course in the heritage of the country of her future husband.

'Did you know it was a peaceful, prosperous nation for many years—independent, even, when other countries buckled under a wider regime?'

'Yes, I did know that.' Aziz had mentioned it, because her own country was the same; a small island in the Aegean Sea between Turkey and Greece, Thallia had enjoyed nearly a thousand years of peaceful, independent rule.

And she would not be the one to end it.

'Perhaps you also know, then, that Sheikh Hashem threatened the stability of Kadar with the rather unusual terms of his will?' He turned back to her, raising his eyebrows, a little smile playing about his mouth.

Elena found her gaze quite unreasonably drawn to that mouth, to those surprisingly lush and sculpted lips. She forced herself to look upwards and met Khalil's enquiring gaze. There was no point, she decided, in feigning ignorance. 'Yes, I am well aware of the old Sheikh's stipulation. It's why I am here to marry Sheikh Aziz.'

'Not a love match, then?' Khalil queried sardonically and Elena stiffened.

'I don't believe that is any of your business.'

'Considering you are here at my behest, I believe it is.'

She pursed her lips and said nothing. The Kadaran people believed it was a love match, although neither she nor Aziz had said as much. People believed what they wanted to believe, Elena knew, and the public liked the idea of a royal fairy-tale. If it helped to stabilise their countries, then so be it. She could go along with a little play-acting. But she wasn't about to admit that to Khalil.

'Pleading the fifth, I see,' Khalil said softly. 'I grew up in America, you know. I am not the barbarian you seem to think I am.'

She folded her arms. 'You have yet to show me otherwise.'

'Have I not? Yet here you are, in a comfortable chair, offered refreshment. Though I am sorry you hurt yourself.' He gestured to her scraped knee, all solicitude. 'Let me get you a plaster.'

'I don't need one.'

'Such abrasions can easily become infected in the desert. A grain of sand lodges in the cut and, the next thing you know, it's gone septic.' He leaned forward, and for a moment the harshness of his face, the coldness in his eyes, was replaced by something that almost looked like gentleness. 'Don't be stupid, Your Highness. God knows I understand the need to fight, but you are wasting your energy arguing with me over such small matters.'

She swallowed, knowing he was right, and hating it. It was petty and childish to refuse medical care, not to mention stupid as he'd said. She nodded and Khalil rose from his chair. She watched as he strode to the entrance of the tent and spoke to one of the guards waiting outside.

Elena remained seated, her fists clenched in her lap, her heart beating hard. A few minutes later Khalil returned to the table with a cloth folded over his arm, a basin of water in one hand and a tube of ointment in the other.

'Here we are.'

To her shock he knelt in front of her and Elena pressed back in her chair. 'I can do it myself.'

He glanced up at her, his eyes gleaming. 'But then you would deny me the pleasure.'

Her breath came out in a rush and she remained rigid as he gently lifted the hem of her skirt over her knee. His fingers barely brushed her leg and yet she felt as if she'd been electrocuted, her whole body jolting with sensation. Carefully Khalil dampened the cloth and then dabbed the scrape on her knee.

'Besides,' he murmured, 'you might miss some sand, and I would hate to be accused of mistreating you.'

Elena didn't answer. She couldn't speak, could barely breathe. Every atom of her being was focused on the gentle touch of this man, his fingers sliding over her knee with a precision that wasn't sensual, not remotely, yet...

She took a careful breath and stared at the top of his head, his hair ink-black and cut very short. She wondered if it would feel soft or bristly, and then jerked her mind back to her predicament. What on earth was she doing, thinking about his hair, reacting to his hands on her skin? This man was her *enemy*. The last thing, the *very* last thing, she should do was feel anything for him, even something as basic as physical desire.

His hand tightened on her knee and everything inside Elena flared to life.

'I think that's fine,' she said stiffly, and tried to draw her leg away from Khalil's hand.

He held up the tube of ointment. 'Antiseptic cream. Very important.'

Gritting her teeth, she remained still while he squeezed some cream onto his fingers and then smoothed it over the cut on her knee. It stung a little, but far more painful was the kick of attraction she felt at the languorous touch of his fingers on her sensitised skin.

It was just her body's basic physical reaction, she told herself as he rubbed circles on her knee with his thumb and her insides tightened. She'd never experienced it like this before, but then she was inexperienced in the ways of men and women. In any case, there was nothing she could do about it, so she'd ignore it. Ignore the sparks that scattered across her skin and the plunging deep in her belly. Attraction was irrelevant; she would never act on it nor allow it to cloud her judgement.

Escape from this man and his plans to ruin her marriage was her only goal now. Her only desire.

CHAPTER TWO

KHALIL FELT ELENA'S body tense beneath his touch and wondered why he had chosen to clean the cut himself. The answer, of course, was irritatingly obvious: because he'd wanted to touch her. Because, for a moment, desire had overridden sense.

Her skin, Khalil thought, was as soft as silk. When had he last touched a woman's skin? Seven years in the French Foreign Legion had given him more than a taste of abstinence.

Of course, the last woman he should ever think about as a lover was Queen Elena, Aziz's intended bride. He had no intention of complicating what was already a very delicate diplomatic manoeuvre.

Kidnapping a head of state was a calculated risk, and one he'd had to take. The only way to force Aziz to call a national referendum was for him to lose his right to the throne, and the only way for that to happen was to prevent his marriage.

His father's will, Khalil mused, had been a ridiculous piece of legal architecture that showed him for the brutal dictator he truly had been. Had he wanted to punish both his sons? Or had he, in the last days of his life, actually regretted his treatment of his first-born? Khalil would never know. But he would take the opportunity his father's strange will offered him to seize the power that was rightfully his.

'There you are.' Khalil smoothed her skirt over her knee, felt her tense body relax only slightly as he eased back. 'I see your skirt is torn. My apologies. You will be provided with new clothes.'

She stared at him, studying him as you would a specimen or, rather, an enemy: looking for weaknesses. She wouldn't find any, but Khalil took the opportunity to gaze back at her. She was lovely, her skin like golden cream, her heavy-lidded eyes grey with tiny gold flecks. Her hair was thick and dark and gleamed in the candlelight, even though it was tangled and gritty with sand.

His gaze dropped to her lips, lush, pink and perfect. Kissable. There was that desire again, flaring deep inside him, demanding satisfaction. Khalil stood up. 'You must be hungry, Your Highness. You should eat.'

'I'm not hungry.'

'Suit yourself.' He took a piece of bread and tore off a bit to chew. Sitting across from her, he studied her once more. 'I am curious as to why you agreed to marry Aziz.' He cocked his head. 'Not wealth, as Thallia is a prosperous enough country. Not power, since you are already a queen. And we know it isn't for love.'

'Maybe it is.' Her voice was low, pleasingly husky. She met his gaze unflinchingly but he heard her breath hitch and Khalil smiled.

'I don't think so, Your Highness. I think you married him because you need something, and I'm wondering what it is. Your people love you. Your country is stable.' He spread his hands, raised his eyebrows. 'What would induce you to marry a pretender?'

'I think you are the pretender, Khalil.'

'You're not the only one, alas. But you will be proved wrong.'

Her grey-gold gaze swept over him. 'You genuinely believe you have a claim to the throne.'

His stomach knotted. 'I know I do.'

'How can that be? Aziz is Sheikh Hashem's only son.'

Even though he'd long been used to such an assumption, her words poured acid on an open wound. A familiar fury rose up in him, a howl of outrage he forced back down. He smiled coldly at this woman whose careless questions tore open the barely healed scars of his past. 'Perhaps you need to brush up on your Kadaran history. You will have plenty of time for leisure reading during your stay in the desert.' Although he knew she wouldn't find the truth in any books. His father had done his best to erase Khalil's existence from history.

She stared up at him unblinkingly. 'And if I do not wish to stay in the desert?'

'Your presence here, I'm afraid, is non-negotiable. But rest assured, you will be afforded every comfort.'

Elena licked her lips, an innocent movement that still caused a hard kick of lust he instantly suppressed. Queen Elena was a beautiful woman; his body, long deprived of sensual pleasures, was bound to react. It didn't mean he was going to do anything about it.

Perhaps the most attractive thing about her, though, was not her looks but her presence. Even though he knew she had to be frightened, she sat tall and proud, her grey eyes glinting challenge. He admired her determination to be strong; he shared it. Never surrender, not even when the whole world seemed to be against you, every fist raised, every lip curled in a sneer.

Had she faced opposition and hardship? She had, he knew, suffered tragedy. She'd taken the throne at nineteen years of age, when her parents had died in a terrorist bombing. She was only twenty-three now and, though she looked very young, she seemed older in her bearing, somehow. In her confidence.

She rose from her seat, every inch the elegant queen. 'You cannot keep me here.'

He smiled; he almost felt sorry for her. 'You'll find that I can.'

'Aziz will send someone to fetch me. People will be looking.'

'Tomorrow. By that time any tracks in the desert, any evidence of where you've gone, will have vanished.' He glanced towards the tent flap, which rustled in the wind. 'It sounds as if a storm is brewing.'

Elena shook her head slowly. 'How did you manage it? To get a false message to him, convince the pilot to land somewhere else?'

'Not everyone is loyal to Aziz. In fact, few are outside of Siyad. You know he has not been in the country for more than a few days at a time since he was a boy?'

'I know he is very popular in the courts of Europe.'

'You mean the country clubs. The gentleman playboy is not so popular here.'

Elena's eyes flashed gold. 'That's a ridiculous nickname, given to him by the tabloids.'

Khalil shrugged. 'And yet it stuck.' Aziz, the playboy of Europe, who spent his time at parties and on polo fields. He ran a business too, Khalil knew; he'd started up some financial venture that was successful, if just an excuse for him to party his way through Europe and avoid the country of his birth.

Aziz didn't even *care* about Kadar, Khalil thought with a familiar spike of bitterness. He didn't deserve to rule, even if he hadn't been a bastard son.

'No matter what you think of Aziz, you can't just kidnap a queen,' Elena stated, her chin jutting out defiantly. 'You'd be wise to cut your losses, Khalil, and free me now. I won't press charges.'

Khalil suppressed a laugh of genuine amusement. 'How generous of you.'

'You don't want to face a tribunal,' she insisted. 'How can you become Sheikh if you've committed a crime?

Caused an international incident? You will be called to account.'

'You'll find that is not how things are done in my country.'

'My country, then,' she snapped. 'Do you think my Council, my country, will allow its queen to be kidnapped?'

He shrugged. 'You were merely detained, Your Highness, as a necessary measure. And, since Aziz is a pretender to the throne, you should be grateful that I am preventing a marriage you would undoubtedly regret.'

'Grateful!' Her eyes sparked with anger. 'What if your plan fails?'

He smiled coldly. 'I do not consider failure a possibility.'

She shook her head slowly, her eyes like two grey-gold pools, reminding him of a sunset reflected on water. 'You can't do this. People don't— World leaders don't do this!'

'Things are different here.'

'Not that different, surely?' She shook her head again. 'You're mad.'

Fury surged again and he took a deep, even breath. 'No, Your Highness, I am not mad. Just determined. Now, it is late and I think you should go to your quarters. You will have a private tent here and, as I said before, every comfort possible.' He bared his teeth in a smile. 'Enjoy your stay in Kadar.'

Elena paced the quarters of the elegant tent Assad had escorted her to an hour ago. Khalil had been right when he'd said he'd give her every possible comfort: the spacious tent had a wide double bed on its own wooden dais, the soft mattress piled high with silk and satin covers and pillows. There were also several teak chairs and a bureau for clothes she didn't even have.

Had they brought her luggage from the jet? She doubted it. Not that she'd even brought much to Kadar. She'd only been intending to stay for three days: a quiet ceremony, a quick honeymoon and then a return to Thallia to introduce Aziz to her people.

And now none of it would happen. Unless someone rescued her or she managed to escape, prospects she deemed quite unlikely, her marriage to Aziz would not take place. If he did not marry within the six weeks, he would be forced to relinquish his claim to the throne. He wouldn't need her then, but unfortunately she still needed him.

Still needed a husband, a Prince Consort, and before the convening of the Council next month.

Elena sank onto an embroidered chair and dropped her head into her hands. Even now she couldn't believe she was here, that she'd actually been *kidnapped*.

Yet why shouldn't she believe it? Hadn't the worst in her life happened before? For a second she remembered the sound of the explosion ringing in her ears, the terrible weight of her father's lifeless body on top of hers.

And, even after that awful day, from the moment she'd taken the throne she'd been dogged by disaster, teetering on the precipice of ruin. Led by Markos, the stuffy, sanctimonious men of the Thallian Council had sought to discredit and even disown her. They didn't want a single young woman as ruler of Thallia. They didn't want *her*.

She'd spent so much time trying to prove herself to the men of her Council who questioned her every action, doubted her every word. Who assumed she was flighty, silly and irresponsible, all because of one foolish mistake made when she'd been just nineteen and overwhelmed by grief and loneliness.

Nearly four years on, all the good she'd done for her country—all the appearances she'd made, the charities she'd supported and the bills she'd helped draft—counted for nothing. At least, not in Markos's eyes. And the rest of the Council would be led by him, even in this day and age. Thallia was a traditional country. They wanted a man as their head of state.

Tears pricked under her lids and she blinked them back furiously. She wasn't a little girl, to cry over a cut knee. She was a woman, a woman who'd had to prove she possessed the power and strength of a man for four endless, stormy years.

It couldn't end now like this, just because some crazed rebel had decided he was the rightful heir to the throne.

Except, Elena had to acknowledge, Khalil hadn't seemed crazed. He'd been coldly composed, utterly assured. Yet how could he be the rightful heir? And did he really think he could snatch the throne from under Aziz's nose? When she didn't show up in Siyad, when the Kadaran diplomat who had accompanied her sounded the alarm, Aziz would come looking. And he'd find her, because he was as desperate as she was.

Although, considering she was being held captive in the middle of the desert, perhaps she was now a little more desperate than Aziz.

He could, she realised with a terrible, sinking sensation, find another willing bride. Why shouldn't he? They'd met only a handful of times. The marriage had been her idea. He could still find someone else, although he'd have to do it pretty quickly.

Had Khalil thought of that? What was preventing Aziz from just grabbing some random woman and marrying her to fulfil the terms of his father's will?

Elena rose from the chair and once more restlessly paced the elegant confines of her tent. Outside the night was dark, the only sound the sweep of the sand and the low nickering of the tethered horses.

She *had* to talk to Khalil again and convince him to release her. That was her best chance.

Filled with grim determination, Elena whirled around and stalked to the opening of her tent, pulled the cloth aside and stepped out into the desert night, only to have two guards step quickly in front of her, their bodies as impenetrable as a brick wall. She gazed at their blank faces, at the rifles strapped to their chests, and lifted her chin.

'I want to speak to Khalil.'

'He is occupied, Your Highness.' The guard's voice was both bland and implacable; he didn't move.

'With something more important than securing the throne?' she shot back. The wind blew her hair about her face and impatiently she shoved it back. 'I have information he'll want to hear,' she stated firmly. 'Information that will affect his—his intentions.'

The two guards stared at her impassively, utterly unmoved by her argument. 'Please return to the tent, Your Highness,' one of them said flatly. 'The wind is rising.'

'Tell Khalil he needs to speak to me,' she tried again, and this time, to her own immense irritation, she heard a pleading note enter her voice. 'Tell him there are things I know, things he hasn't considered.'

One of the guards placed a heavy hand on her shoulder and Elena stiffened under it. 'Don't touch me.'

'For your own safety, Your Highness, you must return to the tent.' And, pushing her around, he forced her back into the tent as if she were a small child being marched to her room.

Khalil sat at the teakwood table in his private tent and with one lean finger traced the route through the desert from the campsite to Siyad. Three hundred miles. Three hundred miles to victory.

Reluctantly, yet unable to keep himself from it, he let his gaze flick to a corner of the map, an inhospitable area of bleak desert populated by a single nomadic tribe: his mother's people.

He knew Abdul-Hafiz was dead, and the people of his mother's tribe now supported him as the rightful ruler of Kadar. Yet though they'd even named him as Sheikh of their tribe, he hadn't been back yet to receive the honour.

He couldn't face returning to that barren bit of ground where he'd suffered for three long years.

His stomach still clenched when he looked at that corner of the map, and in his mind's eye he pictured Abdul-Hafiz's cruel face, his thin lips twisted into a mocking sneer as he raised the whip above Khalil's cringing form.

'The woman is asking for you.'

Khalil turned away from the map to see Assad standing in the doorway of his tent, the flaps drawn closed behind him.

'Queen Elena? Why?'

'She claims she has information.'

'What kind of information?'

Assad shrugged. 'Who knows? She is desperate, and most likely lying.'

Khalil drummed his fingers against the table. Elena was indeed desperate, and that made her reckless. Defiant. No doubt her bid to speak to him was some kind of ploy; perhaps she thought she could argue her way to freedom. It would be better, he knew, to ignore her request. Spend as little time as possible with the woman who was already proving to be an unwanted temptation.

'It is worth investigating,' he said after a moment. 'I'll see her.'

'Shall I summon her?'

'No, don't bother. I'll go to her tent.' Khalil rose from his chair, ignoring the anticipation that uncurled low in his belly at the thought of seeing Queen Elena again.

The wind whipped against him, stinging his face with grains of sand as he walked across the campsite to Elena's tent. Around him men hunkered down by fires or tended to their weapons or animals. At the sight of all this industry, all this loyalty, something both swelled and ached inside Khalil.

This was, he knew, the closest thing he'd had to family in twenty-nine years.

Dimah was family, of course, and he was incredibly thankful for what she'd done for him. She had, quite literally, saved him: provided for him, supported him, believed in him.

Yes, he owed Dimah a great deal. But she'd never understood what drove him, how much he needed to reclaim his inheritance, his very self. These men did.

Shaking off such thoughts, he strode towards Elena's tent, waving the guards aside as he drew back the flaps, only to come up short.

Elena was in the bath.

The intimacy of the moment struck him like a fist to the heart: the endless darkness outside, the candlelight flickering over the golden skin of her back, the only sound the slosh of the water against the sides of the deep copper tub as Elena washed herself—and then the hiss of his sudden, indrawn breath as a wave of lust crashed over him with the force of a tsunami.

She stiffened, the sponge dropping from her hand, and turned her head so their gazes met. Clashed. She didn't speak, didn't even move, and neither did Khalil. The moment spun out between them, a moment taut with expectation and yet beautiful in its simplicity.

She was beautiful, the elegant shape of her back reminding him of the sinuous curves of a cello. A single tendril of dark hair lay against the nape of her neck; the rest was piled on top of her head.

As if from a great distance Khalil registered her shuddering breath and knew she was frightened. Shame scorched him and he spun on his heel.

'I beg your pardon. I did not realise you were bathing. I'll wait outside.' He pushed outside the tent, the guards coming quickly to flank him, but he just shook his head and brushed them off. Lust still pulsed insistently inside him, an ache in his groin. He folded his arms across his chest and willed his body's traitorous reaction to recede.

Yet, no matter how hard he tried, he could not banish the image of Elena's golden perfection from his mind.

After a few endless minutes he heard a rustling behind him and Elena appeared, dressed in a white towelling robe that thankfully covered her from neck to toe.

'You may come in.' Her voice was husky, her cheeks flushed—although whether from the heat of the bath or their unexpected encounter he didn't know.

Khalil stepped inside the tent. Elena had already re-treated to the far side, the copper tub between them like a barrier, her slight body swallowed up by the robe.

'I'm sorry,' Khalil said. 'I didn't know you were in the bath.'

'So you said.'

'You don't believe me?'

'Why should I believe anything you say?' she retorted. 'You haven't exactly been acting in an honourable fashion.'

Khalil drew himself up, any traces of desire evaporating in the face of her obvious scorn. 'And it would be honourable to allow my country to be ruled by a pretender?'

'A *pretender*?' She shook her head in derisive disbelief, causing a few more tendrils of hair to fall against her cheek. Khalil's hand twitched with the sudden, absurd urge to touch her, to brush those strands away from her face. He clenched his hand into a fist instead.

'Aziz is not the rightful heir to the throne.'

'I don't *care*!' she cried, her voice ringing out harsh and desperate. Khalil felt any soft longings in him harden, crystallise into determination. Of course she didn't care.

'I realise that, Your Highness,' he answered shortly. 'Although why you wish to marry Aziz is not clear to me. Power, perhaps.' He let her hear the contempt in his voice but she didn't respond to it, except to give one weary laugh.

'Power? I suppose you could say that.' She closed her eyes briefly, and when she opened them he was surprised to see so much bleak despair reflected in their grey-gold depths. 'All I meant was, none of it really matters to me, being here. I understand this—this conflict is very important to you. But keeping me here won't accomplish your goal.'

'You don't think so?'

'No.' Her mouth twisted in something like a smile. 'Aziz will just marry someone else. He still has four days.'

'I'm aware of the time that is left.' He regarded her thoughtfully, the bleakness still apparent in her eyes, the set of her shoulders and mouth both determined and courageous. He felt another flicker of admiration as well as a surge of curiosity. *Why* had she agreed to marry Aziz? What could such a marriage possibly give her?

'So why keep me here?' she pressed. 'If he can fulfil the terms of his father's will with another woman?'

'Because he won't.'

'But he will. We barely know each other. We've only met once before.'

'I know.'

'Then why do you think he would be loyal to me?' she asked and he felt a sudden flash of compassion as well as understanding, because he'd asked that question so many times himself. Why would anyone be loyal to him? Why should he trust anyone?

The person he'd loved most in the world had betrayed and rejected him utterly.

'To be frank,' he told her, 'I don't think loyalty is the issue. Politics are.'

'Exactly. So he'll just marry someone else.'

'And alienate his people even more? They love the idea of this wedding. They love it more than they do Aziz. And if he were to discard one woman for another...' *As our father did.* No, he had no wish to divulge that information to Elena just yet. He took a quick breath. 'It would not be popular. It would destabilise his rule even more.'

'But if he's going to lose his crown anyway...'

'But he won't, not necessarily. Did he not tell you?' Uncertainty flashed across her features and Khalil curved his mouth in a grim smile. 'The will states that, if Aziz does not marry within six weeks, he must call a national referendum. The people will then choose the new sheikh.'

She stared at him, her eyes widening. 'And you think that will be you?'

He let out a hard laugh. 'Don't sound so sceptical.'

'Who *are* you?'

'I told you, the next ruler of Kadar.' Her gaze moved over his face searchingly, and he saw despair creep back into her eyes.

'But Aziz could still go ahead and marry someone else while I'm stuck here in the desert. What happens then?'

'If he does that, it might lead to a civil war. I don't think he wishes for that to happen. Admittedly, Your Highness, I am taking a risk. You are right in saying that Aziz could marry someone else. But I don't think he will.'

'Why not just meet him and ask him to call the referendum?'

He shook his head. 'Because he knows he won't win it.'

'And if it comes to war? Are you prepared?'

'I will do what I must to secure my country's rule. Make no mistake about that, Queen Elena.' She flinched slightly at his implacable tone and something in Khalil softened just a little. None of this was Elena's fault. She was a casualty of a conflict that didn't involve her. In any other circumstance, he would have applauded her courage and determination.

'I'm sorry,' he said after a pause. 'I realise your plans to marry Aziz have been upset. But, considering how they were made so recently, I'm sure you'll recover.' He didn't mean to sound quite so cutting, but he knew he did, and he saw her flinch again.

She looked away, her gaze turning distant. 'You think so?' she said, not really a question, and again he heard the bleak despair and wondered at its source.

'I know so, Your Highness. I don't know why you decided to marry Aziz, but since it wasn't for love your heart is hardly broken.'

'And you know about broken hearts?' she answered with another weary laugh. 'You don't even seem to have one.'

'Perhaps I don't. But you didn't love him?' That *was* a question, of a sort. He was curious, even if he didn't want to be. He didn't want to know more about Elena, to wonder about her motives or her heart.

And yet still he asked.

'No,' she said after a moment. 'Of course I didn't—don't—love him. I barely know him. We met twice, for a couple of hours.' She shook her head, let out a long, defeated sigh, and then seemed to come to herself, straightening again, her eyes flashing once more. 'But I have your word you will release me after four days?'

'Yes. You have my word.' She relaxed slightly then, even as he stiffened. 'You don't think I'd hurt you?'

'Why shouldn't I? Kidnappers are usually capable of other crimes.'

'As I explained, this was a necessary evil, Your Highness, nothing more.'

'And what else will be a *necessary evil*, Khalil?' she answered back. He didn't like the hopelessness he saw in her eyes; it was as if the spark that had lit her from within had died out. He missed it. 'When you justify one thing, it becomes all too easy to justify another.'

'You sound as if you speak from experience.'

'I do.'

'Your own.'

A pause and her mouth firmed and tightened. 'Of sorts.'

He opened his mouth to ask another question, but then closed it abruptly. He didn't want to know. He didn't need to understand this woman; he simply needed her to stay put for a handful of days. He was sorry, more or less, for her disappointment. But that was all it was, a disappointment. An inconvenience, really. Her future, her very life, was not riding on a marriage to a stranger.

Not like his was.

'I promise I will not hurt you. And in four days you will be free.' She simply stared at him and, with one terse nod, he dismissed her, leaving the tent without another word.

CHAPTER THREE

ELENA WOKE SLOWLY, blinking in the bright sunlight that fil-
tered through the small gap in the tent's flaps. Her body
ached with tiredness; her mind had spun and seethed all
night and she hadn't fallen asleep until some time near
dawn.

Now she stretched and stared up at the rippling canvas
of the tent, wondering what this day would bring.

She'd spent hours last night considering her options.
She'd wondered if she could steal someone's mobile phone,
make contact. Yet who would she call—the operator, to
connect her to the Kadaran palace? Her Head of Council, who would probably be delighted by the news of her
capture? In any case, she most likely couldn't get a signal
out here.

Then she'd wondered if she could make a friend of one
of the guards, get him to help her. That seemed even less
likely; both of the guards she'd met had appeared utterly
unmoved by her predicament.

Could she cause a fire, so its smoke might be caught by
a satellite, a passing helicopter or plane?

Each possibility seemed more ludicrous than the last,
and yet she refused to admit defeat. Giving in would mean
losing her crown.

But the longer she stayed here, the more likely it was
Aziz would marry someone else, no matter what Khalil
said or thought. Or, even if he didn't, he wouldn't marry

her. Maybe he would call this referendum and win the vote. He wouldn't need her at all.

But she still needed him, needed someone to marry her in the next month as she'd promised her Council, someone *she* was willing to marry, to father her children…

The thought caused her stomach to churn and her heart to sink. Her plan to marry Aziz had been desperate; finding another groom was outlandish. What was she going to *do*?

Sighing, she rose from the bed. A female voice sounded outside her tent, and a second later a woman entered, smiling and bearing a pitcher of fresh water.

'Good morning, Your Highness,' she said, ducking a quick curtsey, and Elena murmured back her own greeting, wondering if this woman might be the ally she was looking for.

The sight of the water in the woman's hands reminded her of her bath last night—and Khalil seeing her in it. Even now she felt her insides clench with a nameless emotion at the memory of his arrested look. The heat in his eyes had burned her with both pleasure and pain. To be desired, it was a fearsome thing—exciting, yes, but terrifying too, especially from a man like Khalil.

It had been foolish, she supposed, to take a bath, but when the two surly, silent guards had brought in the huge copper tub and filled it with steaming water, Elena had been unable to resist.

She'd been tired and sandy, every muscle aching with physical as well as emotional fatigue, and the thought of slipping into the rose-scented water, petals floating on top, had been incredibly appealing. A good wash would clear her head as well as clean her body and Khalil, she'd assumed, would not see her again that night.

And yet he'd seen her… Oh, how he'd seen her. She blushed to remember it, even though logically she knew he couldn't have seen much. The high sides of the tub would have kept her body from his sight, and in any case her back had been to him.

Even so she remembered the feel of his stilled gaze on her, the heat and intensity of it and, more alarmingly, her own answering response, everything inside her tightening and tautening, *waiting...*

'Is there anything else you need, Your Highness?' the woman asked, her voice pleasantly accented.

Yes, Elena thought, *my freedom*. She forced a smile. She needed this woman to be her friend. 'This is lovely, thank you. Were you the one who arranged the bath last night?'

The woman ducked her head. 'Yes, I thought you would like a wash.'

'It was wonderful, thank you.' Elena's mind raced. 'Where do you get the water? Is there an oasis here?'

'Yes, just beyond the rocks.'

'Is it very private? I'd love to have a swim some time, if I could.'

The woman smiled. 'If Sheikh Khalil approves, then I'm sure you could. It is lovely for swimming.'

'Thank you.' Elena didn't know if the oasis might provide her with an opportunity either to escape or attempt some kind of distraction to alert anyone who might be looking for her, but at least it was an option, a chance. Now she just had to get Khalil to agree to let her have a swim.

'When you are ready, you may break your fast outside,' the woman said. 'Sheikh Khalil is waiting.'

That was the second time the woman had called Khalil 'sheikh'. Was he a sheikh in his own right, Elena wondered, or did she already consider him as having the throne of Kadar? She wanted to ask Khalil just what made him feel so sure of his position, but she knew she wouldn't. She didn't want to know more about this man or, heaven forbid, find some sympathy for him. Her physical awareness of him was alarming enough.

A few minutes later, dressed in a pair of khakis and a

plain button-down shirt that had been provided for her, her hair neatly plaited, Elena stepped out of her tent.

The brilliance of the desert sun, the hard, bright blue of the sky and the perfect clarity of the air left her breathless for a moment. She was dazzled by the austere beauty of the desert, even though she didn't want to be. She didn't want to feel anything for any of it.

Khalil was eating by himself under an awning that had been set up above a raised wooden platform. He rose as she approached.

'Please. Sit.'

'Thank you.' She perched on the edge of a chair and Khalil arched an amused eyebrow.

'Courteous today, are we?'

Elena shrugged. 'I choose my battles.'

'I look forward to the next one.' He poured her coffee from an ornate brass pot; it looked thick and dark and smelled of cardamom. 'This is Kadaran coffee,' he told her. 'Have you ever tried it?'

She shook her head and took a tentative sip; the taste was strong but not unpleasant. Khalil nodded his approval. 'Would you have taken on Kadaran ways, if you'd become Aziz's bride?'

Elena stiffened. 'I could still become his bride, you know. He might find me.'

The look Khalil gave her was arrogant and utterly assured. 'I wouldn't get your hopes up, Your Highness.'

'Yours certainly seem high enough.'

He shrugged, one powerful shoulder lifting slightly, muscles rippling underneath the linen *thobe* he wore. 'As I told you before, the people of Kadar do not support Aziz.'

Surely he was exaggerating? Elena thought. Aziz had mentioned some instability, but not that he was an unpopular ruler. 'Outside of Siyad, you said,' she recalled. 'And why wouldn't they support him? He's the Sheikh's only son, and the succession has always been dynastic.'

Khalil's mouth tightened, his tawny eyes flashing fire before he shrugged again. 'Maybe you should take my advice and brush up on your Kadaran history.'

'And is there a book you suggest I read?' She raised her eyebrows, tried to moderate her tone. She was not doing herself any favours, arguing with him. 'Perhaps one I can take out of the library?' she added, in a poor attempt at levity.

Khalil's mouth twitched in a smile of what Elena suspected was genuine amusement. It lightened and softened him somehow, made him even more attractive than when he was cold and forbidding. 'I have a small library of books with me. I'll be happy to lend you one, although you won't find the answers you're looking for in a book.'

'Where will I find them, then?'

He hesitated and for a moment Elena thought he was going to say something else, something important. Then he shook his head. 'I don't think any answers would satisfy you, Your Highness, not right now. But when you're ready to listen, and consider there might be more to this story than what you've been told by Aziz, perhaps I'll enlighten you.'

'I should be so lucky,' she retorted, but for the first time since meeting Khalil she felt a flicker of real uncertainty. He was so *sure*. What if his claim had some legitimacy?

But, no, he was an insurgent. An impostor. He *had* to be. Anything else was unthinkable.

To her surprise Khalil leaned forward, placed his hand over hers. Elena stiffened under that small touch and it seemed as if the solid warmth of his hand spread throughout her whole body. 'You don't want to be curious,' he murmured. 'But you are.'

'Why should I be curious about a criminal?' she snapped, and he just smiled and removed his hand.

'Remember what I said. There is another side to the story.' He turned to go and Elena stared at him in frustration; she'd completely missed her opportunity to ask him about the oasis.

'And what am I meant to do for four days?' she called. 'Are you going to keep me imprisoned in my tent?'

'Only if you are foolish enough to attempt to escape.' Khalil turned to face her, his voice and face both hard once more.

'And if I did?'

'I would find you, hopefully before you were dead.'

'Charming.'

'The desert is a dangerous place. Regardless of the scorpions and snakes, a storm can arise in a matter of minutes and bury a tent, never mind a man, in seconds.'

'I know that.' She pressed her lips together and stared down at her plate; Khalil had served her some fresh fruit, dates, figs and succulent slices of melon. She picked up a fork and toyed with a bit of papaya.

'So I may trust you won't attempt an escape?' Khalil asked.

'Do you want me to promise?'

'No,' he answered after a moment. 'I don't trust promises. I just don't want your death on my conscience.'

'How thoughtful of you,' Elena answered sardonically. 'I'm touched.'

To her surprise he smiled again, revealing a surprising dimple in one cheek. 'I thought you would be.'

'So, if I'm not stupid enough to try and escape, may I go outside?' she asked. 'The woman who brought me water said there was an oasis here.' She held her breath, tried to keep her face bland.

'You mean Leila, Assad's wife. And, yes, you may go to the oasis if you like. Watch out for snakes.'

She nodded, her heart thumping with both victory and relief. She had a plan. She could finally *do* something.

'Are you going somewhere?' she asked, her gaze sliding to the horses that were being saddled nearby. If Khalil was gone, all the better.

'Yes.'

'Where?'

'To meet with some of the Bedouin tribes in this area of the desert.'

'Rallying support?' she queried, an edge to her voice, and he lifted his eyebrows.

'Remember what I said about arguing?'

'How was that arguing? I'm not going to just give up, if that's what you want. "Attack is the secret of defence",' she quoted recklessly. '"Defence is the planning of an attack".'

Khalil nodded, a slight smile on his lips. '*The Art of War* by Sun Tzu,' he said. 'Impressive.' She simply stared at him, chin jutted out, and he quoted back at her, '"He who knows when he can fight and when he cannot will be victorious".'

'Exactly.'

He laughed softly, shaking his head. 'So you think you can win in this situation, Your Highness, despite all I've said?'

'"The supreme art of war is to subdue the enemy without fighting".'

He cocked his head, his gaze sweeping over her almost lazily. 'And how do you intend to subdue me?'

Surely he hadn't meant those words to have a sensual intent, a sexual innuendo, yet somehow they had. Elena felt it in the warmth that stole through her body, turning her bones liquid and her mind to mush.

Khalil held her gaze, his eyes glowing gold and she simply stared back, unable to reply or even think. Finally her brain sputtered back into gear and she forced out, '"Let your plans be dark and impenetrable as night".'

'Clearly you've studied him well. It makes me curious, since your country has been at peace for nearly a thousand years.'

'There are different kinds of wars.' And the war she fought was scarily subtle: a murmured word, a whispered rumour. She was constantly on the alert for an attack.

'So there are. And I pray, Your Highness, that this war for the throne of Kadar might be fought without a single drop of blood being spilled.'

'You don't think Aziz will fight you?'

'I hope he knows better. Now, enough. I must ride. I hope you enjoy your day.'

With that he strode towards the horses, his body dark and powerful against the brilliant blue sky, the blazing sun. When he had gone Elena felt, absurdly, as if something was missing that she'd both wanted and enjoyed.

After Khalil had left, riding off into the desert with several of his men, great clouds of dust and sand billowing behind them, Elena went back to her tent. To her surprise, she saw a book—*The Making of Modern Kadar*—had been placed on her bedside table. Was Khalil being thoughtful, she wondered, or mocking?

Curious, she flipped through the book. She already knew the basics of Kadar's history: its many years of peace, isolated as it was on a remote peninsula, jutting out into the Arabian Sea. While war had passed it by, so had technology, and for centuries it had remained as it had always been, a cluster of tribal communities with little interest beyond their nomadic life of shepherding. Then, in the early 1800s, Sheikh Ahmad al Bakir, the great-great-grandfather of Hashem, had united the tribes and created a monarchy. He'd ruled Kadar for nearly fifty years, and since then there had only been peace and prosperity.

None of it told her why Khalil believed he was the rightful ruler and not Aziz, Hashem's only son. The book didn't even hint at any insurgency or civil unrest; if it was to be believed, nothing had caused so much as a flicker of unease in the peaceful, prosperous rule of the House of al Bakir.

She tossed the book aside, determined not to wonder any more about Khalil. She didn't need to know whether his claim had any merit. She wasn't going to care.

She just wanted to get out of here, however she could. Resolutely, she went in search of Leila. The guards outside her tent summoned her, and Leila was happy to show her the way to the oasis. She even brought Elena a swimming costume and a packed lunch. It was all so civilised, Elena almost felt guilty at her deception.

Almost.

Alone in her tent, she searched for what she needed. The legs of the table were too thick, but the chairs might do.

Kneeling on the floor of the tent, the sound muffled by a pillow, she managed to snap several slats from the back of a chair. She stuffed the slats in the bag with the picnic and with her head held high walked out of the tent.

The guards let her pass and Leila directed her down a worn path that wound between two towering boulders.

'"Threading the needle", it's called,' Leila said, for the path between the rocks was incredibly narrow. 'It is a beautiful spot. See for yourself.'

'And you're not worried I'll make a run for it?' Elena asked, trying to keep her voice light. Leila's face softened in sympathy, causing another flash of guilt that she ruthlessly pushed away. These people were her captors, no matter how kind Leila was being. And she *had* to escape somehow.

'I know this is difficult for you, Your Highness, but the Sheikh is a good man. He is protecting you from an unhappy marriage, whether you realise it or not.'

Now *that* was putting quite a spin on things. 'I wasn't aware that Khalil was concerned with the happiness of my marriage,' Elena answered. 'Only with being Sheikh.'

'He is Sheikh already, of one of the desert tribes,' Leila answered. 'And he is the rightful heir to the throne of

Kadar. A great injustice was done to him, and it is finally time to make it right.'

Again Elena felt that uncomfortable flicker of uncertainty. Leila sounded so sure…as sure as Khalil. 'What injustice?' she asked before she could think better of it. Leila shook her head.

'It is not for me to say. But if you had married Aziz, Your Highness, you would have been marrying an impostor. Very few people outside of Siyad believe Aziz should be Sheikh.'

It was what Khalil had said, yet Elena could not accept it. 'But *why*?'

Leila's forehead creased in a troubled frown. 'You must ask Sheikh Khalil—'

'He's not really Sheikh,' Elena interjected, unable to keep herself from it. 'Not of Kadar. Not yet.'

'But he should be,' Leila said quietly, and to Elena she sounded utterly certain. 'Ask him,' the older woman advised. 'He will tell you the truth.'

But did she want to know the truth? Elena wondered as she walked between the towering rocks towards the oasis. If Khalil had a legitimate claim to the throne, what did it mean for her—and her marriage?

Would she still marry Aziz if he wasn't the rightful Sheikh? Would her Council even want her to? The point, Elena reminded herself, was most likely moot—unless she got out of here.

After walking between the boulders she emerged onto a flat rock overlooking a small, shimmering pool shaded by palm trees. The sun sparkled on the water as if on a metal plate, the sky brilliant blue above. The air was hot, dry and still, perfect for a swim.

She glanced around, wondering if the guards had followed her, but she could see no one. Just in case, she made a show of putting down her bag, spreading her towel on the rock. She slathered herself with sunscreen before she stripped down to the plain black swimming costume Leila had provided.

She glanced around again; she was definitely alone. No one had followed her from the camp.

And why should anyone? She was but a five-minute walk from her tent, in the middle of the desert, the middle of nowhere. In every direction the desert stretched, endless sand and towering black rocks, both bleak and beautiful.

There was, Elena knew, nowhere to go, nothing to do but wait and hope that Aziz found her.

Or send a signal.

She reached for her bag and took out the slats she'd broken from the chair. A few weedy-looking plants grew by the oasis's edge, and she took them and made a small, rather pathetic-looking pile. She wasn't going to get much of a blaze from this, Elena realised disconsolately, but it would have to do. It was her only chance. If someone saw the smoke from her fire, they might investigate, might look for her.

Resolutely, she started rubbing the sticks together.

Fifteen minutes later she had blisters on both hands and the sticks were a little warm. She hadn't seen so much as a spark. Frustrated, she laid the sticks aside and rose from the rock. The air was hot and still and the shimmering waters of the oasis looked extremely inviting.

Balancing on her tiptoes, she executed a neat dive into the pool. The water closed around her, cool and refreshing, and she swam under water for a few metres before she surfaced, treading water, not knowing what was on the bottom and not particularly wishing to touch it with her bare feet.

Even if she managed to start a fire, she thought, what would distinguish it from any other camp fire? She'd have to get a really big blaze going for someone to take notice. She'd have to set the whole camp on fire.

Her plan, Elena realised, was ridiculous. The sense of purpose that had buoyed her all morning left her in a depressing rush. Yet even so she decided to try again. It wasn't as if she had many, or any, other options.

She swam to the side of the oasis and hauled herself, dripping, onto the rock ledge. Drying herself off, she knelt before the sticks again and started to rub.

Five minutes later she saw the first tiny spark kindle between the sticks. Hope leapt in her chest and she rubbed harder; some of the dried plants and leaves she'd gathered caught the spark and the first small flame flickered. She let out a cry of triumph.

'Don't move.'

Everything in Elena stilled at the sound of that low, deadly voice. She looked up, her heart lurching against her ribs at the sight of Khalil standing just a few feet away. His eyes were narrowed, his mouth thinned, everything about him tense and still.

Her heart started to pound and then it seemed to stop completely as Khalil slowly, steadily, raised the pistol he'd been holding and pointed it straight at her.

CHAPTER FOUR

THE SOUND OF the pistol firing echoed through the still air, bounced off the boulders and rippled the still waters of the oasis.

Dispassionately Khalil watched as the snake leapt and twisted in the air before falling a few feet away, dead.

He turned back to look at Elena and swore softly when he saw her sway, her face drained of colour, her pupils dilated with terror. Without even considering what he was doing, or why, he strode forward, caught her in his arms and drew her shuddering body to his chest.

'I killed it, Elena,' he said as he stroked her dark hair. 'It's dead. You don't need to be afraid now.'

She pushed away from him, her whole body still trembling. 'What's dead?'

Khalil stared at her for several seconds as the meaning of her question penetrated. He swore again. 'I shot the snake! Did you not see it, but three feet from you, and ready to strike?'

She just stared at him with wide, blank eyes, and forcibly he took her jaw in his hand and turned her head so she could see the dead viper. She blanched, drawing her breath in a ragged gasp.

'I thought…'

'You thought I was aiming at you?' Khalil finished flatly. His stomach churned with a sour mix of guilt and anger. 'How could you think such a thing?' He didn't wait for her answer, for he knew what it would be: *because you kidnapped me.* 'I promised you I wouldn't hurt you.'

'And you also said you didn't trust anyone's promises. Neither do I, Khalil.' She tried to move away from him but she stumbled, her body still shaking, and Khalil pulled her towards him once more. 'Don't—'

'You've had a shock.' He sat down on the rock, drawing her onto his lap. It was a jolt to his system, to feel a warm body against his, yet it also felt far too good, familiar in a way that made no sense, yet felt intrinsically *right*.

He felt the stiffness in her body, saw the way she angled her face away from him and knew that just as he was she was trying to keep herself apart, stand on pride. He saw so much of himself in her and it unnerved him. It touched him in a way he didn't expect or even understand. From the moment he'd met Elena she'd *done* things to him. Not just to his body, but to his heart.

Gently he stroked her damp hair away from her face. She let out a shuddering breath and relaxed against him, her cheek against his chest. Something deep and fierce inside Khalil, some part of him he hadn't thought still existed, let out a roar of both satisfaction and need.

He tucked a tendril behind her ear just as he'd wanted to yesterday. Her eyes were closed, her dark lashes sweeping her pale cheeks.

'You pointed that gun at me,' she whispered, her voice sounding distant and numb.

'I pointed it at the *snake*,' Khalil answered. He knew she was in shock, trying to process what had happened, but he still felt a flash of anger, a stirring of guilt. He should have made her feel safer. She should have been able to trust him.

This, when you trust no one?

'A black snake,' he continued, keeping his voice steady and calm. 'They can be deadly.'

'I didn't even see it.' He thought she was recovering

from the shock but then she let out a little shuddering sob and pressed her face against his chest.

His whole body jolted with the fierce pleasure of having her curl into him, seek his comfort. When had anyone ever done that? When had anyone wanted something real and tender from him? And when had he felt it in response, this yearning and protectiveness?

He could not remember a time, and it forced him to acknowledge the stark emptiness of his life, the years of relentless and ruthless striving, utterly without comfort.

'There, there, *habiibii*. You're safe now. Safe.' The words were strange to him, yet he spoke them without thinking, stroking her hair, his arms tight around her. He could feel her shoulders shake and he could tell from her ragged breathing she was doing her best to keep herself from crying. His throat tightened with emotion he hadn't felt in decades.

After a moment she pushed away from him, her eyes still dry, her face pale but resolutely composed.

'I'm sorry. You must think I'm being ridiculous.' She sat stiffly in his lap now, her chin lifted at a queenly angle. Already Khalil missed the feel of her against him.

'Not at all,' he answered. He suppressed the clamour of his own feelings, forced it all back down again. 'I realise that a great deal has happened to you in a short amount of time.' He hesitated, choosing his words with care, wanting and even needing her to understand. To believe him. 'I'm sorry for the fear and unhappiness I have caused you.'

For a second, no more, he thought she did. Her face softened, her lips parting, and then she gave a little shake of her head and scrambled off his lap. 'Even though it was entirely preventable?'

Their moment of startling intimacy was over and Khalil, half-amazed at his own reaction, felt a sudden piercing of grief at its loss.

* * *

Elena stood on the rock, trying to calm her thundering heart—and ignore the ache Khalil's touch had created in her. She couldn't remember the last time she'd been held so tenderly, spoken to so gently.

He's your captor, she reminded herself grimly. *He kidnapped you.* But in that moment he'd been incredibly kind, and her body and heart had responded to it like a flower unfurling in the sunlight.

When had someone comforted her, touched her, understood her? She'd lived such a solitary existence, first as an only child, then as an orphan queen. The one person she'd let close had betrayed her utterly.

Just as Khalil will betray you. At least he was honest about his intentions.

Khalil gazed at her, his expression inscrutable, any remnant of tenderness erased completely from his harsh features. He glanced at her pathetic pile of plants and broken chair slats; the tiny flame she'd been kindling had gone out. 'What on earth were you doing?' he asked. He turned back to her, his mouth twisting with bemusement. 'Were you building a *fire*?' She didn't answer and his mouth curved into a smile as he shook his head. She almost thought she heard admiration in his voice. 'You were building a signal fire, weren't you?'

Elena lifted her chin. 'And if I was?'

'It's the most pathetic signal fire I've ever seen.' Khalil smiled, inviting her to share the joke, his teasing gentle, compassion kindling in his eyes—a compassion she hadn't seen before and hadn't thought he possessed.

Elena felt an answering smile tug at her own mouth. It *was* pathetic. And it felt good to joke, to laugh, even with Khalil. Especially with Khalil. 'I know. I realised it wasn't going to work. It would be far too small if it had even caught at all. But I had to do something.'

Khalil nodded, his expression serious once more. 'I understand that, Elena,' he said quietly. 'You know, we are a lot alike. We both fight against what we cannot change.'

'It looks to me like you're trying to change something,' she retorted, and he inclined his head in acknowledgement.

'Yes, now. But there was a time when I couldn't. When I was powerless and angry but determined to keep fighting, because at least it reminded me I was alive. That I had something to fight for.'

And, God help her, she knew how that felt. The last four years, she'd felt that every day. 'If you know what that feels like,' she asked in a raw voice, 'then how can you keep me prisoner?'

For a second, no more, Khalil looked conflicted. Torn. Then his eyes veiled and his mouth firmed, everything about him hardening. 'We are not as alike as all that,' he said shortly. 'You might be a prisoner, Elena, but you are treated with respect and courtesy. You have every comfort available.'

'Does that really matter—?'

'Trust me,' he cut her off, his voice cold now, implacable. 'It matters.'

'When have you felt like a prisoner?'

He stared at her for a long moment then gave a little shake of his head. 'We should return to the camp.'

She still wanted answers, even if she shouldn't ask the questions, shouldn't get to know this man any more. Yet she did, because he understood her in a way no one else did. She wanted, she realised, to understand him. 'Why did you come looking for me?'

'I was worried about you.'

'That I'd escape?'

A tiny smile lightened his features. 'No, I'm afraid not. I was worried you might encounter a snake, and I was very nearly right. They like to sun themselves on these rocks.'

'You did warn me.'

'Even so.'

She shook her head, her throat suddenly tight because everything about this was so strange. Khalil was her captor. Her enemy. But he'd also treated her with more gentleness than any other human being that she could remember, and if he had a legitimate claim to the throne…

'What is it, Elena?' he asked quietly.

'I don't know what to think,' she admitted. 'I don't even know if I want to ask you.'

'Ask me what?'

She took a breath, let it out slowly. 'Your side of the story.'

Something flared in his eyes, something she couldn't name, but it had her body responding, heat unfurling low in her belly. Then it died out and his expression hardened once more. 'You don't want to change your mind.'

'You don't know what this marriage means for me, Khalil.'

'Then why don't you tell me?'

'What good would it do? Would you lose the chance of your crown so I can keep mine?'

He raised his eyebrows, his expression still uncompromising. 'Are you in danger of losing it?'

She didn't answer, because she'd already said too much and the last thing she wanted to do was admit to Khalil how shaky her throne really was. So far she'd managed to hide the threat Markos posed to her. If it became public, she knew it would just give him power. She could already imagine the newspaper headlines about the teenaged queen and the stupid mistake she'd made, trusting someone, thinking he loved her.

She wouldn't do that again.

And certainly not with Khalil.

Yet even so part of her yearned to tell him the truth, to unburden herself, have someone understand, sympathise and even offer advice.

Like Paulo had?

Why on earth was she thinking of trusting Khalil when she knew to trust no one? What about this man made her want to break her own rules?

Because he understands you.

'Like you said, we should return to the camp,' she said and with her head held high she walked past him, back through the boulders.

As soon as she got back to her tent, Elena stripped off her swimming costume and dressed in the clothes she'd been given that morning. She felt more trapped now than she had since Khalil had first forced her into the car, but the prison this time was one of her own making. Her own mind. Her own heart.

She knew it was the coward's way not to listen to Khalil, not to ask what his side of the story was. Would she really want to marry Aziz if he wasn't the rightful Sheikh?

And yet he had to be, she told herself as she sat down on the bed. *He had to be.*

Because if he wasn't…

It didn't even matter, she reminded herself with a gusty sigh, dropping her head into her hands. She wasn't going to marry Aziz. No matter how gentle and tender he'd been with her today, Khalil still intended keeping her until the six weeks were up. Soon Aziz would have no reason to marry her.

Whether she wanted to or not.

She looked up, her gaze unfocused as she recalled the way Khalil had held her; the soft words he had spoken; the way he'd stroked her hair; the thud of his heart against her cheek.

She felt deep in her bones that he'd been sincere, and the realisation both terrified and thrilled her. She didn't have real relationships. She didn't know how. She'd been shy as a child, her parents distant figures, her only company a nanny and then a governess. Even if she'd wanted, yearned, for such things, she hadn't known how to go about getting them—and then Paulo had broken her trust and destroyed her faith in other people and, even worse, her faith in herself and her own judgement.

Was she misjudging Khalil now? Was it simply her pathetic inexperience with men and life that made her crave more of that moment, more tenderness, more contact?

Nothing about their relationship, if she could even use that word, was real.

Yet it *felt* real. She felt as if Khalil understood and even liked her for who she was. Maybe that was just wishful thinking, but whatever her association with Khalil was she knew she needed to know the truth. To ask for his side of the story…and face the consequences of whatever he told her.

She let out a shuddering breath, the decision made.

A little while later Leila slipped into the tent, smiling and curtseying as she caught sight of Elena. 'I've brought fresh clothes and water for washing. Sheikh Khalil has invited you to dine with him tonight.'

'He has?' Surprise, and a damning pleasure, rippled through her. 'Why?'

Leila's smile widened. 'Why shouldn't he, Your Highness?'

Why should he?

His reasons didn't matter, she told herself. This could be her opportunity to ask Khalil about his claim to the throne. And if she felt a little flare of anticipation at seeing him, at spending time with him, then so be it.

'Look at the dress he has brought you,' Leila said and, opening a box, she withdrew a dress of silvery grey from folds of tissue paper.

It was both beautiful and modest, the material as delicate and silky as a spider's web. Elena touched it before she could stop herself.

'I'm not sure why I need to wear that,' she said sharply,

drawing her hand away as if the fragile material had burned her. The temptation to try it on, to feel feminine and beautiful, was overwhelming.

Leila's face fell and she laid the dress down on the bed. 'You would look beautiful in it, Your Highness.'

'I don't need to look beautiful. I'm being held captive in a desert camp.' *And she needed to remember that. To stay strong.*

She turned away abruptly, hating that she sounded petulant and childish, and hating even more that she was tempted to wear the dress and have dinner with Khalil.

Hear his side of the story.

Quietly Leila folded the dress and returned it to the box. Elena felt even worse. 'Shall I tell Sheikh Khalil you wish to remain in your tent tonight?'

Conflicted, Elena turned back to Leila. 'I don't—' She stopped, took a breath. She was being a coward, hiding in her tent. She needed to face her fears. Face Khalil. If she learned just what his side of the story was, she'd be able to make a more informed decision about her own future. She'd know all the facts. Know her enemy.

Even if he didn't feel like her enemy any more.

'You may tell Khalil I'll eat with him,' Elena said. 'Thank you, Leila.' She glanced down at the dress, an ache of longing rising in her. It was such a lovely gown. 'And you may leave the dress.'

An hour later Leila escorted Elena to Khalil's private tent. Her heart started thudding and her palms felt damp as she stepped inside the luxurious quarters.

She felt self-conscious in the dress Leila had brought, as if she were dressing up for a date, but she also enjoyed the feel of the silky fabric against her skin, the way it swirled around her ankles as she moved. And, a tiny, treacherous voice whispered, she liked the thought of Khalil seeing her in it.

Everything in her rebelled at the realisation. She shouldn't want to please Khalil. She *couldn't* start to feel something for him. It would be beyond stupid—it would be dangerous.

As she came into the tent, she saw candlelight flickering over the low table that had been set with a variety of dishes. Silk and satin pillows were scattered around it in the Arabic style of dining, rather than sitting in chairs as she was used to.

Khalil emerged from the shadows, dressed in a loose, white cotton shirt and dark trousers; he'd taken off the traditional *thobe* she'd seen him in before. With his golden eyes and midnight hair, his chiselled jaw glinting with dark stubble, he looked like a sexy and dangerous pirate. Dangerous, she told herself, being the operative word.

Elena swallowed audibly as Khalil's heated gaze swept over her. 'You look lovely, Your Highness.'

'I'm not sure what the point of this dress is,' Elena retorted. 'Or this meal.' She was feeling far too vulnerable already, and attack was her best defence. She'd learned that in the Council Room; it had helped keep the crown on her head for four years.

When Markos had mocked her plans for better childcare provision, saying how women didn't need to work, Elena had come back with the percentages of women who did. When he'd belittled her idea for an arts festival, she'd pointed out the increased tourist revenues such events would bring. She'd refused to back down, and it was probably why he hated her. Why he wanted to end her rule.

Khalil had been walking towards her with graceful, predatory intent, but he stopped at her sharp words and raised an eyebrow. 'You complained this morning about being kept in your tent like a prisoner. I thought you would enjoy having company, even if it is mine.' A smile flickered over his face and died. 'Likewise, I thought you might prefer a dress to the admittedly more suitable khakis. I'm sorry if I was wrong.'

Now she felt ridiculous and even a little ashamed, almost

as if she'd hurt his feelings. Khalil waited, his expression ironed out to blandness. 'This is all very civilised,' Elena finally managed.

'It's meant to be civilised, Elena,' he answered. 'I have told you before, I am neither a terrorist nor a thug. Your stay here is, I'm afraid, a necessary—'

'Evil,' she filled in before she could help herself.

'Measure,' Khalil answered. Suddenly and surprisingly, he looked weary. 'If you are going to fight me all evening, perhaps you would prefer to eat in your tent. Or will you try to set fire to this one?'

Elena knew then that she didn't want to fight any more. What was the point? Khalil wasn't going to let her go. And she was wearing a beautiful dress, about to eat a lovely meal with a very attractive man. Maybe she should just enjoy herself. It was a novel concept; so much of her life as queen, and even before she'd ascended the throne, had been about duty. Sacrifice. When had anything been about pleasure?

She gave him a small smile and glanced consideringly at the creamy candles in their bronze holders. 'That would make a big enough signal fire.'

Khalil chuckled softly. 'Don't even think of it, Elena.'

'I wasn't,' she admitted. 'I've come to realise that setting a fire won't do me much good.'

'You have another idea?' he asked and walked forward to take her hand, the slide of his fingers across hers shooting sparks all the way up to her elbow.

'Well, I was thinking of trying to charm you into letting me go,' Elena answered lightly. She did a little twirl in her dress. 'The dress might help.'

Khalil's eyes gleamed. 'You'd tempt a saint, but I'm afraid I'm made of sterner stuff. Flirting won't get you very far.'

She drew back, a blush scorching her cheeks. 'I wasn't *flirting.*'

'No?' Khalil arched his eyebrows as he drew her down to the table. 'Pity.'

Even more disconcerted by his response, Elena fussed with positioning herself on the silken pillows, arranging the folds of her dress around her. Khalil sat opposite her, reclining on one elbow, every inch the relaxed and confident sheikh.

Sheikh. Yes, lying on the pillows, the candlelight glinting on his dark hair, he looked every inch the sheikh.

'Let me serve you,' Khalil said, and lifted the lids on several silver chafing dishes. He ladled some lamb stewed in fragrant spices onto her plate, along with couscous mixed with vegetables.

'It smells delicious,' Elena murmured. 'Thank you.' Khalil raised an eyebrow.

'So polite,' he said with a soft laugh. 'I'm waiting for the sting.'

'I'm hungry,' she answered, which was no answer at all because she didn't know what she was doing. What she felt.

'Then you must eat up,' Khalil said lightly. 'You are too thin, at least by Kadaran standards.'

She *was* thin, mainly because constant stress and anxiety kept her from eating properly. 'And you are familiar with Kadaran standards?' she asked. 'You said something about living in America before, didn't you?'

'I spent my adolescence in the United States,' he answered, his tone rather flat. He handed her a platter of bread, his expression shuttered, and Elena felt a surge of curiosity about this man and his experience.

'Is that why your English is so good?'

A smile flickered across his face, banishing the frown that had settled between his brows when she'd asked about where he had lived. 'Thank you. And, yes, I suppose it is.'

Elena sat back, taking dainty bites of the delicious lamb. 'How long have you been back in Kadar?'

'Six months. Is this an inquisition, Elena?' That smile now deepened, revealing the dimple Elena had seen before. '"Know your enemies and know yourself, and you can win a hundred battles".'

'You are quite familiar with *The Art of War*.'

'As are you,' he observed.

'How come you know it so well?'

'Because my life has been one of preparing for battle.'

'To become Sheikh of Kadar.'

'Yes.'

'But you're already a sheikh, aren't you? Leila told me...'

He shrugged. 'Of a small tribe in the northern desert. My mother's people.'

He was silent and so was she, the only sounds the wind ruffling the sides of the tent, the gentle clink of their dishes. Elena gazed at him, the harsh planes of his face, the sculpted fullness of his lips. Hard and soft, a mass of contradictions, this gentle kidnapper of hers. Her stomach twisted. What was she *doing*? How stupid was she being, to actually consider believing this man, trusting him?

She could tell herself she was here because she needed to know her enemy, needed to make an informed decision about her future, but Elena knew she was fooling herself. She was here because she wanted to be here. And she wanted to trust Khalil because she liked him. As a person. As a man.

'I want to hear the other side of the story,' she said quietly, and Khalil glanced up at her, his expression watchful, even wary.

'Do you,' he said, not a question, and she nodded and swallowed.

'Everyone around you is so sure, Khalil, of your right to the throne. I don't think they're brainwashed or deluded, so...' She spread her hands, tried for a smile. 'There must be some reason why people think you are the rightful sheikh. Tell me what it is.'

* * *

Tell me what it is. A simple request, yet one that felt like peeling back his skin, exposing his heart. Admitting his shame.

Khalil glanced away from Elena, his gaze distant, unfocused. He'd said before he'd tell her his side of the story when she was ready to listen, and here she was—ready.

The trouble was, he wasn't.

'Khalil,' Elena said softly. His name sounded right on her lips in a way that made everything in Khalil both want and rebel.

What was he doing? How had he got to this place, with this woman? It had started, perhaps, from the first moment he'd laid eyes on her. When, in what could be considered courage or folly or both, she'd attempted to escape. When he'd seen both fear and pride in her eyes and known exactly how she'd felt.

When he'd held her in his arms and she'd curled into him, seeking the solace that he'd freely, gladly, given.

And now she wanted more. Now she wanted the truth, which he'd told her he would tell her, except now that she'd actually asked he felt wary, reluctant. *Afraid.*

What if she didn't believe him? *What if she did?*

Finally Khalil spoke. 'My mother,' he said slowly, 'was Sheikh Hashem's first wife.'

Elena's eyes widened, although with disbelief, confusion or simply surprise he couldn't tell. 'What—who was your father?'

He bared his teeth in a smile that was a sign of his pain rather than any humour or happiness. 'Sheikh Hashem, of course.'

A hand flew to her throat. 'You mean you are Aziz's *brother*?'

'Half-brother, to be precise. Older half-brother.'

'But…' She shook her head, and now she definitely seemed disbelieving. Khalil felt something that had started to unfurl inside him begin to wither. *Good*. It was better this way. She wouldn't believe him, and he wouldn't care. It would be easy then. Painful, but easy. 'How can that be?' she asked. 'There's no mention of you anywhere, not even in that book!'

He laughed, the sound hard and bitter, revealing. 'So you read the book?'

'A bit.'

'There wouldn't be a mention of me in it. My father did his best to erase my existence from the world. But the Bedouin tribes, my mother's people, they have not forgotten me.' He hated how defensive he sounded. As if he needed to prove himself, as if he wanted her to believe him.

She didn't matter. Her opinion didn't matter. Why had he even asked her to dinner? Why had he given her that dress?

Because you wanted to please her. Because you wanted to see her again, touch her again...

Fool.

'Why would your father wish to erase your existence, Khalil?'

He gave her a glittering, challenging stare. 'Do you know who Aziz's mother is?'

Elena shrugged. 'Hashem's wife. Her name, I believe, is Hamidyah. She died a few years ago, Aziz told me.'

'Yes, she did. And, before she was my father's second wife, she was his mistress. She bore him a bastard, and my father claimed him as one. Aziz.' He let out a slow breath, one hand clenching involuntarily against his thigh. 'Then my father tired of my mother, his first wife, but Kadaran law has always dictated that the reigning monarch take only one wife.' He gave her the semblance of a smile. 'Not a moral stance, mind you, simply a pragmatic one: fewer contenders for the throne. I suspect it's why Kadar has enjoyed so many years of peace.'

'So you're saying he got rid of his wife? And—and of you? So he could marry Hamidyah?' Elena was gazing at him with an emotion he couldn't decipher. Was it confusion, disbelief or, God help him, pity? Did she think he was deluded?

'You don't believe me,' Khalil stated flatly. His stomach felt like a stone. He wasn't angry with her, he realised with a flash of fury he could only direct at himself; he was hurt.

'It seems incredible,' Elena said slowly. 'Surely someone would have known…?'

'The desert tribes know.'

'Does Aziz?'

'Of course he does.' The words came fast, spiked with bitterness. 'We met, you know, as boys.' Just weeks before he'd been torn from his family. 'Never since, although I've seen his photograph in the gossip magazines.'

Elena shook her head slowly. 'But if he knows you are the rightful heir…'

'Ah, but you see, my father is cleverer than that. He charged my mother with adultery and claimed I was not his son. He banished me from the palace when I was seven years old.'

Elena gaped at him. '*Banished…*'

'My mother as well, to a remote royal residence where she lived in isolation. She died just a few months later, although I didn't know that for many years. From the day my father threw me from the palace, I never saw her again.' He spoke dispassionately, even coldly, because if he didn't he was afraid of how he might sound. What he might reveal. Already he felt a tightness in his throat and he took a sip of wine to ease it.

'But that's terrible,' Elena whispered. She looked stricken, but her response didn't gratify Khalil. He felt too exposed for that.

'It's all ancient history,' he dismissed. 'It hardly matters now.'

'Doesn't it? This is why you're seeking the throne, as—'

'As revenge?' He filled in. 'No, Elena, it's not for revenge. It's because it's my *right*.' His voice throbbed with conviction. 'I am my father's first-born. When he set my mother aside he created deep divisions in a country that has only known peace. If you've wondered why Aziz does not have the support of his whole country, it's because too many people know he is not the rightful heir. He is popular in Siyad because he is cosmopolitan and charming, but the heart of this country is not his. It is mine.' He stared at her, his chest heaving, willing her to believe him. Needing her to.

'How can you be sure,' she whispered, 'that your mother didn't have an affair?'

'Of course I'm sure.' He heard his voice, as sharp as a blade. Disappointment dug deep. No, a feeling worse than disappointment, weaker—this damnable hurt. He took a steadying breath. 'My mother knew the consequences of an affair: banishment, shame, a life cut off from everyone and everything she knew. It would not have been worth the risk.'

'But you would have just been a boy. How could you have known?'

'I knew everyone around her believed her to be innocent. I knew her serving maids cried out at the injustice of it. I knew no man ever stepped forward to claim her or me, and my father couldn't even name the man who'd allegedly sired me. My father's entire basis for banishing both my mother and me was the colour of my eyes.'

Elena stared at him, her own golden-grey eyes filled with not confusion or disbelief but with something that was nearly his undoing: *compassion*.

'Oh, Khalil,' she whispered.

He glanced away, afraid of revealing himself. His jaw worked but he could not form words. Finally he choked out, 'People protested at the time. They said there wasn't enough proof. But then my mother died before he actually married Hamidyah, so it was, in the end, all above board.'

'And what about you?'

He couldn't admit what had happened to him: those years in the desert, the awful shame, even though part of him wanted to, part of him wanted to bare himself to this woman, give her his secrets. To trust another person, and with more than he ever had before, even as a child. He suppressed that foolish impulse and lifted one shoulder in what he hoped passed as an indifferent shrug. 'I was raised by my mother's sister, Dimah, in America. I never saw my father again.'

'And the people accepted it all?' she said quietly, only half a question. 'Aziz as the heir, even though they must have remembered you…'

'My father was a dictator. No one possessed the courage to question his actions while he was alive.'

'Why did Sheikh Hashem make such a strange will?' Elena burst out. 'Commanding Aziz to marry?'

'I think he was torn. Perhaps he realised the mistake he'd made in banishing me, but did not want to admit it. He was a proud man.' Khalil shrugged again. 'Forcing Aziz to marry would make him commit to Kadar and give up his European ways. But calling a national referendum if he didn't…' Khalil smiled grimly. 'My father must have known it was a chance for me to become Sheikh. Maybe that is just wishful thinking on my part, but I'd like to think he regretted, even if just in part, what he did to my mother and me.'

'And do you think people would accept you, if you did become Sheikh?'

'Some might have difficulty but, in time, yes. I believe they would.'

He stared at her then, willing her to tell him she believed him. Wanting, even needing, to hear it.

She looked away. Khalil's insides clenched with a helpless, hopeless anger.

Then she turned back to him, her eyes as wide and clear as twin lakes. 'Then we really are alike,' she said quietly. 'For we are both fighting for our crowns.'

CHAPTER FIVE

KHALIL'S GAZE HAD blazed anger but Elena saw something beneath the fury: *grief.* A grief she understood and felt herself. And, even though she didn't want to, she felt a sympathy for Khalil, a compassion and even an anger on his behalf. He'd been terribly wronged, just as Leila had said.

She thought of him as a boy, being banished from his family and home. She imagined his confusion and fear, the utter heartbreak of losing everything he'd known and held dear.

Just as she had.

She'd been a bit older, but her family had been wrenched from her in a matter of moments, just as Khalil's had. She was fighting to keep her rightful title, just as Khalil was.

With a jolt she realised what this meant: she believed him. She believed he was the rightful heir.

For a second everything in her rebelled. *You believed before. You trusted before. And this man has kidnapped you—how can you be so stupid?*

Yet she'd heard the sincerity in Khalil's voice. She'd felt his pain. She knew him in a way she hadn't known anyone else, because they were so alike.

She believed him.

'How are you fighting for your crown, Elena?' he asked quietly.

She hesitated, because honesty didn't come easily, and letting herself be vulnerable felt akin to pulling out her fingernails one by one. She'd hardened her heart in the last four years. She'd learned to be tough, to need no one.

And yet Khalil had been honest with her. He'd told her his story and she'd seen in his eyes that he'd wanted, even needed, her to believe him.

She took a deep breath. She thought of Andreas Markos and his determination to discredit her—her Council and country's desire for a king, or the closest thing to it. Her own foolish choices. 'It's complicated.'

'Most things are.'

He waited and Elena sifted through all the things she could say. 'My country, and my Council, would like a male ruler.'

'And you wanted that to be Aziz?'

She heard incredulity in his tone and bristled. 'Not like that. We had an agreement—he would attend state functions with me as Prince Consort, act as ruler in name only. It would satisfy the people and, I hoped, my Council. But he wouldn't actually have been involved in any decision making.'

'And you would have been satisfied with that?'

'It was what I wanted.'

'Why not find a man who could truly be your equal, your partner? Who could help you to rule, who could support you?'

Briefly, painfully, she thought of Paulo. 'You speak as though such a thing is simple. Easy.'

'No. Not that. But I wonder why you settle.'

She swallowed past the sudden tightness in her throat. 'What about you, Khalil? Do you want an equal, a partner in marriage as well as in ruling?'

Surprise flashed briefly in his eyes before his expression hardened. 'No.'

'Then why do you think I would want one? Simply because I am a woman?'

'No...' He gazed at her thoughtfully. 'I only asked, because if you needed to marry to please your country it seems wise to pick a man who could be your friend and helpmate, not a stranger.'

'Well, unfortunately for me, I don't have a friend and helpmate waiting in the wings.' She'd meant to sound light and wry but cringed at the self-pity she heard in her voice instead. 'I've been alone for a long time,' she continued when she trusted herself to sound more measured. 'I'm used to it now, and it's more comfortable for me that way.' Even if, since meeting Khalil, she'd started to realise all she'd been missing out on. 'I imagine you might be the same.'

'Yes, I am.'

'Well, then.'

Khalil leaned back in his seat, his gaze sweeping over her in thoughtful assessment. 'So you made this arrangement with Aziz to please your Council?'

'Appease them, more like.' Elena hesitated, not wanting to admit more but knowing she needed to. 'The Head of Council, Andreas Markos, has threatened to call a vote at the next convening.' She took a breath, then forced herself to finish. 'A vote to depose me and abolish the monarchy.'

Khalil was silent for a moment. 'And, let me guess, put himself forward as head of state? Prime Minister, perhaps?'

Amazingly she found herself smiling wryly. 'Something like that.'

'And you think he won't if you are married?'

'I'm gambling that he won't,' Elena admitted. 'It's a calculated risk.'

'I understand about those.'

'Yes, I suppose you do.' They smiled at each other, and as the moment spun out Elena wondered at herself. How could they be joking about her captivity? How could she feel, in that moment, that they were co-conspirators, somehow complicit in all that had happened? Yet she did, and more than that. So much more than that.

'The Thallian people like me, for the most part,' she

continued after a moment. 'And a royal marriage would be very popular. Markos would have a difficult time getting the Council to vote against me if the country approved.'

'I imagine,' Khalil said quietly, 'that your people like you very much indeed, Elena. I think you must be a good queen. You are clearly very loyal to your people.'

Pleasure rippled through her at the sincerity she heard in his voice. It meant so much, more than she'd ever even realised, to have someone believe in her.

'I'm trying to be a good queen,' she said in a low voice. 'I know I've made mistakes—' and she didn't want to talk about those '—but I love Thallia and its people. I want to celebrate its traditions, but also bring it into the twenty-first century.'

Khalil arched an eyebrow. 'And have you had much success so far?'

Elena ducked her head, suddenly shy. She wasn't used to talking about her accomplishments; so often they went unrecognised, by her Council, at any rate. 'A bit. I've introduced some new policies to protect women's rights. I've initiated a review of the national curriculum for primary schools. The education in Thallia has been one of its weaknesses.'

Khalil nodded, encouraging, and shyly Elena continued, 'I also helped to start an annual festival to celebrate the country's music and dance. It's a small thing, but important to our heritage. Thallia is named after the muse of poetry, you know.'

'I didn't know.' His eyes, Elena saw, crinkled when he smiled. She looked away.

'I know it doesn't sound like much.'

'Why belittle yourself or what you've done? There are enough people to do that for you. I've learned that much.'

'We've both persevered,' Elena said quietly. She met his gaze and held it, feeling an overwhelming solidarity with this man who had once been her enemy. They were so alike. He understood her, and she understood him, more than she'd ever expected.

'And this Markos,' Khalil said after a moment. 'He has that power—to call such a vote?'

'Unfortunately he does. Our Constitution states that the monarch cannot enact a law that isn't approved by the majority of the Council, and the Council can't pass one that isn't endorsed by the King or Queen.' Elena gave a rather bleak smile. 'But there's one important caveat: if the Council votes unanimously, the monarch is forced to acquiesce.'

'Even to your own demise?'

'That hasn't happened in a thousand years.' She looked away then, afraid he'd see the fear and shame on her face: the fear that she would be the one to end it. The shame that she wasn't strong enough to keep her crown or the promise she'd made to her father as he'd lain dying.

For Thallia, Elena. You must live for Thallia and the crown.

'You won't be the one to end it, Elena,' Khalil said quietly. The certainty in his voice made her glow inside. 'You're too strong for that.'

'Thank you,' she whispered.

'You have a lot of pressure put on you, for such a young woman,' Khalil continued. Elena just shrugged. 'You are an only child, I presume? The title has always fallen to you?'

'Yes, although for most of my childhood my parents hoped for more children.' Her mouth twisted downwards. 'For a boy.'

'And they were disappointed, I presume?'

'Yes. My mother had many miscarriages, but no more live children.'

'A tragedy.'

'Yes. I suppose it's why they felt a need to keep me so sheltered. Protected.'

'You were doted on?'

'Not exactly.' She thought of how little she'd actually

seen her parents. 'Kept apart, really. I didn't go to formal school until I was thirteen.' When she'd been gawky, over-whelmed and terribly shy. It hadn't been a great introduction to school life.

'And then you became Queen at a young age,' Khalil continued. He reached over to refill her glass with wine. Elena had already finished her first glass; Dutch courage, she supposed, for when she'd been telling him all that truth. She took another sip of wine now as she met his tawny gaze.

'Nineteen,' she said after she had swallowed, felt the liquid slip down her throat and steal seductively through her again.

'I know your parents died in a terrorist bombing,' Khalil said quietly. Elena nodded. She dreaded talking or even thinking about that awful day, hated the memories of the acrid smell of smoke, the stinging pain of broken glass on the palms of her hands, the ringing in her ears—all of it still causing her to wake up in an icy sweat far too many nights.

'I'm sorry,' Khalil continued. 'I know what it is to lose your parents when you are young.'

'Yes, I suppose you do.'

'You must miss them.'

'I do…'

Khalil cocked his head. 'You sound uncertain.'

'No, of course not.' Elena bit her lip. 'It's only that I didn't actually know them all that well. They were away so much… I miss the *idea* of them, if that makes sense. Of what—what I wish we could have been like as a family. That probably sounds strange.'

Khalil shook his head. 'Not strange at all,' he answered quietly, and Elena wondered if he missed the family he could have had too: loving parents, supporting him even now.

Khalil leaned forward, his fingers whispering against her cheek as he tucked a strand of hair behind her ear.

'You look so sad,' he said softly. 'I'm sorry to bring up bad memories.'

'It's okay,' she whispered. Khalil's fingers lingered on her cheek and she wished, suddenly and fiercely, that he wouldn't pull away.

That he would kiss her.

Her lips parted instinctively and her gaze rested on his mouth, making her realise yet again how sculpted and re- ally *perfect* his lips were. She wondered how they would feel. How they would taste. She'd never actually been kissed before, which suddenly seemed ridiculous at the age of twenty-three. But a convent-school education and becoming Queen at just nineteen had kept her from ever pursuing a romantic relationship. First there hadn't been any opportunity, and then she'd been so focused on protect- ing her crown and serving her country there hadn't been any time. Besides, suitable partners for a reigning queen were not exactly plentiful.

Elena knew she shouldn't be thinking of kissing Khalil now. With effort she dragged her gaze up towards his eyes, saw they were molten gold. His fingers tightened on her cheek, his thumb grazing her jawbone, drawing her inexo- rably forward. And Elena went, her heart starting to ham- mer as she braced herself for that wonderful onslaught.

Then Khalil released her, his hand falling away from her face as he sat back in his chair.

Her mind whirled with confusion and disappointment, and her body ached with unfulfilled desire. She scrambled for a way to cover her own obvious longing. 'This is very good,' she said stiltedly, gesturing to her half-eaten meal.

Khalil acknowledged her compliment with a nod. 'Thank you.'

'You have quite an elaborate set-up for a desert camp,' she continued, determined to keep the conversation off dangerous subjects—although every subject felt danger- ous now. Everything about Khalil felt dangerous.

Desirable.

'Comfort need not be sacrificed,' he remarked, taking a sip of wine.

'I suppose you feel very secure?' she asked. 'To have such a…permanent arrangement?'

'These are tents, Elena, as luxurious as they may be. My men and I could disassemble this camp in twenty minutes, if need be.'

'How do you know how to do all this if you grew up in America?'

'All this?' Khalil repeated, raising his eyebrows.

'Tents. Horses. Fighting. All this—this rebel stuff.' She realised she sounded rather ridiculous and she shrugged, half in apology, half in defiance. Heaven help her, she'd had two glasses of wine and she was nearly drunk.

'I served in the French Foreign Legion for seven years,' Khalil told her. 'I'm used to this kind of living.'

'You did?'

'It was good preparation.'

Everything in his life, Elena supposed, had been to prepare for being Sheikh, for taking the throne from the half-brother who didn't deserve it.

Aziz… Why could she barely remember his face now? She'd been going to marry him, yet she'd forgotten what he looked like, or how his voice sounded. And with that thought came another fast on its heels.

She wasn't going to marry him any more. Even if he rescued her, or Khalil released her, she wasn't going to marry Aziz.

It was both a revelation and completely unsurprising. Elena sat back, her mind spinning both from her thoughts and the wine she'd drunk. For the first time, she accepted her fate…even if she had no idea what it would actually mean for her title, her crown, her country.

'I'm not going to marry him,' she blurted. 'Aziz. Not even…not even if he found me in time.'

Something flashed in Khalil's eyes and he sat back. 'What made you change your mind?'

'You did,' she said simply, and she knew she meant it in more ways than one. Not just because he was the rightful Sheikh, but because he'd opened up feelings inside her she hadn't known she'd possessed. She couldn't marry Aziz now, couldn't settle for the kind of cold, mercenary arrangement she'd once wanted.

'I'm glad,' Khalil said quietly. They gazed at each other for a long moment, and everything in Elena tensed, yearned…

Then Khalil rose from the table. 'It is late. You should return to your tent.'

He reached for her hand, and Elena let him pull her up. She felt fluid, boneless; the wine must have really gone to her head.

He kept hold of her hand as they stepped outside the tent, the night dark and endless around them. The air was surprisingly cold and crisp, which had a sobering effect on Elena.

By the time they'd crossed the camp to her tent, Khalil's hand still loosely linked with hers, she wasn't feeling tipsy at all, just embarrassed. The evening's emotional intimacies and revelations were enough now to make her cringe.

'Goodnight, Elena.' Khalil stopped in front of her tent, sliding his hand from hers. He touched her chin with his fingers, tipped her head up so she was blinking at him, the night sky spangled with stars high above him.

For a moment as she looked up at him, just as when they'd been in his tent, she thought he might kiss her. Her lips parted and her head spun and her heart started thudding in a mix of alarm, anticipation and a suspended sense of wonder.

Khalil lowered his head, his mouth a whisper away from hers. 'Elena,' he murmured; it sounded like a question. Everything in Elena answered, *yes*.

She reached up to put her hands on his shoulders; her body pressed against his, the feel of his hard chest sending little shocks of sensation through her.

His hands slid up to frame her face, his fingers so gentle on her skin. She felt his desire as well as her own, felt his yearning and surprise, and thought, *We are alike in this too. We both want this, but we're also afraid to want it.*

Although perhaps Khalil didn't want it, after all, for he suddenly dropped his hands from her and stepped back. 'Goodnight,' he said again, and then he started walking back to his tent and was soon swallowed up by the darkness.

CHAPTER SIX

ELENA DIDN'T SEE Khalil at all the next day. She spent hours lying on her bed or sitting outside her tent, watching the men go about the camp and looking for Khalil.

She missed him. She told herself that was absurd, because she barely knew him. She'd only met him two days ago, and hardly in the best of circumstances.

Yet she still found herself reliving the times he'd touched her: the slide of his fingers on her jaw; the press of his chest against her cheek. She replayed their dinner conversation in her mind, thought about his lonely childhood, his determination to be Sheikh. And realised in just three days he would let her go and she would never see him again.

A thought that made a twist of bewildering longing spiral inside her.

Then the next morning Khalil came to her tent. He loomed large in the space and shamelessly she let her gaze rove over him, taking in his broad shoulders, his dark hair, his impossibly hard jaw.

'I need to go visit some of the desert tribes,' he told her without preamble. 'And I'd like you to go with me.'

Shock as well as a wary pleasure rippled through her in a double wave. 'You…would?'

He arched an eyebrow and gave her a small smile. 'Wouldn't you like to see something other than the inside of this tent?'

'Yes, but…why do you want me to go?' A terrible suspicion took hold of her. 'You aren't…you aren't going to show me off as some trophy of war, are you? Show your people how you captured Aziz's bride?' Just the idea made her stomach churn. Why *shouldn't* he do such a thing? He'd captured her, after all. She was his possession, his prize.

Khalil's face darkened, his eyebrows drawing together in a fierce frown. 'No, of course not. In any case, the people I'm visiting wouldn't be impressed by such antics.'

'Wouldn't they?'

'They are loyal to me. And I would never act in such a barbaric fashion.'

'Then why are you taking me?'

Khalil stared at Elena, the question reverberating through him. *Then why are you taking me?*

The simple answer was because he wanted to. Because he'd been thinking about her since they'd had dinner together, since she'd shown how she believed him. Believed *in* him. And having someone's trust, even if it was just a little of it, was as heady and addictive as a drug. He wanted more. He wanted more of Elena and he wanted more of the person he felt he was in her eyes. The man he wanted to be.

The realisation had kept him from her for an entire day, fighting it, fighting the need and the desire, the danger and the weakness of wanting another person. Of opening himself to pain, loss and grief.

By last night he'd convinced himself that taking her to see the desert tribes who supported him was a political move; it would strengthen his position to have Aziz's former bride on his side.

Gazing at her now, her hair tumbled over her shoulders, her heavy-lidded eyes with their perceptive grey-gold gaze trained on him, he knew he'd been fooling himself.

This wasn't some political manoeuvre. This was simply him wanting to be with Elena.

'I'm taking you,' he said, choosing his words slowly,

carefully, 'because I want you to meet the people who support me.'

Her eyes widened. Her lips parted and then curved in a tremulous smile. 'You do?'

Khalil's hands curled into fists. Everything in him resisted this admission, this appalling weakness. Where was his ruthless determination now? All he wanted in this moment was to see Elena's smile deepen. 'I do.'

'All right,' she said, and Khalil felt relief and even joy pour through him. He smiled, a wider smile than he'd ever felt on his face before, and she grinned back.

Something had changed. Something was changing right here between them and, God help him, but he couldn't stop it. He didn't even want to.

'We should leave within the hour. Can you ride?'

'Yes.'

'Then dress for riding. Leila will find you the appropriate clothes.' With a nod, he started to leave, then turned back to face her. 'Thank you, Elena,' he said quietly, meaning it utterly, and the smile she offered him felt like a precious gift.

An hour later Elena met him on the edge of the camp, where he was saddling the horses they would take. Khalil nodded his approval of her sensible clothing, headscarf and boots, a familiar tightness in his chest easing just at the sight of her.

'We should waste no time in departing. It is half a day's ride and I intend for us to arrive before nightfall.'

She glanced, clearly surprised, at the two horses. 'We're going alone?'

'Three men will accompany us, but they will ride separately. We will meet up with the guards before we enter the camp, so all will be appropriate.'

'Appropriate?'

'In the desert, a man and woman generally do not ride alone.'

She nodded slowly, accepting, her gaze darting between the horses and him.

Khalil acknowledged he was breaching protocol in so many ways. 'You'll be safe with me, Elena,' he said and she looked back at him.

'I know that.'

'Do you?' He felt a smile spread across his face. 'Good.'

'I trust you,' she said simply, and for a moment he couldn't speak. He'd kidnapped her, after all. He didn't deserve her trust, yet she gave it. Freely. Wholly.

'Thank you,' he finally said.

She stepped closer to him, so he caught the scent of roses. 'Are we travelling alone because it's safer? I mean, so Aziz won't find us?'

She spoke without any rancour, yet Khalil felt that churning guilt once more, and more acutely this time, because for the first time something felt stronger than his burning need to be Sheikh.

He refused to name just what it was.

'Yes,' he answered. 'Does that…distress you?'

Her clear gaze searched his and she smiled wryly. 'Not as much as it should.'

He acknowledged her point with a small nod. 'Things are changing.'

'They've already changed,' she said quietly, and something in him both swelled and ached.

He shouldn't want things to change. Change meant losing his focus, losing his whole sense of self. What was he, if not the future Sheikh of Kadar? Everything in his life had been for that purpose. He'd had no room for other ideas or ambitions, and certainly none for relationships.

Yet he knew Elena was right. Things had already changed…whether he'd wanted them to or not.

'Let's go,' he said, a bit more gruffly than he intended, and he laced his fingers together to offer Elena a foothold.

She rode just like she walked or stood, with inherent

elegance and pride. Her back was ramrod straight as she controlled the excited prancing of her horse.

'How well can you ride?' he asked and her eyes sparkled at him.

'Well.'

Khalil's mouth curved. 'Let's see about that,' he said, and with a shout he took off at a gallop. He heard Elena's surprised laughter echo behind him as she gave chase.

Elena felt the kind of thrill of exhilaration she hadn't experienced since she'd been a child riding in Thallia as she followed Khalil. It felt wonderful to be on a horse again, the desert flashing by in a blur of rocks and sand. She had had no time for such pursuits since she'd been queen. She hadn't ridden like this in years.

The only sound was her horse's hooves galloping across the sand. She spurred the beast on, eager to catch up with Khalil—or even pass him. Although he hadn't said, she knew it had become a race.

Glancing behind him, Khalil pointed to a towering, needle-like boulder in the distance that Elena knew must be the finish line. She nodded back and crouched low over the horse as the wind whistled past. She was only a length behind him, and in the last dash to the finish line she made up half a length, but Khalil's horse still crossed a beat before hers.

Laughing, she reined the animal in and patted his sweat-soaked neck. 'That was close.'

'Very close,' Khalil agreed. His teeth gleamed white in his bronzed face. He wore a turban to keep out the sun and sand, and somehow it made him look more masculine. More desirable. 'Foolish, perhaps, to race,' he continued. 'There is a small oasis here. We'll let the horses drink before we continue.'

'A small oasis? I'd thought the next one was a day's ride by camel.'

Khalil just shrugged and Elena let out a huff of indignation. 'So you lied to me?'

'I wanted to discourage you from doing something foolish, something that most certainly wouldn't end well.'

'I could have escaped now,' Elena pointed out. 'I was on a horse, with water and food in my saddlebags.'

Khalil gazed at her evenly. 'I know. But you didn't.'

'No.' She hadn't even thought of it, hadn't been remotely tempted. The knowledge should have shamed her, but instead she felt almost ebullient.

They led the horses to the oasis, and as the animals drank Khalil gazed at the horizon with a frown.

'What's wrong?' Elena asked.

'It looks like a storm might rise.'

'A storm?' She gazed up at the endless blue sky, hard and bright, in incredulity. 'How on earth can you tell?'

'Look there.' Khalil pointed to the horizon and Elena squinted. She could see a faint grey smudge, but that was all. If Khalil hadn't pointed it out, she wouldn't have noticed it.

'Surely that's far away.'

'It is now. Storms in the desert can travel all too quickly. We should ride. I want to get to the camp before the storm gets to us. We'll need to meet up with the guards as well.'

They saddled up once more and headed off at a brisk canter. The sun was hot above, the sand shimmering in the midday heat. Elena kept her gaze on the horizon, noticing with each passing hour that the faint smudge was becoming darker and wider. The stiff breeze she'd felt at camp had turned into a relentless wind.

After several hours of tense riding, Khalil guided them to a grouping of boulders. 'We will not be able to outride the storm,' he said. 'We'll have to shelter here for the night and try to meet up with my men in the morning.'

Elena slid off her horse, glancing at the forbidding-looking rocks with some apprehension. 'Where are we, exactly?'

Khalil gave her the glimmer of a smile. 'In the middle of the desert.'

'Yes…' Standing there next to her horse, the desert endless around her, the sky darkening rapidly and the wind kicking up sand, she suddenly felt acutely how strange this all was. How little she knew Khalil, even if her heart protested otherwise.

'Elena.' Khalil stood in front of her and she blinked up at him, nearly swaying on her feet. 'I will keep you safe.'

She believed him, Elena knew. She trusted him, even if it was foolish. When had any other person been concerned for her safety? Paulo had said he had, but he'd been lying. Her father had, but only for the sake of his country, and he'd paid with his life.

Looking up at Khalil, Elena was struck as forcefully as a fist with the knowledge that he would keep her safe because he cared for her as a person, not as a pawn, or even as a queen. Simply because of who she was—and who he was. The knowledge nearly brought tears to her eyes.

'You look as if you are going to collapse,' he said gently. 'Come. I have food and drink.' He took her by the hand, his warm, callused palm comforting as it closed around her own far smaller one, and led her towards the group of immense black boulders.

He was clearly familiar with the territory, for he led her with confidence through the maze of rocks, coming to a stop in front of a large, flat rock sheltered by a huge boulder above it.

He drew her underneath it and she sat down with her back against the boulder, the overhanging rock providing shelter from the rising wind and swirling sand. He removed his turban so she pulled off her headscarf and ran a hand over her dishevelled hair.

'Drink,' he said and handed her a canteen of water.

She unscrewed the top of the canteen and took a much-needed and grateful sip of water.

'And there's food,' Khalil said, handing her a piece of flat bread and some dried meat. She ate both, as did he, both of them silently chewing as the wind picked up and howled around them.

After she'd finished eating Elena drew her knees up to her chest and watched Khalil put the remnants of their meal back in the saddlebags.

He was a beautiful man, she thought, not for the first time; his sculpted mouth and long lashes softened a face of utterly unyielding hardness. As he tidied up she saw several whitened scars on the inside of his wrist and she leaned forward.

'How did you get those?'

Khalil tensed, his mouth thinning. 'Rope burns,' he said shortly, and Elena stared at him in confusion.

'Rope?'

'It was a long time ago.' He turned away, clearly not wanting to say anything further, although Elena wanted to ask. She wanted to know. Rope burns on his wrists… Had he been *tied up*?

She sat back against the rock and watched as he settled himself opposite her. 'Now what?' she asked.

His smile gleamed in the oncoming darkness. 'Well, I'm afraid I didn't bring a chessboard.'

She gave a little laugh. 'Pity. I'm actually quite good at chess.'

'So am I.'

'Is that a challenge?'

His gaze flicked over her. 'Maybe.'

Excitement fizzed through her. Were they actually flirting? About *chess*? 'Perhaps we'll have a match some time,' she said, and realised belatedly how that made it sound— as if they would have some kind of future beyond her time here. Even though she'd accepted she wouldn't marry Aziz, it didn't mean she had any kind of future with Khalil. She'd be deluding herself to think otherwise.

In two days he was going to let her go.

Why did that make her feel so...*bereft*?

'What are you thinking about?' Khalil asked quietly and she turned back to him, wondering if she dared to admit the truth.

'That in two days I might never see you again.' She took a breath, held it, and forced herself to continue. 'I don't like that thought, Khalil.'

She couldn't make out his expression in the darkness. 'Elena,' he said, and it sounded like a warning.

'I know this is going to sound ridiculous,' she continued, *needing* to be honest now, 'but you're the first real friend I've ever had.'

She tensed, waiting for incredulity, perhaps his discomfort or even derision. Instead he looked away and said quietly, 'That's not ridiculous. In many ways, you're the first friend I've had too.'

Her breath caught in her chest. 'Really?'

He turned back to her, the glimmer of a smile just visible in the moonlight. 'Really.'

'Not even at school? In America?'

She felt him tense but then he shook his head. 'Not even then. What about you? No school friends?'

'Not really.' She hugged her knees to her chest, remembering those lonely years in convent school. 'I was terribly shy in school, coming to it so late. And, looking back, I think the fact that I was a princess intimidated the other girls, although at the time I was the one who was intimidated. Everyone else made it look so easy. Having friends, having a laugh. I envied them all. I wanted to be like they were, but I didn't know how. And then later, after school...' She thought for one blinding moment of Paulo and her throat tightened. 'Sometimes it just doesn't seem worth the risk.'

'The risk?'

She swallowed and met his gaze unflinchingly. It was amazing how easy, how *necessary,* honesty felt sometimes. 'Of getting hurt.'

Khalil didn't speak for a long moment. Okay, so honesty wasn't so easy, Elena thought as she shifted where she sat. She had no idea what he felt about what she'd said.

'Have you been hurt, Elena?' he finally asked, and in the darkness his voice seemed like a separate entity, as soft as velvet, caressing the syllables of her name.

'Hasn't everyone, at one time or another?'

'That's not really an answer.'

'Have *you* been hurt, Khalil?'

'That's not an answer either, but yes, I have.' He spoke evenly, but she still felt the ocean of pain underneath. 'My father hurt me when he chose to disown and banish me.'

'Oh, Khalil.' She bit her lip, remorse rushing through her. 'I'm sorry. That was a thoughtless question for me to ask.'

'Not at all. But I want you to answer my question. What were you talking about when you said friendship wasn't worth the risk?'

'I had a friend once,' Elena said slowly. 'And he let me down rather badly. He—betrayed me.' She shook her head. 'That sounds melodramatic, but that's what happened.'

'He,' Khalil said neutrally, and with a dart of surprise she wondered if he was actually jealous.

'Yes, he. But it wasn't romantic, not remotely.' She sighed. 'It was stupid, really. I was stupid to trust him.'

'So this man is why you don't trust people?'

'I've learned my lesson. But I trust you, Khalil.'

She heard his breath come out in a rush. 'Maybe you shouldn't.'

'Why do you say that?'

'Do I need to remind you why you're here in the first place, Elena? I *kidnapped* you.'

She heard genuine remorse in his voice and she reached out and touched his hand, her fingers skimming across his skin. 'I know you did, Khalil, but I also understand why you did it.'

'You're justifying my actions to me?' he asked with a wry laugh, and Elena managed a laugh back.

'I don't know what I'm doing,' she answered honestly. 'And I don't know what I'd do if you let me go right now. I don't know how I'd feel.'

She held her breath, waiting for his reply, needing him to say something—but what?

'I don't know how I'd feel either,' Khalil answered in a low voice, and that was enough. That was more than enough.

Whatever was happening between them, Khalil recognised it as well. Just as he'd said before, *things were changing*.

Things had changed.

'The temperature is dropping,' Khalil said after a moment. 'Here.' He handed her a blanket and Elena wrapped it around herself. The wind howled; the night air was cold and crisp as she huddled against the rock, trying to make herself comfortable.

After a moment she heard Khalil sigh. 'Elena. Come here.'

'Come—where?'

'Here.' He patted his lap. 'You're obviously cold and I know of only one way to warm you right now.'

Her cheeks heated as she thought of other ways he could warm her. Ways she'd never even experienced before. 'But...'

'You've been on my lap before,' he reminded her.

Yes, and she'd enjoyed it far too much. Elena hesitated, torn between the fierce desire to be close to Khalil again and the ever-present need to keep herself safe. What could happen between them, after all? In two days she would return to Thallia, and without a husband. If she had any sense, she'd keep her distance from Khalil.

It seemed she didn't have any sense. She scooted across the rock, hesitating in front of him, not quite sure actually how to get on his lap.

Khalil had no such hesitation. Without ceremony or any awkwardness at all he slid his arms around her waist and hauled her onto him. Once there, she found it amazingly easy to curl into him just as she'd done before, her legs lying across his, her cheek pressed against his chest.

'Now that's better,' Khalil said, and his voice was a comforting rumble she could feel reverberate right through her. He stroked her hair, his fingers smoothing over the dark strands.

'Sleep,' he said, his voice a caress, and obediently she closed her eyes even though she knew she would be less likely to sleep warm and safe on Khalil's lap than when she'd been huddling by herself in the cold.

She was too aware of everything: the solid strength of his chest, the steady rise and fall of his breathing. The warmth of him, his arms snuggled safely around her, and even the scent of him, a woodsy aftershave mingled with the smell of horse and leather.

He continued to stroke her hair, pulling her gently into his chest so she snuggled in even more deeply, her lips barely brushing the warm, bare skin of his throat. Never had anything felt so familiar. So right.

She slept.

And woke in the clutches of a nightmare.

She hadn't had one of her old nightmares in a long time, mainly because she never slept deeply enough to have any dreams at all. Now lulled to sleep in the warmth and safety of Khalil's arms, it came for her.

Smoke. Screams. Blood. Bombs. In her dreams it was always the same: a chaos of terror, bodies strewn over the floor, shattered glass cutting into her palms. And the worst part of all: the heavy weight of her father on her back, his body shielding hers from the explosion, the last words he ever spoke whispered into her ear along with his last breath.

'For Thallia.'

'Elena. *Elena*.'

She came to consciousness with Khalil's hands on her shoulders, shaking her gently, and tears on her face. She drew a shuddering breath and felt panic clutch at her even though she was awake, for the darkness and the howling wind reminded her of that terrible night.

'It was just a dream, Elena.' She felt Khalil's hands slide up to cup her face, his forehead pressing into hers as if he could imbue her with his warmth, his certainty. 'Whatever it was, it was just a dream.'

She closed her eyes, willing her heart rate to slow, the terrible images that flashed through her mind in brutal replay to fade. 'I know,' she whispered after a long moment. 'I know.'

The touch of his palm cradling her cheek felt achingly, painfully sweet. 'What do you dream of, Elena?' he whispered and her throat went tight, too tight to speak. He ran his thumb lightly over her lips. 'What haunts you so?'

'Memories,' she managed, her voice choked, suffocated. She reached up to wipe the remnants of tears from her face. 'Memories of when my parents died.'

Khalil's hands stilled on her face. 'You were there?'

'Yes.'

'Why didn't I know that?'

'It was kept out of the press, out of respect for my family. That's what I wanted. It was hard enough, dealing with what had happened, without everyone gawking at me.'

'Yes.' Khalil slid his arms around her and pulled her closer to him. 'I can imagine it was. Do you want to talk about it?'

Amazingly, she did. Normally she never talked about her parents' deaths to anyone. She didn't even like remembering it. But, safe in Khalil's arms, she felt the need to tell him her story. Share her pain.

'You know they died in the bombing,' Elena began slowly. 'And as far as I know, my mother died instantly. But my father—my father and I were alive after the bomb went off.'

Khalil didn't say anything, just held her close. After a moment Elena continued. 'I can't remember much after the first bomb went off. I was thrown across the room and I landed on my back. I must have been unconscious for a little while, because I remember waking up, feeling completely disorientated. And everything…' She drew a shuddering breath. 'Everything was madness. People screaming and crying. So much blood…' She shook her head, closing her eyes as she pressed her face into the solid warmth of Khalil's chest.

'I crawled across the floor, looking for my parents. There was broken glass everywhere but I didn't even feel it, although later I saw my hands were covered in blood. It was so strange, so surreal… I felt numb and yet utterly terrified. And then I found my mother…' She stopped then, because she never let herself think about that moment even though sometimes she felt as if it never left her thoughts: her mother's lifeless face, her mouth opened in a soundless scream, her staring eyes.

She'd turned from her mother's body and had seen her father stumbling towards her, terror etched on every feature.

'There was a second bomb,' she told Khalil, her voice muffled against his chest. 'My father knew somehow. Maybe he guessed, or saw something. But he ran towards me and threw his body over me as it went off. The last thing he said…' Another deep, shuddering breath. '"For Thallia",' she quoted softly. 'He said "For Thallia" because he was saving my life for our country, so I could be queen.'

Khalil was silent for a long moment, his arms snugged

around her. 'And you think that was the only reason he was saving your life,' he surmised quietly. 'For the monarchy, not for you. Not because you were his daughter. Because he loved you.'

His words, so softly and surely spoken, cut her to the heart, because she knew they were true and she was amazed that Khalil had been able to see that. Understand it.

'I never knew what they felt,' she whispered. 'I hardly ever saw them, all through my childhood. They were devoted to Thallia, but they never spent time with me.' She let out a shuddering breath. 'And then they were gone in a single moment, and I didn't know if I missed them because they were dead or because I never actually knew them in the first place.' She closed her eyes. 'Is that awful?'

'No, it's understandable.'

'But it seems so ungrateful. My father gave his life for me.'

'You've a right to your feelings, Elena. They loved you, but how were you to know it if they didn't show it until they'd died?'

She pressed her face even harder against his chest, willing the tears that threatened to recede. She wasn't even sure what she was crying for. Her parents' deaths? The lack of relationship she'd had while they'd been alive? Or simply the swamping sense of loss she felt, as if she'd experienced it for ever?

Until Khalil.

She twisted to look up at him. 'I've never told anyone all that.'

'I'm glad you told me.'

'I'm glad I did too.' She hesitated, because she felt a need to reassure him and, perhaps herself, that she knew this wasn't real—that whatever intimacy had sprung between them was separate from what was going on in their lives. It didn't really count.

Yet she said nothing, because it *felt* like it counted. It

felt like the only thing that counted. Khalil had given her something, or maybe he'd just showed her she already had it: a capacity to share, to trust. To love.

She looked up at him, searching his face, wanting to know what he was feeling, if he felt the same pull of attraction and empathy that she did. But then she met his gaze and saw the fire burning there and her breath caught in her chest as desire, raw, fierce and overwhelming, crashed over her.

His face was so close to hers she could feel his breath fanning against her cheek, see the dark glint of stubble on his chin. His lips were no more than a whisper away from hers and, as she stared up at him and heard his breath hitch, she knew without a doubt she wanted to close that small distance between their mouths.

She wanted him to kiss her.

His head dipped and her heart seemed to stop and then soar. His lips were so close now that if she moved at all they would be touching his. They would be kissing.

Yet she didn't move, transfixed as she was by both wonder and fear, and Khalil didn't move either.

The moment stretched between them, suspended, endless.

His breath came out in a shudder and his hands tightened around her face. She tried to say something but words eluded her; all she could do was feel. Want.

Then with another shuddering breath he closed that small space between their mouths and his lips touched hers in her first and most wonderful kiss.

She let out a tiny sigh both of satisfaction and surrender, her hands coming up to tangle in the surprising softness of his hair. Her lips parted and Khalil deepened the kiss, pulling her closer as his tongue delved into her mouth, and everything in Elena throbbed powerfully to life.

She'd never known you could feel like this, want like this. It was so intense and sweet it almost felt painful. She pressed against him, acting on an instinct she hadn't realised she possessed. Khalil slid his hand from her face to cup her breast, and a shocked gasp escaped her mouth as exquisite sensation darted through her.

Khalil withdrew, dropping his hand and easing back from her so she felt a rush of loss. He reached up to cover her hands with his own and draw them down to her own lap.

'I shouldn't have…' he began then shook his head. Even in the moonlit darkness she could see the regret and remorse etched on his harsh features.

'I wanted you to,' she blurted and he just shook his head again.

'You should sleep again, if you can,' he said quietly and Elena bit her lip, blinking hard. She wondered, with a rush of humiliation, if she'd actually been the one to kiss him. In that moment it had been hard to tell, and she'd wanted it so much…

Had she actually thrown herself at him?

'Sleep, Elena,' he said softly, and he repositioned her on his lap so her head was once again pillowed by his chest. He stroked her hair just as he had before and Elena closed her eyes, even though sleep seemed farther away than ever.

What had just happened? And how could she feel so unbearably, overwhelmingly disappointed?

CHAPTER SEVEN

DAWN BROKE OVER the dunes, turning the sand pink with pale sunlight. The storm had died down and the desert had reshaped itself into a new landscape of drifts and dunes. Leaving Elena sleeping in their rocky shelter, Khalil went to check on the horses and get his bearings.

And also to figure out just what he was going to say to her when she awoke.

That kiss had been completely unplanned. Incredibly sweet. And it had left Khalil in an extremely uncomfortable state of arousal for the rest of the night.

He hadn't been able to sleep with Elena on his lap, her hair brushing his cheek, her soft body relaxed and pliant against his. His whole body, his whole *self*, had been in a state of unbearable awareness, exquisite agony.

Sleep had been the farthest thing from his mind.

But now, in the cold light of day, reality returned with an almighty thud. He could not act on his attraction to Elena. He could not nurture any softer feelings for her. He had a goal, a plan, and neither included the Queen of Thallia beyond keeping her captive and then letting her go.

Except, somehow he had forgotten that when he'd held her in his lap. When he'd shared dinner with her in his tent, and invited her to accompany him to visit the desert tribes. When he'd encouraged her to share about her life, and had told her a little bit about his. When he'd let her into his mind and even his heart. *When he'd kissed her.*

He'd told her things had changed, and he felt the change in himself. He was losing sight of his priorities and chasing rainbows instead. How could he be such a fool? How could he let his focus slip, even for a second?

It was time to get back on track, Khalil knew. To forget the fanciful feelings he'd been harbouring for Elena. What an idiot he was, to feel something soft even for a moment! To trust her. Care for her. It would only end badly... in so many ways. He knew that from hard experience. He wasn't about to repeat the mistake of trusting someone, loving someone.

Not that he loved her, Khalil told himself quickly. He barely knew her. Things had become intense between them because they were in an intense situation, that was all.

He let out a long, low breath and headed for the horses. The animals had weathered last night's storm well enough and were happy for Khalil to feed and water them. He'd just finished and was turning back to check on Elena when he saw her standing between the towering black rocks, looking tired and pale, yet also tall and straight...and so very beautiful.

His gut tightened. His groin ached. And as he stood and stared at her he was reminded of her nightmare, of the vulnerability she'd shown and the secrets she'd shared. He thought of her witnessing the death of her parents, the utter horror of the terrorist attack, and a howl of need to protect her rose up inside him. In that moment last night he'd almost told her his own terrible memories. Laid bare his own secrets.

Almost.

Now he pushed the memories away and gave her a measured smile. 'Good morning. Are you rested?'

'A bit.' She took a step closer to him and he saw uncertainty in her eyes. Questions loomed there that he didn't want her to ask. Had no intention of answering, not even in the seething silence of his own mind.

'We can eat and then we should ride. The settlement we've been aiming for is only another hour or so from here, and I hope my men will be waiting for us there. We can explain to the tribe how we became separated in the storm.'

She nodded slowly, her gaze sweeping over him like a sorrowful searchlight. Khalil tried not to flinch under it; that guilt was coming back, along with a powerful desire to pull her into his arms and bury his face in her hair, to comfort her—and himself.

What a joke. He was the last person qualified to give or receive comfort. The last person to think of caring or being cared for. He half-regretted taking her on this god-forsaken trip; he wished he'd left her to stew in her tent. But only half, because even now, when he knew better and had told himself so, he was still glad to see her. Was glad she was here with him.

'Come,' he said, and beckoned her back towards their rocky shelter. They ate the remaining flat bread and dried meat in silence, and then Khalil saddled the horses while Elena watched.

A moment later they were riding across the desert, the sky hard and blue above them, the air dry, and becoming hotter by the minute.

He watched her out of the corner of his eye, admired her long, straight back, the proud tilt of her head. She would never be bowed, he thought with a surge of almost posses-sive admiration. She would never allow herself the possi-bility of defeat. Looking at her now reminded him of how it had felt to hold her: the soft press of her breasts against his chest; the way her hair had brushed his cheek; the smell of her, like rosewater and sunshine.

His horse veered suddenly to avoid a rock, startling Khalil, and he swore under his breath. Already he was losing his concentration again, forgetting his focus. All because of Elena.

Not that he could blame her for his own lack of control. No, he blamed himself, and this sudden need that opened up inside him like a great, yawning chasm of emptiness longing to be filled. He wasn't used to feeling such a thing; for thirty years he'd basically been on his own. The only person he'd let close in all that time was Dimah, and that relationship had had its own problems and pitfalls.

No, he wasn't used to this at all. And he didn't like it. At all.

Liar.

Two hours after starting off, they finally rode into a small Bedouin settlement on the edge of an oasis. There had been no sight of his men, and uneasily Khalil wondered how it would look to the Sheikh for him to ride in alone with Elena. He pushed the thought from his mind. There was nothing he could do about it now.

He'd been here once before on one of his tours of duty through the desert, getting to know the people he was meant to rule, rallying support. Much to his amazement, they had welcomed him.

Such a response still surprised him after all these years: that anyone could accept him. Want him.

Yet he still didn't trust it, because he knew all too well how the people you loved, the people you thought loved you back, could turn on you. Utterly.

Several men came up as he swung off the horse, offering their greetings and taking the horses away before leading Khalil to the Sheikh's tent. He glanced back at Elena who was looking pale but composed as several women hustled her off to another tent.

Deciding she could handle herself for the moment, Khalil went to greet the tribe's Sheikh and explain why he was here. It would be better, he knew, to leave Elena alone for a while.

For ever.

* * *

Several clucking women surrounded Elena and she was carried along with them to a tent, bemused by their interest, and more than a little hurt by the stony look she'd seen on Khalil's face as he'd turned away.

So he regretted their kiss last night. Clearly. And she should regret it too; of course she should. Kissing Khalil was a very bad idea. Caring about him was even worse.

The trouble was, she couldn't regret it. She ached with longing for another kiss—and more. For *him*.

She'd come to this desert tribe because she'd wanted to, because she wanted to see the people who cared about Khalil.

As she cared about him.

More, it seemed, than he wanted her to.

Once in the tent, the women fluttered around her like colourful, chattering birds, touching her hair, her cheek, the clothes she wore that were now grimed with dust and dirt. Elena didn't understand anything they said, and it appeared none of them spoke either English or Greek, the two languages in which she was fluent. They all seemed wonderfully friendly, though, and she let herself be carried along by the wave of their enthusiasm as they fetched her fresh clothing and led her down to the oasis where the women of the village bathed.

After a moment's hesitation at the water's edge, she took off her clothes as the other women were doing and immersed herself in the warm, silky water. After a night in the desert and hours of hard riding it felt wonderful to wash the dirt from her body, scrub the sand from her scalp. She enjoyed the camaraderie of the women too, watching as they chattered, laughed and splashed, utterly at ease with one another. She was gratified by their willingness to include her even though she was a stranger who didn't even speak their language.

After she had bathed she slipped on the unfamiliar garments the women gave her: a cotton chemise and then a loose, woven dress with wide sleeves embroidered with red and yellow. She left her hair down to dry in the sun and accompanied the women back up to the camp where a meal had been laid out.

She looked for Khalil, and tried to ignore the flicker of disappointment she felt when she could not find him.

In the camp the women ushered her into their circle and plied her with a delicious stew of lentils, flat bread and cardamom-flavoured coffee similar to what she had drunk with Khalil. As they ate and chatted, they mimed questions which Elena did her best to answer in a similar fashion.

Within an hour or two she felt herself start to fade, the exhaustion from the night spent outside and the endless hours on horseback making her eyelids begin to droop. The women noticed and, laughing, brought her to a make-shift bed piled high with woven blankets. Grateful for their concern, Elena lay down in it, and her last thought before sleep claimed her was of Khalil.

She woke the next morning to bright sunlight filtering through the flaps of the tent that was now empty save for herself. Today, she acknowledged with a heaviness she knew she shouldn't feel, was the last day of her imprisonment. Aziz's six weeks were up. He would have married someone else or forfeited his title. Either way, she wasn't needed, and Khalil could let her go.

A thought that mere days ago would have brought relief and even joy, not this sick plunging in her stomach. She didn't want to leave Khalil, and she didn't want to face her country and Council alone. How would she explain what had happened? She supposed she'd go with what Khalil had originally suggested: 'a necessary detainment'. Perhaps she would tell the Council she'd changed her mind about the marriage when she realised Aziz's claim to the throne wasn't legitimate.

She spared a second's thought then for the man she'd

intended to marry, a moment's regret. He'd been kind to her. Looking back, she saw how his easy charm had hidden a deeper part of himself, something dark, perhaps painful. What had his experience of Khalil's banishment, his sudden arrival at the palace, felt like? How had it affected him? She supposed she would never know.

Just as she would never truly know Khalil. She'd had glimpses of a man who was both tender and strong, who had the ruthless determination to kidnap a monarch but the gentleness to cradle her and wipe away her tears. A man she knew she now cared about, whom she might never see again after today.

Sighing, Elena swung her legs onto the floor and combed her hands through her tangled hair, wondering where everyone was and just what this day would bring.

When she was as presentable as she could make herself, she stepped outside the tent, blinking in the bright sunlight. People bustled around the camp, busy with various tasks and chores; she could not see Khalil.

A woman from the night before approached her with a smile and gestured for her to come forward. Elena followed her, stopping suddenly as she caught sight of Khalil talking with a group of men. The woman followed Elena's transfixed gaze and giggled, saying something Elena didn't understand, but she had an uncomfortable feeling she'd got the gist of.

This was confirmed a few moments later when Khalil broke apart from the men to join her by a fire where she'd been eating some bread and tahini for breakfast.

'Good morning.'

She nodded back her own greeting, her mouth full of bread and her cheeks starting to heat. It was ridiculous, to have this kind of reaction to him, but it was also undeniable. All she could picture was the look of both tenderness and hunger on his face right before he'd kissed her. All she could remember was how wonderful it had felt—and how much more she had wanted.

Still did.

'You slept well?'

She swallowed her mouthful of bread and nodded once more. 'Yes, I was exhausted.'

'Understandable.'

His expression was unreadable, his tawny eyes veiled, and Elena had a terrible feeling he was going to leave it at that. Something that had become almost easy between them now felt stilted and awkward. Which was, she acknowledged, perhaps as it should be, and yet…

She felt the loss.

'What happens now?' she asked, more just to keep the conversation going than any real desire to know, although she should *want* to know, considering this was her future. Her life. She forced herself to say the words that had been throbbing through her since she'd woken that morning. 'The six weeks are up.'

'I know.'

She gazed up at him, tried to read his expression, but he looked utterly impassive. 'Are you going to let me go?'

'I promised I would.'

She nodded jerkily, feeling bereft and unable to keep herself from it.

'We should stay here for another night, if you are amenable. There is a wedding in the tribe and a big celebration is planned this evening.' He hesitated, and it almost looked as if he were blushing. 'We are the guests of honour.'

'We are? I could understand why you might be, but—'

'The members of the tribe are under the impression that we are newly married,' he interjected in a low voice. 'I have not corrected it.'

'What?' Elena bolted upright, gaping at him before she could think to close her mouth. So that was why the woman had looked at Khalil and giggled. 'But why are they under that impression?' she asked, her voice coming out in something close to a squeak. 'And why haven't you corrected it?'

'They are under it because it is the only reason they know of why a man and woman would be travelling alone together. If the storm hadn't arisen, we would have entered the camp with my men—'

'But couldn't you have explained about the storm?'

'That would not have been a good enough reason. The desert tribes are traditional. I didn't explain because to do so would have brought disapproval and shame upon both of us.' His mouth and eyes both hardened. 'Something I should have considered more carefully. I acted foolishly in asking you to accompany me.'

Elena blinked, trying to hide the hurt his recrimination made her feel. He regretted her company, along with that kiss. She drew a breath, forced herself to think about the practicalities. 'And what happens when they discover we're not married?'

'Ideally, they won't. At least, not while we're here.'

'Eventually, though…'

'Eventually, yes. But by that time I will be installed as Sheikh and I will be able to make any apologies or explanations that are necessary. To do so right now would invite even more instability.' He sighed, shifting his weight restlessly. 'I admit, I don't like lying, not even by silence—but this is a critical time, not just for myself, but for Kadar. The less unrest there is, the better.'

'So I am meant to pretend to be your wife?' Elena asked, her voice a hushed and disbelieving whisper.

Khalil's gaze seemed to burn into hers. 'Only for one day and night. Will that be so hard, Elena?'

She felt her body flood with warmth, her face flush. No, it wouldn't be hard at all—that was the problem. She looked away, willing her blush to recede. 'I don't like lying,' she muttered.

'Nor do I. But there is no choice. Although I would have

hoped that such a pretence would not be quite so abhorrent to you.' His eyes glowed with both knowledge and memory, reminding her of their kiss. It felt as if he were taunting her that he knew she wanted him, that such a fantasy would not be unpleasant at all but far, far too desirable.

Elena broke their locked gaze first, looking away from all the knowledge in Khalil's eyes. 'And after tonight?' she asked when she trusted her voice to sound as level as his had been. 'Then you'll let me go?'

'Yes. I'll take you to Siyad myself. Now that Aziz will be forced to call a referendum, there is no need for me to remain in the desert.'

She swallowed, her mind spinning with all this new information. 'What will happen to Aziz?'

Khalil shrugged. 'He will return to Europe, I imagine. He has a house in Paris. He can live the playboy life he so enjoys.'

'That's not fair,' Elena protested. 'He might be a playboy, but he has his own business, and he's done a lot of good—'

Khalil flung up a hand. 'Please. Do not defend Aziz to me.' She fell silent and he gazed at her, his mouth thinning. 'Are you so disappointed,' he asked after a moment, 'not to marry Aziz?'

'Only because of what it means for my country. My rule.'

'You are a strong woman, Elena. I think you could stand up to your Council without a husband propping you up.'

She let out a short laugh, not knowing whether to feel offended or flattered. 'Thank you for that vote of confidence, I suppose.'

'I didn't mean it as a criticism. You've shown me with your actions how strong and courageous you are. I think you could face your Council on your own, convince this Markos not to depose you. The vote has to be unanimous, doesn't it?'

'Yes.' She eyed him shrewdly even as she fought a lonely

sweep of desolation. 'Are you trying to make me feel better, or ease your own guilt at having wrecked my marriage plans?'

He looked surprised by the question, or perhaps his own answer. 'Both, I suppose. Although a few days ago I wouldn't have given your plans a single thought.' He shook his head wonderingly, and then his expression hardened once more and he rose from her side. 'I will be busy meeting with various leaders of the local tribes today, but I will see you at the wedding festivities tonight.'

She nodded, still smarting from their conversation, and all Khalil hadn't said. That he didn't feel.

She spent the rest of the day with the women, preparing for the wedding that evening. She helped make bread and stew meat, then when the food was finished and the sun was high in the sky the women headed back down to the oasis to prepare themselves for the festivities.

The bride was a lovely young girl with thick, dark hair, liquid eyes and a nervous smile. Elena watched as the women prepared her for her wedding: a dress of bright blue with rich embroidery on the sleeves and hem, hennaed hands and feet and a veil made of dozens of small copper coins.

What would her own wedding have looked like? she wondered as she watched the women laugh and joke with the young bride. A solemn, private ceremony in one of the reception rooms of the Kadaran palace, no doubt, witnessed by a few of Aziz's staff. Nothing fancy, nothing joyful or exciting.

And the wedding night? She shivered suddenly to think how she would have been giving her body to Aziz, a man she barely knew. Would she have felt for him even an ounce of the desire she felt for Khalil?

Inexorably her mind moved onto the man who always seemed to be in her thoughts. The man everyone here thought was her husband. Wouldn't it be wonderful, she thought suddenly, longingly, to pretend just for one day, for one night, that he was? That she was young and giddy with love, just as this pretty bride was?

What was the harm in that—in a single day of pretending?

Tomorrow she would return to reality. Soon she would be back in Thallia, facing a disapproving Council, forced to tell them her marriage plans had been cancelled. Perhaps facing the end of a monarchy that had lasted for nearly a thousand years—all because she hadn't been strong or smart enough to hold onto her crown.

Yes, one day of pretending sounded wonderful.

And so Elena let herself be carried along once more by the women; she didn't protest when they dressed her in a gown of silvery blue, lined her eyes with kohl, placed copper bangles on both arms and a veil of coins over her face. She understood they wanted to celebrate her recent marriage, just as the young bride was celebrating hers, and she didn't resist.

She wanted to celebrate it too.

The sky was deep indigo and studded with millions of stars when the ceremony began. The entire tribe had assembled and Elena watched, enchanted, as the ceremony played out amidst a riot of colour, music and dance. The women and men sat separately, and although she looked for him she could not find Khalil amidst the men gathered under a tent. She wondered if he would even recognise her in the Bedouin dress, headscarf and veil, wondered what he would think of her like this.

After the ceremony people circulated freely to enjoy food, music and dance. Several giggling women pushed Elena towards a group of men and then she saw him standing there, dressed in a traditional white cotton *thobe* richly embroidered with red and gold.

Khalil seemed to stare right through her and Elena knew

he didn't recognise her. Emboldened by the women who had pushed her forward, or perhaps simply by the desires of her own heart, she walked towards him.

'Greetings, husband,' she said softly. She'd meant to sound teasing but her voice came out earnest instead. Khalil glanced down at her, clearly startled, and then heat filled his eyes and his whole body tensed.

'Elena.'

'What do you think?' She twirled around and her dress flared out, the coins covering the lower part of her face jingling as she moved.

'I think you look lovely.' He placed a hand on her shoulder to stop her in mid-twirl, and drew her closer to him. 'Very lovely indeed. Sometimes something hidden is more alluring than something seen.'

Suddenly she was breathless, dazed by the look of undisguised admiration in his eyes. 'Do you really think so?' she whispered.

'Yes. And now I think the people of the tribe are expecting us to dance.'

'Dance?'

'I know the steps. Follow my lead.' And with one hand on her waist, the other clasped with hers, he led her to the circle of dancers.

The next hour passed in a blur of music and dance, every second one of heightened, almost painful awareness. Khalil's hand in hers, his body next to hers, his gaze fastened to hers, everything in her pulsing with longing. She'd never felt so beautiful or desirable, so heady with a kind of power she'd never, ever experienced before.

When she moved, Khalil's gaze followed her. When she spoke, he leaned forward to listen. She felt as if she were, at this moment, the centre of his universe. And it was the most wonderful feeling in the world.

She never wanted it to end.

But of course it did; the bridal couple was seen off and

people began to trail back to their dwellings. Elena turned to Khalil, uncertainty and hope warring within her. He gazed down at her, his expression inscrutable.

'They have arranged for us to share a tent tonight. I hope you don't mind.'

Mind? No, she didn't mind at all. 'That's…that's all right,' she managed.

Smiling faintly, Khalil threaded his fingers through hers and drew her away from the others…towards the tent they would share.

CHAPTER EIGHT

KHALIL KNEW HE was a little drunk. He hadn't had any alcohol to drink; none had been served. Yet he still felt dazed, almost drugged with possibility. With something deeper and stronger than mere lust, even if part of him wanted to give it that name, make it that simple.

He held the tent flap open for Elena and watched as she moved past him, her Bedouin clothing emphasising the sinuous swing of her hips, her graceful gait. Once in the tent she turned to him and he saw the expectation in her eyes, felt it in himself.

Tonight, to all intents and purposes, they were married. Husband and wife.

'Did you have a good time this evening?' he asked and she nodded.

'Yes... I don't know when I've had a better time, actually.' She let out a little laugh, sounding self-conscious, uncertain. 'I haven't gone to many parties before.'

'Not gone to parties? Not even royal or state functions?'

She shook her head, her grey eyes heartbreakingly wide above her veil. 'I've gone to those, but they weren't...they weren't fun. I could never just be myself. I was always Queen Elena and sometimes it felt like an act.'

'A danger of wearing the crown so young, I suppose. But you should be proud of yourself, Elena, and all you have accomplished.'

He took a step towards her, the need to touch her growing with every moment they spent together. His palms itched and he had to keep himself from reaching for her. 'And were you yourself tonight, Elena? Looking as you do, like a Bedouin girl?'

'Strangely, yes.' She let out another laugh, this one breathy. 'I felt more free tonight than I have in a long time.'

'Free—and yet captive.' He didn't know why he felt the need to remind her of the truth of their situation just then, only that he did. Perhaps he was trying to remind himself to hold onto reality when all he really wanted was to slip the veil from her face and the dress from her body.

'I don't feel like a captive any more, Khalil. I want to be here with you. You might have brought me here, but I'm choosing this now.'

He saw a bold purpose in her eyes now. The innocent, it seemed, had become a seductress. A siren. She walked towards him, lowering the veil of coins away from her face, and placed her hands on his chest. He gazed down at her long, slender fingers, felt them tremble against him. 'Tonight I want to forget everything, Khalil. Everything but you.'

Desire pulsed through him, blurred his brain along with his vision. 'Elena—'

'*Please.*'

He covered her hands with his own; he'd meant to remove them but as soon as he touched her he knew he wouldn't. He knew he needed at least this much, because there wouldn't be much more.

There couldn't be.

'Elena,' he said again, and she shook her head, her hair escaping from underneath her veil, tumbling about her shoulders as dark as a desert night.

'Don't, Khalil,' she whispered. 'Don't say no to me now.'

'Do you even know what you're asking?' he demanded, his voice low, raw and ragged with a desire he couldn't deny.

'Yes, I do.' She met his gaze. 'I'm asking you to make love to me. With me.'

Khalil's breath escaped in a hiss. 'Yes, but you don't know what that means.'

Her eyes flashed sudden fire. 'Don't tell me what I know or don't know, Khalil. I'm perfectly aware of what it means. What I'm asking.'

He arched an eyebrow. 'Are you sure about that, Elena? Because, if I'm not very much mistaken, I believe you're a virgin.'

She flushed but didn't lower her challenging gaze. 'Practical experience isn't required to make an informed choice.'

He almost laughed then, both amused by and admiring of her boldness and courage. His hands tightened on hers as he considered the possibility.

One night... One wonderful, amazing, incredible night...

'It's dangerous,' he began, and she shook her head.

'I know there are ways to prevent a pregnancy, if you don't have any protection.'

Her cheeks had turned fiery and he almost laughed. 'Oh, you do? As it happens, I have protection.'

Surprise made her jaw drop. 'You do?'

'Not,' he continued swiftly, 'because I intended to use it.'

She eyed him sceptically. 'Really?'

'I just like to be prepared.'

She looked uncertain then, even vulnerable. 'Have you had many lovers, then?'

'Not as many as you're thinking, and none in the last year. I've been too busy with other things.' *And none like you.* Untouched. Innocent. Amazing. He couldn't believe he was seriously thinking about taking Elena up on her offer. About making love to her.

'When I said it was dangerous, Elena, I didn't mean an unplanned pregnancy. I was talking about the...the emotional risks.'

She flinched and then recovered her composure. 'I'm aware of the risk, Khalil,' she told him. 'And I'm not under the illusion that this would be anything but one night. I'm not asking for more from you.'

'I know that.'

'Then what's the problem?' He just shook his head, both torn and tempted. Her smile turned flirtatious, even sultry. 'I suppose I'll just have to seduce you.'

Surprise flared deep inside him, along with an almost unbearable arousal. 'I don't think that's a good idea,' he managed. He knew she wouldn't have to do much and he would cave completely. He would take her in his arms and lose himself in her kiss, in her body.

He took a defensive step backwards and Elena's mouth curved in the kind of wicked little smile he hadn't known she was capable of.

'Scared, Khalil?'

'Tempted, Elena. And I'd rather not be.'

'Are you sure about that?' Slowly she lifted her arms, the wide sleeves of her dress falling back to reveal her slender wrists, and began to unwind her headscarf. Her kohl-lined eyes were wide and dark as she slowly unwrapped the garment, and Khalil simply watched, entranced by the utterly feminine and sensual act of undressing.

He heard his breath come out in something close to a pant as she dropped the headscarf and then shrugged out of her dress.

Underneath she wore only a thin chemise of bleached cotton, the material nearly transparent. He could see the temptingly round fullness of her breasts, the shadow between her thighs. He stifled a groan.

She moved closer, her eyes full of an ancient feminine power. She knew how she affected him and it made her bold.

It made her irresistible.

Her hands slid up his chest and he knew she could feel

how his heart was racing. His mind had stalled at the sight of her and it now kicked desperately into gear.

'I really don't think this is a good idea, Elena.'

'Too bad, then, that I do.' She stood on her tiptoes and brushed a butterfly kiss across his mouth. 'That's only the second kiss I've ever had,' she whispered against his lips. 'The first was two nights ago, when you held me on your lap.'

He closed his eyes. He was the only man who had ever kissed her? Didn't she realise how much she was giving him, offering him freely? Didn't she know how hurt she might be afterwards? No matter what she said or promised now, she was young. Inexperienced. Innocent.

He forced his eyes open, wrapped his hands around hers and attempted to draw them away from him. 'I don't want to hurt you, Elena.'

'You won't.'

'You don't know that. You *can't* know that, because you've never done this before.'

'And when am I going to get a chance to do it, Khalil?' she asked, her honest gaze clashing with his. 'I was going to give myself to a man I barely knew for the sake of my country. That possibility has been taken away from me now. You've taken it away from me, and I think it's only fair you offer me something in return. You owe me a wedding night.'

He let out a ragged laugh. 'I never thought of it that way.'

'Think of it that way now,' she said, and kissed him again. Her lips were soft, warm and open and her breasts brushed his chest. Khalil's arms came around her without him having made a conscious decision to embrace her, yet suddenly he was. He pulled her closer, fitting her softness against his body, pressing against her, craving the contact. And as her lips parted and she innocently, instinctively deepened the kiss, he knew he was lost.

This was what she wanted. Needed. Elena wound her arms around Khalil's neck as he took over her tentative kiss and made it his own. Made it theirs. His tongue slid into her mouth, exploring its contours and causing shivers of amazed pleasure to ripple through her. She had never known a kiss could be so consuming. So...*much*.

He slid one hand from her shoulder to cup her breast, his palm warm and sure. Elena shuddered under his touch. The intensity of her pleasure was almost painful, and yet achingly exquisite. And, while this was so much more than she'd ever felt or experienced before, it still wasn't enough. She felt an ache deep inside for more and she acted on it.

She pushed the *thobe* from his shoulders, and wordlessly Khalil shrugged out of it; the loose linen shirt and trousers he wore underneath followed. He was completely naked and utterly beautiful, long, lean, lithe and yet incredibly powerful, his body rippling with muscle. Now more than ever he reminded her of a panther, beautiful, awe-inspiring and just a little bit scary.

This was scary. Wonderful, exciting, new—and scary. She took a deep breath and waited for him to make the next move because she wasn't sure what it should be.

He lifted the hem of her chemise and she raised her arms so he could take it off her. She wore nothing underneath and, as his gaze roved over her nakedness, she felt a twinge of embarrassment, extinguished when he ran a gentle hand from her shoulder to thigh.

'You are so beautiful, Elena.'

'You are too,' she whispered and he laughed softly and tugged on her hand, leading her towards the bed.

He lay down on the soft covers and drew her down next to him so they were facing each other. Elena's breath was already coming in short gasps; her senses were on overload simply by lying next to Khalil, his naked body so close to hers. His chest rippled with muscle and his belly was taut and flat. Her gaze dipped lower and then moved up again;

she might have been talking a big game but she was still inexperienced. Still a little nervous.

Khalil took her hand and placed it on his bare chest. 'We can stop,' he said quietly; it amazed her how he always seemed to know what she was thinking, feeling. 'We can always stop.'

'I don't want to stop,' she told him with a shaky laugh. 'That doesn't mean I'm not going to be a little nervous, though.'

'Understandable,' he murmured, and kissed her again, a kiss that was slow and soft and wonderful. A kiss that banished any lingering fears or feelings of nervousness. A kiss that felt like a promise, although of what Elena couldn't say.

He slid his hand down her body, rested it on the flat of her tummy, waited. Everything in Elena quivered with anticipation. She wanted him to touch her...everywhere.

Still kissing her, he moved his hand lower. He waited again for the acceptance that she gave, his fingers brushing between her thighs, everything in her straining and yearning for even more.

And as he touched her with such wonderful, knowing expertise she realised she wanted to touch him too. She felt a new boldness come over her, a certainty to take what she wanted—and give him what he wanted. She smoothed her hands over his chest, slid her fingers across the ridged muscles of his abdomen. She wrapped them around the length of his arousal, causing his breath to come out in a hiss of pleasure which increased her own and made her bolder still.

With each caress the pressure in her built, a desperate need demanding satisfaction. And even she, in her innocence and inexperience, knew how it would finally be satisfied.

She rolled onto her back as he put on the condom and then positioned himself over her, braced on his forearms, his breath coming out in a ragged pant as he waited. 'Are you sure...?'

'Of course I'm sure, Khalil,' she half-laughed, half-sobbed, because by then she was more than sure. She was ready.

And then he entered her, slowly, the sensation so strange and yet so right at the same time. He went deeper, and with an instinct she hadn't known she possessed she arched her hips upwards and wrapped her legs around his waist. Pulled him deeper into herself.

'Okay?' he muttered and she almost laughed.

'Yes. Yes. More than okay.' And she was. She felt powerful in that moment, as well as loved. As if, with Khalil, she could do anything. She could be the person she was meant to be. She'd thought trusting someone, loving someone, made you weak, left you open and vulnerable to hurt. But right now she felt utterly strong. Completely whole.

And then he started to move, and the friction of his body inside hers increased that ache of pleasure deep within her, a sensation that built to such strength she felt as if it would explode from her, as if she would fly from the force of it, soaring high above the little camp, above everything.

And then it happened, everything in her peaking in an explosion of pleasure: she cried out, one long, ragged note, and fell back against the pillows, her body still wrapped around Khalil's, his head buried in the curve of her shoulder.

Neither of them spoke for several long minutes; Elena could feel the thud of Khalil's heart against her own, both of them racing. She stared up at the ceiling of the tent and wondered how she'd gone as long as she had without experiencing such incredible intimacy. Feeling such an amazing sense of rightness and power.

Slowly Khalil moved off her. He lay on his back, staring up at the ceiling, and Elena felt the first pinprick of uncertainty. Suddenly he seemed remote.

'I didn't hurt you,' he said, not quite a question, and she shook her head.

'No.'

'Good.' He rose then, magnificent in his nakedness, and went to dress.

'Khalil…' She rose up onto her elbows. 'Don't.'

'Don't what?'

'You owe me a wedding night, not a wedding hour,' she told him, trying to sound teasing even though nerves leapt in her belly and fluttered in her throat. 'Come back to bed.'

He stared at her for an endless moment, his *thobe* clenched in one hand, and Elena thought he would refuse—walk out of the tent and leave her alone with nothing but memories and regret. Then with a slight shrug he dropped the garment. He returned to the bed, sitting on its edge, away from her. She saw several faded white scars criss-crossing his back, and wondered at them. Now, she knew, was not the time to ask.

'I don't want to hurt you, Elena,' he said quietly. 'And I don't mean physically.'

She swallowed hard. 'I know you don't.'

He gave a slight shake of his head. 'The closer we become, *seem*…'

Seem. Because tonight's intimacy wasn't real, at least not for him. 'I understand, Khalil,' she told him. 'You don't have to warn me again. Tonight is a fantasy. Tomorrow it ends. Trust me, I get that. I accept it.'

He let out a weary sigh and gently she laid a hand on his shoulder, her fingers curling around warm skin, and pulled him back towards her. After a second's resistance, he came, lying next to her, folding her into his arms and then hauling her against his chest.

It felt like the only place she'd ever really belonged.

For tonight.

Neither of them spoke for several long minutes; Khalil stroked her hair and Elena rested one hand on his chest, perfectly content.

Almost.

The knowledge that this was only temporary, only tonight, ate away at her happiness, poked holes in this moment's peace. She tried to banish that knowledge; she wanted to dwell only in the fantasy now.

Closing her eyes, she imagined that they were in fact wed, that the ceremony tonight had been theirs. That they lay here as husband and wife, utterly in love with each other.

As she embroidered each detail onto the cloth of her imagination, she knew she was being foolish. Understood that envisioning such a thing, such a life, even if only as a fantasy, was dangerous.

Khalil didn't want a relationship, a loving relationship, and she didn't either. At least, she shouldn't. She'd never wanted it before. She'd chosen not to look for love, not to trust someone with her heart, her life. She'd done it once before—not romantically, but the betrayal had still wounded her deeply. Had made her doubt not just other people but herself.

How could she have trusted someone who had used her so spectacularly?

And how could she ever risk herself to trust again?

No, she was better off without love or romance. Keeping it as a fantasy, a single night.

And maybe, if she kept telling herself that, she'd believe it.

'What are you thinking about, Elena?' Khalil asked, his voice a quiet rumble in his chest.

'Nothing—'

'Not nothing,' he interjected quietly. 'You've gone all tense.'

And she realised she had; she was lying stiff in his arms, her hand curled against his chest. Gently he reached up and flattened her fist, smoothing her fingers out before resting his hand on top of hers. 'What were you thinking about?' he asked again.

She sighed. 'Just…some memories.'

'The same memories that give you nightmares?'

'No. Different ones.'

'Not good ones, though.'

'No.' She let out a little sigh. 'Not particularly.'

'I'm sorry,' he said after a moment, and somehow that felt like exactly the right thing to say.

'So am I. But I don't want to think about bad memories tonight, Khalil. I want to be happy. Just for tonight.'

He squeezed her hand lightly. 'I won't stop you.'

'I know, but…' She wanted more than his acquiescence; she wanted his participation. 'Can we—can we pretend?' she asked, her voice quavering slightly with nervousness. 'Can we pretend, just for tonight, that we're…that we're in love?' She felt his body tense underneath her hand and she hurried to explain. 'I know we're not. I don't want us to be, not for real. I don't want to love someone like that.' Khalil remained ominously silent, so she continued stiltedly, 'I just want to feel like I do for one night. To forget everything else and just enjoy feelings I can't afford to have in real life.' She sounded ridiculous, Elena realised. What was she really asking? For him to *pretend* to love her?

How absurd. How pathetic.

And Khalil still hadn't said anything.

'Maybe it's a stupid idea,' Elena muttered. Inwardly she cringed at the whole ridiculous proposition she'd put before him. 'I didn't mean… You don't have to worry that I'll suddenly…' Her throat tightened and she was about to force herself to go on, to reassure him that she wouldn't fall in love with him or start expecting emotions and commitments from him simply because they'd had sex, but then Khalil spoke first.

'For one night,' he said slowly. 'I think I can manage that…my darling.'

Surprise gave way to mirth and even joy, and she let out

a bubble of laughter, shaking her head. 'Now, that rolled off the tongue quite nicely,' she teased.

'Did it not, dearest?' He raised his eyebrows, turning to her with an enquiring smile. 'What shall I call you, then, essence of sweetness?'

She turned her head towards the pillow to muffle her laughter. '*Essence of sweetness?* Where do you come up with that stuff?'

'It comes naturally, my dewy petal,' he purred. 'Can't you tell?'

Tears of laughter started in her eyes. Her stomach ached. And she felt the biggest, sloppiest grin spreading over her face. 'Sorry, but I can't tell.'

Khalil rose on his arms above her, a wicked smile curving his mouth and glinting in his eyes. 'What a dilemma,' he answered softly. 'Since I don't seem able to tell you how I love you, then perhaps I should show you.'

And then Elena's laughter stopped abruptly as he did precisely that—showing her with his mouth, his hands and body. And he showed her very well indeed.

CHAPTER NINE

KHALIL AWAKENED TO sunlight streaming into their tent and Elena's hair spread over his chest. He'd slept the whole night with his arms around her, his body entwined with hers, and it had felt good.

Unbearably good.

What on earth had possessed him to participate in her little game? Pretend to be in *love?* And, never mind the danger involved in that all too enjoyable charade, what about the fact that he'd slept with her at all? That he'd taken her virginity? No matter what she'd assured him about understanding the emotional risks, he knew it was dangerous. Dangerous for her, and even dangerous for him, because already he wanted her again—and not just in bed.

In his life.

And there was no place for Queen Elena of Thallia in his life.

The next few days and weeks were crucial to his campaign to retake the throne that was rightfully his. He couldn't waste a moment's energy or thought on anything but his goal, a goal he'd nourished and cherished since he'd been seven years old and had been dropped into the desert like a dog no one wanted. Treated like one too, kicked and beaten and abused.

And, in any case, he didn't do love. He didn't know how. Trusting another person with *anything,* much less his heart—dried-up, useless organ that it was—was next to impossible for him. He wanted to trust people, men like Assad who had sworn their loyalty to him, but he still always felt that prickle of wary suspicion between his shoulder blades. He was still, always, waiting for the sudden slap, the knife in the back. The betrayal.

When you lived your life like that, love had no place in it. Relationships had no place, save for expediency.

And as for Elena? He glanced down at her, her face softened in sleep, her dark, lush lashes feathering her cheeks. Her lips were slightly pursed, one hand flung up by her head. Despite his mental list of reasons to walk away right now, desire stirred insistently. He knew just how he could wake her up...

Swearing under his breath, Khalil extracted himself from Elena's embrace and rolled from the bed. He heard her stir behind him, but he was already yanking on his clothes, his back determinedly to her.

A serving maid entered, blushing, with a pitcher of hot water and inwardly Khalil swore again. The news of their night together would spread throughout the whole tribe. They would know he had consummated a union that he intended to reject shortly.

And his plan to explain later why he'd been travelling alone with Elena would no longer work. He'd acted dishonourably and the tribe would know it. When they found out he and Elena weren't married, they would feel both betrayed and angry, and how could he blame them?

It was a fiasco, and all because he'd wanted her so damn much. How could he have been so weak?

'Khalil...?'

He turned to see her sitting up in bed, her dark hair tumbling wildly about her shoulders, her hooded grey eyes sleepy but with a wariness already stealing into them.

'We need to get moving,' he said brusquely. 'Assad is coming with a vehicle this morning. He'll take us to a new camp and then we'll move onto Siyad. You'll be back in Thallia this time tomorrow, I hope.'

She looked away, hiding her face, but he still felt the hurt he knew he'd caused her. Damn it, he'd *warned* her about this. He couldn't blame Elena, though. He could only blame himself. He'd known she was a virgin, inexperienced and innocent. She was bound to read more into their night together, even if she'd said she wouldn't.

Hell, he'd read more into it. Felt more than he was comfortable with.

And now he had no idea what to do, how to make things right: with Elena; with the tribe; with this country of his that teetered on the brink of civil war, made worse by his own foolish choices.

What an unholy mess.

After Khalil had left the tent Elena rose slowly from the bed and reached for the Bedouin-style dress he'd stripped from her body the night before.

Had it only been the night before? It felt like a lifetime ago. Felt like a different life, one where she'd known pleasure, joy and love.

It was only pretend, you idiot.

Sighing, she slipped on the chemise, only to see her Western clothes lying neatly folded by the pitcher of water. She took off the chemise and washed quickly, scrubbing the scent of Khalil from her body, before putting on the clothes she'd come here in.

Time to return to reality.

By the time she'd eaten breakfast—with the other women, Khalil not in sight—some of her equilibrium had been restored, along with her determination.

She'd had setbacks before, been hurt before. And this time she had no one to blame but herself. Khalil had been honest with her, unlike Paulo had been. He'd told her what she could and couldn't expect, and he'd been true to his word. She could not fault him.

And so she wouldn't. She'd had her night, her fantasy, and she'd treasure it—but she wouldn't let it consume or control her. Life had to go on and, with the end of her captivity looming ever nearer, she needed to think about her return to Thallia.

Just the thought made her feel as if she'd swallowed a stone.

After breakfast Khalil came for her, his *thobe* billowing out behind him, the set of his face exceptionally grim. Even scowling he was handsome, with the dark slashes of his eyebrows and those full, sculpted lips. His eyes seemed to glow fire.

'Are you ready? We should leave as soon as possible.'

Elena rose from where she'd been sitting by the fire and brushed the crumbs from her lap. 'I'm ready now.'

Nodding, Khalil turned away, and wordlessly Elena followed him. Assad was waiting by an SUV with blacked-out windows. Elena slid inside, fighting a weird sense of déjà vu. She'd been driven in a car like this when she'd first been captured. Now she was being driven to a freedom she wasn't sure she wanted.

They rode through the unending desert, Assad driving while Khalil and Elena sat in the back, not speaking, not touching.

Despite the ache Khalil's stony silence caused her, Elena forced herself to think practically. In two days she would, God willing, be back in Thallia. What would Andreas Markos have done in her absence? Would he have heard of her abduction, or would Aziz have managed to keep it secret?

She'd only been in the desert for a handful of days, even if it had felt like a lifetime. Perhaps Markos and the rest of her Council weren't yet aware of what had happened.

'Have you heard any news?' she asked Khalil abruptly,

and he turned, eyebrows raised. 'Has Aziz admitted that I'm missing? Does my Council know?'

'Aziz has admitted nothing. I doubt your Council is aware of events.'

'But how has he explained—?'

'He hasn't. He hired someone to pretend to be you and it seems everyone, including your Council, has believed it.'

Shock left her speechless for a moment. 'He did? But—'

'They appeared on the palace balcony two days ago. From a distance the woman fooled the people, or so it would seem. That's all I know.' He arched an eyebrow. 'Your Council wasn't expecting to hear from you, I presume?'

'Not until I returned.' She'd been meant to be on her honeymoon. 'You should have told me,' Elena said and Khalil eyed her coolly.

'What purpose would it have served?'

'It just would have been good to know.' She stared out of the window, tried to sift through her tangled feelings. She wasn't exactly surprised that Aziz had come up with an alternative plan; she'd suggested as much to Khalil. She wasn't hurt by his actions either. But she felt…something and with a jolt she realised it *was* hurt—not for what Aziz had done, but for what Khalil hadn't. Not telling her had been a tactical move, a way of treating her like a political pawn rather than a—what?

Just what was she to him now?

Nothing, obviously. She closed her eyes and thought of him covering her with kisses last night, both of them laughing. *It was pretend. You knew that.*

But it still hurt now.

'I'll be able to tell you more when we return to camp,' Khalil said. He drummed his fingers against the window, clearly restless. 'What will you do when you return to Thallia?' he asked. Elena opened her eyes.

'Do you really care?'

'I'm asking the question.'

'And the answer is, I don't know. It depends what state my country is in. My government.'

'Your Head of Council won't have had time to call a vote to abolish the monarchy.'

'No, but he will as soon as he can.'

'You could marry someone else in the meantime.'

'Suitable husbands are a little thin on the ground.'

'Are they?' He turned back to the window, frowning deeply. Elena had no idea what he was thinking. 'Just what was your arrangement with Aziz?' he asked, still staring out of the window.

'I told you.'

'I mean in practical terms.'

Bewildered, she almost asked him why he wanted to know. Why he cared. Then, with a mental shrug, she answered, 'It was a matter of convenience for both of us. We'd split our time between Thallia and Kadar, rule independently.'

'And that pleased your Council?'

'My Council was not aware of all the terms of the marriage. They probably assumed I'd be more under Aziz's influence.'

'And they didn't mind a stranger helping to rule their country?'

'He's royal in his own right, and as I explained they're traditional. They want me under a man's influence.'

Khalil nodded slowly, his forehead knitted in thought. 'And what about heirs?'

A blush touched her cheeks. 'Why are we talking about this, exactly?'

'I'm curious.'

'And you want me to satisfy your curiosity?' Her temper flared. 'What for, Khalil? None of it is going to happen anyway, and in any case it has nothing to do with you.'

He turned to her with a granite stare. 'Humour me.'

Her breath came out in a rush. 'We planned for two children, an heir for each of our kingdoms.'

'And where would these children have been raised?'

'Initially they would stay with me, and when they were older they would split their time between the two countries.' She looked away, uncomfortably aware of how cold and clinical it sounded. 'I know it's hardly an ideal solution, but we were both desperate.'

'I realise that.'

'Like I said, it doesn't matter anyway.'

'But you still feel you need a husband.'

She sighed and leaned her head back against the seat, closing her eyes once more. 'I do, but maybe you're right. Maybe I can face my Council on my own, convince them not to call the vote.'

'It's a risk.'

She opened her eyes. 'You don't sound nearly as encouraging as you did before.'

He shrugged. 'You have to choose for yourself.'

'Seeing as there's nothing to choose, as I have no prospective husband, this whole conversation seems pointless.'

'Maybe,' Khalil allowed, and turned back to the window. 'Maybe not.'

He could marry her. The thought made everything in him rear up in shocked panic. Marriage had never been on his agenda. Yet ever since he'd seen that serving girl this morning, and realised the repercussions of his night with Elena, the thought had been rattling around in his brain like a coin in a box.

He could marry her—marry the woman who was intended as the Sheikh of Kadar's wife. It would help strengthen his claim, stabilise his throne, and it would give Elena what she wanted too.

Why not?

Because it's dangerous. Because the emotional risks you warned her about apply to you too.

Because you care about her already.

Elena had spoken of a cold, convenient union, but would it be like that if he was her husband? Would he be able to keep himself from caring for, even loving, her?

Did he even want to?

His mind spun and seethed. He felt the clash of his own desires, the need to protect himself and the urge to be with her—care for her.

And did Elena even care for him? Just what kind of marriage would she want them to have?

Once back at the camp—which to Elena looked like just another huddle of tents, horses, cars and camels amidst the dunes and black rocks—Khalil strode away and Leila met Elena and brought her to her private tent.

'A bath, perhaps,' she murmured and Elena thanked her, nodding wearily. She felt overwhelmed by every aspect of life at the moment: the end of things here, her responsibilities in Thallia, her non-relationship with Khalil.

A quarter of an hour later she watched as two men filled the copper tub with steaming water. Leila scattered it with rose petals and brought a thick towel and some lovely smelling soap, and Elena's throat suddenly went tight with emotion.

'Thank you. This is so kind…'

'It is nothing, Your Highness. You could use a little pampering, I think.'

The older woman's sympathy was almost her undoing. Elena nodded, swallowing past the tightness in her throat as Leila quietly left.

As she soaked in the tub Elena's thoughts returned relentlessly to Thallia and matters of state. She had no husband. She could explain why and, since it looked as if

Khalil would become Sheikh, she thought her Council would accept it.

But in a few weeks' time, if she were still single, Markos would call for the vote to abolish the monarchy. Somehow she had to convince him not to call it, or at least convince her Council not to vote against her.

Could she do it on her own? Did she dare risk her crown in such a way? Khalil believed in her, perhaps more than she believed in herself. Just remembering the warmth of his smile, the confidence she'd seen in his eyes, made her ache.

No, she couldn't risk it. A royal wedding and a devoted husband were what had been going to save her, no matter what Khalil said about her being strong enough to face her Council alone. He didn't know what she was up against. Didn't understand what she'd been through.

Sighing, Elena leaned her head back against the tub. The only way to avoid such a disaster would be to prove Markos wrong—to return with a husband.

Too bad that was impossible.

Unless she married Khalil.

Elena smiled mirthlessly as she imagined Khalil's horrified reaction to such an idea. He would never agree to marry her. He'd been appalled by the possibility that she might harbour any tender feelings for him. He'd sounded contemptuous of her arrangement with Aziz.

Elena sat up suddenly, water sloshing over the sides of the tub. Marrying her could potentially be beneficial for Khalil. She'd seen the approval of the Bedouin they'd been with, how they'd liked seeing him with his bride.

And since he'd already acted as if they were married…

Could it be possible? Did she even dare suggest a thing? The potential rejection and humiliation she faced made her flinch.

Then, in a sudden, painful rush of memory, Elena recalled her father throwing himself over her, saving her life from the explosions and gunfire around them. Sacrificing himself...for Thallia. For the monarchy.

How could she not do whatever it took to ensure her reign?

An hour later she was dressed in another outfit Leila had brought her, a simple dress of rose-coloured cotton. She twisted her hair up in a chignon and wished she had some make-up or jewellery to make her feel more prepared. She was going to talk to Khalil. Beard the lion in his den.

Taking a deep breath, Elena square her shoulders and exited the tent. Two guards immediately moved in front of her, blocking her way.

Fury surged through her, shocking her with its intensity. 'Really?' she asked them. 'After everything, you still think I'm going to run off into the desert?'

They stared back at her blandly. 'Do you want for something, Your Highness?'

A husband. She took another deep breath. 'I would like to speak to Khalil.'

'He is not—'

'Available? Well, make him available. I need to speak to him, and it's important.'

Leila came hurrying over, her face creased with concern. 'Your Highness? Is something wrong?'

'I'd like to speak to Khalil,' Elena stated. Her voice wobbled and, furious with herself, she bit her lip. Hard. 'Do you know where he is, Leila?' she asked, and thankfully this time her voice was steady.

Leila gazed at her, a certain sorrowful knowledge in her eyes, and Elena had the sudden, awful suspicion that Leila knew she and Khalil had slept together.

'Yes, I know where he is,' she said quietly. She spoke in Arabic to the two guards, but her voice was too low for Elena to make anything out. Then she turned back to her and said, 'Come with me.'

Elena went. Leila led her to a tent on the opposite side of the camp, pausing outside the entrance to turn back to her.

'Khalil has been through much, Your Highness,' she said quietly. 'Whatever has happened between the two of you, please remember that.'

So Leila had definitely guessed, then. Elena forced the realisation away and met her gaze squarely. 'I just want to talk to him, Leila.'

'I know.' The older woman smiled sadly. 'But I can tell you are hurting, and I am sorry for it. Khalil is hurting too.'

Khalil hurting? *I don't think so.* But Elena was still considering Leila's words as she stepped into the tent and looked upon Khalil.

He was seated at a folding table, his dark head bent as he scrawled something on a piece of paper. He didn't look up, just lifted one hand, signalling her to wait.

'One moment, Assad, please.'

'It's not Assad.'

Khalil glanced up swiftly then, his gaze narrowing as it rested on Elena. She stared back, levelly, she hoped, but after a taut few seconds she knew she was glaring.

'Elena.'

'*Khalil.*' She mimicked his even tone, slightly sneering it. Oops. Not the way she'd wanted to start this business-like meeting, but then Leila was right. She *was* hurting, even if she didn't want to be.

He sat back, resting his arms lightly on the sides of his chair. 'Is there something you need?'

'You had said you would look at the news,' Elena reminded him. 'Find out if people know what has happened.'

'So I did. I haven't seen anything so far. Aziz is keeping quiet.'

'And how will you return me to Thallia?' she asked coolly. 'Royal jet? Economy class? Or will you roll me up in a carpet like Cleopatra and then unroll me in the throne room of the Thallian palace?'

'An interesting possibility.' His gaze rested on her, assessing, penetrating. 'Why are you so angry, Elena?'

'I'm not angry.'

'You sound angry.'

'I'm frustrated. There's a difference.'

'Very well, then. Why are you frustrated?'

'Because I came to Kadar with a plan to save my throne and I no longer have one.'

'You mean marriage.'

'Yes.'

His gaze narrowed. 'And what would you like me to do about it?'

'I'm glad you asked.' Elena took a deep breath, tried to smile as she met his narrowed gaze. 'I'd like you to marry me.'

CHAPTER TEN

SHE'D BEATEN HIM to it, Khalil thought bemusedly, even as an elemental panic clawed at his insides. He'd been considering marriage to Elena as a solution to both of their problems since this morning. Yet looking at her now, seeing the hope and determination blazing in her eyes, everything in him resisted. There had to be another solution.

Slowly he shook his head. 'That's impossible, Elena.'

'Why is it impossible?' she demanded.

'Because I have no wish or reason to marry you, Elena.' Better to be brutal. Nip it in the bud, if he could. 'You may be desperate, but I am not.'

She flinched, but only slightly. 'Are you sure about that, Khalil?'

'Quite sure. You asked for a wedding night, Elena, not a marriage.'

'Well, now I'm asking for a marriage.'

'And I'm telling you the answer is no.' He rose from his chair, fought the panic that was crashing over him in tidal waves. 'This discussion is over.'

She raised her eyebrows, a small smile playing about her mouth. A mouth he'd kissed. Tasted. He forced his gaze upwards but her eyes just reminded him of how they'd been filled with need and joy when he'd slid inside her. Her hair reminded him of how soft and silky it had felt spread across his chest. Everything about her was dangerous, every memory a minefield of emotion.

'You don't even want to think about it?' she challenged and he folded his arms.

'I do not.'

'You almost sound scared, Khalil,' she taunted, and fury pulsed through him because he knew she was right. Talking about marriage scared the hell out of him, because he was afraid it wouldn't be the cold, convenient arrangement she'd intended to have with Aziz. She'd want more. *He* would.

And that was far, far too dangerous.

'It's simply not an option,' he told her shortly.

'Even though you've already told people we're married?'

He felt his jaw bunch, his teeth grit. 'I didn't tell anyone.'

'Semantics, Khalil. The result was the same. And, no matter what you tell yourself or me, there will still be repercussions for you.'

'I'm perfectly aware of that, Elena.' He heard a patronising note enter his voice and knew it was the lowest form of self-defence. Everything she was saying was true, yet still he fought it. 'As I told you before, by the time people learn the truth I will be established in Siyad as Sheikh.'

'And that's how you want to start your rule? Based on a lie?'

He pressed his lips together, forced the anger back. 'Not particularly, but events dictated it be thus. I will deal with the consequences as best as I can.' All because of his own stupid weakness concerning this woman.

'And what if your people decide you might be lying about other things? What if they assume you lied about your parentage and Aziz is the true heir?'

Just like his father had lied. He would be no better, and the realisation made him sick with both shame and fury. 'Are you trying to argue your way into a marriage the way you argued your way into my bed?' he demanded, and she flinched then, her face crumpling a little before she quickly looked away. Khalil swore softly. 'Elena,' he said quietly, 'I understand you feel you need a husband. But I am not that man.'

He couldn't be.

'It makes sense,' she whispered. She still wouldn't look at him and the fury left him in a weary rush. He wanted to pull her into his arms. Kiss her sadness away.

But he couldn't marry her. He couldn't open himself up to that weakness, that risk, that *pain*.

'I can see how it might make sense to you,' he said carefully. 'You need a convenient husband.'

'And you need a convenient wife.' She swung around to face him with a challenging stare. 'Your people want you to marry. We saw that when we were with them. They think you're married to me already! One day you'll need an heir—'

'One day.' Khalil cut her off swiftly. 'Not yet.'

'I won't ask anything of you that you wouldn't want to give,' Elena continued doggedly. 'I won't fall in love with you, or demand your time or attention. We can come to an arrangement, like I had with Aziz—'

'Don't mention his name,' Khalil said, his voice coming out like the crack of a whip. Elena's eyes widened; she was startled, and so was he.

Where was all this emotion coming from? This anger and...*hurt*? Because the thought of her with Aziz made his blood boil and his stomach churn. He couldn't bear to think of her with anyone else, not even a man he knew she didn't love, barely knew.

They stared at each other, the very air seeming to spark with the electric charge that pulsed between them: anger and attraction. Desire and frustration.

'I won't, then,' Elena said quietly. 'But you could at least think of it, Khalil. You'll have to marry some day. Why not me? Unless...' She paused, nibbling her lip. 'Unless you're holding out for love.'

'I am not.'

'Well, then.'

He just shook his head, unwilling to articulate just why he was rejecting her proposal out of hand. He couldn't admit to her that he was actually *scared*. 'What about you? You're not interested in love?'

She hesitated, and he saw the truth in her eyes. She was. She wouldn't admit it to him, but she was. 'I can't afford to be interested in love.'

'You might decide one day you want someone who loves you,' he pointed out, trying to sound reasonable when in fact he felt incredibly, insanely jealous at the thought of another man loving her. *Touching* her.

'I won't,' she told him. 'I won't let myself.'

'Even if you wanted to?'

'Are you worried I'm going to fall in love with you, Khalil?'

No—he was terrified that he was already in love with her. Khalil spun around. 'Put like that, it sounds arrogant.'

'I'll try to keep myself from it.' She spoke lightly, but he had a feeling she was serious. She didn't want to fall in love with him, and why should she? He would only hurt her. He wouldn't love her back.

Except maybe you already do.

'We've both been hurt before,' Elena said after a moment. 'I know that. Neither of us wants that kind of pain again, which is why an arrangement such as the one I'm suggesting makes so much sense.'

It did. He knew it did. He shouldn't be fighting it. He should be agreeing with her, coolly discussing the arrangements.

Instead he stood there, silent and struggling.

Elena didn't want his love, wouldn't make emotional demands. In that regard, she would make the perfect wife.

And yet looking at her now he saw the welter of hope and sadness in her eyes. Felt it in himself. And he knew that no matter how they spun it, no matter what they agreed on, marriage to Elena would be dangerous. Because, even if some contrary part of him actually longed for the things he said he couldn't do, didn't want—love, intimacy, trust, all of it—the rest of him knew better. Knew that going down that road, allowing himself to feel, yearn and ache, was bad, bad news.

No matter how practical Elena's suggestion might be, he couldn't take it.

'I'm sorry, Elena,' he said. 'But I won't marry you. I can't.'

She stared at him for a moment, her wide, grey eyes dark with sadness, and then turning darker still with acceptance. Slowly she nodded.

'Very well,' she said, and without another word she turned and left the tent.

Khalil stared at the empty space she'd left, his mind spinning, his heart aching, hating that already he felt so bereft.

It had been worth a shot, Elena told herself as she walked back to her tent, escorted by the same men who guarded her. They didn't speak and neither did she, because she knew she wouldn't be able to manage a word. Her throat ached and she was afraid that if she so much as opened her mouth she'd burst into tears.

Back in her tent she sat on her bed, blinking hard to contain all the pain and hurt she felt. Then suddenly, almost angrily, she wondered why she bothered. Why not have a good cry? Let it all out? No one was here to hear her or think her weak or stupid or far too feminine.

She lay down on her bed, drew her knees up to her chest and swallowed hard. Crying—letting herself cry—was so hard. She'd kept everything in for so long because she'd had to. Men like Markos were always looking for chinks in her armour, ways to weaken her authority. Shedding a single tear would have been just handing them ammunition. The only time she ever cried was when she had nightmares.

In Khalil's arms.

She hadn't consciously, deliberately accessed that hidden, vulnerable part of herself for years, and it was hard to reach it now, even when she wanted to. Sort of.

She took a shuddering breath and clutched her knees harder, closed her eyes and felt the pressure build in her chest.

Finally that first tear fell, trickling onto her cheek. She dashed it away instinctively, but another came, and another, and then she really was crying. Her shoulders shaking, the tears streamed as ragged sobs tore from her throat. She pressed her hot face into the pillow and let all the misery out.

It was not just sadness about her wrecked wedding, or Khalil, but about so much more: the needless deaths of her parents and the fact that she hadn't been able to grieve for them as she should have. Her broken relationship with Paulo, her shattered trust. The four lonely years she'd endured as Queen, working hard for the country she loved, suffering Markos's and other councillors' sneers and slights, trying desperately to hold onto the one thing her parents wanted her to keep.

And yes, she realised as she sobbed, she was crying about Khalil. He'd helped her in so many ways, opened her up, allowed her to feel and trust again. She'd miss him more than she wanted to admit even to herself. More than he'd ever want to know.

Khalil turned back to the reports he'd been studying, reports detailing Kadar's response to Aziz, polls that confirmed outside of Siyad he was not a popular choice as Sheikh. It was news that should have encouraged him, but he only felt restless and dissatisfied—and it was all because of Elena. Or, really, all because of him and his reaction to her and her proposal.

He should have said yes. He should have been strong and cold and ruthless enough to agree to a marriage that would stabilise his country, strengthen his claim. Instead he'd let his emotions rule him. His fear had won out, and the realisation filled him with self-fury.

'Your Highness?'

Khalil waved Assad forward, glad to think about something else. 'You have news, Assad?'

Assad nodded, his face as stony and sombre as always. Khalil had met him eight years ago, when he'd joined the French Foreign Legion. They'd fought together, laughed together and saved each other's lives on more than one occasion. And, when the time had been right for Khalil to return to Kadar, Assad had made it possible. He'd gathered support, guarded his back.

None of this would have been possible without Assad, yet Khalil still didn't trust him. But that was his fault, not his friend's.

'Is something the matter?' he asked and Assad gave one terse nod.

'Aziz has married.'

Khalil stilled, everything inside him going cold. He'd always known this was a risk, yet he was still surprised. 'Married? How? Who?'

'We're not sure. Intelligence suggests someone on his staff, a housekeeper or some such.'

'He married his housekeeper?' *Poor Elena.* No matter what she had or hadn't felt for Aziz, it would still be a blow. And with a jolt Khalil realised he shouldn't even be thinking about Elena; he should be thinking about his rule.

Aziz had fulfilled the terms of his father's will. He would be Sheikh.

And Khalil wouldn't.

Abruptly he rose from his chair, stalked to the other

side of the tent. Emotion poured through him in a scalding wave, emotion he would never have let himself feel a week ago. Before Elena.

She'd accessed that hidden part of himself, a part buried so deep he hadn't thought it existed. Clearly it did, because he felt it all now: anger and guilt. Regret and fear. *Hurt.*

'All is not lost, Khalil,' Assad said quietly, dropping the honorific for once. 'Aziz is still not popular. Secretly marrying a servant will make him even less so.'

'Does that even matter?' Khalil bit out. 'He's fulfilled the terms of the will. He is Sheikh.'

'But very few people want him to be.'

'So you're suggesting a civil war,' Khalil stated flatly. 'I didn't think Aziz would go that far.' And he wasn't sure he would either, no matter what he'd thought before. Felt before.

Risking so much for his own crown, endangering his people, was not an option he wanted to consider now.

Things were changing. *They'd already changed.*

He wasn't the cold, ruthless man he'd once been, yet if he wasn't Sheikh…

What was he?

'A civil war is not the only option,' Assad said quietly. 'You could approach Aziz, demand a referendum.'

Khalil let out a mirthless laugh. 'He has everything he wants. Why would he agree?'

'There is something to be said for a fair fight, Your Highness,' Assad answered. 'Aziz might want to put the rumours and unrest behind him. If he wins the vote, his throne is secure.'

And Khalil would have no chance at all. He would have to accept defeat finally, totally—another option he didn't like to consider.

'There are a lot of people in Siyad,' he said with an attempt at wryness, and Assad smiled.

'There are a lot of people in the desert.'

'Aziz might not even agree to see me. We haven't seen each other since we were children.'

'You can try.'

'Yes.' He nodded slowly, accepting.

'You still have the stronger position,' Assad stated steadily. 'You always have. The people are loyal to you, not to Aziz.'

'I know that.' He felt his throat go tight. Did he really deserve such loyalty? And did he dare trust it? He knew how quickly someone could turn on you. Only the day before his father had thrown him out of the palace, he'd sat in on one of Khalil's lessons, had chucked him under the chin when Khalil had said his times tables.

Stupid, childish memories, yet still they hurt. They burned.

'So you will speak to Aziz?'

Khalil ran his fingers through his hair, his eyes gritty with fatigue. A thousand thoughts whirled through his mind, and one found purchase: one way forward, one way to solidify his position and strengthen his claim to the throne.

Now more than ever, he needed to marry Elena.

Aziz's bride. The woman the country had already accepted as the Sheikh's wife-to-be. The woman at least one tribe already thought was his wife.

He'd reacted so forcefully against it because he didn't want to risk his emotions or his heart. So, he wouldn't. Just like her, he couldn't afford to look for love. He'd keep a tight rein on his emotions and have the kind of marriage both he and Elena wanted: one of mutual benefit…and satisfaction.

Just the thought of being with Elena again sent desire arrowing through him.

'The servant is not even Kadaran,' Assad said quietly, and Khalil wondered if his friend and right- hand man had guessed the progression of his thoughts.

'Neither is Elena,' Khalil answered, and Assad smiled faintly. Khalil now knew he had been thinking along the same lines.

'She is a queen, an accepted choice. Marrying her would work in your favour.'

'I know.' Khalil took a deep breath, let it out slowly. 'I know.'

'Then…?'

'I'll go find her.' And by this time tomorrow, perhaps, he would be married.

The camp was quiet and dark all around him as Khalil walked towards Elena's tent. A strange mix of emotions churned within him: resolve, resignation and a little spark of excitement that he tried to suppress.

Yes, he would enjoy Elena's body again. But this would be a marriage of convenience. No more play-acting at love. No more pretending. No more *feeling*.

The guards stepped aside as he came to the tent and drew the curtain back—and stopped short when he saw Elena curled up on her bed, her face pressed into her pillow, sobbing as if her heart would break.

Or had already been broken…by him.

'Elena…Elena!'

Elena felt hard hands on her shoulders drawing her up from her damp pillow and then cradling her against an even harder chest.

Khalil. For a second she let herself enjoy the feel of him. Then she remembered that she'd been bawling her eyes out and twisted out of his embrace.

'You should have knocked,' she snapped, dashing the tears from her cheeks. She probably looked frightful, her face blotchy, her eyes red and swollen…

She sniffed. *And* her nose was running. Perfect.

'Knock?' Khalil repeated, one eyebrow raised in eloquent scepticism. 'On the flap of a tent?'

'You know what I mean,' she retorted. 'You should have made your presence known.'

Khalil regarded her quietly for a moment. 'You're right,' he finally said. 'I should have. I'm sorry.'

'Well.' She sniffed again, trying desperately for dignity. 'Thank you.'

'Why were you crying, Elena?'

She shook her head as if she could deny the overwhelming evidence of her tears. 'It's been a couple of very long days,' she muttered. 'I was... I'm just tired.'

'You weren't crying as if you were just tired.'

'Why do you care?' she demanded. Perhaps going on the offensive was best.

Khalil opened his mouth, then shut it again. 'I don't *care*,' he answered. 'But I want to know.'

'I've got a lot going on in my life that has nothing to do with you, Khalil. Maybe I'm crying about *that*.' She wasn't about to admit that she had been crying about him along with everything else that had gone wrong in her life.

'I wasn't assuming you were crying about me,' he stated quietly. His voice was calm but he sounded as if he was trying not to grit his teeth.

'Weren't you?' Elena retorted. 'Ever since spending the night together you've been completely paranoid that I'm obsessing over you, and I can assure you, I'm not.'

'What a relief.'

'Isn't it?'

They glared at each other. Elena folded her arms and tried to stare him down; Khalil's eyes sparked annoyance and his mouth was compressed.

'Why did you come into my tent, anyway?' she finally asked, their gazes still clashing. 'Have you learned something? Some news?'

'Yes, I have.'

Her stomach rolled and she felt her nails bite into her

palms. 'What have you heard? Has Markos called for a meeting?'

'I haven't heard any news from Thallia, Elena. I think they still believe you are safely with Aziz.' Khalil's mouth was still a hard line but his expression seemed softer somehow, his eyes almost sad. 'It's Aziz,' he said after a pause. 'He's married someone else, just like you said he would.'

'He has?' Her eyes widened as she considered what this meant for Khalil. 'He did it within the six weeks?'

'Yes.'

'Then he fulfilled…?'

'The terms of my father's will.' Khalil nodded. 'Yes, he did. But you…? You're not sad?'

She stared at him in disbelief. 'About Aziz? I gave up on him a while ago, Khalil.'

'Yes, but…still…he chose someone else. Rather quickly.'

'So did I.' She gave him a look filled with dark humour. 'At least Aziz received a positive answer to his proposal.'

'Yes…' He shook his head, almost as if to clear it. 'About that proposal…'

'Trust me, you don't need to remind me how much you don't want to marry me, Khalil. I got that the first time.'

'I'm sorry if I seemed…negative.'

She rolled her eyes. 'That's an understatement.' Better to joke than to cry. In any case, she wasn't sure she had any tears left, just a heavy sense of weariness, a resignation that nothing was going to be easy. That she'd probably lose her crown.

'You surprised me,' he said. 'I wasn't expecting… I've never expected…'

'I know.' She shook her head, exasperated, exhausted and definitely not needing to hash through all this again. 'Why are we even talking about this, Khalil?'

'Because,' he answered evenly, 'I've changed my mind.'

She blinked and then blinked again, the meaning of his words penetrating slowly. 'You've what?'

'I've changed my mind,' he repeated clearly. 'I want to marry you.'

Elena opened her mouth, then closed it again. 'Well,' she finally managed. 'That was a charming proposal.'

'Don't be absurd, Elena. This is about convenience, for both of us.'

'You didn't seem to think so an hour ago.'

'Aziz's marriage has made me realise I need to strengthen my position.'

'But if he's married,' Elena said slowly, 'he's fulfilled the terms of the will. How can you fight that?'

'I can't. I don't want to start a war. The only thing I can do is confront him openly—demand he call the referendum. Perhaps I should have done that before, but it seemed too easy for Aziz to refuse. Perhaps it still is.'

'And marrying me will strengthen your position when it comes to a vote.'

Khalil gazed at her evenly. 'Yes.'

'That's quite a sacrifice for you to make,' she said a bit sharply. 'Just to look good for a vote.'

'I am the rightful Sheikh, Elena,' Khalil said, his voice rising with the force of his conviction. 'That is who I *am*, who I always will be. I've lived my entire life waiting for the day I took the throne. Every choice I've made, every single thing I've done, has been to that end. Not for revenge, but for justice. Because it is right—' He broke off, forced a smile. 'In any case, marrying you is not a sacrifice.'

'No?'

'We are friends, are we not? And we have enjoyed each other's bodies. Neither of us wants anything more.' He smiled, reached out to touch her face. 'It's a match made in heaven.'

'That's an about-face if I've ever seen one,' she huffed.

'I admit, your proposal shocked me. I reacted emotionally rather than sensibly.'

'I didn't think you had emotions.'

'You know I do, Elena.' His gaze seemed to burn into hers. 'I will be honest. This—' he gestured between them '—scares me.'

Elena felt as if a giant fist had taken hold of her heart. 'It scares me too, Khalil.'

'So that is why we will agree to this convenient marriage,' he answered with a small smile. 'Because neither of us wants to be hurt again.'

'Right,' Elena agreed, but to her own ears her voice sounded hollow. They didn't want to be hurt again—but she wondered if she or Khalil would be able to keep themselves from it.

CHAPTER ELEVEN

ELENA GAZED OUT of the window of the royal jet at the perfect azure sky and marvelled at how quickly things had changed. Just forty-eight hours earlier she'd been sobbing into her pillow, stuck in the middle of the desert with no possibilities and no hope.

Now she was flying back to Thallia with Khalil by her side, planning a wedding in just a few days' time, and everything was possible.

Well, almost everything. She snuck a sideways glance at Khalil who sat opposite her, his face looking as if it had been chiselled from marble. A deep frown had settled between his brows and his mouth was its usual hard line. He'd barely spoken to her since he'd reconsidered her marriage proposal, a proposal which Elena had wondered more than once whether she should have accepted.

Yet in the moment before she'd agreed, when he'd been waiting for her answer, she'd seen a look of uncertainty on his face, almost as if he were bracing himself for a blow. As if he expected her to reject him.

That moment of vulnerability had been gone in an instant, but it still lingered in Elena's mind. In her heart. Because it made Khalil a man with softness and secrets, a man she was starting to understand and know better and better.

Which, Elena acknowledged, violated the terms of this very convenient marriage. It was what she had first suggested, after all. If some contrary, feminine part of her wanted something different, something more…well, too bad.

She had other, more important things to think about. Like the fact that she was going to face her Council in just a few hours, and with a different fiancé in tow. She glanced again at Khalil, grateful that he'd agreed to accompany her to Thallia and marry in a private ceremony in the palace. It had made sense, rather than something furtive and hurried in the desert; both of them wanted this marriage to be accepted by the public as quickly as possible.

After she'd presented him to her Council, they'd return to Siyad and Khalil would demand Aziz call the referendum. Khalil had told her Aziz had retreated with his bride to a remote royal palace for his honeymoon. The announcement from the palace had simply said the Sheikh had wed, not the name of his bride. Siyad buzzed with speculation, but no one knew what was really going on. Khalil had said Aziz was just buying time. Things would come to a head when they returned from Thallia and Elena hoped that both of their countries—and thrones—would be secure.

Even then she didn't know what life with Khalil would look like, or even where or how they would live. She and Aziz had discussed all these details, outlined everything in a twenty-page document that had been drawn up by lawyers from both of their countries.

But everything with Khalil was unknown. Looking at his grim expression, she wasn't sure she wanted to discuss it now.

Instead she tried to plan what she would say to her Council. To Markos. No doubt he'd be contemptuous of her sudden change of groom. Perhaps he would claim she was being deceived by Khalil, as she had been by Paulo.

She thought of all the things Markos could say, all the contempt he could pour on her, and in Khalil's presence, and inwardly she cringed.

'What's wrong?' Khalil asked, turning to fix her with a narrowed gaze, and Elena realised her reaction had been visible too.

'Nothing…' she began, only to acknowledge she would have to tell Khalil about her mistakes. Better to hear it from her than Markos.

And actually, she realised, she *wanted* to tell him. She wanted to be honest, to share her burden with someone. To trust him with the truth.

'Elena?' Khalil prompted, and she took a deep breath.

'Khalil…I need to tell you some things.'

His gaze swept over her. 'All right.'

Elena took another deep breath. She wanted to tell Khalil, but it was still hard. 'I was young when I became queen,' she began. 'As you know. My parents had just died and I suppose I was feeling…vulnerable. Lonely.'

'Of course you were, Elena.' His face softened in sympathy. 'You'd had an isolated childhood and then you lost the two people who were closest to you.'

'Even if they weren't all that close.'

'Still, they were your parents. You loved them, and they loved you.'

'Yes.' She nodded, feeling a sudden, surprising peace about what Khalil had so simply and surely stated. Her parents had loved her. No matter how little they might have shown it during their lives, they'd loved her in their own way.

'So what happened when you became queen?' he asked after a moment, his voice gentle, and Elena gave him a rather shaky smile.

'My mother's brother, Paulo, came to stay with me after the funeral. I hadn't known him very well—he spent most of his time in Paris or Monte Carlo. I don't think my father liked him all that much. He'd stayed away, in any case.'

'And after the funeral?'

'He was very kind to me.' She sighed, a weary acceptance and regret coursing through her. 'He was funny and charming and in some ways he felt like the father I'd never had. The one I'd always wanted. Approachable. Genuine. Or so I thought.'

'He wasn't, I presume.' Khalil's frown deepened. 'This is the man who betrayed you.'

'Yes, he did, yet I trusted him. I listened to him, and I came to him for advice. The Council didn't want me to rule—Andreas Markos had tried to appoint himself as Regent.'

'But you're of age.'

'He made the case that I didn't have enough political experience. And he was right, you know. I didn't. I'd gone to a few royal functions, a few balls and events and things. But I didn't have the first clue about laws or policies. About anything real or important.'

'You learned, though. I've read some of the bills you helped draft online, Elena. You're not a pretty princess sitting on her throne, you're an active head of government.'

'Not at first.'

'The Council should have given you time to adjust to your new role.'

'Well, they didn't, not really.'

Khalil shook his head. 'So what happened with Paulo?'

'He advised me on some real-estate deals: government subsidies for tourist developments on our coastal region. I thought he was helping me, but he was just lining his own pockets.'

'How could you have known?'

'It wasn't just that,' she hastened to explain, practically tripping over herself to tell him the whole sordid truth. She needed him to know, craved for him to accept the whole of her and what she'd done. 'Every piece of advice he gave me was to benefit himself. And there were worse things. He forged my signature on cheques. He even stole some of my mother's jewels, which weren't hers to begin with. They were part of the crown jewels and they belonged to the government.'

She closed her eyes, filled with remorse and shame. 'I was completely clueless, pathetically grateful for all his support. Markos uncovered it, and had him sent to prison. Kept the scandal from breaking in the press, thankfully—not for my sake, but for Thallia's.'

'That must have been very hard.'

'Yes.' Her throat was so tight it hurt to speak, but she kept going. 'You know what's really sad? Sometimes I still miss him. He completely betrayed me in every way possible, and I actually miss him.' She shook her head, suddenly near tears, and Khalil reached over and covered her hand with his own.

'He seemed kind to you, and during a time when you craved that kindness. Of course you miss that.'

'Do you miss your father?' she blurted, and Khalil stilled, his hand tensing over hers.

'I've hated my father for so long,' he said slowly. 'And I can't ever forget what he did.' His face contorted for a second, and she knew how difficult this was for him to admit. 'But I do miss his kindness to me. His—his love.'

'Of course you do,' she murmured and Khalil gave her a wry and rather shaky smile.

'I never realised that before. I was too busy being angry.'

'Are you still angry?'

'I don't know what I am,' he said, sounding both surprised and confused, and then he shook his head. 'We weren't talking about me, though. We were talking about you. You shouldn't blame yourself, Elena, for trusting a man who did his best to endear himself to you.'

'I should have known better.'

Khalil shook his head, his hand tightening on hers. 'You were young and vulnerable. It wasn't your fault.'

'The Council thinks it was. Or, at the very least, it completely undermined any confidence they might have had in me. Markos has been working steadily to discredit me ever since.'

Khalil frowned. 'How?'

'Rumours, whispers. Gossip that I'm flighty, forgetful. So far I've managed to keep him from destabilising me completely. I hope—I hope my record speaks for itself.' She turned to him, needing him to believe her just as he had once needed her to believe him. 'I've worked hard since the whole Paulo debacle, Khalil. I've poured my life into my country, just as my father wanted me to. Everything I've done has been for Thallia.'

'I know it has,' Khalil said quietly. He squeezed her hand. 'Your devotion to your country is something I've never questioned.' He gave her a small smile. 'After all, you were willing to marry for it.'

'As were you.'

'Hopefully it was a wise decision on both our parts.' He removed his hand from hers and sat back, his brow furrowed.

Elena suspected he regretted the intimacy of their conversation. She knew that wasn't part of their marriage deal. And yet, watching him covertly, remembering how her body yearned and her heart ached for him, Elena wondered how she could have fooled herself into thinking she'd ever be satisfied with a marriage of convenience.

With Aziz it had been different. He'd been a stranger, and she'd given little thought to their marriage beyond the hard practicalities. Now she wondered how she could have been so blind. So naïve. How could she have coped with such a cold approach to marriage, to motherhood? *How would she now?*

She stared out of the window, realisations trickling despondently through her. She didn't want a loveless arrangement any more. She wanted more from her marriage. More from Khalil.

She glanced back at Khalil; he looked distant and pre-occupied. The things she wanted now seemed more un-likely than ever.

Khalil stared out of the window as the jet descended towards the runway, the waters of the Aegean Sea sparkling jewel-bright in the distance. He could see the domes and towers of Thallia's ancient capital, the sky a bright blue above, the sun bathing everything in gold.

He turned to look at Elena and saw how pale she'd gone, her hands clenched together in her lap so tightly her knuckles shone bony and white. He felt a shaft of sympathy for her, deep and true, in that moment. She'd endured so much, yet had stayed so strong, even if she didn't think she was. Even if she didn't trust herself.

He trusted her. He believed in her, believed in her strength, her courage, her goodness. The knowledge made something in him break open, seek light. He leaned forward and reached for her hand. She turned to him, clearly startled, her eyes wide with apprehension.

'You're stronger than they are, Elena,' he said quietly. 'And smarter. They may think you need me, but you don't. You are a legitimate and admirable ruler all on your own.'

Her cheeks went pink and her eyes turned shiny. For a moment Khalil thought she might cry. Then her lips curved in a wobbly smile and she said, 'Thank you, Khalil. But you're wrong—I do need you. I needed you to tell me that.'

They left the plane, blinking in the bright sunlight as they took the stairs down to the waiting motorcade. The paparazzi, thankfully, weren't present; Elena had told him there would be a press briefing from the palace after they met with her Council.

He hadn't liked leaving Kadar, but he understood the necessity of it. A marriage made deep in the desert was essentially no marriage at all. They both needed the positive publicity, the statement their marriage would make not just to Elena's Council but to Aziz.

I took your bride. I'll take your throne. Because both are mine by right.

Khalil felt the old injustice burn, but not as brightly or hotly as it had before. In that moment, looking at her pale face, he was more concerned for Elena than anything that was happening in Kadar. The realisation surprised him, yet he didn't fight it, didn't push the feelings away. He reached for Elena's hand once more and she clung to him, her fingers slender and icy in his.

'Welcome back to Thallia, Your Highness.'

Khalil watched Elena greet the royal staff who had lined up by the fleet of cars. She nodded and spoke to each one by name, smiling graciously, her head held high.

She looked pale but composed, elegant and every inch the queen despite the fear he knew she had to be feeling. Admiration and something deeper swelled inside him. Queen Elena of Thallia was magnificent.

Two hours later they were at the palace, waiting outside the Council Room. Elena had changed into a modest dress in blue silk, feminine yet businesslike, her heavy, dark hair pulled back in a low coil. Khalil wore an elegantly tailored business suit and, as they waited to be admitted to the Council Room, he wondered what this Markos was playing at. Was he keeping Elena waiting on purpose, to unnerve her? A petty show of power? Based on what Elena had already told him, it seemed likely.

He turned to Elena. 'You should go in there.'

'I'm meant to wait until I'm summoned.'

'You are Queen, Elena. You do the summoning.'

'It's not like that, Khalil.'

'It should be. You're the one who can change things, Elena. Remember that. *Believe* it.'

She stared at him uncertainly for a moment and he imagined how hard it must have been for her, all of nineteen years old, devastated by grief and so utterly alone, trying to assert herself against the sanctimonious prigs of her Council. The fact that she was still here, still strong, both amazed and humbled him.

'You can do it,' he said softly. 'You can do anything you set your mind to, Elena. I know that. I've seen it.'

She gave him a small, tremulous smile. 'Except maybe make a fire in the middle of the desert.'

He felt himself grin back at her. 'There were a few flames going there. If that snake hadn't come along...'

'If you hadn't come along,' she shot back, her smile widening, and then she drew herself up and turned towards the double gold-panelled doors.

He watched as she threw open the doors, grinned at the sight of twelve slack-jawed, middle-aged men rising hastily to their feet as Elena walked into the room.

'Good afternoon, gentlemen,' she greeted them regally, and Khalil had to keep from letting out a cheer.

Elena could feel her heart thudding so hard it hurt and she could hear the roar of her blood in her ears. She kept her head high, her smile polite and fixed, as she gazed at each member of the Council in turn, saving Markos for last. Her nemesis's eyes were narrowed, the corners of his mouth turned down, and she felt a flash of relief. If he'd made any headway with the rest of the Council, he'd have been looking at her in triumph, not irritation. She was safe...so far.

'Queen Elena. We have been wondering where you had gone.' Marko's gaze flicked to Khalil. 'A honeymoon in the desert?' he suggested with only the faintest hint of a sneer, but as always it was enough. He made it sound as if she'd run off with her bodyguard, heedless of her country or its demands.

'There has been no honeymoon yet,' Elena answered crisply. 'But things, as you have surmised, have changed. I wisely ended my engagement to Aziz al Bakir when I realised he was not the legitimate claimant to the throne of Kadar. Marriage to an impostor would hardly benefit Thallia, would it…Andreas?'

Markos's eyes flashed annoyance or perhaps even anger. 'And who is this, then?' he asked, his gaze flicking back to Khalil.

'This is Khalil al Bakir, sheikh of a northern desert tribe and Aziz's older brother. He is the rightful heir to the throne of Kadar.' Elena felt the sudden surprise tense Khalil's body, felt it in herself. She'd spoken with a certainty she felt right through her bones.

'I have chosen to marry Khalil instead, in an arrangement similar to the one I had with Aziz.' She looked at each councillor in turn, felt herself practically grow taller. Khalil had been right. She was strong and smart enough, yet she was still achingly glad he was by her side. 'I trust that this will be agreeable to all of you, as it was before?'

'You change husbands at the drop of a hat,' Markos said, his lip curling in contempt. 'And we are meant to take you at your word?'

For a second Elena felt herself falter, everything in her an apology for past sins, but in her moment of damning silence Khalil spoke. 'Yes,' he stated coolly. 'As she is your queen and sovereign, you will most certainly take her at her word. Queen Elena has demonstrated her loyalty to her country again and again. It will not be called into question simply because once long ago she gave her trust and her loyalty to a man who should have, by all measures, been worthy of it.' Elena watched in amazement as Khalil nailed each councillor with a hard, challenging stare. 'We will not speak of this again. Ever.'

She barely heard the answering buzz of murmured assurances and apologies; her mind was spinning from what Khalil had said, how he'd stood up for her, supported her. When had someone last done that?

She'd kept herself apart, refused to trust anyone, because it had felt stronger. Certainly less risky. But in that moment she knew she was actually stronger with Khalil, and the knowledge both thrilled and humbled her.

She turned to her Council with a cool, purposeful smile. 'Now, shall we discuss the meeting with the press?'

CHAPTER TWELVE

ELENA CLOSED THE door quietly behind her and leaned against it, her eyes closed, exhaustion making every muscle and sinew ache. It had been a long, stressful, overwhelming and yet ultimately successful day.

She hadn't had a chance to tell Khalil how grateful she was for his support, from the showdown with the Council to his effortless grace and charm before the press. It had been a tense diplomatic moment, supporting Khalil's claim to Kadar's throne publicly, and one her Council had initially balked at. But Khalil had stood by her and it was her turn to stand by him.

Side by side. That was the kind of marriage she wanted. And today it had felt as if Khalil wanted it too.

Maybe all he needed was time to get used to the idea, to learn to love again…

Because she loved him. It had been utter foolishness to pretend she didn't, or wouldn't. She'd been fooling herself as well as Khalil, but now she wanted to be honest. Wanted to admit her feelings for him, her love, respect and desire.

Yes, desire. She'd felt it all day like an in-coming tide, lapping at her senses, washing over her body. Every aspect of him appealed to her, from his hard-headed pragmatism to his sudden sensitivity, to that sensual blaze of heat in his eyes…

They hadn't spoken privately since the plane, since she'd told him about Paulo—and she'd seen no judgement or con-

demnation in his eyes, just understanding and a surprising compassion, which just added to her desire. He was,
she'd realised, not for the first time but with growing certainty, a *good* man.

After the press conference he'd gone to deal with matters relating to Kadar, and she had met with her personal
assistant to review the schedule for the next few days. A
team of lawyers had hammered out an agreement concerning the marriage terms that they'd both signed, and then
they'd eaten dinner with a handful of dignitaries before
parting ways, Khalil to a guest suite in another wing and
she to her own suite of rooms.

Already she missed him. She needed to talk to him, she
realised; they'd set the wedding for tomorrow and yet had
barely discussed the details beyond a clinical meeting with
the legal team. In any case, she didn't want to talk business; she just wanted to be with him.

Swiftly she turned around and opened the door, slipped
from her room and down several corridors to where she
knew Khalil was staying.

She stood in front of his door, her palms slightly damp
and her heart beginning to race. She knocked.

'Enter.'

Elena stepped inside and the whole world seemed to
fall away as her gaze focused on Khalil. He'd undone the
studs of his tuxedo shirt, its tails untucked from his trousers so she could see a bronzed expanse of taut belly, and
her breath instinctively hitched.

Khalil's gaze darkened, although with what emotion she
couldn't tell. 'I thought you were one of the staff.'

'No.'

A tiny smile twitched at the corner of his mouth. 'I realise.'

Hope ballooned inside her, impossible to control. One
smile and she was lost. 'I thought we should talk.'

'About?'

'We're getting married tomorrow, Khalil,' she reminded him with a smile, and his smile deepened.

'I know that, Elena.' He turned to face her fully, his arms folded across that magnificently broad chest. 'Are you having second thoughts? Cold feet?'

Surprise at his question, and the shadow of vulnerability that crossed his face, made her shake her head decisively. 'No.' She took a breath and forced her gaze away from his pectorals. 'Are you?'

'No.'

'Even though you didn't want to marry?'

She shouldn't have pressed, Elena realised. Any levity they'd been flirting with disappeared in an instant. 'You know my feelings on the subject.'

'A necessary evil?'

He inclined his head. 'That might be a bit harsh.'

Elena rolled her eyes, inviting him into the joke, wanting to reclaim the lightness. 'Well, that's a relief.'

He smiled again and Elena felt a giddy rush of joy. She really did love his smile. She loved...

But she wouldn't tell him that now. She knew he wasn't ready to hear it, and she wasn't sure she was ready to say it.

'Why are you here, Elena?' Khalil asked quietly.

'I told you, to talk.'

He took a step towards her, his muscles rippling under his open shirt, his eyes glinting gold with amusement— and knowledge. 'Are you sure about that?'

Suddenly her mouth was dry. Her heart beat harder. 'No,' she whispered.

He took another step towards her and then another, so if she lifted her hand she could touch him. He smiled down at her. 'I didn't think so.'

Of course he didn't think so. Her need for him was obvious, overwhelming and undeniable. And the very force of it made her bold. 'I want you, Khalil.'

Appreciation flared in his eyes. 'I want you too.'

Want. So basic, so huge, yet Elena felt even more than just that. She felt gratitude and admiration, respect and joy, all because of what he'd done, who he was. How he'd helped and strengthened her. She'd never expected to feel that way about someone, to have that person fulfil a need and hope in her she hadn't even known she had.

The need to tell him all that she felt was an ache in her chest, a pressure building inside her, so she opened her mouth to speak, to say even just a fraction of what was in her heart.

But Khalil didn't let her.

He curled his hands around her shoulders and drew her to him, stealing her words away with a kiss. It was better this way, Elena had to acknowledge as she lost herself in the heady sensations. Khalil didn't want her words, her declarations of emotion. He just wanted this.

And so did she.

He drew her to the bed and down upon the silken sheets, stripping the evening gown from her body with one gentle tug of the zip. Neither of them spoke, and the silence felt hushed, reverent. This time tomorrow they would lie in a bed like this one as husband and wife.

But Elena knew she already felt like Khalil's wife in her mind, in her heart. She cared too much for him, she knew, but in this moment, when his hands were touching her with such tenderness and his mouth was on hers, she didn't want to think about *too much*. She didn't want to police herself, or limit her joy. She just wanted to experience all Khalil was offering her…however little that turned out to be.

And, in that moment, it felt like enough.

Afterwards they lay entwined among the sheets, her palm resting over his heart so she could feel its steady thud against her hand. Khalil stroked her arm from shoulder to wrist, almost absently, the touch unthinking and yet incredibly gentle. She felt almost perfectly happy.

If only, she thought, they could stay like this for ever.

It was a foolish wish, nothing more than a dream, yet she was so tired of the scheming and trying, the politics and the uncertainty. She just wanted this. Him. *For ever.*

'When will you speak with Aziz?' she asked softly, because no matter what she wanted reality had to be faced.

'As soon as we return to Kadar I will seek out a meeting. He will hear of our marriage, of course, and I will have to address that.'

'Do you think he'll be angry?'

She felt Khalil tense, and then he shrugged. 'I have no idea. You know him better than I do.'

'I do?' She raised her head, propping herself on one elbow to study his face. 'Did you not know him as a child?'

'I left the palace when I was seven. I only met him once, from memory, when my father wished for his sons to see each other.'

He spoke evenly, but she could still feel the tension in his body, under her hand. She gazed at him, realising afresh how much she didn't know...and how much she wanted to.

'It must have been very hard,' she said softly. 'To have to leave everything you knew.'

'It was strange,' Khalil acknowledged. His expression had become shuttered, his eyes giving nothing away.

She eased away from him so she could look up into his face. 'I know you don't like to talk about it, Khalil, but what happened with your father must have been terrible.' Her gaze fell on the scars that crisscrossed his wrists. 'Why do you have rope burns on your wrists?' she asked softly.

She thought he wouldn't answer. He didn't speak for a long time, and she wondered at the story those scars told, a story she had no idea about but knew she wanted and perhaps even needed to hear.

'I was tied up,' he said finally, his voice flat, emotionless. 'For days. I struggled, and these scars are the result.'

She stared at him in helpless horror. 'Tied up? When—?'

'When I was seven. When my father banished me.'

'But I thought you went to America with your aunt.'

'She found me when I was ten. For three years I lived with a Bedouin tribe in a far corner of Kadar. The sheikh liked to punish me. He'd tie me up like a dog, or beat me in front of everyone. I tried to escape, and I always failed. So, believe me, I understood how you felt as a prisoner, Elena. More than you could possibly know.' He let out a shuddering breath and unthinkingly, just needing to touch him, she wrapped her arms around him, held on tight.

'I'm sorry.'

'It was a long time ago.'

'But something like that stays with you for ever, Khalil!' She remembered now how he'd told her it mattered how she was treated. 'But this man, this sheikh—why did he treat you so terribly?'

Khalil gave a little shrug. 'Because he was a petty, evil man and he could? But, no, the real reason I suppose is because my mother was his cousin and she brought shame to his family with her alleged adultery. In any case, Abdul-Hafiz already had a grudge against her family for leaving the tribe and seeking their fortunes in Siyad.' His arms tightened around her. 'That's why my father banished me to that tribe—he returned me to my mother's people, knowing they would revile me. And so they did, at least at first. The irony, perhaps, is that I rule them now as their sheikh.'

He was trying to speak lightly but she still heard the throb of emotion underneath. Elena couldn't even imagine all he wasn't saying: the abuse, the torture and utter unkindness. To tie up a seven-year-old boy for *days*? To beat him so his back was covered with scars? Fury warred with deep sorrow, and she pressed her cheek against his back, her body snug against his.

'I'm so glad you escaped.'

'So am I.'

Yet could anyone really escape such a terrible past? Elena knew Khalil bore as many scars on his heart as he did on his wrists and back. No wonder he didn't trust any-one. No wonder he had no use or understanding of loving relationships.

Could she be the one to change him? Save him?

She shied away from such questions, knowing how dangerous they were, yet already the answers were rushing through her.

Yes. Yes, she could. She wanted to try, she needed to try, because she loved him and couldn't imagine a life without him. Without him loving her.

And she began in that moment, rolling onto her stomach and pressing her lips to his wrist, kissing the places where he'd been hurt the most. Underneath her, she felt Khalil shudder.

'Elena…'

She kissed her way across his body, touching every scar, taking her time with her tongue and her lips, savouring him, showing her love for him with her body because she couldn't with her words. Not yet.

And Khalil accepted her touch, his hands coming up to clutch her shoulders as she moved over him and then gently, wonderfully, sank onto him, taking him into her body, filling them both up to the brim with wonder and joy and pleasure.

His eyes closed and his breath came out in a shudder as she began to move, pouring out everything in her heart in that ultimate act of love—and praying Khalil understood what she was saying with her body.

Sleep was a long time coming that night. Khalil stared up at the canopied bed, his arms around Elena as her breathing evened out, and he wondered why on earth he'd told her so much, had said things he hadn't admitted to anyone, not even Dimah or Assad. He hated to think of anyone knowing the truth of his utter humiliation as a child, yet he'd willingly told Elena. In that moment he'd wanted to, had wanted someone to understand and accept him totally.

And her response had nearly undone him. The sweet selflessness of her touch, the giving of her body... He still wasn't sure he knew what love was, but he imagined it might feel like that. And, if it did, he wanted more. He wanted to love someone and know he was loved back.

Foolish, foolish, foolish. Insanity. This was a marriage of cold convenience, not love or trust or intimacy. He'd told Elena he wanted none of that, and he'd meant it.

How had he changed?

Yet he knew he had. He'd been changing since the moment he'd met her, since he'd seen a reflection of himself in her. She'd begun changing him even then, softening him, opening up his emotions, unlocking his heart.

How could he go back to the cold, barren life he'd once known?

How could he not?

He'd learned to trust her with so many things—with his feelings. With the truth. Could he trust her with his heart?

Their wedding took place in the palace chapel, with only the Council members and their wives, as well as a few ambassadors and diplomats, in attendance.

Elena wore a cream silk sheath dress and a matching fascinator, no veil or bouquet, or really anything bridal at all. She'd picked the outfit with the help of her stylist when she'd arrived in Thallia, thinking only of what image she wanted to present to her public. She'd wanted to seem like a woman in control of her country and her destiny, perfectly prepared to begin this businesslike marriage.

She hadn't wanted to look like a woman in love, yet she knew now that was what she was. And as she turned to Khalil to say her vows she wished, absurdly, perhaps, for a meringue of a dress and a great, big bouquet, a lovely lace veil and a father to give her away.

Never mind, she told herself. *It's the marriage that matters, not the wedding.* Yet what kind of marriage would she have with Khalil?

Last night had been so tender, so wonderful and intimate in every way, physically and emotionally. Yet this morning he seemed his usual, inscrutable self, stony-faced and silent, dressed in traditional Kadaran formal wear, a richly embroidered *thobe* and loose trousers. He looked magnificent—and a little frightening, because Elena had no idea what he was thinking or feeling.

The ceremony passed in a blur. Vows were spoken, words read, then Khalil drew her to him and pressed his mouth against hers in a cool kiss.

She still had no idea what was going on behind those veiled eyes.

Elena circulated through the guests at a small reception after the ceremony, her gaze tracking Khalil's movements around the room, even as she chatted with councillors who oozed satisfaction now that she was wed and taken care of.

She felt as if everything had changed for her—but had it for him? Should she even hope it had? It might be better—wiser, safer—not to let things change for herself. Not to open herself up to all of the pain and possibility that loving someone meant.

It was too late for that, she knew. She couldn't stop what she felt for Khalil, just as she couldn't keep the waves from crashing into the sea or the moon from rising that night. Her love for him simply *was*.

After the reception they retired to a suite of rooms in its own private wing, as much of a bridal chamber as the palace had.

Elena took in the champagne chilling by the canopied bed, the fire crackling in the fireplace, the frothy nightgown some accommodating member of staff had laid out for her.

'It's all a bit much, isn't it?' she said with an attempt at wryness. She felt, bizarrely, as if they were pretending, as if they were going through the motions of marriage and love when last night she'd felt they'd known the real thing.

'It's thoughtful,' Khalil answered with a shrug. He hesitated, his gaze pinned to hers even though Elena had no idea what he felt or what he intended to say. 'You looked beautiful today. You still do.'

A thrill of surprised pleasure rippled through her. 'Thank you.'

'I couldn't take my eyes off you.'

'I couldn't take my eyes off you, either,' she admitted with a shy smile.

His answering smile was assured. 'I know.'

'Oh—you!' Elena gasped with a shocked laugh. 'You sound unbearably arrogant, you know.'

'But it's true.'

'It would be more gentlemanly for you not to remark on it.'

'Why?' he asked as he reached for her. 'When the feeling is mutual?'

She stared up at him, suddenly breathless. *Just how much was mutual?*

He feathered a few kisses along her jaw. 'And this is what I've been wanting to do all day long.'

'Why didn't you, then?' Elena managed as she tilted her head back to give him greater access.

Khalil pressed a kiss to the tender hollow of her throat. 'What do you think your stuffy councillors would have thought if I'd dragged you out of that ballroom and returned you with messed hair, swollen lips and a very big smile on your face?'

Elena let out a choked laugh, her mind blurring as Khalil's mouth moved lower. 'I think they would have been pleased. I'd have been put in my place as a dutiful wife.'

'I like the sound of those duties,' Khalil answered as he

tugged at the zip of her dress. 'I think you need more instruction on just how to carry them out.'

Her dress slithered down her body, leaving her in nothing but her bra and pants, her whole body on fire from the heat of Khalil's gaze. 'I think I do,' she agreed…then they didn't speak for quite a while after that.

Later they lay in bed just as they had last night, hands linked and limbs entwined. Sleepily, utterly sated, Elena thought how this did feel like for ever. Maybe they could be this happy…for ever.

'I need to go to Paris,' Khalil said. His fingers tightened briefly on hers as he stared up at the bed's canopy. 'To see my Aunt Dimah. She moved there a few years ago. She should hear of our marriage from me. And I'd like you to meet her.'

'Of course,' Elena said simply. She was glad to share in any part of Khalil's life that he wanted her to.

'And after that,' he continued, 'we will return to Kadar. I received a message from Aziz today, just before the wedding. He has agreed to meet with me.'

'That's good news, isn't it?'

'I hope it is. I hope I will be able to convince him to call the referendum.'

'And if he refuses?'

Khalil stared up at the ceiling. 'I don't know,' he said quietly. 'I don't—I don't want war. But I can't imagine giving up my claim to the throne, either. It's everything to me.' He turned to her then, a new, raw vulnerability shadowing his eyes. 'Not everything,' he amended. 'Not any more. But it's important, Elena.'

'I know it is.'

'Everything I've been, everything I've done, has been for Kadar. For my title.'

'I know,' she said softly. She leaned over and kissed him. 'I know how important this is, Khalil, and I believe in you just as you've believed in me. You'll succeed. You'll convince Aziz and win the vote.'

He smiled and squeezed her fingers. 'I pray so.'

'I know it.'

'I'd like you to be with me when the referendum is called,' Khalil said after a moment. 'It's important for the people to see you support me. But it shouldn't take long, and afterwards you can return to Thallia. Those were the terms of our agreement.'

Elena thought of the soulless piece of paper they'd both signed just yesterday, outlining the nature of their marriage: so cold, so clinical. She felt his fingers threaded through hers, his legs tangled with hers, and she mentally consigned that piece of paper and all of its legalese to the rubbish heap. 'I'll need to return to Thallia, of course,' she said. 'But do you want me to stay longer?' She twisted to face him, and was gratified to see a light blaze in Khalil's eyes.

'Yes,' he said simply, and she squeezed his hand, never feeling more certain of anything in her life. She loved this man and she would go anywhere with him.

'Then I'll stay,' she said simply, and Khalil closed the space between them and kissed her.

CHAPTER THIRTEEN

THE NEXT MORNING they boarded the royal jet to Paris. Since last night Elena had felt closer to Khalil than ever before, even though neither of them had put a name to what they felt. Perhaps it was too early to put such fragile feelings into words; in any case, Elena was simply glad to be sharing Khalil's life, and that he wanted her to.

'You must be very close to your aunt,' she said as the plane took off and they settled into their seats. A royal steward brought a tray of coffee and pastries into the main cabin.

Khalil poured milk into both of their coffees, his mouth twisting in something like a grimace. 'I am, but it is a complicated relationship.'

'How so?'

'When Dimah found me, I'd been in the desert for three years. I was…' He paused, his gaze on the bright blue sky visible from the plane's windows. 'Difficult. No, that is putting a polite spin on it—feral is a better description.'

Feral. Elena swallowed and blinked back sudden tears. Emotions, ones she'd suppressed and denied for so long, were always so close to the surface now; Khalil had made her feel, want and love again. 'I hate to think of what you endured, Khalil.'

'It was a long time ago,' he answered. 'But I admit, it affected me badly. I'd been treated like an animal for three years, so even after Dimah found me I acted like one. I didn't trust anyone. I barely spoke.' He shook his head, his features tightening. 'She was very patient. She took me to New York to live with her and her husband. She brought me to learning specialists and therapists, people who helped me adjust to this strange new life.'

'And you did adjust?'

Khalil grimaced. 'Some. But I haven't ever felt truly at home in America. No one understood me, or knew what I experienced. Not even really Dimah.'

'Did you tell her?'

'A little. I don't think she really wanted to know. She wanted me to forget Kadar completely, but returning to claim my birthright has always been what has motivated me. Dimah has never understood that.'

Surprise flashed through her. 'Why not?'

'The memories are too painful for her, I suppose. She grew up in Siyad, but she always longed to leave. When my mother died, she was heartbroken. She left to marry an American businessman and never wanted to return.'

'But she knows it is your right.'

'What she knows is that she provided a good life for me in America. She sent me to boarding school and university, helped me start my own consulting business before I joined the French Foreign Legion. She thought all those things would help me to forget Kadar, but I always saw them as stepping stones to returning. I don't think she has ever understood how much it has meant to me.'

'And yet the two of you are close,' Elena said quietly. 'Aren't you?'

'Yes, we are close. She saved me, quite literally.' The smile he gave her was bleak. 'I owe her a debt I can never repay, and I hope that one day she understands that I am attempting to redress it by claiming my birthright and becoming Sheikh.'

'Even though she doesn't want you to.'

'Yes.' He paused, his gaze moving once more to the

sky. 'Claiming my rightful inheritance will expunge any stain from my mother's memory. It's not just for my sake that I am pursuing this path. It's to right old wrongs, to repair the very fabric of my country that was torn when my father decided to pursue his own selfish whims instead of justice. Putting aside my mother with no real reason rent the country in two. I want to repair it.'

'And I want to help you, Khalil,' Elena said. She reached over and took his hand, and he squeezed her fingers in response. Encouraged by this show of affection, she took a deep breath and said some of what was in her heart. 'I know we agreed to live virtually separate lives in that document we signed, but I don't want to live that way any more.' She gazed into Khalil's clear, amber eyes, unable to tell what he thought about what she'd just said. 'You once asked me whether I wanted a loving, equal partner for a husband, someone who could support me. I said I didn't because I'd never even imagined someone like that existed.'

'Neither did I,' Khalil answered quietly and her hopes soared.

'Then you feel differently now too?'

'I don't know what I feel, Elena. I never expected or wanted any of this.' He sighed restlessly, but didn't let go of her hand. 'I feel like I've experienced something with you that I never thought I would. I want more of it. More of you. More of *us*.'

'I want that too,' she whispered.

'But this is all new to me. And frankly it's frightening.' He gave her a wry smile, but she still saw bleakness in his eyes. 'I haven't trusted anyone like this since I was seven years old with a child's simple heart. Since my father told me I wasn't his son.'

'I know, Khalil. And I want to be worthy of your trust and—and even of your love.' She held her breath, waiting for his reaction, wanting him to say it back: *I love you*. She hadn't said it quite as clearly as that, but still she thought he must know how she felt.

'I want to trust you,' Khalil answered after a long moment. He took a deep breath, squeezing her fingers once more. 'I want to love you.'

And in that moment it seemed so wonderfully simple, the way forward so very clear. They both wanted a loving relationship, a proper marriage. Why shouldn't they have it? Why shouldn't it be possible?

As they left the airport for Dimah's townhouse near the Ile de la Cité Khalil marvelled at the change in himself. He felt like some shell-less creature, pink, raw and exposed, everything out there for another person's examination. It was a strange and uncomfortable feeling, but it wasn't necessarily *bad*.

He'd been glad to tell Elena about his childhood, his aunt, his own fears and weaknesses. He'd never talked that way to another soul, yet he craved that kind of honesty with Elena.

He just didn't know what to do next. How it all would actually *work*. Take one step at a time, he supposed. For now he needed to think about Dimah.

He'd phoned her from Thallia, so she was waiting as their limo drew up to her townhouse and their security detail quickly got out to check the surrounding area.

Dimah came out to the front steps, her face wreathed in a tremulous smile, her wispy white hair blowing in the breeze. She looked so much older, Khalil thought with a pang, and he'd last seen her less than a year ago when he'd stopped in Paris on the way to Kadar.

'Dimah.' He put his arms around her, feeling her fragility. 'This is my wife, Queen Elena of Thallia.'

'Your Highness,' Dimah murmured and curtseyed. No matter how frail she looked or felt, she was still every inch the lady.

'I'm so pleased to meet you,' Elena said, and took Dimah's thin hand in both of her own.

Once inside, Dimah arranged for refreshments to be brought to the main salon, chattering with Elena about women's things while Khalil's mind roved over his arranged meeting with Aziz next week.

He'd been amazed that his half-brother had agreed to meet with him; it had given him hope. Perhaps Aziz really would see sense. Perhaps he would call the referendum.

And what about his wife?

Perhaps a quick and quiet annulment would get the nameless woman Aziz had married out of the way. Yet the fact that Aziz had been willing to marry so quickly made Khalil uneasy. It made him wonder if his half-brother wished to be Sheikh more than he'd thought he did.

'Khalil, you are not even paying attention,' Dimah chided. Her eyes were bright, her cheeks flushed. 'But I don't blame you. Anyone can tell you are in love!'

He felt Elena start next to him, saw her glance apprehensively at him. Was she worried for his sake or her own? He smiled and reached for her hand. It felt amazingly easy. 'You're right, Dimah,' he said. 'My mind is elsewhere.'

Elena beamed.

'I'm afraid I must excuse myself,' he said a few minutes later as he rose from his chair. 'I have business to attend to. But we will dine with you tonight, Dimah, if that is acceptable?'

She waved a hand in easy dismissal. 'Of course, of course. Go ahead. I want to get to know Elena properly.'

Suppressing a wry smile, Khalil gave his bride a look of sympathy before striding from the room.

'I can't tell you how pleased I am Khalil has found you,' Dimah said once she was alone with Elena. 'Anyone can tell how in love you are.'

Elena smiled, felt that tremulous joy buoy her soul.

'Do you think so?' she murmured, craving the confirmation of Khalil's feelings. 'I want to love you' was, she acknowledged, a little different from 'I love you'.

'I know it,' Dimah declared. 'I've waited so long for Khalil to find someone to love, and to love him back. I pray now he'll forget all this foolishness with Kadar.'

Elena tensed, unsure how to address such a volatile subject. 'The sheikhdom of Kadar is his legacy, Dimah,' she said gently. 'It's his birthright. He will not forget it.'

'He should,' Dimah said, her voice rising fretfully. 'He *should*. I keep telling him. There is nothing good for him there.' She bit her lip, her eyes filling with tears, and Elena frowned.

'Why do you want him to forget it?' she asked. 'Wouldn't you like to see him restored to his rightful place, and your sister's memory—'

'No.' Dimah cut her off swiftly. 'No. We mustn't talk about that.' She shook her head, seeming to come to herself. 'I want to hear more about you and your wedding. Tell me about happy things. Tell me about when you first realised Khalil loved you.' She smiled eagerly, like a child waiting for a story, sounding so certain of something Elena still wondered about.

Yet in that moment she knew she wanted to be like Dimah and believe. She wanted to hear and speak of happy things, to be certain that, no matter what happened with kingdoms or countries or thrones, she could be sure of her love for Khalil…and his love for her.

Gazing at Dimah's expectant face, Elena felt her own doubts begin to melt away. If Dimah could already see how Khalil loved her, then surely he did? Elena saw it in his eyes, felt it in his touch.

Maybe Khalil wasn't sure what love looked or felt like,

but Elena believed he loved her. She loved him. Nothing else mattered.

Nothing could change that.

Leaning forward, she began to tell Dimah all about how she and Khalil had fallen in love.

CHAPTER FOURTEEN

THE NEXT MORNING Elena came downstairs with Khalil to find Dimah standing in the centre of the salon. 'I need to talk to you,' she said, looking pale and resolute, and Khalil frowned.

'Dimah, what is it?'

'I need to tell you something.' Dimah closed the doors to the salon and turned to them, her fingers knotted anxiously together. 'I should have told you before, Khalil, a long time before. I never wanted to, but...' She trailed away, clearly nervous, and Khalil shook his head.

'I don't understand.'

Elena felt a sudden, terrible thrill of foreboding. She had a mad impulse to tell Dimah not to say anything. Not to change anything. Last night they'd all chatted and laughed over dinner, and then Khalil had taken Elena upstairs and made sweet love to her for half the night. She'd fallen asleep in his arms, perfectly content. Utterly secure in his feelings for her, and hers for him.

Yet now, standing there, looking at Dimah's anxious face, remembering her fretful pleas yesterday about Khalil forgetting Kadar, Elena's stomach knotted. Without even thinking about what she was doing, she flung out one hand.

'Don't.'

Khalil turned to stare at her incredulously. 'Do you know what she's going to say, Elena?'

'No, but…' What could she say? That she had some sort of premonition?

'But what? What do you know, Elena?' Khalil rounded on her and Elena blinked up, stunned at how quickly he had become suspicious, even angry. Dimah hadn't said anything, Elena didn't even know what she was going to say, yet here was Khalil, glaring at her accusingly.

'Khalil,' she whispered and he turned back to Dimah.

'What do you need to tell me, Dimah?'

'I should have told you a long time ago, Khalil.' For once Dimah's voice was low, certain, which made Elena all the more anxious. What was she going to say? 'Perhaps even when you were a boy, but I was afraid. Afraid first for you, and how you would take it, and then afraid for me. How you would feel about me keeping such a secret.'

Khalil stared at her, his expression shuttered. 'You are speaking in riddles.'

'Only because I am still afraid to tell you the truth,' Dimah admitted quietly. 'But I can see you have changed, Khalil. I know you love Elena—'

'Don't tell me what I feel.' Khalil cut her off brusquely and everything in Elena cringed and shrank. What was happening, and how had it all gone so wrong, so quickly?

Because it hadn't been strong enough to begin with.

'Khalil.' Dimah faced him directly, bravely, as if she were facing a firing squad—a death sentence. 'Hashem is not your father.'

His expression, amazingly, did not change. It did not so much as flicker. He didn't even blink.

'Say something,' Dimah said softly and a muscle in his jaw bunched.

'Nonsense.'

'You don't believe me?' Dimah blinked, incredulous.

'Why are you telling me this now, Dimah, after so many years?' He nodded towards Elena. 'Is it because of Elena? Because you think I've changed?'

Elena flinched; he sounded so contemptuous.

'Partly. You have more to live for now, Khalil, than being Sheikh.'

He clenched his hands into fists. 'But you're lying. Hashem is my father.'

Dimah cocked her head and in that moment Elena imagined the older woman was looking at Khalil as she had when he'd first come to her, wild and angry and so very terrified. 'Why would I lie, Khalil?'

He shrugged, the movement abrupt, aggressive. 'You never wanted me to return to Kadar. Maybe my marriage to Elena has given you the opportunity—'

'What opportunity? To deny you your birthright?'

'It *is* my birthright.'

'No,' Dimah said with heavy finality. 'It is not.'

Khalil shook his head. He held himself rigid, his gaze unblinking. '*No.*'

Everything in Elena ached as she realised what he was facing: the loss of his life's purpose, his very self. No wonder he wanted to deny it.

'I know it is a terrible thing for you to accept—'

'How can I accept it?' he demanded, and for a moment it seemed as if he almost wanted an answer to the question. 'Why would you not tell me for twenty-five years?'

'I told you, I was afraid!' Dimah's voice rang out, harsh and desperate. 'The more time passed, the more difficult it became. I did not want you to think badly of me, or your mother. Her memory seemed like the only thing that sustained you.'

'And you are tainting her memory now!' Elena saw the agony in his eyes. 'She was always so gentle with me. How could you do such a thing, Dimah? How could you accuse her of such a crime?'

'Oh, Khalil.' Dimah's voice broke. 'I'm a pitiful old woman, I know. I should have said something before. Long before. I closed my eyes to your ambition because I thought you would let go of it, in time. When Aziz became Sheikh, at least. I hoped that, in telling you now, I might finally set you free from this fruitless hope you've clung to for so long. That you'd be happy with the life you are making with Elena.'

'Why would my father make his will so open-ended, if I was not his son?' Khalil demanded.

'Maybe because Aziz has never seemed interested in Kadar,' Dimah offered helplessly. 'I don't know why, Khalil. But I do know what is true, and I'm sorry I didn't tell you sooner.'

Elena stepped forward and reached out one trembling hand. 'Khalil,' she began, but he jerked away from her.

'This suits you, doesn't it?' he said in a snarl. 'Now you'll have just what you wanted—a puppet prince at your beck and call.'

She blinked, stung. 'That's not fair. And that's not what I want at all.'

'It's certainly not what I want,' Khalil snapped. 'I'll never forget Kadar and my birthright and everything that has ever been important to me. Everything I've ever *been*.' His voice broke on the last word and he turned away from her, his head bowed.

'I'm sorry,' Dimah said quietly. 'I should have spoken before. I knew I had to speak now, since you were intending on returning to Kadar.'

'How would you even know such a thing as this? My mother—'

'Told me. She wrote me a letter, admitting everything. She even had a photograph of him, Khalil. Of your father.'

'*No.*' The one word was a cry of anguish and it broke Elena right open. Without even thinking of what she was doing or how Khalil might react, she went to him.

'Khalil.' She put her arms around his rigid body. 'Khalil.'

Tears started in her eyes. What could she say to him? How could she make this better?

'It can't be true,' Khalil said, and she heard then the agonised acceptance in his voice. He believed. He didn't want to believe, but he did.

'I can show you the letter, if you like,' Dimah said quietly. 'The photograph.'

Khalil gave a little shake of his head, then shrugged out of Elena's embrace, his back to them both. 'Who was he?' he asked, his voice barely audible.

'One of the palace guards,' Dimah answered in a whisper. 'You have his eyes.'

Khalil let out a sound that was almost a moan. Then he shook his head. 'I can't—' He stopped, stared blankly for a moment. 'I need to be alone,' he said, and walked out of the room without looking at either of them again.

It couldn't be true. *It couldn't, it couldn't, it couldn't.*

He sounded like a little boy, Khalil thought with a surge of fury. Like a terrified little boy, begging for mercy.

Don't hit me. Please don't hit me. Where is my mother? My father? Please...

The tears had run down his dirty face and Abdul-Hafiz had just laughed.

Now Khalil swore aloud and slammed his fist against the wall, causing a dent, bruising his hand and bloodying his knuckles.

It *couldn't* be true.

Yet he knew it was. And with that awful truth came the even more terrible realisation that everything he'd built his life on had been for nothing.

Every choice he'd made, every hope he'd had, had been for clearing his mother's name and claiming his legacy. His birthright. It had been who he was, and now that it had been taken away he was left spinning, empty, exposed. He had nothing. He *was* nothing.

He would not, would never, be Sheikh of Kadar.

Neither, he acknowledged with leaden certainty, would he be Elena's husband.

Elena paced the salon of Dimah's townhouse, her mind spinning, her heart aching. Khalil had left that morning, right after that awful confrontation, and although it was nearing midnight he had still not returned.

Dimah had gone to bed, after reassuring her that Khalil would return soon and things would look better in the morning. Elena had felt like shaking her. Things wouldn't look any better in the morning, not for Khalil. She knew what kind of man he was, how strong and proud. How he'd built everything on the foundation that the throne of Kadar was his by right. To have it taken away would devastate him…and he would be too proud to admit it.

And how would he be feeling, knowing that the man he'd thought was his father wasn't? That the truths he'd insisted on believing for so long, that had been sustaining him, were actually lies?

She longed to see him, to put her arms around him and comfort him. To tell him it didn't matter to her whether he was Sheikh or not. She didn't care who his parents were, or if he had a title. She wanted to tell him she loved him properly, not just hint at it. She wanted that love to make a difference.

And yet, deep down inside, she was afraid it wouldn't.

She heard the front door open and the slow, deliberate tread of a person who seemed utterly weary, even defeated. Elena hurried to the door, her heart thumping in her chest.

'Khalil.'

He turned to face her, the lines of his face haggard and yet his expression strangely, terribly blank.

'Elena. I didn't think you would still be awake.'

'Of course I'm awake!' she cried. 'I've been worried about you, Khalil, wondering how you are, how you're coping—'

'Coping?' He spoke the single word with contempt. 'Don't worry about me, Elena.'

'Of course I worry about you.' She bit her lip then took a deep breath. 'I love you, Khalil.'

He let out a hard laugh and Elena flinched. 'A little late for that, Elena.'

'Late? Why?'

'Because there is no reason for us to be married any more.'

'What?' Shock reverberated through her so her body practically vibrated with it. She stared at him in disbelief. 'No reason? Why is that, Khalil?'

He stared at her evenly, unmoved. 'You know why.'

'I know you no longer have a claim to the throne of Kadar. I know you've suffered a great disappointment. But I am still your wife. We're still *married*.'

'We'll get an annulment.'

'An annulment? How? We've made love, Khalil.'

'It can be done.'

She shook her head slowly, shock warring with hurt. Then both were replaced by a deep, hard anger. 'You coward,' she said, and her voice was cold. 'You selfish, thoughtless *coward*. You think because you have no need of me and our convenient marriage you can just forget your vows? Forget me?'

'How is this marriage convenient for you, Elena? I have no title, no claim. *I'm* the pretender. Do you think your Council will approve your marriage to me? Or will Markos just use it as a reason to depose you, consider it another foolish choice you've made?'

She blinked back tears. 'I don't care.'

'You should.'

'Forget my Council!' Elena cried. 'Forget our countries

or convenience. You told me you wanted to love me, Khalil. What happened to that? Did you decide you didn't want to any more? Or were you lying?' Her voice and body both shook as she demanded, 'Do you have no honour at all?'

'This isn't about honour,' Khalil retorted. 'I'm setting you free, Elena.'

'Setting me free? You haven't even asked if I want that kind of freedom. Don't hide behind excuses, Khalil. You're a better man than that.'

'Am I?' he demanded, his voice ringing in the sudden silence. 'Am I really, Elena? I don't even know what I am any more, if I am not my father's son. If I am not—' He drew a ragged breath. 'I've built my life on something that is a lie. Everything I've done, everything I've been…it's gone. So what am I now?'

'You are,' Elena said quietly, 'the man I love. I didn't fall in love with the Sheikh of Kadar, Khalil. I fell in love with the man who kissed my tears and held me in his arms. Who protected and encouraged and believed in me. I fell in love with that man.'

'And that man no longer exists.'

'He does.'

Khalil shook his head then stared at her openly, emptily. 'What am I going to do now, Elena? What purpose can I serve? Who can I even be?'

A tear trickled down Elena's cheek. 'You can be my husband, Khalil. You can be the Prince Consort of Thallia. You can be the father to our children.' He didn't answer, so she continued, her voice rising with determination. 'You can be the man you've always been, Khalil. A man with pride and strength and tenderness. A man who commands people's loyalty and who works hard for it. Why limit yourself? Why defined by who sired you, or a title? There is so much more to you than that. So much more to *us*.'

She took a step towards him, her hands outstretched. 'Kadar is in your blood, Khalil. It's still your country, and you are still Sheikh of your own tribe. You told me you wanted to repair your country, and you still can. Aziz will need you to help him. Kadar needs you. People will look to you for the way forward, for peace.'

Khalil didn't talk for a long moment. Elena held her breath, hardly daring to hope, to believe…

To trust.

Now, more than ever, she needed to trust him. 'Khalil,' she said softly, his name a caress, a promise.

'Don't you even care?' he asked after an endless moment. 'Doesn't it matter to you that I'm no one now? I'm just some nameless bastard.'

And then she realised he needed to trust her as much as she needed to trust him. To trust her to love him, even now. Especially now. 'I told you, you're my husband, and I am your wife. It doesn't matter, Khalil. It doesn't matter at all.'

She saw a flicker of hope in his eyes, like the first light of dawn, then he shook his head. 'Your Council—'

'You told me I didn't need a husband to stand up to my Council, and I don't. I'm stronger now, Khalil. You've made me strong.' Another step, and she was touching him, her hand curling around his arm. 'But I need a husband to be my helpmate and equal. Someone I can love and support, who will love and support me. Standing side by side with me.'

Khalil closed his eyes briefly. 'I feel as if everything I've ever known, everything I've counted on, has been ripped away from me. Destroyed.'

'I haven't,' Elena said softly. 'I'm still here.'

He reached for her hand. 'After so many years of anger, I don't know what to feel now. My father had a right to banish me.'

'Did he? He could have treated you far more kindly than he did.'

'And my mother…'

'You don't know what her situation was, Khalil. How unhappy she was, or what drove her to it.'

He nodded slowly. Elena knew it would take a long time for him to find peace with these revelations,, but she wanted to help him

He turned to her, his eyes wide and bleak, his voice raw. 'I love you, Elena. I didn't think I even knew what love was, but you've showed me in so many ways. You've believed in me, trusted me even when I didn't deserve to have that trust. I still don't know if I do. I don't know what the future can look like,' he told her, a confession. 'I don't know how to *be*.'

'We'll figure it out together.' She stood in front of him, letting all her hope and love shine in her eyes. 'I love you, Khalil. And you love me. That's all that matters.'

His face crumpled for a second and then he pulled her into his arms. 'Oh, Elena,' he said, and he buried his face in her hair. 'Elena. I love you so much. I'm sorry for being a fool. For being afraid.'

'You think this doesn't scare me?' Elena answered with a wobbly laugh, and she felt Khalil's smile against her hair.

'Then maybe we'll be scared together.'

'That sounds good to me.'

Khalil's arms tightened around her. 'I don't deserve you.'

'I could say the same thing.'

He kissed her then, softly, and it was a kiss that held so much tenderness and love that her heart swelled. 'I still don't know what will happen. What—what the future looks like. I'll have to talk to Aziz, renounce my claim…'

'I know.'

'You're right. I can still help Kadar. I want to.'

'They need you, Khalil. I need you.'

He pressed his forehead against hers, his hands framing her face. 'I love you.'

She smiled against his palm. 'You told me that before, but I don't think I'll ever get tired of hearing it.'

'Me neither.'

'I love you, Khalil.'

He closed his eyes. 'I never thought I'd ever hear anyone say that to me.'

'I'll say it. I'll keep saying it.'

He kissed her again, pulling her even closer to him. 'Don't ever stop saying it, Elena. And I won't either. No matter what happens.'

'No matter what happens,' she promised.

Neither of them knew just what the future held. Khalil would need to grieve; they both needed to grow. And their love, Elena knew, would keep them strong.

* * * * *

*If you enjoyed this book,
look out for Aziz's story in*
COMMANDED BY THE SHEIKH
by Kate Hewitt.
Coming next month.

'This is wrong.' Aksel's eyes rested on her slender figure and her rose-flushed face. 'You should not have come to Storvhal.'

Mina felt sick as the realisation sank in that he was rejecting her. 'Last night—' she began. But he cut her off.

'Last night was a mistake that I am not going to repeat.'

'Why?'

Mina was unaware of the raw emotion in her voice, and Aksel schooled his features to hide the pang of guilt he felt.

She bit her lip. Her pride demanded that she should accept his rejection and try to salvage a little of her dignity, but she did not understand why he had suddenly backed off. 'Is it because I'm deaf? You desired me when you didn't know about my hearing loss,' she reminded him when he frowned. 'What else am I supposed to blame for your sudden change of heart?'

'My heart was never involved,' he said bluntly. 'Learning of your hearing impairment is not the reason why I can't have sex with you again.'

'Then what *is* the reason?' The frustration Mina had felt as a child when she had first lost her hearing surged through her again now. She wished she could hear Aksel. It wasn't that she had a problem reading his lips, but not being able to hear his voice made her feel that there was a wide gulf between them.

'I can't have an affair with you. I am the Prince of Storvhal, and my loyalty and duty must be to my country.'

Chantelle Shaw lives on the Kent coast, five minutes from the sea, and does much of her thinking about the characters in her books while walking on the beach. An avid reader from an early age, her schoolfriends used to hide their books when she visited—but Chantelle would retreat into her own world, and still writes stories in her head all the time.

Chantelle has been blissfully married to her own tall, dark and very patient hero for over twenty years and has six children. She began to read Harlequin Mills & Boon® romances as a teenager, and throughout the years of being a stay-at-home mum to her brood found romantic fiction helped her to stay sane!

Her aim is to write books that provide an element of escapism, fun, and of course romance for the countless women who juggle work and home-life and who need their precious moments of 'me' time. She enjoys reading and writing about strong-willed, feisty women and even stronger-willed sexy heroes. Chantelle is at her happiest when writing. She is particularly inspired while cooking dinner, which unfortunately results in a lot of culinary disasters! She also loves gardening, taking her very badly behaved terrier for walks and eating chocolate (followed by more walking...at least the dog is slim!).

Chantelle is on Facebook and would love you to drop by and say hello.

Recent titles by the same author:

SECRETS OF A POWERFUL MAN
  (The Bond of Brothers)
HIS UNEXPECTED LEGACY
  (The Bond of Brothers)
CAPTIVE IN HIS CASTLE
AT DANTE'S SERVICE

Did you know these are also available as eBooks?
Visit www.millsandboon.co.uk

A NIGHT IN THE PRINCE'S BED

BY
CHANTELLE SHAW

Published in Great Britain 2014
by Mills & Boon, an imprint of Harlequin (UK) Limited,
Eton House, 18-24 Paradise Road, Richmond, Surrey, TW9 1SR

© 2014 Chantelle Shaw

ISBN: 978-0-263-24994-1

A NIGHT IN THE
PRINCE'S BED

CHAPTER ONE

HE WAS HERE. Again.

Mina had told herself that she would not look for him, but as she stepped out from the wings her eyes darted to the audience thronged in the standing area in front of the stage, and her heart gave a jolt when she saw him.

The unique design of Shakespeare's Globe on London's South Bank meant that the actors on stage could see the individual faces of the audience. The theatre was a modern reconstruction of the famous Elizabethan playhouse, an amphitheatre with an open roof, above which the sky was now turning to indigo as dusk gathered. To try to recreate the atmosphere of the original theatre, minimal lighting was used, and without the glare of footlights Mina could clearly see the man's chiselled features; his razor-edged cheekbones and resolute jaw shaded with stubble that exacerbated his raw masculinity.

His mouth was unsmiling, almost stern, yet his lips held a sensual promise that Mina found intriguing. From the stage she could not make out the colour of his eyes, but she noted the lighter streaks in his dark blond hair. He was wearing the same black leather jacket he had worn on the three previous evenings, and he was so devastatingly sexy that Mina could not tear her eyes from him.

She was curious about why he was in the audience

again. It was true that Joshua Hart's directorial debut of William Shakespeare's iconic love story *Romeo and Juliet* had received rave reviews, but why would anyone choose to stand for two and a half hours to watch the same play for three evenings in a row? Maybe he couldn't afford a seat in one of the galleries, she mused. Tickets for the standing area—known as the yard—were inexpensive and popular, providing the best view of the stage and offering a unique sense of intimacy between the audience and the actors.

Mina tried to look away from him, but her head turned in his direction of its own accord, as if she were a puppet and he had pulled one of her strings. He was staring at her, and the intensity of his gaze stole her breath. Everything faded—the audience and the members of the cast on stage with her—and she was only aware of him.

On the periphery of her consciousness Mina became aware of the lengthening silence. She sensed the growing tension of the actors around her and realised that they were waiting for her to speak. Her mind went blank. She stared at the audience and sickening fear churned in her stomach as she registered the hundreds of pairs of eyes staring back at her.

Oh, God! Stage-fright was an actor's worst nightmare. Her tongue was stuck to the roof of her mouth and sweat beaded on her brow. Instinctively she raised her hands to her ears to check that her hearing aids were in place.

'*Focus,* Mina!' A fierce whisper from one of the other actors dragged her from the brink of panic. Her brain clicked into gear and, snatching a breath, she delivered her first line.

'"How now, who calls?"'

Kat Nichols, who was playing the role of Nurse, let out an audible sigh of relief.

"'Your mother.'"

"'Madam, I am here. What is your will?'"

The actress playing Lady Capulet stepped forward to speak her lines, and the conversation between Lady Capulet and the Nurse allowed Mina a few seconds to compose herself. Her hesitation had been brief and she prayed that the audience had been unaware of her lapse in concentration. But Joshua would not have missed it. The play's director was standing in the wings and even without glancing at him Mina sensed his irritation. Joshua Hart demanded perfection from every member of the cast, but especially from his daughter.

Mina knew she had ignored one of acting's golden rules when she had broken the 'fourth wall'—the imaginary wall between the actors on stage and the audience. For a few moments she had stepped out of character of the teenage Juliet and given the audience a glimpse of her true self—Mina Hart, a twenty-five year-old partially deaf actress.

It was unlikely that anyone in the audience was aware of her hearing impairment. Few people outside the circle of her family and close friends knew that as a result of contracting meningitis when she was eight she had been left with serious hearing loss. The digital hearing aids she wore were small enough to fit discreetly inside her ears and were hidden by her long hair. The latest designed aids enabled her to have a telephone conversation and listen to music. Sometimes she could almost forget how lonely and cut off she had felt as a deaf child who had struggled to cope in a world that overnight had become silent.

Although Mina had complete confidence in her hearing aids, old habits remained. She was an expert at lip-reading and from instinct rather than necessity she watched Lady Capulet's lips move as she spoke.

"'Tell me, daughter Juliet, how stands your dispositions to be married?'"

The exquisite poetry of Shakespeare's prose was music to Mina's ears and touched her soul. Reality slipped away. She was not an actress, she *was* Juliet, a maid of not yet fourteen who was expected to marry a man of her parents' choosing, a girl on the brink of womanhood who was not free to fall in love, unaware that by the end of the night she would have lost her heart irrevocably to Romeo.

Speaking in a clear voice, Juliet replied to her mother.

"'It is an honour that I dream not of.'"

The play continued without further hitches, but in one corner of her mind Mina was aware that the man in the audience didn't take his eyes off her.

Shakespeare's tale of star-crossed lovers was drawing to its tragic conclusion. After standing for more than two hours, Prince Aksel Thoresen's legs were beginning to ache, but he barely registered the discomfort. His eyes were riveted on the stage, as Juliet, kneeling by her dead husband Romeo, picked up a dagger and plunged the blade into her heart.

A collective sigh from the audience rippled around the theatre like a mournful breeze. Everyone knew how the ill-fated love story ended, but as Juliet's lifeless form slumped across the body of her lover Aksel felt a sudden constriction in his throat. All the members of the cast were skilled actors, but Mina Hart, who played Juliet, was outstanding. Her vivid and emotive portrayal of a young woman falling in love was electrifying.

Aksel's decision to visit Shakespeare's Globe three nights ago had been at the end of another frustrating day of discussions between the governing council of Storvhal and British government ministers. Storvhal was a principality stretching above Norway and Russia in the Arctic Circle. The country had been governed by the Thoresen royal dynasty for eight hundred years, and Aksel, as monarch and head of state, had supreme authority over his elected council of government. It was a position of great privilege and responsibility that he had shouldered since the death of his father, Prince Geir. He had never admitted to anyone that sometimes the role that had been his destiny from birth felt like a burden.

His visit to London had been to discuss proposals for a new trade agreement between Britain and Storvhal, but negotiations had been hampered by endless red tape. A trip to the theatre had seemed a good way to unwind, away from the rounds of diplomatic talks. He had certainly not expected that he would develop a fascination with the play's leading actress.

The play ended, and as the actors walked onto the stage and bowed to the audience Aksel could not tear his eyes from Mina. This was the last evening that the play would be performed at the Globe. It was also his last night in London. Having finally secured a trade agreement with the UK, tomorrow he was returning to Storvhal and his royal duties, which, as his grandmother constantly reminded him, meant that he must choose a suitable bride to be his princess and produce an heir.

'It is your duty to ensure the continuation of the Thoresen royal dynasty,' Princess Eldrun had insisted in a surprisingly fierce voice for a woman of ninety who had recently been seriously ill with pneumonia. 'It is my greatest wish to see you married before I die.'

Emotional blackmail from anyone else would have left Aksel unmoved. From childhood it had been impressed on him that duty and responsibility took precedence over his personal feelings. Only once had he allowed his heart to rule his head. He had been in his twenties when he had fallen in love with a beautiful Russian model, but the discovery that Karena had betrayed him was only one of the reasons why he had built an impenetrable wall around his emotions.

His grandmother was the single chink in his armour. Princess Eldrun had helped her husband, Prince Fredrik, to rule Storvhal for fifty years and Aksel had immense respect for her. When she had fallen ill and the doctors had warned him to prepare for the worst he had realised just how much he valued her wise counsel. But even for his grandmother's sake Aksel was not going to rush into marriage. He would choose a bride when he was ready, but it would not be a love match. Being Prince of Storvhal allowed Aksel many privileges but falling in love was not one of them, just as it had not been for his Viking ancestors.

Perhaps it was the knowledge that his grandmother's health was failing that had caused his uncharacteristic emotional response to the tragedy of *Romeo and Juliet*, he brooded. Today was the twelfth anniversary of when his father had been killed in a helicopter crash in Monaco— the playground of the rich and famous where Prince Geir had spent most of his time—to the dismay of the Storvhalian people. In contrast to his father Aksel had devoted himself to affairs of state and slowly won back support for the monarchy, but his popularity came with a price.

In Storvhal he could rarely escape the limelight. The media watched him closely, determined to report any sign of him becoming a party-loving playboy as his father had been. There would be no opportunities for him to go out alone as he had been able to do in London. If he went to the theatre he would have to sit in the royal box, in full view of everyone in the auditorium. He would not be able to stand unrecognised in a crowd and be moved almost to tears by the greatest love story ever told.

He stared at Mina Hart. The cast wore Renaissance costumes and she was dressed in a simple white gown made of gauzy material that skimmed her slender figure. Her long auburn hair framed her heart-shaped face and she looked innocent yet sensual. Aksel felt his body tauten with desire. For a moment he allowed himself to imagine what might happen if he were free to pursue her. But the inescapable truth was that his life was bound by duty. For the past three evenings he had escaped to a fantasy world, but now he must step back to reality.

This was the last time he would see Mina. He studied her face as if he could imprint her features on his memory, and felt a curious ache in his chest as he murmured beneath his breath, 'Goodbye, sweet Juliet.'

'Are you coming for a drink?' Kat Nichols asked as she followed Mina out of the theatre. 'Everyone's meeting up at the Riverside Arms to celebrate the play's successful run.'

Mina had planned to go straight home after the evening performance but she changed her mind when Kat gave a persuasive smile. 'Okay, I'll come for one drink. It's strange to think that we won't be appearing at the Globe any more.'

'But maybe we'll be appearing on Broadway soon.' Kat gave Mina a sideways glance as they walked the short distance to the pub. 'Everyone knows that your father has been in negotiations to take the production to New York. Has he said anything to you about what's going to happen?'

Mina shook her head. 'I know everyone thinks Joshua confides in me because I'm his daughter, but he doesn't treat me any differently from the rest of the cast. I had to audition three times for the role of Juliet. Dad doesn't give me any special favours.'

If anything, her father was tougher on her than other members of the cast, Mina thought ruefully. Joshua Hart was himself a brilliant actor, and a demanding perfectionist. He was not the easiest man to get on with, and Mina's relationship with him had been strained since the events that had happened while she had been filming in America had led Joshua to accuse her of bringing the Hart name into disrepute.

Kat was not deterred. 'Just imagine if we do appear on Broadway! It would be a fantastic career opportunity. You never know, we might even get spotted by a top film director and whisked off to LA.'

'Take it from me, LA isn't so wonderful,' Mina said drily.

Kat gave her a close look. 'I've heard rumours, but what did actually happen when you went to America to make a film?'

Mina hesitated. She had become good friends with Kat, but even so she could not bear to talk about the darkest period of her life. Her memories of the film director Dexter Price were still painful two years after their relationship had ended in a storm of newspaper headlines. She couldn't believe she had been such a gullible fool to have fallen in love with Dex, but she had been alone in LA for her first major film role—young, naïve, and desperately insecure about her hearing impairment. The American film industry demanded perfection, and she had felt acutely conscious of her disability.

She had been grateful for Dexter's reassurance, and within a short time she had fallen for his blend of sophistication and easy charm. Looking back, Mina wondered if one reason why she had been drawn to Dex was because he had reminded her of her father. Both were powerful men who were highly regarded in the acting world, and Dex had given her the support she had always craved from Joshua Hart. When Mina had found out that Dex had lied to her it was not only his betrayal that had left her heartbroken, but the fact that once again her father had failed to support her when she had needed him.

'Mina?'

Kat's voice jolted Mina from her thoughts. She gave her friend an apologetic smile as they reached the pub and she opened the door. 'I'll tell you about it another time.'

The pub was busy and fortunately the din of voices was too loud for Kat to pursue the subject. Mina spotted some of the play's cast sitting at a nearby table. 'I'll get the first round,' she told Kat. 'Save me a seat.'

As she fought her way to the bar Mina decided she would have one drink and then leave. The noisy pub made her feel disorientated and she longed for the peace and quiet of her flat. She suspected that there were a few journalists amongst the crowd. Rumours that Joshua Hart's production of *Romeo and Juliet* might go to New York were circulating, and for the past week the paparazzi had been hanging about the theatre hoping for a scoop.

Mina squeezed through the crowd of people gathered in front of the bar and tried to catch the barman's eye. 'Excuse me!'

The barman walked straight past her and she wondered if he hadn't heard her. The loud background noise inside the pub made it difficult for her to hear her own voice and so regulate how loud or softly she spoke. Moments later the same thing happened again when another barman ignored her and went to serve someone else. It was situations like this that made her conscious of her hearing impairment. Her hearing aids worked incredibly well, but as the bar staff continued to take no notice of her she felt a resurgence of her old insecurities about her deafness. She felt invisible, even though she could see herself in the mirror behind the bar.

As she watched her reflection a figure appeared at her shoulder. Mina tensed as she met his gaze in the mirror and her heart slammed against her ribs as she recognised him. It was *him*—the man who had been in the audience—and close up he was even more gorgeous than she'd thought when she had seen him from the stage.

His eyes were a brilliant topaz-blue, glittering like gemstones beneath his well-defined brows that were a shade darker than his streaked blond hair. When Mina had seen him at the theatre the firm line of his mouth had looked forbidding, but as she watched him in the mirror he gave her a smoulderingly sexy smile that made her catch her breath.

'Perhaps I can be of assistance?'

The gravelly huskiness of his voice caused the tiny hairs on the back of Mina's neck to stand on end. She could not place his accent. Slowly she turned to face him, conscious that her pulse was racing.

'One advantage of my height is that I can usually attract the attention of bar staff,' he murmured. 'Can I buy you a drink?'

His stunning looks and sheer magnetism ensured that he would *never* be ignored. Mina flushed when she realised that she was staring at him. 'Actually, I'm trying to order drinks for my friends…but thanks for the offer.'

Her voice trailed off as her eyes locked with his. She could feel the vibration of her blood pounding in her ears as she studied his lean, handsome face. He was ruggedly male and utterly beautiful. Was this how Juliet had felt when she had first set eyes on Romeo? Mina wondered. In her character study of the role of Juliet she had tried to imagine how it felt to be a teenage girl who had fallen desperately in love at first sight with a young man. It had been more difficult than Mina had expected to step into Juliet's shoes. Could you really feel such intense emotion for someone you had just met, before you had got to know them?

Her common sense had rejected the idea. The story of *Romeo and Juliet* was just a fantasy. But now, in a heartbeat, Mina understood that it was possible to feel an overwhelming connection with a stranger. Even more startling was her certainty that the man felt it too. His eyes narrowed on her face and his body tensed like a jungle cat watching its prey.

Someone pushed past her on their way to the bar and knocked her against the stranger. Her breasts brushed his chest and an electrical current shot through her. Every nerve ending tingled and her nipples instantly hardened and throbbed. For a few seconds she felt dizzy as the heat of his body and the spicy scent of his aftershave hijacked her senses and filled her with a fierce yearning that pooled hot and molten in the pit of her stomach.

With a little gasp she jerked away from him. He was watching her intently, as if he could read her mind. In a desperate attempt to return to normality, she blurted out, 'You were at the theatre tonight. I saw you. Did you enjoy the play?'

His bright blue eyes burned into her. '*You* were—astonishing.'

He spoke in a low, intense voice, and Mina was startled to see colour flare briefly along his sharp cheekbones. She had the impression that he had intended to make a casual response to her question but the words had escaped his lips before he could prevent them.

Thinking about his lips was fatal. Her eyes focused on the sensual curve of his mouth and her breath caught in her throat.

'You came last night, too…and the night before that,' she said huskily.

'I couldn't keep away.' He stared deeply into her eyes, trapping her with his sensual magic so that Mina could not look away from him. Weakness washed over her and butterflies fluttered in her stomach. She swayed towards him, unable to control her body's response to the invisible lure of male pheromones and sizzling sexual chemistry.

A bemused expression crossed the man's face and he shook his head as if he was trying to snap back to reality. He pulled a hand through his dark blond hair, raking it back from his brow.

'Tell me what your friends want to drink and I'll place your order.'

Friends? The spell broke and Mina glanced around the busy pub. Somehow she gathered her thoughts and reeled off a list of drinks. The stranger had no trouble catching the attention of the bar staff and minutes later Mina paid for the round and wondered how she was going to carry a tray of drinks across the crowded room.

Once again the stranger came to her rescue and picked up the tray. 'I'll carry this. Show me where your friends are sitting.'

Kat's eyes widened when she spotted Mina approaching the table followed by a tall, fair-haired man who resembled a Viking. The stranger put the tray of drinks down on the table and Mina wondered if she should invite him to join her and her friends. She wished Kat would stop staring at him.

'Thanks for your help. I'm Mina, by the way.' Worried that she might not hear him in the noisy pub, she watched his mouth closely so that she could read his lips.

Amusement flashed in his blue eyes. 'I know. Your name was on the theatre programme.' He held out his hand. 'I'm Aksel.'

'That's not an English name,' Mina murmured, trying not to think about the firm grip of his fingers as she placed her hand in his. The touch of his skin on hers sent a tingling sensation up her arm and she felt strangely reluctant to withdraw her hand again.

He hesitated fractionally before replying, 'You're right. I am from Storvhal.'

'That's near Russia, isn't it—in the Arctic Circle?'

His brows lifted. 'I'm impressed. Storvhal is a very small country and most people haven't a clue where it is.'

'I'm addicted to playing general knowledge quizzes,' Mina admitted. 'The location of Storvhal often comes up.'

God, did that make her sound like a boring nerd who spent a lot of time on her own? People often assumed that actors led exciting and glamorous lives, but that was far from the truth, Mina thought wryly. There had been plenty of times when she'd been between acting roles and had to take cleaning jobs or stack shelves in a supermarket. Most actors, unless they made it big in the American film industry, struggled to earn a good living. But Mina was not driven by money and had been drawn to the stage because acting was in her blood.

The Harts were a renowned theatrical family, headed by Joshua Hart, who was regarded as the greatest Shakespearean actor of the past thirty years. Mina had wanted to be an actress since she was a small child and she had refused to allow her hearing loss to destroy her dream.

But the dream had turned sour in LA. Making a film there had been an eye-opener and she had hated the celebrity culture, the gossip and backbiting. The events in LA had had a profound effect on her and when she had returned to England she had re-evaluated what she wanted to do with her life, and she had recently qualified as a drama therapist.

One thing she was certain of was that she never wanted her private life to be splashed across the front pages of the tabloids ever again. It still made her shudder when she remembered the humiliation of reading explicit and inaccurate details about her relationship with Dexter Price in the newspapers. The paparazzi did not seem to care about reporting the truth, and Mina had been a target of their ruthless desire for scandal. She had developed a deep mistrust of the press—and in particular of the man she had just spotted entering the pub.

She froze when she recognised him. Steve Garratt was the journalist who had exposed her affair with Dexter. Garratt had written a scurrilous article in which he had accused Mina of sleeping with the film director to further her career while Dexter's wife had been undergoing treatment for cancer. Most of the article had been untrue. Mina had never been to bed with Dex—although she had been in love with him, and ready to take the next step in their relationship, before she had discovered that he was married. But no one had been interested in her side of the story, certainly not Steve Garratt.

What was Garratt doing here in the UK? It was unlikely to be a coincidence that he had turned up at the same time as rumours were rife that Joshua Hart's production of *Romeo and Juliet* might be performed on Broadway. Garratt was after a story and Mina's heart sank when the journalist looked over in her direction and gave her a cocky smile of recognition.

As he began to thread his way across the pub she felt a surge of panic. She could not bear the embarrassment of the journalist talking about the LA scandal in front of her friends from the theatre company. The story had been mostly forgotten after two years, and she had hoped it would remain dead and buried.

She glanced at the good-looking man who had introduced himself as Aksel. They were strangers, she reminded herself. The curious connection she felt with him must be a figment of her imagination.

'Well, it was nice to meet you,' she murmured. 'Thanks for your help.'

Aksel realised he was being dismissed. It was a novel experience for a prince and in different circumstances he might have been amused, but inexplicably he felt a rush of jealousy when he noticed that Mina was staring at a man who had just entered the pub. Was the man her boyfriend? It was of no interest to him, he reminded himself. He was regretting his decision to follow Mina into the pub, and her obvious interest in the man who was now approaching them was a signal to Aksel that it was time he left.

'You're welcome.' His eyes met hers, and for a split second he felt a crazy urge to grab hold of her hand and whisk her away from the crowded pub to somewhere they could be alone.

What the hell had got into him tonight? he asked himself irritably. His behaviour was completely out of character and he must end his ridiculous fascination with Mina Hart right now. 'Enjoy the rest of your evening,' he bade her curtly, and strode out of the pub without glancing back at her.

* * *

'Mina Hart, what a pleasant surprise!' Steve Garratt drawled. He smelled of stale cigarette smoke and Mina wrinkled her nose as he leaned too close to her.

'I find nothing pleasant about meeting you,' she said coldly. 'And I doubt you're surprised to see me. You're here for a reason, and I can guess what it is.'

The journalist grinned to reveal nicotine-stained teeth. It was warm inside the pub and his florid face was turning pinker. 'A little bird told me you'll soon be making your Broadway debut.'

'Who told you that?' Mina asked sharply. She glanced at his shifty expression and realised that he was hoping to goad her into giving him information.

'Come on, sweetheart. Everyone wants to know if your father will be directing *Romeo and Juliet* in New York. He must have told you whether it's going to happen. All the hacks are hoping to break the story. Give me an exclusive and I'll make sure you get good reviews if you do open on Broadway.'

'Joshua hasn't told me anything, but even if he had confided in me I wouldn't tell you. You're a weasel, Garratt. You nose around in people's private lives looking for scandal and if none exist you make up lies—like you did to me.' Mina broke off, breathing hard as she struggled to control her temper.

The journalist gave a cynical laugh. 'Am I supposed to feel sorry for you? Don't give me that bull about journalists respecting celebrities' private lives. Actors need publicity. You don't really believe that a film starring an unknown English actress would have been a box-office success on its own merits, do you? People went to see *Girl in the Mirror* because they were curious about the bimbo who screwed Dexter Price.'

Steve Garratt's mocking words made Mina's stomach churn. The pub felt claustrophobic and she was suddenly desperate for some fresh air. She pushed past the journalist, unable to bear being in his company for another second. 'You disgust me,' she told him bitterly.

Kat was chatting with the other members of the cast and Mina did not interrupt them. They would guess she had gone home, she told herself as she made her way across the crowded pub towards the door. Outside, it was dark. The October nights were drawing in and Mina's lightweight jacket did not offer much protection against the chilly wind. Head bowed, she walked briskly along the pavement that ran alongside the river. The reflection of the street lights made golden orbs on the black water, but soon she turned off the well-lit main road down a narrow alleyway that provided the quickest route to the tube station.

Her footsteps echoed loudly in the enclosed space. It wasn't late, but there was no one around, except for a gang of youths who were loitering at the other end of the alleyway. From the sound of their raucous voices Mina guessed they had been drinking. She thought about turning back and going the long route to the station, but she was tired and, having grown up in central London, she considered herself fairly streetwise. Keeping her head down, she continued walking, but as she drew nearer to the gang she noticed they were passing something between them and guessed it was a joint.

Her warning instincts flared. Something about the youths' body language told her that they were waiting for her to walk to the far end of the alley. She stopped abruptly and turned round, but as she hurriedly retraced her steps the gang followed her.

'Hey, pretty woman, why don't you want to walk this way?' one of them called out.

Another youth laughed. 'There's a film called *Pretty Woman*, about a slag who makes a living on the streets.' The owner of the voice, a skinhead with a tattoo on his neck, caught up with Mina and stood in front of her so that she was forced to stop walking. 'Is that what you do—sell your body? How much do you charge?' As the gang crowded around Mina the skinhead laughed. 'Do you do a discount for group sex?'

Mina swallowed, trying not to show that she was scared. 'Look, I don't want any trouble.' She took a step forwards and froze when the skinhead gripped her arm. 'Let go of me,' she demanded, sounding more confident than she felt.

'What if I don't want to let go of you?' the skinhead taunted. 'What are you going to do about it?' He slid his hand inside Mina's jacket and she felt a surge of fear and revulsion when he tugged her shirt buttons open. The situation was rapidly spiralling out of control. The youths were drunk, or high—probably both—and on a cold autumn night it was unlikely that anyone was around to help her.

'You'd better let me go. I'm meeting someone, and if I don't show up they'll start looking for me,' she improvised, thinking as she spoke that her friends at the pub would assume she had gone home.

The skinhead must have sensed that she was bluffing. 'So, where's your friend?'

'Here,' said a soft, menacing voice.

Mina's gaze shot to the end of the alleyway that she had entered a few minutes earlier and her heart did a somersault in her chest. The light from the street lamp behind him made his blond hair look like a halo. Surely no angel could be so devastatingly sexy, but to Mina, scared out of her wits, he was her guardian angel, her saviour.

The skinhead, surprised by the interruption, had loosed his grip on her arm, and Mina wrenched herself free.

'Aksel,' she said on a half-sob, and ran towards him.

CHAPTER TWO

'IT'S ALL RIGHT, Mina, you're safe,' Aksel murmured. He felt the tremors that shook her slender frame. When she had raced down the alleyway he had instinctively opened his arms and she had flown into them. He stroked her auburn hair, one part of his brain marvelling at how silky it felt. At the same time he eyed the gang of youths and felt a cold knot of rage in the pit of his stomach when the skinhead who had been terrorising Mina stepped forwards.

'Can't you count, mate? There's six of us and only one of you,' the gang leader said with a show of bravado.

'True, but I am worth more than the six of you combined,' Aksel drawled in an icy tone that cut through the air like tempered steel. He never lost his temper. A lifetime of controlling his emotions had taught him that anger was far more effective served ice-cold and deadly. 'I'm willing to take you all on.' He flicked his gaze over the gang members. 'But one at a time is fair, man to man—if you've got the guts of real men.'

He gently put Mina to one side and gave her a reassuring smile when her eyes widened in fear as she realised what he intended to do.

'Aksel...you can't fight them all,' she whispered.

He ignored her and strolled towards the skinhead

youth. 'If you're the leader of this pack of sewer rats I guess you'll want to go first.'

The skinhead had to tilt his head to look Aksel in the face, and doubt flickered in his eyes when he realised that his adversary was not only tall but powerfully built. Realising that he was in serious danger of losing face, he spat out a string of crude profanities as he backed up the alleyway. The other youths followed him and Aksel watched them until they reached the far end of the alley and disappeared.

'You have got to be nuts!' Mina sagged against the wall. Reaction to the knowledge that Aksel had saved her from being mugged or worse was setting in and her legs felt wobbly. 'They could have been carrying a weapon. You could have been hurt.'

She stared at him and felt weak for another reason as she studied his chiselled features and dark blond hair that had fallen forwards onto his brow. He raked it back with his hand and gave her a disarming smile that stole her breath.

'I could have handled them.' He frowned as Mina moved and the edges of her jacket parted to reveal her partially open shirt. 'That punk had no right to lay a finger on you. Did he hurt you?' Aksel felt a resurgence of the scalding anger that had gripped him when he had seen the skinhead gang leader seize hold of Mina. A lifetime of practice had made him adept at controlling his emotions, but when he had seen her scared face as the gang of youths crowded round her he had been filled with a murderous rage.

'No, I'm fine. *Oh…*' Mina coloured hotly as she glanced down and saw that her shirt was half open, exposing her lacy bra and the upper slopes of her breasts. She fumbled to refasten the buttons with trembling fin-

gers. Nausea swept over her as her vivid imagination pictured what the gang of youths might have done to her if
Aksel had not shown up.

'Thank you for coming to my rescue—again,' she said
shakily, remembering how he had helped her order drinks
at the bar earlier. The memory of how she had thrown
herself into his arms when he had appeared in the alley
brought another stain of colour to her cheeks. 'By the
way, I'm sorry I behaved like an idiot and hugged you.'

His lips twitched. 'No problem. Feel free to hug me
any time you like.'

'Oh,' Mina said again on a whispery breath that did not
sound like her normal voice. But nothing about this evening was normal, and it was not surprising she felt breathless when Aksel was looking at her in a way that made
her think he was remembering those few moments when
he had caught her in his arms and held her so close to
him that her breasts had been squashed against his chest.

Keen to move on from that embarrassing moment, she
quickly changed the subject. 'What are you doing here?'

Aksel had been asking himself the same question
since he had left the Globe Theatre after the performance.
His car had been waiting for him, but as his chauffeur
had opened the door he'd felt a surge of rebellion against
the constrictions of his life. He knew that back at his
hotel his council members who had accompanied him
from Storvhal would be waiting to discuss the new trade
deal. But Aksel's mind had been full of the Shakespearean tragedy that had stirred his soul, and the prospect of
spending the rest of the evening discussing politics had
seemed unendurable.

No doubt Harald Petersen, his elderly chief advisor
and close friend of his grandmother, would be critical of
the fact that he had dismissed his driver and bodyguard.

'I am sure I don't need to remind you that Storvhal's wealth and political importance in the world are growing, and there is an increased risk to your personal safety, sir,' Harald had said when Aksel had argued against the necessity of being accompanied by a bodyguard while he was in London.

'I think it's unlikely that I'd be recognised anywhere other than in my own country,' Aksel had pointed out. 'I've always kept a low media profile at home and abroad.' Unlike his father, whose dubious business dealings and playboy lifestyle had often made headlines around the world.

After he had sent his driver away, Aksel had strolled beside the river when he had spotted Mina entering a pub, and without stopping to question what he was doing he had followed her inside. His immediate thought when he had met her at the bar was that, close up, she was even more beautiful than he'd thought when he had seen her on stage. He'd looked into her deep green eyes and felt as if he were drowning.

'When you left the pub, I assumed I would never see you again.' Her soft voice pulled Aksel back to the alleyway.

'I was about to get into a taxi when I saw you come out of the pub. I watched you turn down this alleyway and decided to follow you. A badly lit alley doesn't seem a good place to walk on your own at night.'

Mina gave him a rueful glance. 'I'm on my way home and this is the quickest way to the station.'

'Why didn't you stay with your friends?' Aksel hesitated. 'You looked over at a man who walked into the pub and I thought he must be someone you knew.'

Aksel must be referring to Steve Garratt. Supressing a shudder, Mina shook her head. 'He was no one—just…a guy.' She swallowed, thinking that the only reason she had left the pub and started to walk to the station alone at night was because she'd wanted to get away from the journalist she despised.

She had a flashback to the terrifying moment when the gang of youths had surrounded her, and the colour drained from her face.

'Are you all right?' Aksel looked at her intently. 'You're in shock. Do you feel faint?'

Mina was not going to admit that she felt close to tears. 'I probably feel wobbly because I'm hungry. I'm always too nervous to eat before a performance,' she explained ruefully. 'That's why I was going home to get something to eat.'

His sensual smile evoked a coiling sensation in the pit of Mina's stomach.

'I have an idea. Why don't you have dinner with me? My hotel isn't far from here, and it has an excellent restaurant. I'm sure you won't feel like cooking a meal when you get home,' he said persuasively.

'I...I couldn't impose on you any further.' For a crazy moment she wanted to accept Aksel's invitation. It would be madness, she told herself. He was a stranger she had met in a pub and she knew nothing about him other than that he came from a country most people had never heard of. She looked at him curiously. 'Are you on holiday in England?'

'A business trip—I'm flying home tomorrow.'

She crushed her ridiculous feeling of disappointment. 'What line of business are you in?'

Was it her imagination, or did an awkward expression flit across his face before he replied? 'I work as an advisor for my country's government. My visit to London was with a delegation to discuss trade policies with Britain.'

Mina could not hide her surprise. With his streaked blond hair and leather jacket he looked more like a rock star than a government advisor. 'It sounds interesting,' she murmured.

His laughter echoed through the alleyway; a warm, mellow sound that melted Mina's insides. 'I would have expected an actress to be more convincing at pretending that my job sounds fascinating,' he said softly. 'Can I persuade you to have dinner with me if I promise I won't bore you with details about trade policies?'

As she met his glinting, bright blue gaze Mina thought it would be impossible for Aksel to bore her. Her common sense told her to walk back out to the main street and hail a taxi to take her home. She would be mad to go to dinner with a stranger, even if he was the sexiest man she had ever laid eyes on. She had followed her heart in LA but her experience with Dexter Price had left her wary and mistrustful, not just of other men but of her own judgement.

'I'm not dressed for dinner at a restaurant.' She made another attempt to ignore the voice of temptation that was telling her to throw caution to the wind and go with Aksel. Besides, it was the truth. Her cotton gypsy skirt and cheesecloth shirt were very boho chic, according to Kat, but not a suitable outfit to wear to dinner.

'You look fine to me,' Aksel assured her in his seductive, gravelly voice. 'There's just one thing. You've done your buttons up in the wrong order.'

He moved closer, and Mina caught her breath as he lifted his hands and fastened her shirt buttons properly. He smelled of sandalwood cologne, mingled with a clean, fresh fragrance of soap and another barely discernible scent that was intensely male and caused Mina's stomach muscles to tighten.

As if he sensed her indecision, Aksel gave her another of his sexy smiles that set Mina's pulse racing. 'I understand the hotel restaurant serves a rich chocolate mousse that is utterly decadent. What do you say to us both sampling it this evening?'

His gravelly voice was electrifying, or maybe it was the expression in his eyes as he'd put a subtle emphasis on the word decadent. They both knew he hadn't been thinking about chocolate dessert as he'd said it, and Mina was unable to control the tiny tremor that ran through her.

He frowned. 'You're cold. Here...' Before she could protest he slipped off his leather jacket and draped it around her shoulders. The silk lining was warm from his body and Mina felt a wild, wanton heat steal through her veins. He caught hold of her hand and led her back to the entrance of the alleyway, but then he stopped and glanced down at her, his expression enigmatic.

'I have a taxi waiting. I'll ask the driver to take us to my hotel, or take you home. It's your choice.'

It was crunch time, Mina realised. She sensed that if she chose to go home Aksel would not argue. It would be sensible to refuse his offer of dinner, but a spark of rebellion flared inside her. Since she had returned from LA she had built a shell around herself and stayed firmly inside her comfort zone, afraid to try new experiences. But what harm could there be in agreeing to have dinner with Aksel, who had rescued her from the youths and behaved like a perfect gentleman? Was she going to run a mile from every handsome man she met and allow what had happened with Dexter Price to affect her for the rest of her life?

She hoped he could not tell that butterflies were dancing in her stomach. 'All right, you win. You've seduced me with talk of chocolate mousse, and I'd like to come back to your hotel.'

The moment the words left her lips she realised how suggestive they sounded and colour rushed into her cheeks. 'To have dinner, I meant,' she added quickly. Oh, God, why had she said seduced? She didn't want him to guess that she wished he would kiss her, she thought numbly as her eyes locked with his.

He gave a husky laugh and lowered his head towards her so that his warm breath whispered across her lips. 'I know you meant dinner,' he assured her. His smile was wolfish as he said softly, 'Seduction will come later.'

And then Aksel did what he had wanted to do since he had first set eyes on Juliet three nights ago, what he had ached to do since he had drowned in Mina's deep green gaze when he had met her in the pub. He cupped her face in his hands and brushed his mouth over hers, once, twice, until she parted her lips beneath his.

Mina dissolved instantly when Aksel slanted his mouth over hers. She had fantasised about him kissing her since she had first noticed him in the audience three nights ago, and now fantasy and reality merged in a fire-storm of passion. Her heart pounded as he pulled her hard against him. His body was all powerful muscle and sinew but the heat of his skin through his shirt made her melt into him as he deepened the kiss and it became achingly sensual.

'Oh,' she whispered helplessly as he probed his tongue between her lips. Her little gasp gave Aksel the access he desired, and he slid his hand beneath Mina's hair to cup her nape while he crushed her mouth beneath his. The sweet eagerness of her response drew a ragged groan from him. He could have kissed her for ever, but one part of his brain reminded him that he was a prince and he was breaking every rule of protocol by kissing a woman he barely knew in a public alleyway.

Reluctantly he lifted his mouth from hers. 'Will you come with me, Mina?'

Mina stared into Aksel's eyes that glittered as brightly as the stars she could see winking in the black strip of sky above the alleyway. Her common sense warned her to refuse, but on a deeper instinctive level she knew she would be safe with him. She nodded mutely and followed him out of the alley to the main road where a taxi was waiting.

She couldn't stop looking at him, drinking in the chiselled masculine beauty of his face and his sensual mouth that had wreaked havoc on hers. And he could not stop looking at her. They were both blind to everything around them, and as they climbed into the taxi neither of them noticed the man who had just emerged from the pub and watched them from the shadows before he got into his car and followed the taxi at a discreet distance.

Some time soon his common sense was going to return, Aksel assured himself as he gave the taxi driver the name of his hotel and leaned back against the seat. He glanced at Mina and was shocked by how out of control she made him feel. He wanted to kiss her again. Hell, he wanted to do a lot more than kiss her, he acknowledged derisively. His body throbbed with desire, and only the knowledge that the taxi driver was watching them in the rear-view mirror stopped him from drawing her into his arms and running his hands over the soft contours of her body that she had pressed against him when they had kissed in the alleyway.

The taxi driver's curiosity reminded Aksel that he had not thought things through when he had invited Mina to dinner. Journalists from Storvhal had accompanied the trade delegation to London and they would jump at the chance to report that the prince had entertained a beautiful actress at his hotel. It was the kind of story his enemies would seize on to fuel rumours that he was turning into a playboy like his father had been.

Scandal had followed Prince Geir like a bad smell, Aksel remembered grimly. During his reign there had even been a move by some of the population to overthrow the monarchy. The protest groups had grown quiet since Aksel had become Prince of Storvhal, but he was conscious of the necessity to conduct his private life with absolute discretion.

While he was debating what to do, his phone rang and presented him with a solution to the problem. Aksel knew that his personal assistant was completely trustworthy, and he instructed Benedict to arrange a private dinner for him and a guest.

Mina did not recognise the language Aksel was speaking when he answered his phone, but she guessed it was Storvhalian. It was a more guttural sound than Italian, which she had learned to speak a little when she had spent a month in Sicily with her sister Darcey.

Listening to Aksel talking in an unfamiliar language reminded Mina that she knew nothing about him other than that he worked as some kind of advisor for his government. She had also discovered that he was an amazing kisser, which suggested he'd had plenty of practice at kissing women, she thought ruefully. She glanced at his chiselled profile and acknowledged that with his stunning looks he was likely to be very sexually experienced. Maybe he had a girlfriend in Storvhal. She stiffened as another thought struck her. Maybe he had a wife.

He finished his phone conversation and must have

mistaken the reason for her tension because he said softly, 'Forgive my rudeness. I am used to speaking to my PA in my own language.'

'It's late to be talking to a member of your staff.' Mina hesitated. 'I wondered if it was a girlfriend who called you…or your wife.'

His brows lifted. 'I'm not married. Do you think I would have asked you to dinner—hell, do you think I would have kissed you if I was in a relationship?'

Mina held her ground. 'Some men would.'

'I'm not one of them.'

The quiet implacability of his tone convinced her. Perhaps she was a fool to trust him, but Mina sensed that Aksel had a strong code of honour. He had a curious, almost regal air about him that made her wonder if his role in the Storvhalian government was more important that he had led her to believe. Perhaps he was actually a member of the government rather than an advisor.

But would a government minister have kissed her with such fierce passion? Why not? she mused. Not all politicians were crusty old men. Aksel was an incredibly handsome, sexy, *unmarried* man who was free to kiss her, just as she was free to kiss him. Heat flooded through her as she recalled the firm pressure of his lips on hers, the hunger that had exploded in her belly when he had pushed his tongue into her mouth.

'You spoke as if you have personal experience of the type of man who would cheat on his wife.'

Mina shrugged. 'I was just making a general comment.' She sensed from the assessing look Aksel gave her that he wasn't convinced, but to her relief he did not pursue the subject as the taxi came to a halt outside one of London's most exclusive hotels.

'You didn't say you were staying at The Erskine,' she

muttered, panic creeping into her voice as she watched a doorman dressed in a top hat and tailcoat usher a group of people into the hotel. The men were in tuxedos and the women were all wearing evening gowns. Mina glanced doubtfully at her gypsy skirt and flat ballet pumps. 'I'm definitely not wearing the right clothes for a place like this.'

'I'd forgotten that there's a charity function being held at the hotel this evening.' Aksel frowned as a flashbulb went off and he saw a pack of press photographers outside the hotel, telescopic lenses extended to snap pictures of celebrities attending the event. The last thing he wanted was to be photographed entering the hotel with a beautiful and very noticeable actress. It was the kind of thing that would trigger frantic speculation about his love-life back in Storvhal. He leaned forwards and spoke to the taxi driver, and seconds later the car pulled away from the kerb.

'There's another entrance we can use,' he told Mina. 'I've arranged for us to have dinner privately,' he explained as she slipped his leather jacket from her shoulders and handed it back to him. 'I'm not dressed for a black-tie event either.'

As the taxi turned down a narrow side street Mina checked her phone and read a text message from Kat, reminding her that Joshua Hart had asked the cast to meet at the Globe Theatre at nine a.m. the following day. After quickly texting a reply, she scrambled out of the taxi after Aksel. She stumbled on the uneven pavement and he shot an arm around her waist to steady her. The contact with his body made her catch her breath, and her pulse accelerated when he pulled her close. Keeping his arm around her, Aksel escorted her through an unremarkable-looking door into the hotel. Neither of them noticed the car that had pulled up behind the taxi.

Although they had entered the hotel via a back entrance, they still had to walk across the lobby: an oasis of marble and gold-leaf décor, which this evening was filled with sophisticated guests attending the charity function. Mina felt like a street urchin in her casual clothes and was glad that Aksel whisked her over to the lifts, away from the haughty glances of the reception staff.

As the doors closed she was intensely aware of him in the confined space and her heart lurched when he reached out a hand and brushed her hair back from her face. She tensed. Her hearing aids were tiny but they were fitted into the outer shell of her ears and were visible to someone standing close to her. There seemed no point telling him about her hearing loss when she would not see him again after this evening. He had already told her that he was returning to Storvhal tomorrow. She did not understand why he had asked her to have dinner with him, or why she had agreed, and she suddenly felt out of her depth. What on earth was she doing in a luxurious five-star hotel with a man she did not know?

'What's wrong?' he asked softly. 'If you've changed your mind about dinner I can arrange for you to be taken home.' He paused, and his husky voice sent a shiver across Mina's skin. 'But I hope you'll stay.'

She could feel her blood pounding in her ears, echoing her erratic heartbeat. It terrified her that he had such a devastating effect on her. 'It's ridiculous for two strangers to have dinner,' she blurted out. 'I don't know anything about you.'

'You know that I am a fan of Shakespeare—and chocolate mousse.' His blue eyes glinted as bright as diamonds. 'And I have discovered that you have an incredible talent for acting, and kissing.'

Her breath caught in her throat. 'You shouldn't say that,' she whispered.

'Do you want me to say you're bad at kissing?' His lips twitched with amusement but the expression in his eyes was serious. 'I can't lie, angel, you are amazing, and all I can think of is how much I want to kiss you again.'

Mina did not know if she was relieved or disappointed when the lift stopped and the doors slid smoothly apart. As she followed Aksel along a carpeted corridor the voice of caution inside her head told her to race back to the lift. Her eyes widened when he opened a set of double doors into an exquisitely decorated room where a polished dining table set with silver cutlery and candles reflected the ornate chandelier suspended above it. Vases of oriental lilies placed around the room filled the air with their sweet perfume, and the lamps were dimmed to create an ambiance that was unsettlingly intimate.

Aksel strolled over to the bar and picked up a bottle of champagne from an ice bucket. He popped the cork with a deftness that suggested he was no stranger to champagne, filled two tall flutes and handed one to Mina.

'We'll have a drink while we look at the menu.'

Mina watched his throat move as he swallowed a mouthful of champagne. His dark blond hair had fallen forwards onto his brow again and she longed to run her fingers through it. Conscious that she was staring at him, she took a gulp of her drink and belatedly realised that champagne on an empty stomach was not a good idea. The bubbles hit the back of her throat and seemed to instantly enter her bloodstream, making her head spin.

'Come and sit down.' Aksel draped his jacket over the arm of a sofa and sat down, patting the empty space beside him. He hooked his ankle over his thigh and stretched one arm along the back of the sofa, causing his black silk shirt to strain across his broad chest. He looked indolent and so dangerously sexy that the thought of joining him on the sofa made Mina's heart hammer.

'Um…I'd like to use the bathroom before we eat.'

'The first door on your left along the corridor,' he advised.

Get a grip, Mina told herself sternly a few moments later as she stared at her flushed face in the bathroom mirror. She looked different, more alive, as if a lightbulb had been switched on inside her. Even her hair seemed to crackle with electricity, and her eyes looked enormous, the pupils dilated, reflecting the wild excitement that she could not control. She traced her tongue over her lips, remembering how the firm pressure of Aksel's mouth had forced them apart when he had kissed her.

She held her wrists under the cold tap, hoping to lower her temperature that seemed in danger of boiling over. Maybe if she took her jacket off she would cool down— but the sight of her pebble-hard nipples jutting provocatively beneath her thin shirt put paid to that idea. The jacket would have to stay on. It was better to look hot than desperate!

Oh, hell! Tempting though it was to hide in the bathroom, she had to go out and face him. You're an actress, she reminded herself. You can play cool and collected if you pretend he's in the audience and don't make eye contact with him.

Taking a deep breath, she returned to the dining room and to avoid looking at Aksel she picked up her glass and finished her champagne. He was standing by the window, but turned when she came in and walked towards her.

'I'd love to know what thoughts are going on behind

those mysterious deep green eyes,' he murmured as she swept her long eyelashes down.

'Actually, I was wondering why someone who can afford to stay at a five-star hotel would choose to buy the cheapest ticket at the theatre and stand for a two-hour performance, not just once, but on three evenings. But I suppose,' Mina voiced her thoughts, 'as you are in London on a business trip, your employer would pay for your hotel. You must be very good at your job for your government to put you up at The Erskine.'

Aksel hesitated. Although Mina had heard of Storvhal, she clearly had no idea of his identity, and he did not feel obliged to reveal that he was the ruling monarch of the principality. For one night he wanted to forget his royal responsibilities.

'It's true that my accommodation was arranged for me,' he murmured. 'The first evening when I visited the Globe the only tickets available were for the yard in front of the stage. I probably could have booked a seat in the gallery on the second and third night, but I'll admit I chose to stand so that I had a clear view of you.'

His voice roughened. 'The first time I saw you walk onto the stage you blew me away.'

Mina felt as if the air had been sucked out of her lungs. She understood what he meant because she had felt exactly the same when she had seen him in the audience: utterly blown away by his raw sexuality. Her eyes flew to his face, and the primitive hunger in his gaze mirrored the inexplicable, inescapable need that was flowing like a wild river through her body.

'Aksel...' She had meant it to sound like a remonstration but his name left her lips on a breathy whisper, an invitation, a plea.

'Angel.' He moved towards her, or maybe she moved

first. Mina did not know how she came to be in his arms,
only that they felt like bands of steel around her as he
pulled her into the hard, warm strength of his body and
bent his head to capture her mouth in a kiss that set her
on fire.

CHAPTER THREE

MINA REMEMBERED HOW she had run into Aksel's arms when she had fled from the youths in the alleyway. Her instincts had told her she would be safe with him, and she felt that same sense of security now, as if—ridiculous as it seemed—she belonged with him.

He kissed her with increasing passion until she trembled with the intensity of need he was arousing in her. When he eventually lifted his mouth from hers she pressed her lips to his cheek. The blond stubble on his jaw scraped against her skin, heightening her awareness of his raw masculinity. She arched her neck as he traced his lips down her throat, but when he smoothed her hair back behind her ear she quickly turned her head so that he did not see her hearing aids.

He moved his hands over her body, shaping her shoulders, tracing the length of her spine and finally cupping her bottom. She gasped when he jerked her against his pelvis and she felt the unmistakable hard ridge of his arousal. Perhaps she should have felt shocked, or pulled away from him, but she had no control over the molten warmth of her own desire.

'You have no idea how many times in the last three days I have imagined doing this—holding you, kissing you—' Aksel's voice lowered to a husky growl '—making love to you.'

Mina's heart turned over at the thought of where this was leading. Was she really contemplating making love with a man she had only spoken to for the first time a few hours ago? It was madness—and yet hadn't she thought of him constantly since she had spotted him in the audience three nights ago? She had tried to tell herself that she had become too absorbed in the role of Juliet, and had been looking for a real-life Romeo. Fantasising about the blond man in the audience had been just that—a fantasy. But being here with Aksel was real, and so was the urgent, all-consuming desire that was making her heart pound in her chest.

A tiny shred of her sanity still remained and she said almost desperately, 'I don't *do* things like this. I don't go back to strangers' hotels…' She broke off helplessly as he gave her a crooked smile.

'Will you believe that this is a new experience for me too, angel?' Aksel raked his hair back from his brow with an unsteady hand. The restrictions of being a prince meant that he had rarely had the opportunity, and never the inclination, to pick up a woman in a bar. He assured himself that he'd had no ulterior motive when he had invited Mina to his hotel other than that he wanted to get to know her a little better. But the minute they had been alone and he had looked into her deep green eyes his usual restraint had been swept away by a storm surge of desire, and now the situation was rapidly getting out of hand.

'I've never felt like this before,' he admitted rawly. 'I have never wanted any woman as desperately as I want you.'

They were supposed to be having dinner, Aksel reminded himself. Perhaps if they sat down at the table and studied the menu the madness that was making him behave so out of character would pass.

'Are you hungry?'

Aksel spoke in such a low tone that Mina struggled to hear him, but as she watched his lips shape the question she remembered that she had not eaten anything since breakfast. She felt light-headed, probably from the effects of the champagne, she acknowledged ruefully. But hunger seemed to heighten her other senses and evoked a different physical need inside her. Just the thought of Aksel making love to her made her gut twist with desire.

'Yes, I'm hungry,' she replied in a husky, sensual voice that did not sound like her own.

'Do you want to order some food?'

She hesitated for a heartbeat. 'It's not food I want,' she whispered.

He said something in his own language. Mina did not understand the words but the glitter in his eyes was unmistakable as he hauled her against him and brought his mouth down on hers in a kiss that plundered her soul. She did not protest when he lifted her into his arms and strode through a door at the far end of the dining room. With her hands linked at his nape and her face pressed against his throat she was barely aware of her surroundings until he set her on her feet and she saw that they were in a huge bedroom dominated by an enormous bed.

It occurred to her vaguely that he must have a very good job for his country's government to have arranged for him to stay in such a luxurious room. But then he placed his mouth over hers once more and she instantly succumbed to the sensual mastery of his kiss. She was barely aware of him removing her jacket or unbuttoning her shirt and sliding it off her shoulders. Her sheer white bra decorated with tiny lace flowers pushed her breasts high and her dark pink nipples tilted provocatively beneath the semi-transparent material.

Aksel made a harsh sound in his throat as he lifted his hand and traced a finger lightly over her breasts. 'You are even more beautiful than I imagined. You take my breath away.'

Mina's heart gave a jolt as he reached behind her and undid her bra, but she made no attempt to stop him. Not even his ragged groan pierced the mist of unreality that had descended over her, and she gave a little shiver of excitement as her bra cups fell away and her breasts spilled into his palms. She lifted her eyes to his face and saw dull colour streak along his high cheekbones. His reaction to her, the feral glitter in his eyes, made her feel intensely aware of her femininity and her sexual allure. After what had happened with Dexter she had deliberately kept her body hidden beneath shapeless clothes, unwilling to risk attracting any man's attention. But the past and all its humiliating horror seemed far away.

Her sense of unreality deepened. It seemed incredible that her fantasies about the man in the audience were coming true. She had imagined him kissing her, undressing her, and now, as Aksel unzipped her skirt and it fluttered to the floor, Mina allowed herself to sink deeper into the dream.

'Sweet Juliet,' he murmured as he bent his head and closed his lips around the tight bud of her nipple. The sensation was so exquisite that she cried out and arched her body like a slender bow, offering him her breasts and gasping with pleasure when he suckled her nipples in turn until they were swollen and tender.

She wanted to touch him as he was touching her and tore open his shirt buttons, parting the edges of his black silk shirt to reveal his golden tanned body. His skin gleamed like satin stretched taut over the defined ridges of his abdominal muscles. Dark blond hairs covered his chest and arrowed down over his flat stomach. Mina traced the fuzzy path with her fingers, but hesitated when she reached the waistband of his trousers as a voice of caution inside her head reminded her that her last sexual experience had been three years ago with a boyfriend she had dated for over a year.

Her heart-rate slowed and thudded painfully beneath her ribs. She must be crazy to think of having sex with a stranger. Aksel had proved that she could trust him when he had rescued her from the youths in the alleyway, and she was certain that if she called a halt now he would accept her decision. The sensible thing to do would be to tell him that she had changed her mind, but as she stared at his sculpted face with its slashing cheekbones and sensual mouth she could not formulate the words. The fire in his ice-blue eyes melted her resolve to walk away from him, and desire pooled hotly between her thighs when he stroked the bare strip of skin above the lace band of her hold-up stockings.

He held her gaze as he eased her panties aside and ran a finger up and down her moist opening until he felt her relax, allowing him to gently part her and slide deep into her silken heat.

'Beautiful,' he murmured when he discovered how aroused she was. He kissed her again with a blatant sensuality that drugged her senses so that she was barely aware of him removing the rest of her underwear before stripping out of his own clothes. He moved away from her for a moment, and she drew a shaky breath as she watched him take a protective sheath from the bedside drawer and slide it over his erection.

'I'm sure you agree that we don't want to take any risks,' he murmured.

Mina nodded mutely, shocked to realise that she was so caught up in the heat of sexual excitement she had not given a thought to contraception. Luckily Aksel was thinking clearly, but the fact that he was prepared for sex emphasised that his level of experience was far greater than hers. Doubt crept into her mind and she hoped he would not find her disappointing.

Her thoughts were distracted as he drew her into his arms once more. His powerful, muscular body reminded Mina of a golden-haired Norse god, but although he looked as formidable as a Viking warrior his hands were gentle as he cupped her bottom and lifted her against him.

She caught her breath when she felt the solid length of his erection jab into her belly.

'Wrap your legs around me,' he bade her tautly.

Trembling with anticipation, she gripped his shoulders for support and locked her ankles behind his back. Carefully he guided his thick shaft between her thighs and Mina buried her face against his neck to muffle her soft moan as he possessed her with a devastating powerful thrust. Her internal muscles stretched as he filled her. He withdrew slowly and then drove into her again, each thrust harder than the last so that her excitement swiftly mounted to fever pitch.

His shoulder muscles rippled beneath her hands as he supported her, making her aware of his immense strength. The sensation of him moving inside her was amazing, incredible, and indescribably beautiful. The world was spinning faster and faster, drawing her into a vortex of pleasure that grew more intense as he increased his pace. It was all happening too quickly. She gasped, feeling overwhelmed by Aksel's urgent passion and her equally urgent response to him.

'Angel, I'm sorry, I can't wait,' he groaned. He tightened his grip on her bottom and thrust so deeply into her that Mina wondered how much more she could take before her body shattered. She looked into his brilliant blue eyes and saw her need reflected in his burning gaze. His expression was almost tortured and she sensed he was fighting for control. He tipped his head back so that the veins on his neck stood out, and at the moment he exploded inside her Mina felt the first powerful ripples of her orgasm radiate out from her central core, and she gave a keening cry as she fell with him into ecstasy.

It was a long time before the world settled back on its axis, but eventually reality returned, bringing with it a tidal wave of guilt.

'I...I should go,' Mina whispered. She could taste tears at the back of her throat and forced herself to swallow them. There would be time for recriminations later, but her immediate aim was to slide off the bed where Aksel had laid her a few moments ago, and get dressed with as much dignity as possible—given the circumstances.

She stifled the urge to laugh hysterically as she considered the circumstances. It wasn't every night that she had wild and abandoned sex with a stranger—or any kind of sex, for that matter. A little moan of pain and shame rose in her throat and she bit down hard on her lip as she forced herself to look at the blond Viking sprawled beside her. Now that they were lying down she could admire the full glory of his naked body, the long legs and lean hips, the powerful abdominal muscles and broad chest.

Her eyes jerked to the one area of his body that she had avoided looking at. Even half aroused he was—

magnificent. Her stomach squirmed as she remembered how big he had felt when he had slowly filled her. Oh, God, what had she been thinking? Pretty much the same thoughts that were in her head now, Mina acknowledged with a choked sound of self-disgust.

She sat up and told herself it was ridiculous to feel shy that he was looking at her bare breasts when—let's face it—he'd done a lot more than simply look.

'Hey—angel?' Aksel propped himself up on one elbow and frowned when Mina quickly turned away from him. His gut clenched as he glimpsed a betraying shimmer in her eyes. *She was crying!* The idea that he had caused her to cry filled him with guilt. He had acted like a barbarian, he thought disgustedly. It was no excuse that for the first time in his life his iron self-restraint had been breached by her achingly sweet response to him. 'What's wrong?' he asked softly. 'Where are you going?'

Were there rules for this sort of occasion? If so, Mina did not know the rules. 'I thought I'd go home...now that...now that we've...' She watched his frown deepen and hoped he wasn't going to suggest they had dinner. The idea of sitting in that plush dining room while they were served by waiters who could probably guess what they'd had for an appetiser sent a shudder through her.

She tensed as he cupped her jaw and tilted her face to him.

'I didn't mean to make you cry, angel,' he said roughly. 'I'm sorry—I was too fast—too impatient...'

'*No*—' Mina did not want him to take the blame. He had nothing to blame himself for. 'It's not your fault—it's mine. It's just that I've never in my life gone to bed with a complete stranger...' her voice wobbled '...and I'm embarrassed.'

He did not seem to have listened to her, and doubt and remorse darkened his eyes. 'Angel...I should have—'

She shook her head, desperate to reassure him. 'You did everything right. It was...perfect.' She swallowed, thinking of those moments when she had come apart in his arms. Nothing had prepared her for the physical or emotional intensity of her orgasm. She had connected with him on a deeply fundamental level—as if they were each two halves of a whole—and even now she could not forget that feeling. 'It was beautiful,' she said huskily.

'For me too.' Aksel was surprised to find it was the truth. He leaned forwards and brushed his mouth over hers, felt the soft tremble of her lips and gently pulled her down so her head lay on his chest, and he stroked her hair. She reminded him of a young colt, nervous and unsure, ready to run away at any moment. Certainly she was not like the sophisticated women who occasionally shared his bed. Not at the palace, of course. Royal protocol demanded that only his wife could sleep with him in the prince's bedchamber. But he owned a private house a few kilometres out of Storvhal's capital city, Jonja, where he took his lovers, and also a cabin in the mountains where he took no one.

Making love with Mina had been unlike anything he'd ever experienced with other women. But he had known it would be. He'd known when he'd watched Juliet on stage and had been captivated by her sweet innocence mixed with exquisite sensuality that she would fulfil all his fantasies.

'I'm glad it was as good for you as it was for me,' he murmured. He rolled over, pinning her beneath him, and smiled when he heard her indrawn breath as he pushed his swelling, hardening shaft between her unresisting thighs. 'Something so good should be repeated, do you agree, angel?'

* * *

Life, Aksel mused, had a habit of throwing up problems when you least expected them. He rolled onto his side and studied his current problem. Mina's long auburn hair streamed across the pillows like a river of silk and her dark eyelashes lay on her cheeks in stark contrast to her creamy complexion. The sunlight filtering through the blinds revealed a sprinkling of tiny golden freckles on her nose. She looked curiously innocent and yet incredibly sexy as she moved and the sheet slipped down to expose one milky-pale breast tipped with a rose-pink nipple.

Aksel felt himself harden and he almost gave in to the delicious throb of desire that flooded through him. Only the realisation that if it was light outside then it could not be very early forced him to abandon the idea of drawing Mina into his arms. The clock showed that it was seven a.m. His private jet was scheduled to fly him and the members of the trade delegation back to Storvhal at eight-thirty, and he had a series of meetings booked for the afternoon before he was due to host a dinner party at the palace this evening.

Cursing beneath his breath, he sprang out of bed before he succumbed to the temptation of Mina's delectable body. Striding into the en-suite bathroom, he acknowledged that he had thrown his personal rule book out of the window when he had spent the night with her at his hotel. She was hardly the first woman he'd had sex with. He was thirty-five and did not live the life of a monk. But he chose his lovers from the tight-knit group of Storvhal's aristocracy. The women he met socially understood the need for discretion and ensured that details of the prince's private affairs never came to the attention of the media.

Falling asleep with Mina in his arms in a haze of sated exhaustion had compounded his folly, Aksel thought ruefully as he stood beneath an ice-cold shower. Meeting her had thrown up all kinds of problems, starting with the fact that she did not know who he was. Maybe that was why making love with her had been so amazing. Last night he had been able to forget for a few hours that he was a prince. He had just been a man blown away by his desire for a beautiful young woman who had captivated him since he had seen her in the role of Juliet.

But now the fantasy was over and he must focus on his royal duties. Frowning, Aksel reached for a towel embroidered with the monogram of the hotel. He knew he should feel grateful that he lived a life of great privilege, but he had learned during the twelve years that he had been monarch that personal freedom was the greatest privilege of all, and this morning more than at any other time in his life he was acutely aware that it was a luxury denied to him.

Mina breathed a sigh of relief as she peeped from beneath her lashes and watched Aksel walk into the bathroom. The sight of his broad back and taut buttocks evoked a melting sensation in the pit of her stomach. It was not only his golden hair and skin that reminded her of a Norse god. Last night he had demonstrated his formidable strength and energy—not to mention inventiveness, she thought, flushing hotly as memories of the various ways he had made love to her crowded her mind.

When she'd woken a few minutes ago and felt his erection nudge her thigh, her pulse had quickened with anticipation. But she'd pretended to be asleep when she had realised that the batteries in her hearing aids had died.

She had no idea how he would react if she revealed that she was partially deaf. They might have enjoyed a night of wild and totally amazing sex, but Aksel was still a stranger she had met in a pub, and in the cold light of day Mina felt a growing sense of shame at her wantonness. Her behaviour had been completely out of character, but Aksel did not know that.

She did not have a clue what the protocol was when you woke up in a man's hotel bedroom. What was she supposed to say to him? Thanks very much for the best sex I've ever had? She bit her lip. Okay, she'd behaved like an idiot and she felt vulnerable and out of her depth. It was imperative that she took control of the situation, and her first priority was to change the batteries in her hearing aids.

Conscious that Aksel might emerge from the bathroom at any moment, Mina did not waste time collecting up her clothes that were scattered across the floor, and instead wrapped a silk sheet from the bed around her before going to look for her handbag. Last night she had been too engrossed in Aksel to take much notice of her surroundings, but now she realised that this must be the hotel's penthouse suite. The door from the bedroom led into a luxurious sitting room, and beyond that was the dining room.

Her bare feet sank into the thick-pile carpet. She could only guess how much it would cost to stay in the lavish suite, and she wondered exactly what job Aksel did for his government.

In the dining room, the curtains had been opened and the table was set out for breakfast. The aroma of coffee and freshly baked rolls was enticing and Mina realised she was starving. Her handbag was on the chair where she had left it, and luckily the spare batteries she always carried with her were charged. It took a couple of seconds to replace the batteries in her hearing aids. She felt less vulnerable when she could hear again and her urgency to sneak out of Aksel's suite was replaced with a more acute need to allay her hunger pangs.

She was halfway through eating a roll spread with honey when she sensed that she was no longer alone. Glancing over her shoulder, she saw Aksel watching her from the doorway.

'You look like you're enjoying that,' he murmured.

It was ridiculous to feel embarrassed, Mina told herself. But she was conscious that she was naked beneath the sheet and that her nipples—still swollen from Aksel's ministrations last night—were clearly visible jutting beneath the silk. Colour flared on her cheeks as she remembered how he had kissed every inch of her body and suckled her breasts before he'd moved lower and pushed her legs apart to bestow the most intimate kiss of all.

Her appetite disappeared and she put the roll down on a plate. 'I hope you don't mind. I was hungry.'

'I'm not surprised,' he drawled, his eyes glinting. 'I ordered breakfast for you. After all, it's my fault you missed dinner last night.'

He couldn't take all the blame. It wasn't as if he'd forced her to stay with him, Mina thought guiltily. Her heart thudded as he walked towards her. Last night he had looked like a rock star in his leather jacket, but this morning he was dressed in a superbly tailored grey suit, white silk shirt and an ice-blue tie that matched the colour of his eyes. He was a suave and sophisticated stranger, and Mina clutched the sheet tighter round her. 'I should get dressed,' she mumbled.

'I wish you could stay as you are.' His voice thickened as he cupped her bare shoulders and pulled her towards him. 'Making love to you last night was amazing, and I wish the night could have lasted for ever.'

Mina's heart leapt as he dipped his head and kissed

her. She'd had no idea how Aksel would react after their night of passion, and had mentally prepared for him to state that it had been a mistake. The tenderness in his kiss was unexpected and utterly beguiling. She closed her eyes and melted against him, and the world disappeared as she was swept away by his sensual mastery.

It was a long time before he lifted his mouth from hers. 'You taste of honey,' he said huskily. With obvious reluctance he dropped his hands from her. 'My car is waiting to take me to the airport, but of course I'll take you home first.'

Her heart plummeted as his words catapulted her back to reality. 'You're flying back to Storvhal today, aren't you?'

'I have to, I'm afraid.' Aksel glanced at his watch and his jaw clenched. There was no time now to explain to Mina who he was. He could never escape the responsibilities that came with being a ruling monarch, but he was unwilling to accept that he would never see her again. However, inviting her to Storvhal would be fraught with difficulties.

'What about you? Do you have any plans now that the production of *Romeo and Juliet* has finished its run at the Globe?'

Perhaps later today she would hear if the play was going to Broadway, but Mina saw no point in mentioning it, or that she had an interview arranged for a position as a drama therapist with a health-care trust. She was by no means certain to get the job, and even if she were to be offered it there was still the problem of telling her father that she wanted to pull out of the play.

She shrugged. 'I don't have anything planned for the next couple of weeks. In the acting profession it's known as resting,' she said drily.

'I have to go to Paris at the end of next week. I was thinking about staying on for a couple of days to do some sightseeing.' Aksel paused and looked deeply into Mina's eyes. 'Would you like to meet up and spend the weekend with me?'

He wanted to meet her in Paris—the city of lovers! She strove to sound cool, despite the fact that her heart was racing because he wanted to see her again. 'That could be fun.'

A flame flickered in his blue eyes. 'I can guarantee it.' Unable to resist the lure of her soft mouth, Aksel bent his head, but at that moment his phone rang and he stifled a frustrated sigh when he saw that the call was from his PA. 'Excuse me, I need to take this,' he murmured.

Mina hurried back to the master bedroom. The tangled sheets on the bed were an embarrassing reminder of the passionate night she had spent with Aksel, but she felt better for knowing that it hadn't been a one-night stand. In the en-suite bathroom she bundled her hair into a shower cap and took a quick shower. It would be a mistake to read too much into his invitation to Paris, but the fact that he wanted to spend a weekend with her surely meant that he wanted to get to know her better—and not only in the bedroom.

A lifetime of practice allowed Aksel to greet Mina with an easy smile that disguised his tense mood when she walked back into the room. Her skirt looked even more crumpled after it had spent the night screwed up on the floor, and her long auburn hair fell in silky disarray around her shoulders, but her rather bohemian style was not foremost in his mind as he ushered her into the lift.

'The car is waiting round the back of the hotel,' he told her. He wondered what his PA's terse message meant. 'A situation has arisen' could mean anything. He hoped to God the trade deal hadn't fallen through.

Leading Mina to the rear of the lobby, he opened the door through which they had entered the hotel the previous night. A gust of wind whipped up the steps and lifted the hem of her skirt to reveal her slim thighs and lace stocking tops.

'*Oh…*' She frantically tried to push the lightweight material down. Another gust of wind almost knocked her off her feet and Aksel slid his arm around her waist to clamp her to his side as they walked out of the hotel.

'*Mina—over here!*' a voice called, and a flashbulb flared in the grey street. As Aksel turned his head towards the light the voice called again, '*Prince Aksel— fantastic!* Mina—you're a star. I asked you to give me a scoop, and this is gonna hit the headlines and make me rich!'

'What the hell…?' Cursing, Aksel glanced down at Mina's white face before shooting a furious glare at the man standing on the opposite pavement, holding a long-lens camera.

'Sir…' The chauffeur drew the car up against the kerb and jumped out, but the rear door had already been opened from inside by Aksel's PA.

'Quickly, sir…'

Aksel hardly needed to be told. He bundled Mina into the car before sliding in next to her, and the chauffeur slammed the door. As the car pulled away Aksel ran a hand through his hair and glared at the bespectacled young man sitting opposite him. 'Would you like to tell me what in hell's name is going on, Ben?'

CHAPTER FOUR

AKSEL'S PA, BENEDICT LINDBURG, grimaced. 'The paparazzi are swarming at the front of the hotel. I hoped you would be able to leave through the back door without being spotted.'

Glancing over his shoulder, Aksel could still see the florid-faced press photographer focusing his camera on the back of the car. 'I recognise him,' he said slowly. He looked at Mina, who was huddled into her jacket. 'That man came into the pub last night, and you looked at him as though you knew him.' His eyes narrowed on the twin spots of colour that flared on her white face. 'You told me he was no one in particular.'

He frowned as a curious, almost hunted expression flitted across Mina's face. 'Angel, who was that man? Do you have a problem?'

'With respect, sir, *you* have a problem,' Benedict Lindburg said quietly, handing Aksel a newspaper.

It took him a matter of seconds to skim the front page and he cursed savagely. 'What are the chances of us keeping this story contained?' he asked his PA.

'None,' was the short reply. 'The photo of you and Miss Hart entering the hotel through a back door last night has already been picked up by the media in Storvhal and is headline news. The pictures taken a few moments ago will doubtless already be posted on social media sites.'

Aksel's jaw clenched. 'Damn the paparazzi to hell.'

'I don't understand,' Mina said shakily. She had been shocked into silence when she had seen the journalist Steve Garratt as she and Aksel had emerged from the hotel, but she was puzzled by Aksel's reaction. 'What story? Why does it matter if we were seen going into the hotel last night?'

She recalled her suspicion that Aksel had an important role working for his country's government. Steve Garratt's words pushed into her head. The journalist had called out *Prince Aksel*. She stared at the newspaper photo of her and Aksel entering the hotel with their arms around each other. Above the picture the headline proclaimed *The Prince and the Showgirl!*

Mina turned stunned eyes on Aksel's hard-boned profile, trying frantically to recall any information she had read about Storvhal. The country was a principality— rather like Monaco was—an independent state with close connections to Norway, ruled by a monarch.

Realisation hit her like an ice-cold shower. 'You're a *prince*?' she choked.

'Prince Aksel the Second is head of the Royal House of Thoresen and Supreme Ruler of Storvhal,' the young man with the glasses said in a clipped tone. His expression behind his lenses was disapproving as he studied Mina's crumpled clothes.

She flushed, and asked tightly, 'And you are?'

'Benedict Lindburg, His Highness's personal assistant.'

His Highness! Mina bit her lip and stared at Aksel, wondering if she would wake up in a minute. If last night had seemed unreal, the events unfolding this morning were unbelievable. 'Why didn't you tell me?'

He gave her an odd, intent look. 'So you maintain that you did not know my identity when we met in the pub?'

'Of course I didn't.' Her voice faltered as she watched a muscle flicker in his jaw. There was no hint of his sexy, crooked smile on his mouth. His lips were set in a stern line and his face looked as though it had been sculpted from marble. 'Aksel...' she said uncertainly.

'Someone must have tipped off the press last night and told them that we would be entering the hotel through the back door.'

Aksel's voice was expressionless but inside his head his thoughts ran riot. Nothing made sense. No one had known that he had invited Mina to his hotel—except for Mina herself, his brain pointed out. He tensed as his mind violently rejected the possibility that he had made the most spectacular misjudgement of his life. But a memory slid like a snake into his mind and spewed poison.

'You sent a text message to someone as the taxi drew up outside the hotel,' he reminded her.

Mina's eyes flashed at his accusatory tone. 'I sent a message to my friend Kat to confirm that I would be at a cast meeting at the theatre this morning. I'll show you the damn text if you don't believe me,' she said hotly. Her eyes met Aksel's and she felt chilled by the cold speculation in his gaze.

His PA broke the tense silence. 'Is the meeting to discuss the announcement made in the press this morning that the Joshua Hart Theatre company will be performing *Romeo and Juliet* on Broadway?'

Mina blinked. 'There's been an announcement? I haven't spoken to my father but I have heard he has been in negotiations to take the play to New York.'

'The news about the play has received extra prominence in the media, due no doubt to speculation about your relationship with Prince Aksel,' Benedict Lindburg said stiffly.

Aksel swore beneath his breath. Since he had become ruler of Storvhal he had never lowered his guard, never slipped up—until he had looked into a pair of deep green eyes and lost his head. Shame seared him. Perhaps he was as weak as his father after all. If he was labelled a playboy prince by the press in Storvhal it could cause irreparable damage to his reputation and even to the monarchy.

He stared at Mina and despised himself for wanting to kiss her tremulous mouth. 'The journalist who was waiting for us this morning—he knew your name, and he said he'd asked you to give him a scoop,' Aksel said grimly. 'He *was* the same man who was in the pub.' He recalled the strange expression on Mina's face when she had seen the man the previous evening, and the truth hit him like a blow to his stomach. 'The journalist is a friend of yours, and you tipped him off that I'd invited you to my hotel last night.'

'I didn't!'

Her beautiful eyes widened. A man could drown in those deep green pools, Aksel thought. Hell, he could feel himself floundering, wanting to believe the shocked outrage in her voice. Only a gifted actress could feign such innocence. Mina had played Juliet so convincingly, taunted a voice in Aksel's head. She made a living out of pretence and playing make-believe.

Rage burned inside him, but beneath his anger was a savage feeling of betrayal that despite her denial Mina *must* have spoken to the press. He was aware of the same hollow sensation in his gut that he had felt as a young man, when he had learned that his mother had betrayed him.

When Aksel had found out that Karena did not really love him, he had been hurt. But far worse had been the discovery that his mother had encouraged the Russian model to seduce him, promising her a life of fame, fortune and luxury. After Prince Geir's death, Irina had had strong financial reasons for wanting to maintain a link between Russia and Storvhal, and she had believed it would be beneficial for her if her son married a Russian woman. But when her plan had been revealed, Aksel had realised just how cold and calculating his mother was, and how little she cared about him.

Helvete! If his own mother could betray him, why was he surprised that a woman he had picked up in a bar had done the same? he derided himself. Bitter experience had taught him never to trust any woman and he was furious with himself for being taken in by Mina's air of innocence.

Mina could tell from Aksel's cold expression that he did not believe her. 'I *didn't* know you are a prince,' she repeated. 'Even if I had, why would I have tipped off a journalist?'

'To create publicity for your father's theatre company,' Benedict Lindburg suggested smoothly.

'Keep out of this.' Mina rounded on the PA fiercely. 'You don't know anything about me.'

'As a matter of fact I know everything about you.' The PA handed a folder to Aksel with an apologetic shrug. 'The photo of you and Miss Hart was posted on social media sites shortly after it was taken last night. As soon as I was alerted to it I ran a security check on Miss Hart. My report includes details of Miss Hart's acting career in England and also in the United States.'

The colour drained from Mina's face as she stared at the folder in Aksel's hand. Without doubt his PA had unearthed the story about her relationship—her alleged white-hot affair—with the film director Dexter Price, which some of the media had labelled a publicity stunt to promote the film she had starred in. She had done nothing wrong, Mina reminded herself. She had not deserved to be vilified by the press, but what chance was there of Aksel believing her side of the story when she looked as guilty as hell of tipping off the journalist Steve Garratt.

She looked into Aksel's eyes and felt chilled to the bone. The Viking lover with the sexy smile had turned into a stranger. He had always been a stranger, she reminded herself. Just because he had made love to her as though she were the most precious person on the planet did not prove anything other than that he was very good at sex.

Shame swept through her as she remembered how she had responded to him in bed. She did not know what had come over her. And him a *prince*! She froze when Aksel opened the folder and sought his gaze, her eyes unconsciously pleading. If only they could go back to last night, to the private, magical world they had created.

'Aksel…' she whispered.

For a heartbeat she thought he was going to listen to her. Something flared in his eyes, and he stared at her mouth as if he wanted to kiss her. But then his jaw hardened and he deliberately turned away and looked down at the open file.

Mina could not bear to sit beside him while he read about the most humiliating episode in her life. The traffic was crawling around Marble Arch, and the car came to a standstill. The only thought in Mina's head was to run from Aksel—something she should have done last night, she acknowledged grimly. She must have been out of her mind to have slept with a stranger.

Before he realised her intention she opened the car door and scrambled out into the midst of four lanes of traffic.

Aksel sprang forwards and tried to grab hold of her. 'Don't be an idiot!' he yelled. 'You'll be killed!' His heart was in his mouth as he watched her weave through the cars, taxis and buses. Moments later he glimpsed Mina's long auburn hair as she disappeared down the steps leading to the underground station. Slowly he sank back in his seat, fighting a fierce urge to chase after her.

Benedict pulled the car door shut. The PA was startled when he thought he glimpsed emotion in the Prince of Storvhal's eyes. 'Sir...I'm sorry,' he said hesitantly.

The hot flood of rage inside Aksel had solidified into a cold, hard knot. It was bad enough that Mina had made a fool of him, and worse that his stupidity had been witnessed by a member of his staff.

His jaw tightened. He had certainly been a fool to have thought—even fleetingly—that making love with Mina had been somehow special. She'd had a few clever tricks—that was all. Like the way she had focused her big green eyes intently on his mouth. She'd made him feel as if he were the only man in the world for her.

He glanced at his PA and raised an eyebrow. 'I don't require your sympathy, Ben,' he drawled. 'I simply want you to get on with your job. Have you confirmed my meeting with the Danish Prime Minister yet?'

He must have been imagining things, Benedict told himself. The Ice Prince's face was as emotionless as always. Suitably chastened, the PA murmured, 'I'll do it right away, sir.'

* * *

Mina could hear her father's raised voice from the other end of the corridor.

'Get out of my sight,' Joshua Hart roared. 'I will not put up with guttersnipes from the tabloid press harassing me with tittle-tattle and nonsense.'

Forewarned that journalists must be in her father's office, Mina darted into a broom cupboard moments before two men clutching cameras and recording equipment shot past.

It was no surprise that the other members of the play's cast seemed to be keeping out of the director's way. Joshua in a temper reminded Mina of an angry bear, and she took a deep breath before she peeped cautiously around his office door.

'Oh, it's you.' He greeted her with a scowl. 'I hope you haven't brought any more damn journalists with you.'

'No.' Mina was pretty sure she had managed to slip through a side door of the Globe without being seen by the journalists milling about outside the theatre. She gave him a hesitant smile. 'It's great news about the play going to New York.'

Her father snorted. 'I tried to phone you last night to tell you the news first, before I announced it to the rest of the cast, but you didn't answer. I suppose you were with this chap of yours.' He glared at Mina from beneath his bushy eyebrows. 'It's all over the papers that you are dating a prince.'

Mina's heart sank when she saw copies of several of the morning's newspapers on her father's desk. The photograph on the front page showed her and Aksel entering his hotel through a back door, and it was clear from their body language that they had been on their way to bed.

'I'm not dating him,' she said quickly, but her father did not appear to have heard her.

'I would have thought you'd had enough publicity when you got involved with that film director in America. Heaven knows, you're an adult and you can lead your life how you want,' Joshua exploded. 'But having your love-life plastered across the newspapers is not the sort of publicity I want for the Hart family or my theatre company. Have you thought that this could have a detrimental effect when the play opens on Broadway?'

According to Dexter Price there was no such thing as bad publicity, Mina thought darkly. 'In what way do you mean detrimental?' she asked her father.

'We're performing Shakespeare on Broadway,' Joshua snapped. 'I don't want the production to turn into a soap opera because Juliet is sleeping with a European aristocrat. You know how fascinated the Americans are by that sort of thing.'

Mina bit her lip as she stared at her father's furious face. She had hoped for his support but she should have known that he would be more concerned about the play than her. Joshua had been an unpredictable parent while she was growing up, and Mina and her brother and sisters had learned to deal with his mood swings and artistic temperament.

'I assure you I didn't ask for the publicity,' she said stiffly. 'I won't be seeing Aks…the prince…again so you need not worry that I'll attract adverse press coverage.'

It was obvious from the way Aksel had been so quick to believe the worst of her that he'd never had any intention of meeting her in Paris. He was a prince, for heaven's sake, and she had been a one-night stand. She swallowed the sudden lump in her throat, remembering how he had kissed her with such beguiling tenderness at the hotel that morning. He had made her think that he genuinely did want to see her again. She grimaced. His performance had been worthy of an award for best actor.

'Your mother's worried about you,' Joshua muttered. 'You'd better phone her.' He sat down at his desk. 'I've told the cast to assemble on the stage and I'll be along to discuss the New York project when I've made a couple of calls.'

Kat Nichols was the first person Mina saw when she walked through the theatre.

'Mina! I couldn't believe it when I saw the newspapers. Who would have guessed that the blond hunk from the pub is a *prince*?'

Not me, unfortunately, Mina thought ruefully.

Kat looked at her closely. 'Are you okay? Some of the papers have dragged up a story about you and a film director in LA.' She could not hide her curiosity. 'What did exactly happen between you and Dexter Price?'

Mina bit her lip. Now that the newspapers had reprinted the lies about her, she might as well tell Kat the truth.

'I'd been picked for a lead role in what was touted as the next big blockbuster film,' she said heavily. 'During filming I formed a close relationship with Dexter. I naïvely believed that he wanted to keep our friendship quiet to protect me from gossip. He never took me to popular bars or restaurants where we might be seen together. But a journalist got wind that something was going on and managed to take some damning photos of us.'

She grimaced. 'I only ever kissed Dex, but pictures of us were splashed across the newspapers and appeared to prove that we were having a sordid affair. It turned out that Dex was married—although he had told me he was divorced. Not only that, but his wife had been diagnosed with breast cancer.'

'Oh, God, how awful for her, and for you,' Kat murmured.

'The press labelled me a heartless marriage-wrecker,' Mina said flatly as she relived the nightmare that had unfolded in LA. 'Dex lied to me. I hadn't known he had a wife, let alone that she was seriously ill. I felt so guilty that she had been hurt, but Dex didn't care. He actually said that the publicity about our relationship would be good for the film.'

'What a bastard,' Kat said fiercely.

'I wanted to come home straight away, but I had to finish the film. Too many people would have been affected if I'd pulled out. Luckily there were only two more weeks of filming left but I was hounded by the paparazzi until I left LA.'

'Some journalists have been at the theatre this morning, trying to get members of the cast to talk about you. But no one has,' Kat added quickly.

'No one knows much about me,' Mina said drily. Although she got on well with most of the other cast members, she guarded her privacy. She felt sick knowing that everyone would be gossiping about her personal life, and her temper simmered because once again she had unwittingly become headline news. If Aksel had told her that he was the Prince of Storvhal she would never have agreed to go to his hotel. Her bitter experience with Dex had taught her to steer clear of people who were in the public eye.

She went with Kat to join the other actors, who were gathered on the stage. The buzz of conversation faded and there was an awkward silence until Laurence Adams, who played Mercutio, said brightly, 'That was a great

PR stunt, Mina. The story about your relationship with a prince who is supposedly one of Europe's most eligible bachelors has gone global on the same day that it was announced that our production of *Romeo and Juliet* is going to Broadway. With all the media interest I reckon we'll be a sell-out in New York.'

No way, Mina silently vowed, would she allow any of the cast to know how humiliated she felt. When she had been growing up, being the only deaf child in a mainstream school had taught Mina to develop a tough shell and hide her feelings of insecurity and hurt when she was teased for being 'different'. Acting had become a means of survival, and now she utilised all her theatrical skills to brazen out the embarrassing situation.

Lifting her chin, she said airily, 'Yeah, I'm thrilled that I was pictured with a prince. Apparently the story is on all the American news networks and everyone in New York will know that the play will be opening there soon. I'm sure you're right and we'll perform to a full house every night.'

Several of the cast cheered, but beside her Kat stiffened and muttered warningly, 'Mina—he's here!'

Mina's heart missed a beat. She turned her head to tell Kat that she did not find the joke funny, but the words froze on her lips as she looked up at the gallery and saw a golden-haired Viking staring down at the stage.

Aksel's stern face could have been carved from granite, and even from a distance Mina felt chilled by his icy stare. He did not say a word, but as she replayed her statement in her head, her frustration boiled over.

'I…I didn't mean what I said,' she called up to him.

His silence was crushing. He stared at her for a few more seconds before he swung round and the sound of his footsteps as he strode from the gallery reverberated around the theatre.

'I swear, I didn't know you are a damn prince,' Mina shouted after him. But he did not turn his head and moments later he had disappeared.

He had walked out without giving her a chance to explain! Who was this cold man who had replaced her caring lover of the night before? The fiasco of the damning photograph in the newspaper was *his* fault. His royal status made him a target for the paparazzi. Her stomach lurched as she realised that Steve Garratt must have recognised Aksel in the pub the previous evening. The journalist must have seen her get into the taxi with Aksel and followed them to the hotel. Garratt had certainly got the scoop he'd wanted, she thought bitterly.

She choked back an angry sob. Aksel had refused to listen to her—just as her father so often did not listen. When she had first lost her hearing, Mina had also lost her confidence to speak. Years of speech therapy had helped her to find her voice again, and thanks to her hearing aids she was able to disguise her hearing impairment. But deep inside her there still lingered the insecure little girl who had felt trapped and alone in a silent world. Being deprived of one of her senses made her feel invisible and insignificant.

Damn Aksel for ignoring her, she thought furiously as she ran through the theatre. She would make him listen to her!

But when she reached the exit there was no sign of him and the only people outside the theatre were some journalists. The sound of a car's engine drew her attention to the road, and her heart sank when she saw the sleek black limousine that had collected her and Aksel from the hotel earlier pull away from the kerb.

The journalists spotted her and crowded around the door. 'Miss Hart—are you in a relationship with Prince Aksel of Storvhal?'

'Are you hoping that the prince will visit you while you are performing in New York?'

Kat rushed up as Mina slammed the door shut to block out the journalists' questions.

'Joshua is in a furious temper,' Kat told her breathlessly. 'He's demanding to know why you invited the prince here to the theatre.'

Mina groaned. She could not cope with her father when he was in one of his unreasonable moods. But in fairness she could understand why he was angry with her. The announcement that he would be directing his theatre company's production of *Romeo and Juliet* on Broadway should have been a highlight of Joshua's career, but Mina had unwittingly stolen his thunder. The press were more interested in her relationship with a prince than in the play.

'I have to get away from here,' she muttered.

'My car is parked round the back. We might be able to slip out without being seen. But, Mina…' Kat hesitated, looking concerned. 'I drove past your flat on my way here this morning and saw press photographers outside.'

'I'm not going home,' Mina said grimly. 'Will you give me a lift to the airport?'

Benedict Lindburg, sitting in the front of the limousine with the driver, took one look at Aksel's face as he climbed into the rear of the car and wisely did not say a word.

At least his PA knew when to keep his opinion to himself, Aksel thought darkly as he hit a button to activate the privacy screen that separated him from the occupants in the front of the car. It was unlikely that his chief advisor would show the same diplomacy. He grimaced as his phone rang and Harald Petersen's name flashed on the caller display.

'It's a personal matter,' Aksel explained curtly, in answer to his advisor's query about why the royal flight from London to Storvhal had been delayed.

There was a tiny hesitation before Harald said smoothly, 'I understand that you have cancelled all your meetings for this afternoon. If you have a problem, sir, I hope that I can be of assistance.'

The problem—as Harald damn well knew—was the photograph and the headline *'The Prince and the Show-girl'* that had made the front page of the newspapers in England and Storvhal, and no doubt the rest of the world. But the real problem was *him*, Aksel thought grimly. He cursed the crazy impulse that had caused him to instruct his driver to turn the car around when they had been on the way to the airport, and take him to the Globe Theatre. But his conscience had been nagging. He had remembered the charity function that had been held at the Erskine hotel last night, and the members of the press who had been gathered outside to take pictures of the celebrity guests. It was possible that the paparazzi had been covering other entrances to the hotel, and Aksel had realised that he might have been wrong when he had accused Mina of tipping off a journalist that they would enter via a back door.

The article in the newspaper about her affair with a married film director in LA was damning, but when he'd read the sordid details Aksel had struggled to equate the heartless bimbo described in the paper with the woman who had responded with such sweet eagerness when he had made love to her. There had been a curious innocence to Mina that had touched something inside him. But now he knew it had been an act. Overhearing her at the theatre had ripped the blinkers from his eyes, and the realisation that she was as calculating and mercenary as his mother and Karena filled him with icy rage.

'The photograph in the newspapers of you and the English actress could have repercussions in Storvhal,' Harald Petersen murmured. 'I fear that people will be reminded of your father's playboy image, and it is imperative we think of a damage-limitation strategy. Perhaps you could issue a statement to deny that you are involved with Miss Hart—although that will be less believable now that there is a second photograph of you leaving the hotel with her.' Harald gave a pained sigh. 'I assume you will not be seeing her again. I'm afraid the Storvhalian people will not approve of you having an affair with her, and I am sure I do not need to remind you that your duty to your country must come before any other consideration.'

Aksel's jaw clenched and he tightened his grip on his phone until his knuckles whitened. 'You're right—you don't need to remind me of my duty,' he said harshly. '*Helvete!* You, above all people, Harald, know the sacrifice I made to ensure the stability of the country when Storvhal was on the brink of civil unrest. Only you, amongst my staff, know that Karena gave me an illegitimate child. My son is dead, and for eight years I have kept Finn's brief existence a secret because I understood that I must focus on ruling Storvhal and try to repair the damage my father caused to the monarchy.'

His tone became steely as he fought to disguise the rawness of his emotions. 'Do not throw duty in my face, Harald. I swore when I was crowned that I would fulfil the expectations that the people of Storvhal have of their prince, but I have paid a personal price that will haunt me for ever.'

Aksel ended the call and his head fell back against the leather car seat. He could feel his heart jerking painfully beneath his ribs as he replayed his conversation with his chief advisor in his mind. How *could* Harald have implied that he needed to be reminded of his duty to his country? He had given Storvhal everything. He had spent more than a decade paying for his father's sins, and had striven to be a perfect prince, even though it meant that he'd had to bury his grief for his son deep inside him.

The baby had been born in Russia and tragically had only lived for a few weeks. Losing Finn had ripped Aksel's heart out. Every time his grandmother spoke of the need for him to have an heir Aksel pictured his baby boy and felt a familiar ache in his chest. But his grandmother had no idea how he felt. No one in his life, apart from his chief advisor, knew about Finn.

His thoughts turned again to Mina and for some inexplicable reason the ache inside him intensified. His mouth twisted cynically. He'd had sex with her, but of course she had not touched him on an emotional level, he assured himself. Aksel had buried his heart with his baby son, and the Ice Prince—the name that he knew his staff called him behind his back—was incapable of feeling anything.

CHAPTER FIVE

NOTHING HAD PREPARED Mina for the bone-biting cold as she walked through the doors of Storvhal's international airport into a land of snow and ice.

'Are you sure you want to do this?' Kat had asked when she had dropped Mina off at Heathrow. 'Where on earth is Storvhal, anyway?'

'It's an island that stretches across the northern border of Norway and Russia.'

Kat had eyed Mina's thin cotton skirt and jacket doubtfully. 'Well, in that case you'd better borrow my coat.'

Mina had baulked at the idea of wearing her friend's purple leopard-print coat with a hood trimmed with pink marabou feathers but she hadn't had the heart to refuse. Now she was less concerned about Kat's eccentric taste in fashion, and was simply grateful that the eye-catching coat provided some protection against the freezing temperature, as did the fur-lined boots and gloves she had bought in the airport shop along with a few other essentials. But the coat and boots would not keep her warm for long when a sign on the airport wall displayed a temperature of minus six degrees.

The fact that it was dark at three o'clock in the afternoon was another shock. But she was in the Arctic Circle, Mina reminded herself. According to the tour-

ist guide she had picked up, Storvhal would soon be in
polar night—meaning that there would be no daylight at
all from the end of October until February.

She did not plan to be in Storvhal for long—although
admittedly her exact plans were sketchy. She had been
furious with Aksel when she had flown from England,
and determined to defend herself against his accusation
that she had tipped off the journalist and was therefore
responsible for the photograph of them in the papers. But
now that she had arrived in his icy, alien country she was
starting to question her sanity.

Her sister often teased her for being impulsive. Mina
felt a sudden pang of longing to be in Sicily, at the castle
Torre d'Aquila with Darcey and Salvatore. Her brother-
in-law had made her feel so welcome when she had visited in the summer. It was wonderful that Darcey was so
happy and in love. Mina could not help but feel a little
envious that her sister was adored by her handsome husband. If she ever got married she hoped she would share
a love as strong as theirs.

A blast of icy wind prompted Mina to walk towards a
taxi parked outside the airport terminal. To her relief the
driver spoke good English and he nodded when she asked
him to take her to the royal palace, which was mentioned
in the tourist guide.

'The palace is open to the public during the week.
You should be in time for the last tour of the day,' he
told her. 'It's very spectacular. It was built in the twelfth
century by a Viking warrior who was the first prince of
Storvhal. If you look at the newspaper,' the driver continued, 'you will see that our current prince has made
the headlines today.'

Mina glanced at the newspaper on the seat beside her
and her heart sank. The paper must be a later edition

than the one she had seen earlier, and the photo on the front page was of her and Aksel emerging from the hotel that morning. The wind had whipped her skirt up to her thighs, and her tangled hair looked as if she had just got out of bed. Aksel had his arm around her and wore the satisfied expression of a man who had enjoyed a night of hot sex.

Oh, God! Mina cringed. The taxi driver glanced at her in his rear-view mirror and she was thankful that her face was hidden by the hood of her coat.

'According to the press reports, the prince is having an affair with an English actress. I feel sorry for him,' the driver continued. 'The people of Storvhal take great interest in Prince Aksel's private life. I guess they are afraid that he will turn out like his late father.'

'What was wrong with his father?' Mina was curious to learn any information about Aksel.

'Prince Geir was not a good monarch. People called him the playboy prince because he was more interested in partying with beautiful women on his yacht in Monaco than ruling the country.' The driver shrugged. 'It did not help his popularity when he married a Russian woman. Historically, Storvhalians have mistrusted Russia. Prince Geir was accused of making secret business deals with Russian companies and increasing his personal wealth by selling off Storvhal's natural resources.

'Since Prince Aksel has ruled Storvhal he has avoided any hint of scandal and has restored support for the monarchy,' the driver explained. 'He won't be pleased to have his personal life made public—and I'm sure the princess will be upset.'

Mina's heart lurched sickeningly. 'The *princess*...do you mean Prince Aksel is married?'

The memory of learning that Dexter had a wife and

was not divorced as he had told her was still raw in Mina's mind. Aksel had insisted that he was not married, but he could have lied. She shuddered to think that she might have been a gullible fool for a second time.

The driver did not appear to notice the sudden sharpness in her voice. 'Oh, no, I meant Princess Eldrun—Prince Aksel's grandmother. She ruled Storvhal with her husband, Prince Fredrik, for many years. When he died and Prince Geir inherited the throne the princess did not hide her disappointment that her son was a poor monarch. Geir was killed in a helicopter crash on his way to visit one of his many mistresses. It is common knowledge that Princess Eldrun hopes her grandson will choose a Storvhalian bride and provide an heir to the throne.'

They had been travelling along a main road, but now the taxi driver turned the car onto a gravel driveway that wound through a vast area of parkland. The frozen snow on the ground glittered in the bright glare of the street lamps, and the branches of the trees were spread like white lacy fingers against the night-dark sky. It was hard to believe that it was afternoon, Mina mused.

Her thoughts scattered as the royal palace came into view. With its white walls, tall turrets and arched windows, it looked like a fairy-tale castle, and the layer of powdery, glistening snow clinging to the roofs and spires reminded her of icing on top of a cake. The sight of guards in navy blue and gold uniforms standing in front of the palace gave her a jolt. For the first time it dawned on her that the man she had spent last night with, and who had made love to her with breathtaking passion, was actually a member of a royal dynasty.

The taxi driver dropped her at the public entrance to the palace and Mina joined the queue of people waiting to take a guided tour. An information leaflet explained that the public were allowed into the library and several reception rooms, which had been turned into a museum. The beautiful wood-panelled rooms filled with ancient tapestries and oil paintings were fascinating, but she was not in the mood for sightseeing.

She turned to the tour guide. 'Where can I see the prince?'

'You cannot see him—of course not.' The female guide looked shocked, but her expression lifted as she clearly thought that she had misunderstood. 'Do you mean you wish to buy a photograph of Prince Aksel? We sell souvenirs in the gift shop. The palace is about to close but you can visit the shop on your way out.'

The guide walked away, leaving Mina feeling a fool. Why had she thought that she would be able to stroll into the palace and bump into Storvhal's monarch? It was as likely as expecting to meet the Queen of England when Buckingham Palace was opened to the public in the summer. But the truth was she hadn't thought of anything past her urgency to find Aksel and convince him that she had not betrayed him to the press.

After learning from the taxi driver about Storvhal's royal family, and the unpopularity of Aksel's father, who had been known as the playboy prince, she could understand better why Aksel had reacted so angrily to the press allegations that they were having an affair.

The adrenaline that had been pumping through Mina's veins since she had arrived in Storvhal and mentally prepared herself for a showdown with Aksel drained away, and she felt exhausted—which was not surprising when she'd had very little sleep the previous night, she thought, flushing as erotic memories resurfaced. The knowledge that Aksel was somewhere in the vast palace but she could not meet him was bitterly frustrating.

She glanced out of the window and realised that she must be overlooking the grounds at the rear of the palace. A four-by-four was parked on the driveway and someone was about to climb into the driver's seat. The man was wearing a ski jacket; his hood slipped back, and Mina's heart missed a beat when she recognised the distinctive tiger stripes in his blond hair.

Aksel!

She tapped frantically on the window to gain his attention. He was going to drive away and there was nothing she could do to stop him! He did not look up, and she watched him take a mobile phone out of his jacket and walk back inside the palace.

Mina looked along the corridor and saw the guide shepherding the other people from the tour party into the gift shop. Walking as rapidly as she dared, she hurried past the shop and out of the palace before racing through the grounds. With every step she expected to be challenged by the palace guards, but no one seemed to have noticed her. When she reached the four-by-four she found the engine had been left running, but there was no sign of Aksel.

The freezing air made Mina's eyes sting, and she peered through the swirling snowflakes that had started to fall. She was likely to get frostbite if she stayed outside for much longer but she refused to give up her only opportunity to talk to Aksel. A few more minutes passed, and her toes and fingers became numb. There was nothing for it but to wait inside the vehicle, she decided as she opened the rear door and climbed inside.

The warmth of the interior of the four-by-four enveloped her. Gradually she stopped shivering, and as tiredness overwhelmed her she lay down on the seat and closed her eyes, promising herself that she would only rest them for a minute.

* * *

The snow was falling so thickly that the windscreen wipers could barely cope. Aksel knew that driving into the mountains in mid-October was a risk, but the weather reports had been clear, and he'd decided to visit the cabin for one last weekend before winter set in.

He guessed the blizzard had taken the forecasters by surprise. The road down in the valley was likely to be impassable already and there was no point turning round. Aksel was used to the harsh, fast-changing conditions of the Arctic landscape and wasn't worried that he would make it to the cabin, but he knew there was a chance he could be stranded there if the weather did not improve.

He probably should have listened to his chief advisor's plea to remain at the palace, he thought ruefully. But he had been in no mood to put up with Harald Petersen's pained expression as the chief advisor read the latest press revelations that Storvhal's ruling monarch was having a love affair with an English actress and apparently good-time girl, Mina Hart.

Love affair! Aksel gave a cynical laugh. Emotions had played no part in the night he had spent with Mina. If the press had accused him of having casual, meaningless sex with her it would have been closer to the truth. But he was meant to be above such behaviour, because, as Harald frequently reminded him, the population of Storvhal would not tolerate another playboy prince as his father had been.

Thank God he had managed to keep the story from his grandmother so far. Princess Eldrun's heart was weak and a rumour that her grandson might be following his father's reprobate lifestyle would be a devastating shock for her. Aksel's knuckles whitened on the steering wheel.

Mina's publicity stunt could have dire consequences for his grandmother's health.

A memory flashed into his mind of Mina's stricken face as he had walked away from her at the Globe Theatre earlier in the day. Damn it, he had overheard her admit that the rumours she was having an affair with him had earned her father's production of *Romeo and Juliet* extensive media coverage. So why did he still have a lingering doubt that he might have misjudged her?

Because he was a fool, that was why, he told himself angrily. He should despise Mina, but he could not stop thinking about her and remembering how she had felt in his arms, the softness of her skin when he had lowered his body onto hers. *Damn her*, he thought savagely, shifting position to try to ease the throb of his arousal.

A sudden movement in his rear-view mirror caught his attention. Something—a faceless figure—loomed up on the back seat of the four-by-four. Aksel's heart collided with his ribcage, and he swore, as shock and—hell, he wasn't ashamed to admit it—fear surged through him. His chief advisor's warnings that he should take more care of his personal safety jerked into his mind. But he refused to carry a weapon that had the potential to take a life. He had witnessed the utter finality of death when he had cradled his baby son's lifeless body in his arms. The experience had had a profound effect on him and made him appreciate the immeasurable value of life.

He only hoped that whoever had stowed away in his car valued *his* life. Most of the population of Storvhal supported his rule. However he could not ignore the fact that no leader or public figurehead was completely safe from the threat of assassination. *Was he going to feel a bullet in the back of his neck?*

The hell he was! His survival instinct kicked in and

he hit the brakes hard, causing the faceless figure to fall forwards. Adrenaline pumped through his veins as he leapt out of the truck and pulled open the rear door. The interior light automatically flicked on and Aksel stared in disbelief at the incongruous sight of a figure wearing a purple leopard-print coat with a hood trimmed with pink feathers.

'What in God's name…?' Conscious that the stow-away could have a weapon, Aksel grabbed hold of an arm, and with his other hand yanked the hood back to reveal a tumbling mass of silky auburn hair and a pair of deep green eyes.

'Mina?' His brain could not comprehend what his eyes were telling him. He was halfway up a glacier in the middle of a snowstorm and it was beyond belief that the woman who had haunted his thoughts all day was star-ing mutely at him.

'What are you doing? How did you get into my truck? Hellvete!' He lost his grip on his temper when she made no reply. The snow was swirling around him and he im-patiently raked his damp hair off his brow and glared at her. 'What crazy game are you playing? Answer me, damn you. Why are you pretending to be deaf?'

'I'm not pretending.' At last she spoke in a tremulous voice that Aksel struggled to hear.

Mina stared at Aksel's furious face. She could tell he was shouting at her from the jerky way his lips moved, but she couldn't hear him. She could not hear anything. When she had woken, dazed and disorientated in the back of the four-by-four, it had taken her a few moments to work out why everything was silent. She had realised that her hearing-aid batteries had run down and remem-bered that she had fitted a new set at Aksel's hotel that morning, but the rechargeable batteries in her handbag had probably not been fully charged.

The faint gleam of the car's interior lamp cast shadows on Aksel's face and highlighted his sharp cheekbones and strong jaw. He was forbiddingly beautiful, and, despite the freezing wind whipping into the four-by-four, Mina felt a flood of warmth in the pit of her stomach.

She said shakily, 'I have a severe hearing impairment and rely on hearing aids to be able to hear.' She opened her hand and showed him the two tiny listening devices that she had removed from her ears. 'The batteries are dead, but I can lip-read if I watch your mouth when you speak.'

For one of only a handful of times in his life, Aksel had no idea what to say. 'Are you serious about being unable to hear, or are you playing some sort of sick joke?' he demanded.

'Of course I wouldn't joke about something like that,' Mina snapped. 'I've been deaf since I was a child. Most people don't know I can't hear because my hearing aids allow me to lead a normal life, and I'm good at hiding my disability from strangers,' she added with fierce pride.

'Last night we were as intimate as two people can get,' Aksel reminded her. 'I wouldn't call us strangers. Why didn't you tell me you are unable to hear?'

'I suppose for the same reason that you didn't tell me you are a prince.' Mina shrugged. 'I didn't feel ready to share personal confidences with you. And clearly we are still strangers, because otherwise you wouldn't have believed that I told the press about us.'

Aksel frowned. Snowdrifts were already forming around his legs, and more importantly around the wheels of the truck, and he knew he must keep the vehicle moving or risk becoming trapped on the exposed mountain road. But there were still a couple of questions he needed answered. 'Why the hell are you wearing a fancy-dress costume?'

Mina glanced ruefully at the horrendous purple coat. 'My friend lent me her coat because I only had a thin jacket. Kat has an…unusual fashion sense, but it was kind of her,' she said loyally.

'Do you mean to say that underneath that thing you're not wearing protective cold-weather clothing?'

'I didn't know I would need them when I got into your car at the palace. You had gone inside to talk on your phone and I decided to wait for you, but I fell asleep,' she explained when Aksel gave her a puzzled look.

That cleared up one mystery. 'I'm surprised you didn't bring your journalist friend with you,' he said bitterly.

'I'm not friendly with any journalists.'

'The man in the pub,' he reminded her.

She grimaced. 'I promise you Steve Garratt is no friend of mine.'

Aksel shook the snow out of his hair. He wished he could turn the truck around and drive Mina straight back to the airport, but the weather was worsening and his only option was to take her to the cabin.

'We'll have to save the rest of this discussion for later.' He turned away from her as he spoke. When she did not respond he realised that she had not heard him, and the only way they could communicate was for Mina to read his lips. Things were starting to fall into place—like the way she had focused intently on his face last night. He'd thought that she couldn't take her eyes off him because she found him attractive, but now he knew she had watched his lips when he spoke to disguise the fact that she was deaf.

She must have some guts to be so determined not

to allow her hearing impairment to affect her life, he thought, feeling a grudging admiration for her. He wondered if she felt vulnerable without her hearing aids. He couldn't imagine what it was like to live in a silent world, but he guessed it could be lonely being cut off from ordinary sounds that hearing people took for granted.

A muscle tightened in Aksel's jaw. He did not want to admire Mina, and he did not want to take her to the cabin. She was a dangerous threat to his peace of mind, especially when he could not forget the searing passion that had burned out of control between them last night. With a curse he slammed the rear door and climbed behind the wheel to drive the last part of the journey that could be made in the four-by-four.

'Where are we?' Mina asked as she climbed out of the truck and caught hold of Aksel's arm to make him turn around so that she could see his face. They had arrived at a building that had suddenly loomed out of the snow and seemed to be in the middle of nowhere. Aksel had driven the four-by-four inside the building, and the light from of the car's headlamps revealed that they were in some sort of warehouse. The place wasn't heated and Mina was already shivering from the bone-biting cold.

'This is as far as we can go by road. From here we'll be travelling on the snowmobile.' He pointed to a contraption that looked like a motorbike on skis.

Travelling to where? Mina wondered. She eyed the snowmobile nervously. 'You expect me to ride on that?'

'I didn't expect you to be here at all.' Aksel spoke carefully so that Mina could read his lips. The glitter in his ice-blue eyes warned her that he was furious with her. He strode over to a cupboard and pulled out several items of clothing, and then walked back to stand in front of her so that she could see his face. 'Luckily my sister keeps spare gear here for emergencies.'

Mina seized this tiny snippet of information about the man who had shared his body with her but nothing else. 'I didn't know you have a sister.'

'There are a lot of things you don't know about me.' He ignored her curiosity and handed her the clothes. 'Put a couple of sweatshirts on under the snowsuit. The more layers you wear, the warmer you'll be.'

Mina doubted she would ever feel warm again. She had to take her skirt off before she could step into the snowsuit and her numb fingers would not work properly. But at last she pulled her boots back on and Aksel handed her a crash helmet. He swung his leg over the saddle of the snowmobile and indicated that she should climb up behind him.

'What if I fall off?' she asked worriedly.

'Then you'll be left behind,' was his uncompromising reply, before he closed the visors on both their helmets and cut off communication between them.

Mina had never been so scared in her life, as Aksel drove the snowmobile across the icy wasteland that stretched endlessly in all directions. There was a grab-rail behind her seat, but she felt safer with her arms wrapped around his waist. At least if she fell off he would be aware of it and might stop.

It had stopped snowing, but the freezing air temperature even through the snowsuit made her blood feel as if it had frozen in her veins. The wind rushed past as the snowmobile picked up speed, and she squeezed her eyes shut and clung to Aksel. His muscular body was reassuringly strong and powerful, and an image flitted into Mina's mind of him naked; his golden-skinned chest crushing her breasts, and his massive arousal pushing between her thighs. Her fear faded and she put her trust in the giant Viking who was confidently steering the snow bike across the ice.

In the light from the snowmobile's headlamp the snow was brilliant white, and above them the vast black sky was crowded with more stars than Mina had known existed. The birch forest became sparser the higher into the mountains they went, and at last a log cabin with lights blazing in the windows came into view.

Mina was relieved to see a house, thinking that she would be able to charge her hearing-aid batteries. She always carried the charger with her but the device needed to be plugged into an electricity supply to work.

As Aksel helped her climb off the bike a strange-looking man stepped out of the shadows. He was wearing what looked like a traditional costume, with an animal hide draped around his shoulders. Mina watched him and Aksel talking and could tell that they were not speaking English or any other language she recognised.

'His name is Isku,' Aksel told her when the man got onto a sledge pulled by huskies and drove off into the night. Mina could feel the vibration of the dogs racing across the snow long after they had disappeared from sight. 'His people are called the Sami. They are reindeer herders and still live according to their ancient traditions. Isku's family are camping near here, and he came to the cabin to light the boiler and make a fire.'

Mina was thankful that Aksel hadn't planned to camp out in the sub-zero temperature. The log cabin looked well built to withstand the Arctic storms. Snow was piled high on the roof and a wisp of grey smoke curled up from the chimney. 'It's so pretty,' she murmured. 'It reminds me of the fairy-tale cottage of the Three Bears.'

Aksel unstrapped the bags from the back of the bike

and remembered to turn to her so that she could watch his mouth as he replied. 'There are no brown bears in Storvhal, and it is very rare that polar bears come this high into the mountains. Their territory is lower down near the coast. The largest predators you might see near the house are wolves.'

He noticed the fearful expression in her eyes as she hurried inside and thought it was probably a good thing she could not hear the howling of wolves close by.

Inside the cabin, a fire blazed in the hearth. Mina quickly started to overheat and had to strip out of the snowsuit and the layers of sweatshirts Aksel had lent her. Her face was flushed by the time she was down to her own shirt, and only then did she realise that she must have left her skirt in the four-by-four where she had got changed.

Aksel pulled off his boots and ski jacket and strode over to the drinks cabinet, where he sloshed neat spirit into a glass and gulped it down, savouring the fiery heat at the back of his throat. He glanced at Mina undressing in front of the fire and felt a tightening sensation in his groin. He recognised her shirt was the same one he had peeled from her body at the hotel in London the previous night. God knew where her skirt was, but he wished she would hurry up and put it on because the shirt only fell to her hips, leaving the creamy skin of her bare thighs above the lace band of her stockings exposed.

With her auburn hair tumbling around her shoulders, and her huge green eyes fixed on him, she was incredibly sensual, and Aksel wanted to forget that he was a prince and kiss her until she pleaded with him to pull her down onto the rug and strip off the remainder of her clothes.

He picked up a second glass and the bottle of liqueur

and walked over to join her in front of the fireplace. 'Here.' He half filled the glass and handed it to her.

Mina took a cautious sip of the straw-coloured liquid and choked. 'That's strong! What is it?'

'*Akevitt* is a traditional Scandinavian spirit. The Storvhalian version is flavoured with aniseed.'

A few sips of the fearsome drink would be likely to render her unconscious, Mina thought. She put the glass down on a table and took the battery charger out of her handbag.

'I need to plug this into an electrical socket to recharge the batteries for my hearing aids.'

Aksel frowned. 'There is no electricity at the cabin. The lamps are filled with oil, and the wood-burning stove heats the hot-water tank. The only modern convenience I keep here is a satellite phone so that my ministers can contact me if necessary. Don't you carry spare batteries for your hearing aids?'

'Both the sets I have with me are dead.' Mina had not anticipated being without her hearing aids. Her degree of hearing loss meant that she could hear certain sounds above a high decibel, but even if Aksel shouted at the top of his voice she would be unable to hear him. She chewed on her lower lip. 'I'm sorry I've spoiled your trip, but I'm going to have to ask you to take me back to civilisation.'

He shrugged. 'I can't take you anywhere. The heavy snowfall will have blocked the roads further down the valley, and it's snowing again.'

Aksel folded his arms across his chest and a nerve flickered in his jaw as he surveyed her half-undressed state. 'We could be trapped here for days,' he told her grimly.

CHAPTER SIX

MINA'S HEART SANK as she looked over to the window and saw the blizzard that was raging outside. Evidently they had reached the cabin just in time before the weather worsened.

Aksel slid his hand beneath her chin and tilted her face to his so that she could read his lips. 'Why did you come to Storvhal?'

Mina might not be able to hear the anger in his voice, but the rigid set of his jaw was an indication that his temper was on a tight leash. She had as much right to be angry about the photographs in the newspapers as him, she thought, her own temper flaring. His royal status had made them both a target for the paparazzi.

She focused on his question and decided to be honest. 'Before we left the hotel this morning you asked me to meet you in Paris.'

She paused, hoping that her voice did not sound too quiet or flat-toned. She felt self-conscious not being able to hear herself when she spoke, but speech therapy had taught her breathing techniques, and she took a steadying breath before continuing.

'You said that when we made love it had been perfect.' She stared into his eyes, daring him to deny it. 'But later, at the theatre, why did you walk away without listening to me?'

His eyes blazed. 'You tipped off the press that we spent the night together and used me for a publicity stunt. You know damn well the media hype that you are having an affair with a prince will raise your profile when you perform *Romeo and Juliet* in New York.'

Aksel's nostrils flared with the effort of controlling his anger. 'The journalist who was waiting for us outside the hotel this morning was the man I saw you looking at in the pub. He called out your name. You obviously know him so don't try to deny it.'

'His name is Steve Garratt.' Disdain for the journalist flickered across Mina's face. 'It's true that I recognised him when he came into the pub, but he's not a friend— in fact he's the reason I left early. I hate Garratt after he wrote a load of lies about me.'

She bit her lip. 'I know your PA has dug up all that regurgitated rubbish about my supposed affair with Dexter Price, but most of what has been written about me is untrue. I had no idea that Dexter was married or that his wife was ill. He had told me he was divorced and we grew close while we were working on a film in LA. But Steve Garratt accused me of having a torrid affair with him and made me out to be an unscrupulous marriage-wrecker.' Memories of how hurt and humiliated she had been left feeling by the journalist's assassination of her character, and by Dexter Price's refusal to defend her, churned inside Mina.

'No one ever listens to me,' she burst out. 'Not the press, or my father—or you. I may be deaf but that doesn't mean you can ignore me. I didn't tell *anyone* that you had invited me to your hotel. I didn't know when I met you that you are a prince.'

She wished her hearing aids were working. Standing close to Aksel and looking directly at his face so that she could read his lips created an intense atmosphere between them.

'You were just a man,' she said huskily, 'a handsome stranger. I couldn't take my eyes off you and I agreed to go to your hotel because you…overwhelmed me. Making love with you was the most beautiful experience I've ever had, and I…I thought it might have been special for you too—not just a one-night stand—because you asked me to spend a weekend in Paris with you.'

'It wasn't special.' Aksel ignored the stab of guilt he felt when he saw Mina's green eyes darken with hurt. He had been convinced that she had tipped off the press, but now he was beginning to wonder if he might have been wrong about her. Mina's feeling of disgust for the journalist who had taken photos of them outside the hotel had been evident on her expressive features. However, he reminded himself that she was a talented actress. And his instincts were not infallible. Once he had trusted Karena, he remembered grimly.

'Having sex with you was an enjoyable experience, but it was just sex,' he said bluntly, 'and I can't pretend that last night was anything more than a few hours of physical pleasure.'

It felt brutal to look into her eyes as he spoke such harsh words. Usually when he gave women the brush-off he avoided eye contact with them, he acknowledged with savage self-derision.

'Look…' He raked a hand through his hair, feeling unnerved by Mina's intent gaze. He felt as though she could see into his soul—and that was a dark place he never allowed anyone access to. He wanted to step away and put some space between them, but she needed to read his lips.

'I was carried away by the play. When I saw you on stage I was captivated by Juliet.' A nerve flickered in his jaw again. 'But Juliet isn't real—the woman I saw on stage was make-believe. It was my mistake to have forgotten that fact when we met in the pub.'

It was the only explanation Aksel could find for his behaviour that had been so out of character. In all the years he had been Storvhal's monarch he had never picked up a woman in a bar, never done anything to risk damaging his reputation as a responsible, moral prince who was the exact opposite of his father.

Helvete, he had even hidden his son's brief existence for the sake of the Crown. The secret gnawed like a cancer deep in Aksel's heart.

'I made love to Juliet,' he said, speaking carefully so that Mina would not mistake his words. 'For one night I forgot that I belong to an ancient royal dynasty. I was—as you said—just a man who desired a beautiful woman. But in the morning the fantasy ended. You are an actress, and I am a prince and ruler of my country. Our lives are set to follow different paths.'

Mina flinched at his bluntness. She had told herself she had come to Storvhal to clear her name and persuade Aksel that she had not told the press they had spent the night together. But in her heart she knew that her real reason for finding him was because she had felt a deep connection with him when they had made love, and she had been convinced that he had felt it too. His cold words seemed to disprove her theory.

'In that case why did you invite me to Paris?' she said stiffly.

'You looked upset when I told you that I was about to fly back to Storvhal. It seemed kinder to allow you to believe that I was interested in seeing you again, but we hadn't made a specific arrangement.'

Humiliation swept in a hot tide through Mina. Fool, she silently berated herself. She went cold when she remembered that Aksel had called her Juliet when he had kissed her. At the time she hadn't thought anything of it, but now she knew that he had been making love to a fantasy woman. He had been captivated by Juliet when he had watched her on stage, not by Mina Hart, the actress who played the role. According to Aksel, he hadn't felt any kind of connection to her. She had completely misread the situation.

Or had she?

Her mind flew back to the previous night, and the fierce glitter in Aksel's eyes just before he had climaxed powerfully inside her. For a few timeless moments when they had both hovered on the edge of heaven, she had sensed that their souls had reached out to each other and something indefinable and profound had passed between them.

Last night her hearing aids had been working. Could Aksel really have faked the raw emotion she had heard in the groan he'd made when he had come apart in her arms?

He lifted his glass to his lips and gulped down the fiery *akevitt* in a single swallow. For a split second, Mina saw him flick his gaze over her in a lightning sweep from her breasts down to her stocking tops, and she glimpsed a predatory hunger in his eyes before he glanced away.

Her heart thudded. Aksel might want to deny that he felt anything for her, but she had seen desire in his eyes. She couldn't shake off the feeling that when they had made love the previous night it *had* been special. She had not imagined his tenderness and she was convinced that they had shared more than a primitive physical act.

If he had spoken the truth when he'd stated that he'd just wanted sex with her, why hadn't he looked into her eyes as he had said it? And why was he still determined to avoid her gaze? Mina was adept at reading the subtle nuances of body language, and the tension she could feel emanating from Aksel suggested that he was not telling her the whole truth.

'So, you desired the fantasy Juliet, not Mina the real woman?' she demanded. When he did not look at her she put her hand on his jaw and felt the rough stubble scrape her palm as she turned his face towards her. His eyelashes swept down, but not before she had glimpsed something in his eyes that gave her courage. 'Prove it,' she said softly.

His dark blond brows drew together. 'What do you mean?'

'Kiss me and prove that I don't turn you on.'

'Don't be ridiculous.'

She stood up on tiptoe and brought her face so close to his that when he blinked she felt his eyelashes brush her skin. Being deprived of her hearing made her other senses more acute and she was aware of the unsteady rhythm of his heart as his breathing became shallow.

'What are you afraid of?' she said against his mouth. 'If I kiss you and you don't respond, then I'll know you're telling the truth and you don't want me.'

Are you crazy? taunted a voice inside her head. You won't dare do it! If he rejected her she would die of humiliation. But life had taught Mina that if you wanted something badly enough it was worth fighting for.

If she could only break through Aksel's icy detachment, she was convinced she would find the tender lover he had been last night. She hesitated with her lips centimetres from his and felt his warm breath whisper across her skin. He had tensed, but he hadn't pushed her away, and before she lost her nerve she closed the tiny gap between them and grazed her mouth over Aksel's.

He made no response, not even when she pressed her lips harder against his and traced the shape of his mouth with the tip of her tongue. Desperation gripped her and she began to wonder if last night really had been just a casual sexual encounter for him.

He stood unmoving, as unrelenting as rock, and in frustration she nipped his lower lip with her teeth. His chest lifted as he inhaled sharply, and Mina took advantage of his surprise to push her tongue into his mouth.

He curled his hands around her shoulders and tightened his grip until his fingers bit into her flesh. Mina tensed, expecting him to wrench his mouth free and cast her from him. But suddenly, unbelievably, he was kissing her back.

He moved his mouth over hers, tentatively at first—as if he was still fighting a battle with himself. Relief flooded through Mina and she pressed her body closer to him so that her breasts were crushed against the hard wall of his chest. And all the while she moved her lips over his with aching sensuality, teasing him, tempting him, until Aksel could withstand no more of the sweet torture.

A shudder ran through his huge frame. He loosened his grip on her shoulders and grabbed a fistful of her hair, holding her captive while he demonstrated his mastery and claimed control of the kiss.

It was no slow build-up of passion but a violent explosion that set them both on fire. Mina wondered if her bones would be crushed by Aksel's immense strength as he hauled her hard against him. But she did not care. His raw hunger made her melt into him as she responded to his demanding kisses with demands of her own. She curled her fingers into his hair and shaped his skull before tracing her fingertips over his sculpted face and the blond stubble covering his jaw.

He lifted her up and she wrapped her legs around his waist while he strode through the cabin and into the bedroom. Mina was vaguely aware of a fire burning in the hearth, and an oil lamp hanging on the wall cast a pool of golden light on the bed. The mattress dipped as Aksel laid her down and knelt over her. His eyes were no longer icy but blazed with desire that matched the molten heat coursing through Mina's veins.

She felt fiercely triumphant that her feminine instinct had been right and he wanted *her*. His excuse that he had desired the fantasy Juliet was patently untrue. The erratic thud of his heart gave him away, and his hands were unsteady as he tore open her shirt and pushed it over her shoulders. He slipped a hand beneath her back to unfasten her bra and tugged away the wisp of lace to lay bare her breasts. Mina watched streaks of dull colour flare on his sharp cheekbones, and, even before he had touched her breasts, her nipples tautened in response to the feral gleam in his eyes.

Aksel lifted his head and stared down at Mina. 'You are driving me insane, you green-eyed witch.'

She read his lips and smiled. 'Who am I?'

He frowned. 'You're Mina.'

'Not Juliet?'

Now he understood. 'You're a witch,' he repeated. She made him forget his royal status and his life of responsibility and duty. She made him forget everything but his urgent, scalding need that was unlike anything he'd ever felt for any other woman. He cupped her firm breasts in his hands and flicked his thumb pads across the puckered nipples, smiling when he heard her sharp intake of breath that told him her hunger was as acute as his.

Mina gave a choked cry as Aksel kissed her breasts, transferring his mouth from one nipple to the other and lashing the swollen peaks with his tongue until the pleasure was almost unbearable. She could feel his erection straining beneath his jeans and she fumbled with his zip, eager to take him inside her. There was something excitingly primitive about the way he jerked the denim over his hips; the fact that he was too impatient to possess her to undress properly.

She wrenched his shirt buttons open and spread the material so that she could run her hands through the wiry blond hairs that grew on his chest. He dragged her knickers down her legs, and then his big hand was between her thighs, spreading her wide, touching her where she ached to be touched.

Mina closed her eyes and fell into a dark, silent world where her other senses dominated. The feel of Aksel parting her and sliding a finger into her wetness was almost enough to make her come. She could smell his male scent; spicy aftershave mingled with the faint saltiness of sweaty and the indefinable fragrance of sexual arousal. When he moved his hand she arched her hips in mute supplication for him to push his finger deeper inside her.

It wasn't enough, not nearly enough. She curled her hand around his powerful erection and gave a little shiver of excitement when she remembered how he had filled her last night. She lifted her lashes and studied his chiselled features, and her heart stirred. He wasn't a stranger, she had known him for ever, and she wondered why she suddenly felt shy and nervous and excited all at the same time. She smiled, unaware that her eyes mirrored her confused feelings of hope and anticipation, but Aksel tensed, and silently cursed his stupidity.

Reality struck him forcibly. There were numerous reasons why he must not allow the situation to continue, but the most crucial was that he could not have unprotected sex with Mina. He never brought women to his private sanctuary and he did not keep condoms at the cabin. Perhaps Mina used a method of contraception, but years ago Karena had told him she was on the pill, and since then he had never trusted any woman. His gut ached with sexual frustration but, even though he was agonisingly tempted to plunge his throbbing erection between her soft thighs, he could not, would not, take the risk of making Mina pregnant.

A series of images flashed into his mind. He remembered looking into Finn's crib and pulling back the blanket that was half covering the baby's face. At first he had thought that his son was asleep. He'd looked so peaceful with his long eyelashes curling on his cheeks. The baby's skin was as flawless as fine porcelain—*but his little cheek had felt as cold as marble.*

Pain tore in Aksel's chest as he snatched a breath and forced air into his lungs that felt as though they had been crushed in a vice. There were other reasons why he should resist the siren call of Mina's body, not least the soft expression in her eyes that was a warning sign she hoped for something more from him than sex. He needed to make her understand that nothing was on offer. His emotions were as cold and empty as the Arctic tundra.

'Don't stop,' she murmured. Her words affected Aksel more than he cared to admit. He wondered if she could hear her own voice, or whether she was unaware of the husky pleading in her tone. He looked down at her slender body spread naked on his bed and could not bring himself to reject her when she was at her most vulnerable.

Helvete! How had he allowed things to get this far? He should have tried harder to resist her, but the sweet sensuality of her kiss had driven him out of his mind. She looped her arms around his neck and pulled his head down, parting her lips in an invitation that Aksel found he could not ignore. He slanted his mouth over hers, and desire ripped through him when he tasted her warm breath in his mouth.

She twisted her hips restlessly, pushing her sex against his hand. It would be cruel to deny her what she clearly wanted, Aksel told himself. He could give her pleasure even if he could give her nothing else.

The little moan she made when he slipped a second finger inside her and moved his hand in a rhythmic dance told him she was close to the edge. He forced himself to ignore the burn of his own desire and concentrated on Mina. Her head was thrown back on the pillows, her glorious hair spilling around her shoulders, and she closed her eyes as tremors shook her body.

'Aksel…' Her keening cry tugged on his heart. He did not understand why he wanted to gather her close and rock her in his arms while the trembling in her limbs gradually eased. The sight of tears sliding from beneath her lashes filled him with self-loathing. She had flown all the way to Storvhal to find him because—in her words— she believed that last night had been special for both of them. The brutal truth was going to hurt her feelings, he acknowledged grimly as he withdrew from her.

Mina watched Aksel get up from the bed, and the languorous feeling following her orgasm turned to excitement as she waited for him to strip off his jeans and position himself over her. Despite the pleasure he had just gifted her she was desperate to take his hard length inside her. She did not recognise the wanton creature she became with him. He had unlocked a deeply sensual side to her nature that she had been unaware of, and she was eager to make love with him fully and give him as much pleasure as he had given her.

But instead of removing the rest of his clothes he was pulling up the zip of his jeans. Her confusion grew when he walked over to the door. She sat up and pushed her hair out of her eyes. 'Aksel…what's wrong?'

He turned around so that she could see his face, and her heart plummeted at the coldness in his eyes. She watched his mouth form words that made no sense to her.

'This is wrong.' His eyes rested on her slender figure and rose-flushed face. 'You should not have come to Storvhal.'

Mina felt sick as the realisation sank in that he was rejecting her. 'Last night—' she began. But he cut her off.

'Last night was a mistake that I am not going to repeat.'

'Why?' Mina was unaware of the raw emotion in her voice, and Aksel schooled his features to hide the pang of guilt he felt.

She bit her lip. Her pride demanded that she should accept his rejection and try to salvage a little of her dignity, but she did not understand why he had suddenly backed off. 'Is it because I'm deaf? You desired me when you didn't know about my hearing loss,' she reminded him when he frowned. 'What am I supposed to blame for your sudden change of heart?'

'My heart was never involved,' he said bluntly. 'Learning of your hearing impairment is not the reason why I can't have sex with you again.'

'Then what is the reason?' The frustration Mina had felt as a child when she had first lost her hearing surged through her again now. She wished she could hear Aksel. It wasn't that she had a problem reading his lip, but not being able to hear his voice made her feel that there was a wide gulf between them.

'I can't have an affair with you. I am the Prince of Storvhal and my loyalty and duty must be to my country.'

Mina suddenly felt self-conscious that he was dressed and she was naked when she noticed his gaze linger on her breasts. She flushed as she glanced down at her swollen nipples—evidence that her body had still not come down from the sexual high he had taken her to—and tugged a sheet around her before she slid off the bed and walked towards him.

'I understand that you have many responsibilities.' She remembered the taxi driver saying that Aksel had needed to win the support of the Storvhalian people after his father had been an unpopular ruler. Aksel had admitted that, when they had made love last night, he had been able to briefly forget his royal status.

'You belong to an ancient royal dynasty, but surely the Storvhalian people accept that you are a man first, and a prince second?' she said softly.

She was shocked to see a flash of emotion in his eyes, but it disappeared before she could define it, and she wondered if she had imagined his expression of raw pain.

Aksel grimaced as he imagined how his grandmother would react to Mina's lack of understanding of his role as ruler of Storvhal. It was a role he had prepared for probably since he had taken his first steps. He remembered when he was a small boy, Princess Eldrun had insisted that he must not run through the palace but must walk sedately as befitted the future monarch. His whole life had been constrained by strict rules of protocol, and he had done his best to fulfil the expectations that his grandmother, his government ministers—the entire nation of Storvhal, it often felt like—had of him.

He had even kept secret his son's birth—and death.

He stared at Mina and hardened his heart against the

temptation of her beauty. 'I swore an oath promising my devotion to my country and my people. I will always be a prince first.'

'Do you place duty above everything because you feel you have to make up for the fact that your father wasn't a good monarch?'

He stiffened. 'How do you know anything about my father?'

She gave a wry smile. 'My father says that if you want to hear an honest opinion about politics or any other subject, talk to a taxi driver.'

The gentle expression in Mina's green eyes infuriated Aksel. She did not understand anything about his life. *The sacrifice he had made that would haunt him for ever.*

'Did the taxi driver you spoke to tell you that during my father's reign many of his own ministers supported a move to abolish the monarchy? There were incidents of civil unrest among the population and the House of Thoresen, who have ruled Storvhal for eight centuries, came close to being overthrown.

'My father betrayed Storvhal by selling off gold reserves and other valuable assets belonging to the country to fund his extravagant lifestyle. He was called the playboy prince for good reason and the Storvhalian population disliked that their ruler was setting a bad moral example.

'It has taken twelve years for me to win back the trust of my people.' Anger flashed in Aksel's eyes. 'But now, thanks to your wretched journalist friend and the photographs of me escorting an actress with a dubious reputation into my hotel, rumours abound that I lead a secret double life and I am a playboy like my father.'

Aksel knew as soon as he spoke that he was being unfair. The real blame lay with him. God knew what he had been thinking of when he had invited Mina to his hotel last night. The truth was he hadn't been thinking at all. He had been bewitched by a green-eyed sorceress and risked his reputation and the support of the Storvhalian people to satisfy his sexual desire for a woman whose own reputation, it turned out, was hardly without blemish.

Mina blanched as she read Aksel's lips. How dared he judge her based on what he had read about her in the newspapers? Good grief, she had only ever had one sexual relationship—two if she counted Aksel, she amended. But one night in his bed did not constitute a relationship—as he seemed determined to make clear. The unfairness brought tears to her eyes.

'At the risk of repeating myself, I didn't tell the press about us,' she said tautly. 'I discovered from bitter experience that the paparazzi prefer to print scandal and lies than the truth.'

Even with her talent for acting, could she really sound so convincing if she was lying? Aksel wondered. He had found the newspaper article about her affair with a married film director distasteful, but, hell, the paparazzi could make a vicar's tea party sound sordid.

Glimpsing the shimmer of her tears made him feel even more of a bastard than he'd felt when he had stopped making love to her. He wanted to look away before he drowned in her deep green eyes, but he forced himself to remain facing her so that she could watch his lips when he spoke.

'You should get some sleep. As soon as there's a break in the weather I want to get us off the mountain, and that might mean I'll have to wake you early in the morning. Put another log on the fire before you get into bed and you should be warm enough.'

'What about you?' Mina stopped him as he went to walk out of the room. 'Where are you going to sleep?'

'I'll make up a bed on the sofa in the living room.'

'I feel bad that I've taken your bed.' She hesitated, and glanced at the huge wooden-framed bed. 'It's a big bed and I don't mind sharing.'

'But I do.'

His glinting gaze made Mina feel sure he was mocking her. She flushed. 'Don't worry. I'd keep to my side of the mattress.'

He turned his head away, but not before her sharp eyes read the words on his lips that he had spoken to himself. 'I wish I could be certain that I could keep my hands off you, my green-eyed temptress.'

Mina felt confused as she watched him walk into the living room and pick up the bottle of fiery liqueur *akevitt* before he sprawled on the rug in front of the fire. She had not imagined the feral hunger in his eyes. But Aksel believed that he must put his duty to Storvhal above his personal desires. Perhaps that explained the aching loneliness she had glimpsed, before his lashes had swept down and hidden his expression, she mused as she climbed into the big bed and huddled beneath the covers.

CHAPTER SEVEN

THE FLAMES IN the hearth were leaping high into the chimney when Mina woke. The fire had burned down to embers during the night and she guessed that Aksel had thrown on more logs while she was sleeping. She slid out of bed and pulled back the curtains. It was not snowing at the moment, but the towering grey clouds looked ominous and Aksel's warning that they could be trapped at the cabin for days seemed entirely possible.

Although her watch showed that it was nine a.m. it was barely light. By the end of the month it would be polar night and the sun would not rise above the horizon until next year. The land was an Arctic wilderness: remote, beautiful and icy cold—a description that equally fitted the Prince of Storvhal, Mina thought ruefully.

A movement caught her attention, and she turned her head to see Aksel at the side of the house chopping logs with an axe. Despite the freezing temperature he was only dressed in jeans and a sweater. He paused for a moment to push his blond hair out of his eyes, and Mina's heart-rate quickened as she studied his powerful body. There was not an ounce of spare flesh on his lean hips, and his thigh muscles rippled beneath his jeans as he dropped the axe and gathered up an armful of logs.

Mina often rued her impulsive nature, but she could

not resist opening the window and scooping up a handful of snow from the ledge. She took aim, and the snowball landed between Aksel's shoulder blades. He jerked upright, and she guessed he shouted something, but he was too far away for her to be able to read his lips. He must have heard her slam the window shut because he spun round and his startled expression brought a smile to her lips. It was heartening to know that he might be a prince but he was also a human being.

Having not brought any spare clothes with her, she had no alternative but to put on Aksel's shirt that he had taken off when he had started to make love to her the previous night. The shirt came to midway down her thighs and, feeling reassured that she was at least half decently covered, she made a quick exploration of the cabin. She entered the large kitchen at the same moment that Aksel walked in through the back door, and stopped dead when she saw a snowball in his hands and a determined gleam in his eyes.

'*No…!*' She dodged too late and gave a yelp as the snowball landed in the centre of her chest. 'Don't you dare…!' Face alight with laughter, she backed away from him, her eyes widening when she saw he was holding a second snowball. She raced around the table but he caught her easily and grinned wickedly as he shoved snow down the front of her shirt.

'*Oh…*that's cold.' She gasped as the melting snow trickled down her breasts.

He slid his hand beneath her chin and tilted her face so that she could watch him speak. Amusement warmed his ice-blue eyes. 'You asked for it, angel.'

'That wasn't fair to bring snow into the house. Don't you know the rules of snowball fights?'

He shook his head. 'I've never had a snowball fight.'

'Never?' Mina stared out of the window at the snowy landscape. 'But you live in a land of snow and ice. When you were a child you must have had snowball fights with the other kids at school, and surely you built snowmen?'

'I didn't go to school, and I rarely played with other children.'

She could not hide her surprise. 'That's…sad. I know you are a prince, but in England the children of the royal family are educated at school. Didn't your parents think it was important for you to mix with other children of your own age?'

Aksel's smile faded at Mina's curiosity. 'My grandmother supervised my upbringing because my parents were busy with their own lives. I was taught by excellent tutors at the palace until I went to university when I was eighteen.'

The few years he had spent in England at Cambridge University had been the happiest of his life, Aksel thought to himself. He had enjoyed socialising with the other students who came from different backgrounds, and he had loved the sense of freedom and being able to lead a normal life away from the protocol of the palace. Even the press had left him alone, but that had all changed when his father had died and the new Prince of Storvhal had been thrust into the public spotlight.

Mina recalled something the taxi driver had told her. 'I heard that your mother is Russian, but the people of Storvhal didn't approve of your father's choice of bride.'

'Historically there was often tension between my country and Russia. Seventy years ago my grandfather signed a treaty with Norway, which means that the principality of Storvhal is protected by the Norwegian military.'

Aksel shrugged. 'It is true that my father's marriage

to my mother was not popular, particularly as my mother made it plain that she disliked Storvhal and preferred to be in Moscow. I grew up at the palace with my grandmother. My father spent most of his time with his many mistresses in the French Riviera, and I did not see either of my parents very often.'

Aksel's explanation that his grandmother had 'supervised' his upbringing gave Mina the impression that his childhood had been lacking love and affection. She pictured him as a solemn-faced little boy playing on his own in the vast royal palace.

'You said you have a sister.' She remembered he had mentioned a sibling.

'Linne is ten years younger than me, and she lived mainly with my mother. We were not close as children, although we have a good relationship now.'

'Does your sister live at the palace?'

'Sometimes, but at the moment she is on an Arctic research ship in Alaska. Linne is a glaciologist, which is the subject I studied at university before I had to return to Storvhal to rule the country.'

Although Mina could not hear Aksel's tone of voice, years of experience at lip-reading had given her a special understanding of body language and she glimpsed a hint of regret in his eyes. 'Do you wish you were a scientist rather than a prince?' she asked intuitively.

His expression became unreadable. 'It does not matter what I wish for. It was my destiny to be a prince and it is my duty to rule to the best of my ability.'

Mina nodded thoughtfully. 'I think you must have had a lonely childhood. I know what that feels like. My parents decided to send me to a mainstream school where I was the only deaf child, and I always felt apart from the other children because I was different. My sister was the only person who really understood how I struggled to fit in with my peers.' She gave a rueful smile. 'I don't know how I would have managed without Darcey. She was my best friend and my protector against the other kids who used to call me dumb because I was shy of speaking.'

Aksel gave her a puzzled look. 'In that case, why did you choose to become an actress?'

'All my family are actors. My father is often called the greatest Shakespearean actor of all times, but my mother is also amazingly talented. Performing in front of an audience is in my blood and I decided that I wasn't going to allow my loss of hearing to alter who I am or affect my choice of career.'

Mina sighed. 'I suppose I was determined to prove to my father that I could be a good actress despite being deaf. Dad was supportive, but I know he doubted that I would be able to go on the stage. I wanted to make him proud of me. But at the moment, he's furious,' she said ruefully, remembering Joshua Hart's explosive temper when she had met him at the Globe Theatre after she had spent the night with Aksel.

'Why is your father angry with you?' Why the hell did he care? Aksel asked himself impatiently. He told himself he did not want to hear about Mina's life, but he could not dismiss the image of her as a little girl, struggling to cope with her hearing impairment and feeling ostracised by the other pupils at school. He was glad her sister had stood up for her.

'Joshua was not impressed to see a photograph of me with a prince, and details about my supposed love-life, splashed across the front pages of the newspapers. I am his daughter and the lead actress in his production of *Romeo and Juliet,* and he feels that any sort of scandal

will reflect badly on the Hart family and on the play.'
She bit her lip. 'He accused me of turning Shakespeare
into a soap opera.'

Aksel frowned. 'Surely you told him it was not your
fault that you were snapped by the paparazzi?'

'Of course I did—but like you he didn't believe me,'
Mina said drily.

Aksel's jaw clenched. He felt an inexplicable anger
with Mina's father and wanted to confront Joshua Hart
and tell him that he should be supportive of his beautiful and talented daughter, who had faced huge challenges
after she had lost her hearing, with immense courage.

He stared at Mina and felt a fierce rush of desire at the
sight of her wet shirt—his shirt—clinging to her breasts.
The melting snowball had caused her nipples to stand
erect and he could see the hard tips and the dark pink
aureoles jutting beneath the fine cotton shirt.

Helvete! She had thrown what he had planned to be a
peaceful weekend into turmoil and the sooner he could
take her back down the mountain, the better for his peace
of mind.

'Linne left some spare clothes in the wardrobe. Help
yourself to what you need. There's plenty of hot water
if you want a shower, and food in the larder, if you're
hungry.' He grabbed his jacket. 'I'm going for a walk.'

'Do you think that's a good idea? It's snowing again.'

Aksel followed her gaze to the window and saw swirling white snowflakes falling from the sky. This was the
last time he would come to the cabin before winter set
in and he might not get another chance to visit his son's
grave. He could not explain to Mina that sometimes he
craved the solitude of the mountains.

'I won't be long,' he told her, and quickly turned away
from her haunting deep green gaze.

* * *

The pair of jeans and a thick woollen jumper belonging to Aksel's sister that she found in the wardrobe fitted Mina perfectly. With no hairdrier, she had to leave her hair to dry into natural loose waves rather than the sleek style she preferred. The only item of make-up she kept in her handbag was a tube of lip gloss. She wondered ruefully if Aksel liked the fresh-faced, girl-next-door look, and reminded herself that it did not matter what she looked like because he had made it quite clear that he regretted sleeping with her and had no intention of doing so again.

Returning to the kitchen, she found rye bread, cheese and ham in the larder. There was no electricity at the cabin to power a fridge, but the walk-in larder was as cold as a freezer. She could see no sign of Aksel when she peered through the window that was half covered by ice. His footprints had long since been obliterated by the falling snow and in every direction stretched a barren, white wasteland.

It was more than two hours later when she spotted him striding towards the cabin through snow that reached to his mid-thighs. He stripped out of his snowsuit and boots in the cloakroom and came into the kitchen shaking snow out of his hair. Mina could not control her accelerated heart-rate as she skimmed her eyes over his grey wool sweater that clung to his broad shoulders and chest. His rugged masculinity evoked a sharp tug of desire in the pit of her stomach, but when she studied his face she almost gasped out loud at the bleak expression in his eyes. She wanted to ask him what was wrong—why did he look so *tormented*? But before she could say anything, he walked over to the larder and took out a bottle of *akevitt*, which he opened, and poured a liberal amount of the straw-coloured liqueur into a glass.

She glanced at the kettle on the gas stove. 'I was going to make coffee. Do you want some to warm you up?'

He dropped into a chair opposite her at the table so that she could see his face. His mouth curved into a cynical smile as he lifted his glass. 'This warms my blood better than coffee.'

Mina bit her lip. 'You were gone for a long time. I was starting to worry that something had happened to you.' When he raised his brows, she said quickly, 'You said there are wolves around here.'

'Wolves don't attack humans. In fact they very sensibly try to avoid them. I've been coming to the cabin since I was a teenager, and I know these mountains well.'

'Why do you come to such a remote place?'

He shrugged. 'It's the one place I can be alone, to think.'

'And drink.' Mina watched him take a long swig of the strong spirit, and glanced at the empty liqueur bottle on the draining board that he must have finished last night. 'Drinking alone is a dangerous habit.' She gave him a thoughtful look. 'What are you trying to forget?'

'Nothing.' He stood up abruptly and his chair fell backwards and clattered on the wooden floorboards. 'I come to the cabin for some peace and quiet, but clearly I'm not going to get either with you asking endless questions.'

As she watched him stride out of the room Mina wondered what raw nerve she had touched that had made him react so violently. Aksel gave the impression of being coldly unemotional, but beneath the surface he was a complex man, and she sensed that his emotions ran deep. Had something happened in his past that had caused him to withdraw into himself?

He strode back into the kitchen and leaned over her, capturing her chin in his hand and tilting her head up so she was forced to watch his mouth when he spoke. 'What makes you think you're a damn psychologist?'

'Actually, I have studied psychology, and I am a qualified drama therapist.'

Aksel stared into Mina's eyes and felt his anger drain out of him. She had come too close to the truth for comfort when she had suggested that he drank alcohol as a means of trying to block out the past. It wasn't that he wanted to forget Finn—never that. But sometimes the only way he could cope with the guilt that haunted him was to anaesthetise his pain with alcohol.

He frowned. 'What the hell is a drama therapist?'

'Drama therapy is a form of psychological therapy. Drama therapists use drama and theatre techniques to help clients with a wide range of emotional problems, from adults suffering from dementia through to children who have experienced psychological trauma.' Mina was unaware that her voice became increasingly enthusiastic as she explained about drama therapy, which was a subject close to her heart. 'In my role as a drama therapist, I use stories, role-play, improvisation and puppets—a whole range of artistic devices to enable children to explore difficult and painful life experiences.'

Aksel was curious, despite telling himself that he did not want to become involved with Mina. 'How do you combine being a drama therapist with your acting career?'

'I managed to fit acting work around my drama therapy training, but now that I am a fully qualified therapist I've been thinking about leaving acting to concentrate on a full-time career as a drama therapist.

'I love the stage. I'm a Hart and performing is in my blood. My father would be disappointed if I gave up acting,' Mina admitted. 'But I had been thinking for a while that I would like to do something more meaningful with my life. My sister Darcey trained as a speech therapist after seeing how vital speech therapy was for me when I became deaf. Being ill with meningitis when I was a child and losing my hearing was hugely traumatic. I feel that my experiences have given me an empathy with children who have suffered emotional and physical trauma.

'I didn't become an actress to be famous,' she told Aksel. 'I hate show business and the celebrity culture. When I made that film in America, and the media falsely accused me of having that affair, I saw a side to acting that I don't want to be a part of.

'The photos in the newspapers of me going into a hotel with you and leaving the next morning looking like I'd spent a wild night in your bed are the worst thing that could have happened as far as I'm concerned. The lies written about my relationship with Dexter Price have been reprinted and my reputation is in tatters.' She grimaced. 'You should have been honest when we met, and told me who you are. You might be a prince, but you're not my Prince Charming.'

Aksel's expression was thunderous, but he did not reply. Instead he grabbed the bottle of *akevitt* and walked out of the room, leaving Mina trembling inside and silently calling herself every kind of a fool, because while he had been leaning over her she had ached for him to cover her mouth with his and kiss her until the world went away.

By mid-afternoon the weak sun had slipped below the horizon once more and the snow clouds had been blown away to leave a clear, indigo-coloured sky. Aksel lit the oil lamps, and Mina was curled up in an armchair by the fire, reading. She had been surprised to find that many of the books in the book case were English.

'English is the second official language of Storvhal,' Aksel explained. 'When I became Prince I made it a law that schools must also teach children English. It is important for the population to retain a strong link to their culture, but Storvhal is a small country and we must be able to compete on world markets and communicate using a globally recognised language.'

He lowered his sketch pad where he had been idly drawing, and looked over at Mina. 'Why did your parents send you to a mainstream school?'

'I was eight when I lost my hearing and by that age I had learned speech and language. Mum and Dad were concerned that if I went to a specialist school for deaf children I might lose my verbal skills. But the hearing aids I wore then were not as good as the ones I have now, and I struggled—not so much with my school work, but I found it hard to be accepted by the other children.' She gave a wry smile. 'Luckily I learned to act, and I was good at pretending that I didn't care about being teased. Most people didn't realise that I could lip-read when they called me dumb or stupid.'

'You certainly proved your tormentors wrong by becoming a gifted actress.' Aksel frowned as he imagined the difficulties Mina had faced as a child—and perhaps still sometimes faced as an adult, he mused. She seemed to have no problem understanding him by reading his lips, but he wondered if she felt vulnerable without her hearing aids.

'I'd like to learn more about drama therapy,' he said. 'That type of specialised psychotherapy is not available in Storvhal, but I think it could help a group of children from a fishing village, whose fathers were all drowned when their boats sank during a storm at sea. Twenty families were affected, and the tragedy has touched everyone in the small village of Revika. The local school teachers and community leaders are doing what they can, but the children are devastated.'

'Such a terrible disaster is bound to have left the children deeply traumatised,' Mina murmured. 'Drama therapy could provide a way for the children to explore and express their feelings.'

She gave up trying to concentrate on her book. In truth she had spent more time secretly watching Aksel than reading. In the flickering firelight, his sculpted face was all angles and planes, and she longed to run her fingers through his golden hair.

She glanced at the sketch pad. 'What are you drawing?'

'You.' His answer surprised her.

'Can I see?'

He hesitated, and then shrugged and handed her the pad. Mina's eyes widened as she studied the skilful charcoal sketch of herself. 'You're very good at drawing. Did you study art?'

'Not formally. Drawing is a hobby I began as a child and I'm self-taught.'

Mina handed him back the sketch pad. 'You've made me prettier than I really am.'

'I disagree. I haven't been able to capture your beauty as accurately as I wish I could.'

Her heart leapt, but she firmly told herself she must have made a mistake when she'd read his lips, just as she must have mistaken the reflection of the firelight in his eyes for desire. The atmosphere between them pricked with an undercurrent of tension, and in an attempt to ignore it she turned her attention to a second sketch pad lying on the table.

'Do you mind if I have a look at your work?'

'Be my guest.'

The drawings were mainly done in charcoal or pencil and were predominantly of wildlife that she guessed Aksel had spotted in the mountains. There were several sketches of reindeer, as well as a lynx, an Arctic fox and some stunningly detailed drawings of wolves. The sketches were skilfully executed, but they were more than simply accurate representations of a subject; they had been drawn with real appreciation for wildlife and revealed a depth of emotion in Aksel that he kept hidden in all other aspects of his life.

He was an enigma, Mina thought with a sigh as she closed the sketch pad. She stood up and carried the pad over to Aksel to put back on the shelf, but as she handed it to him a loose page fell out onto the floor. She leaned down to pick it up, but he moved quickly and snatched up the drawing. However he had not been quick enough to prevent Mina from seeing the drawing of a baby. She guessed the infant was very young, perhaps only a few weeks old, she mused, thinking of her sister's twin boys when they had been newborns.

Her eyes flew to Aksel's face. She wanted to ask him about the drawing—a baby seemed an unusual subject for him to have sketched. But something in his expression made her hesitate. His granite-hard features showed no emotion but he seemed strangely tense, and for a second she glimpsed a look of utter bleakness in his eyes that caused her to take a sharp breath.

'Aksel…?' she said uncertainly.

'Leave it, Mina.'

She could not hear him but she sensed his tone had

been curt. He deliberately turned away from her as he slipped the drawing inside the cover of the sketch pad and placed the book on the shelf.

Her confusion grew when he turned off the oil lamps so that the room was dark, apart from the orange embers of the fire flickering in the hearth. Unable to see Aksel's face clearly to read his lips, Mina stiffened when he put a hand on her shoulder and steered her over to the window. But the sight that met her eyes was so spectacular that everything else flew from her mind.

She had heard about the natural phenomenon known as the aurora borealis but nothing had prepared her for the awe-inspiring light show that filled the sky. Swirling clouds of greens and pinks performed a magical dance. Mystical spirits, shimmering and ethereal, cast an eerie glow that illuminated the sky and reflected rainbow colours on the blanket of white snow beneath.

Mina vaguely recalled, from a geography lesson at school, that the aurora—sometimes called the Northern Lights—were caused by gas particles in the earth's atmosphere colliding, and the most stunning displays could only be seen at the north and south poles. But the reason why the aurora took place did not seem important. She was transfixed by the beauty of nature's incredible display and felt humbled and deeply moved that she was lucky enough to witness something so magnificent. As she stared up at the heavens the tension seeped from her body and she unconsciously leaned back against Aksel's chest.

Aksel drew a ragged breath as he struggled to impose his usual icy control over his emotions. Seeing the picture of Finn had been a shock and he'd felt winded, as though he had been punched in his gut. He hadn't known the drawing was tucked in the sketch pad. He must have put it there years ago, but he remembered sketching his son while the baby had been asleep in his crib.

His little boy had been so beautiful. Aksel took another harsh breath and felt an ache in the back of his throat as he watched the glorious light spectacle outside the window. He had seen the aurora many times but he never failed to be awed by its other-worldly beauty. It gave him some comfort to know that Finn was up here on the mountain. If there was a heaven, then this remote spot, with the aurora lighting up the sky, was surely the closest place to paradise.

He recalled the puzzled expression in Mina's eyes when she had seen the sketch. It had been obvious that she was curious about the identity of the baby. What shocked him was that for a crazy moment he had actually contemplated telling her about Finn.

He frowned. Why would he reveal his deepest secret to her when he was not certain that he could trust her? Why, after so many years of carrying his secret alone, did he long to unburden his soul to this woman? Perhaps it was because he recognised her compassion, he brooded. How many people would choose to give up a successful acting career to become a psychotherapist working with traumatised children?

But he doubted Mina would be sympathetic if he revealed the terrible thing he had done. For eight years he had hidden his son's birth from the Storvhalian people, his friends, and even from his grandmother. He had believed he was doing the best thing for the monarchy, but his guilt ate away at him. He did not deserve Mina's compassion, and he had not deserved her mind-blowing sensuality when they had made love.

His mind flew back to two nights ago, and the memory of her generosity and eagerness to please him caused subtle warmth to flow through his veins, melting the ice inside him. He became aware of her bottom pressing against his thighs and an image came into his mind of the peachy perfection of her bare buttocks. The warmth in his veins turned to searing heat and the throb of desire provided a temporary respite from the dull ache of grief in his heart.

In the darkened room he could see the profile of her lovely face and the slender column of her throat. Last night it had taken all his will power to walk away from her, but right now, when his emotions felt raw, it was becoming harder to remember why he must resist her.

He wanted to press his lips to her white neck, wanted it so badly that his fingers clenched and bit into her shoulder, causing her to make a startled protest. She turned her head towards him and her mouth was mere centimetres from his, offering an unbearable temptation. Surely there was no harm in kissing her? He felt a tremor run through her and knew she was waiting for him to claim her lips. He dipped his head lower so that his mouth almost grazed hers. One kiss was all he would take, he told himself.

One kiss would not be enough, a voice inside his head taunted. If he kissed her he would be bewitched by her sensual magic. But the reason he had fought his desire for her last night had not changed. He could not have unprotected sex with her and risk her conceiving his child. Nor would it be fair to allow her to think that he wanted a relationship with her. The brutal truth was that he wanted to lose himself in her softness and forget temporarily the past that haunted him.

Mina stumbled as Aksel snatched his hand from her shoulder. She did not know what had happened to make him move abruptly away from her when seconds earlier he had been about to kiss her. Feeling dazed by the sudden change in him, she watched him light an oil lamp. In the bright gleam it emitted his face was expressionless, his blue eyes as cold as the Arctic winter. He took a step closer to her—reluctantly, she sensed—so that she could read his lips.

'Go and put your snowsuit on,' he instructed. 'The sky is clear, which means we shouldn't get any more snow for a few hours, and I'm going to risk making a dash down the mountain.'

Aksel could not make it plainer that he did not want to spend any more time with her than was necessary. She could not cope with him blowing hot one minute and cold the next, Mina thought angrily. Coming to Storvhal had been an impulsive mistake, and the sooner she could fly home and forget she had ever met a prince, the better.

CHAPTER EIGHT

THE JOURNEY DOWN the mountain was thankfully uneventful. The snow that had fallen earlier in the day had frozen into an ice sheet, which reflected the brilliant gleam of the moon and the countless stars suspended in the dark-as-ink sky.

Halfway down, they swapped the snowmobile for the four-by-four. As Aksel had predicted, the snow was deep in the valley, but snow ploughs had cleared the roads and eventually they reached Storvhal's capital city Jonja and saw the tall white turrets of the royal palace rising out of the dense fog that blanketed the city.

Mina turned to him. 'Why have you brought me here? I thought you were taking me straight to the airport.'

Aksel was forced to stop the car in front of the ornate palace gates while they slowly swung open. He turned his head towards her so that she could watch his lips move. 'All flights are grounded due to freezing fog. You'll have to stay at the palace tonight.'

A bright light flared outside the window. 'What the hell…?' Aksel's jaw tightened when another flashbulb exploded and briefly filled the car with stark white light. 'I hadn't expected press photographers to be here,' he growled. The gates finally parted and he put his foot down on the accelerator and gunned into the palace grounds.

'You'd better prepare yourself for the reception committee,' he told her tersely as he parked by the front steps and the palace doors were opened from within.

'What do you mean?'

'You'll see.'

As Aksel escorted Mina into the palace she understood his curious comment. Despite it being late at night, a dizzying number of people were waiting in the vast entrance hall to greet the prince. Courtiers, palace guards and household staff dressed in their respective uniforms bowed as Aksel walked past. There were also several official-looking men wearing suits, and Mina recognised the young man with round glasses as Aksel's personal assistant, Benedict Lindburg. She knew there must be a buzz of conversation because she could see people's lips moving, but it was impossible for her to lip-read and keep track of what anyone was saying.

The crippling self-consciousness that Mina had felt as a child gripped her now. She hoped no one had spoken to her and thought she was being rude for ignoring them. Instinctively she kept close to Aksel and breathed a sigh of relief when he escorted her into a room that she guessed was his office and closed the door behind him so that they were alone.

Aksel's eyes narrowed on Mina's tense face. 'I did warn you,' he said, stepping closer to ensure that she could see his mouth moving. 'It must be difficult to lip-read when you are in a crowd. At least you can charge up your hearing-aid batteries while you are at the palace.'

'What do all those people want?'

He shrugged. 'There is always some matter or other that my government ministers believe requires my urgent attention.' His life was bound by duty, but for a few moments Aksel imagined what it would be like if he were not a prince and were free to live his life as he chose, free to make love to the woman whom he desired more than any other.

Daydreams were pointless, he reminded himself. 'The fog is forecast to clear by tomorrow afternoon and a member of my staff will drive you to the airport and book you onto a flight,' he told her abruptly. 'Whereabouts in London do you live?'

'Notting Hill—but I won't go back home until the paparazzi have grown bored of stalking my flat.'

Aksel frowned. 'Do you mean you were hounded by journalists?'

'My friend Kat saw a group of them outside my front door. She won't mind if I stay with her for a few days— and hopefully the furore about my alleged affair with a prince will die down soon.' She gave him a wry look. 'Anyway, it's not your problem, is it? You are protected from press intrusion in your grand palace.'

Although that was not absolutely true, Mina acknowledged as she remembered the press photographers who had been waiting at the palace gates. She wondered if Aksel resented living his life in the public eye, subjected to constant media scrutiny. In some ways this beautiful palace was his prison, she realised.

Aksel appeared tense. 'I'm sorry your life has been disrupted. I *should* have told you who I am when we first met.'

'Why didn't you?'

He hesitated. 'You might have thought I was lying to impress you and refused to have dinner with me.'

Mina stared at his mouth, feeling frustrated that she

could not hear him. 'Would you have cared if I had refused?'

His tugged his hand through his hair until it stood up in blond spikes. 'Yes.'

Her frustration boiled over. 'Then why did you leave me alone at the cabin? You let me think you didn't want me.' She bit her lip. The memory of Aksel's rejection felt like a knife wound in her heart. It had hurt far more than when she had discovered that Dexter had lied to her, she realised with a jolt of shock. How was that possible? She had been in love with Dex, but she certainly could not have fallen in love with Aksel after two days.

The glimmer of tears in Mina's eyes made Aksel's gut twist. 'My role as prince comes with expectations that would make it impossible for us to have a relationship,' he said roughly.

'That's another thing you forgot to mention when you took me to bed.'

'*Damn it*, Mina.' He caught hold of her as she turned away, and spun her round to face him. 'Damn it,' he growled as he pulled her into his arms and crushed her mouth beneath his. He couldn't fight the madness inside him, couldn't control his hunger, his intolerable need to possess her beautiful body and make her his as she had been two nights ago.

A knock on the door dragged Aksel back to reality. Reluctantly he lifted his mouth from Mina's and felt guilty when he stared into her stunned eyes. He couldn't blame her for looking confused, when he did not understand his own behaviour. His carefully organised life was spinning out of control and cracks were appearing in the ice wall he had built around his emotions.

He knew she could not have heard the knock on the door, but the interruption had reminded him that he had no right to kiss her. He dropped his arms to his sides. 'I'm needed,' he told her, before he strode across the room and yanked open the door. His mood was not improved by the sight of his chief advisor. 'Can't it wait, Harald?' he demanded curtly.

The elderly advisor frowned as he looked past Aksel and saw Mina's dishevelled hair and reddened lips. 'I'm afraid not, sir. I must talk to you urgently.'

Duty must take precedence over his personal life, Aksel reminded himself. However much he wanted to sweep Mina into his arms and carry her off to his bed, he would not allow desire to make a weak fool of him as it had his father.

He stepped back to allow his chief advisor into the room, and rang a bell to summon a member of the palace staff. When a butler arrived, Aksel said to Mina, 'Hans will show you to your room, and tomorrow he will escort you to the airport.'

It was impossible to believe that his cold eyes had blazed with desire when he had kissed her a few moments earlier, Mina thought. She sensed that his return to being a regal and remote prince had something to do with the presence of the grey-haired, grey-suited man who was regarding her with a disapproving expression.

She was not an actress for nothing, she reminded herself. Her pride insisted that she must hold onto her dignity and not allow Aksel to see that he had trampled on her heart.

She gave him a cool smile and felt a flicker of satisfaction when he frowned. 'Goodbye, Aksel.' She hesitated, and gave him a searching look. 'I hope one day you'll realise that you can't pay for your father's mistakes for ever. Even a prince has a right to find personal happiness.'

As Aksel watched Mina walk out of the room he was

tempted to go after her and kiss her until she lost her infuriating air of detachment and melted in his arms as she had before they had been interrupted by his chief advisor. He knew she was a talented actress—so who was the real Mina? Was she the woman who had kissed him passionately a few minutes ago, or the woman who had sauntered out of his office without a backwards glance?

'Sir?' Harald Petersen's voice dragged Aksel from his frustrated thoughts. 'Benedict Lindburg has informed me that members of the press were at the palace gates when you arrived and they may have seen that Miss Hart was with you.'

'Undoubtedly they saw her,' Aksel said grimly, recalling the glare of camera flashbulbs that had shone through the windscreen of the four-by-four.

The chief advisor cleared his throat. 'Then we have a problem, sir. The Storvhalian people might overlook your affair with an actress in London, but I fear they will be less accepting when it becomes public knowledge that you are entertaining your mistress at the palace as your father used to do. Some sections of the press have already made unfavourable comparisons between you and Prince Geir. The last thing we want is for you to be labelled a playboy prince.'

Harald Petersen sighed. 'You have proved yourself to be a good ruler these past twelve years, but the people want reassurance that the monarchy will continue. For that reason I urge you to consider taking a wife. There are a number of women from Storvhalian aristocratic families who would be suitable for the role. If you give the people a princess, with the expectation that there will soon be an heir to the throne, you are certain to increase support for the House of Thoresen and ensure the stability of the country.'

'What if I do not wish to get married?' Aksel said curtly.

His chief advisor looked shocked. 'It is your duty, sir.'

'Ah, yes, *duty.*' Aksel's jaw hardened. 'Don't you think I have sacrificed enough in the name of duty? For pity's sake,' he said savagely, 'I cannot speak my son's name in public, or celebrate his tragically short life.' He felt a sudden tightness in his throat and turned abruptly away from the older man. 'I cannot weep for Finn,' he muttered beneath his breath.

When he swung back to his advisor his hard-boned face showed no emotion. 'I will consider your suggestion, Harald,' he said coolly. 'You may leave me now.'

'What are we to do about Miss Hart?' Harald said worriedly.

'I'll think of something. Tell Benedict that I do not want to be disturbed for the rest of the evening.'

The following morning, Aksel stood in his office staring moodily out of the window at the snow-covered palace gardens. He tried to ignore the sudden acceleration of his heart-rate when there was a knock on the door and the butler ushered Mina into the room.

'Are your hearing aids working?' he asked as she focused her deep green gaze on his face.

'Yes, I can hear you.' She bit her bottom lip—something Aksel had noticed she did when she was feeling vulnerable. 'Why did you want to see me? I'm about to go to the airport.'

'There's been a change of plan,' he said abruptly. 'We need to talk.'

Mina suddenly realised that they were not alone. The elderly man she had seen the previous evening was in

Aksel's office and the censure in his cold stare made her flush.

'I don't believe we have anything more to say to one another,' she said bluntly.

The older man stepped towards her. 'Miss Hart, you clearly do not understand palace protocol. The prince wishes to talk to you, and you must listen.'

Aksel cursed beneath his breath. 'Mina, may I introduce the head of my council of government and chief advisor, Harald Petersen?' He glanced at the older man. 'Harald, I would like to speak to Miss Hart alone.'

'Please forgive his brusqueness,' he said to Mina when the advisor had left the room. 'Harald is an ardent royalist who worked hard to help me restore support for the monarchy after my father's death. He is naturally concerned that I should not do anything which might earn the disapproval of the Storvhalian people.'

'He must have had a fit when he saw the photographs in the newspapers of you with an actress who the paparazzi labelled the Hollywood Harlot,' Mina said bleakly.

Aksel gave her a searching look. 'Why didn't you sue the newspapers for publishing lies about you?'

'I didn't have the kind of money needed to fight a legal battle with the press, and Dexter refused to deny that we were lovers because the scandal gave publicity to the film. I hoped that the story would be forgotten—and it was until I was photographed with a prince.

'What did you want to talk to me about?' Mina hadn't expected to see Aksel again and was struggling to hide her fierce awareness of him. It didn't help that he looked devastatingly sexy in a pale grey suit and navy-blue silk shirt. She longed to reach out and touch him.

Instead of responding to her question, he said roughly, 'You look beautiful. That dress suits you.'

'I feel awful for wearing your sister's clothes without her knowledge.' She glanced down at the cream cashmere dress that a maid had brought to her room that morning. 'The maid said that my skirt and blouse were being laundered, and I could borrow some clothes belonging to your sister. I'll return the dress and shoes as soon as I get back to London.'

'Don't worry about it. Linne is often sent samples from designers, but she rarely wears any of the clothes. Cocktail dresses aren't very useful on an Arctic research ship,' Aksel said drily.

He dragged his gaze from Mina's slender legs that were enhanced by three-inch stiletto-heel shoes. She had swept her long auburn hair into a loose knot on top of her head, with soft tendrils framing her face, and looked elegant and so breathtakingly sexy that Aksel was seriously tempted to lock his office door, sweep the pile of papers off his desk and make love to her on the polished rosewood surface.

He forced himself to concentrate on the reason he had called her to his office. 'You need to see this,' he said, handing her a newspaper.

Frowning, Mina took it from him and caught her breath when she saw the photograph on the front page of her and Aksel when they had arrived at the palace the previous evening. The photo of them sitting in the four-by-four showed them apparently staring into each other's eyes, but in fact she had been focused on his mouth because at the time her hearing aids hadn't been working and she had needed to read his lips.

Her frown deepened as she read the headline.

Royal Romance—has the Prince finally found love?

'I don't understand. I know there was speculation that we are having an affair, but why would the press suggest that our relationship is serious?'

'Because I brought you to the palace,' Aksel said tersely. 'You are the first woman I have ever invited here. The press don't usually camp outside the palace gates but I should have guessed they would want to follow up the story that we are having an affair. If I had known the photographers were waiting when we came down from the mountains I would have arranged for you to spend the night at a hotel.'

It was what he *should* have done, Aksel acknowledged. But his conscience had refused to leave her at a hotel in a strange country when he knew how vulnerable she felt without her hearing aids.

Mina skimmed the paragraph beneath the headline. 'How did the journalist who wrote this know that I have recently qualified as a drama therapist?' Her eyes widened as she continued reading. 'It says here that you invited me to Storvhal so that I could help the children from the village of Revika whose fathers drowned when their fishing fleet was hit by a terrible storm.'

She lowered the newspaper and glared at Aksel. 'What's going on?'

'Damage limitation,' he said coolly. 'The palace press office released certain details about you, including that you are a drama therapist.

'I've explained that my father's reputation as a playboy prince made him deeply unpopular,' he continued, ignoring the stormy expression in Mina's eyes. 'I cannot risk people thinking that I am like him, and that you are my casual mistress. It will be better if the population believe that I am in a serious relationship with a compassionate drama therapist who wishes to help the children of Revika.'

Mina shook her head. 'I refuse to be part of any subterfuge. You'll have to give a statement to the press explaining that they have made a mistake and we are not in a relationship.'

'Unfortunately that is not an option when the photograph of us entering the palace together is a clear indication that we are lovers. Some of the papers have even gone so far as to suggest that the palace might soon announce a royal betrothal.'

Her jaw dropped. 'You mean…people believe we might get married? That's ridiculous.'

'As my chief advisor often reminds me—the country has long hoped that I will marry and provide an heir to the throne,' Aksel said drily.

'I thought you were expected to choose a Storvhalian bride?'

'I don't think the people would mind what nationality my wife is. It's true that my Russian mother was not popular, but she made it clear that she disliked Storvhal and had no time for the people she was supposed to rule with my father. Your offer to help Revika's children has gone down well in the press. The tragedy of the fishing-fleet disaster has aroused the sympathy of the whole nation and your desire to help the bereaved children appears to have captured the hearts of the Storvhalian people.'

'But I didn't offer to visit the children. You gave the press false information,' Mina said angrily. 'I mean, of course I would like to help them, but my flight to London leaves in an hour.'

'Your ticket has been cancelled. We will have to go along with the media story of a royal romance for a while,' Aksel said coolly. 'In a few weeks, when you go to New

York to perform on Broadway, we'll announce that sadly, due to the pressures of your acting career, we have decided to end our relationship.'

Mina sensed that the situation was spiralling out of her control. 'You've got it all worked out, haven't you?'

'I held an emergency meeting with my chief ministers this morning to discuss the best way to deal with the situation.'

'Had it occurred to you that I might not want to pretend to be in love with you?' she demanded coldly.

His eyes showed no emotion. 'Allowing people to think we are romantically involved could be beneficial to both of us. This afternoon we will visit the village of Revika to meet the children whose fathers were killed in the disaster. It will be a good PR exercise.'

Mina was shocked by his heartless suggestions. 'You can't use those poor children for a…a publicity stunt.'

'That isn't the only reason for the visit. I have spoken to the headmistress of the school in Revika. Ella Holmberg is enthusiastic about the idea of using drama therapy to help the bereaved children. She is concerned that without help to come to terms with their loss, they could suffer long-term emotional damage.'

'That's certainly true,' Mina admitted.

'It's also true that favourable publicity would improve your image and might make people forget the scandal surrounding your relationship with a married film director in America,' Aksel said smoothly.

'I'm not going to visit the children just to improve my image. That's a disgusting suggestion.' Mina marched over to the door. 'I'm sorry, but I'd prefer to stick to the original plan and leave Storvhal. I'm sure the press interest in us will eventually die down and I refuse to pretend that we are romantically involved. I can't bear to have my personal life made public again,' she said huskily.

'What about the fishermen's children?' Aksel's voice stopped her as she was about to walk out of his office. 'They have been desperately affected by the tragedy. I thought you said you had trained as a drama therapist because losing your hearing when you were a child gave you a special empathy with traumatised children? You told me you wanted to do something meaningful with your life—and this is your chance.' He crossed the room and stood in front of her, tilting her chin so that he could look into her eyes. 'I am asking you to come to Revika for the children's sake.'

His words tugged on Mina's conscience. She felt torn between wanting to leave Aksel before she got hurt, and sympathy for the children whose lives had been shattered by the loss of their fathers. It was possible that they might benefit from drama therapy and it would be selfish of her to refuse Aksel's request to visit the children with him.

She looked away from him and her heart thudded beneath her ribs as she made a decision that she hoped she would not regret. 'I'll come with you today to make an assessment of how best to help the children. But it's likely they will need a programme of drama therapy lasting for several months.'

Aksel gave a satisfied nod. 'There is one other thing. My grandmother has asked to meet you.' Sensing Mina's surprise, he explained. 'When Princess Eldrun saw the photograph of us in today's newspapers she was dismayed because the picture reminded her of how my father had been a playboy during his reign and an unpopular monarch. My grandmother is old and frail, and to avoid upsetting her I reassured her that we are in a serious relationship.'

'I can't believe you did that!' Mina's temper flared. 'It seems awful to lie to your grandmother, even to protect her from being upset. I've told you I don't feel comfortable with the idea of fooling people, and I can't pretend to your grandmother that I'm in love with you.'

'No?' He moved before she guessed his intention and shot his arm around her waist as he lowered his head to capture her mouth. Mina stiffened, determined not to respond to him, but her treacherous body melted as he deepened the kiss and it became flagrantly erotic and utterly irresistible. With a low groan she parted her lips beneath his, but when she slid her arms around his neck he broke the kiss and stepped back from her.

'That was a pretty convincing performance,' he drawled. 'I have no doubt my grandmother will believe that you are smitten with me.'

She blushed and clenched her hand by her side, fighting a strong urge to slap the mocking smile from his face. 'You were very convincing yourself.' She was shocked to see colour rising on his cheeks. The flash of fire in his eyes told her that he was not as immune to her as he wanted her to believe, and she was certain he could not have faked the raw passion in his kiss.

'Perhaps we won't have to lie?' she murmured.

His eyes narrowed. 'What do you mean?'

She looked at him intently and noted that he dropped his gaze from hers. 'Who's to say that a relationship won't develop between us while we are pretending to be in love?'

'I say,' Aksel told her harshly. 'It won't happen, Mina, so don't waste your time looking for something that will never exist.' He breathed in the light floral scent of her perfume and felt his gut twist. 'I'm different from other people. I don't feel the same emotions.'

'Is it because you're a prince that you think you should put duty before your personal feelings—or is there another reason why you suppress your emotions?' she asked intuitively.

The image of Finn's tiny face flashed into Aksel's mind. The memory of his son evoked a familiar ache in his chest. He equated love with loss and pain and he did not want to experience any of those feelings again.

'I don't have any emotions to suppress,' he told Mina brusquely. 'I'm empty inside and the truth is I don't want to change.'

CHAPTER NINE

SHE MUST HAVE been mad to have agreed to Aksel's crazy plan to pretend that their relationship was serious, Mina thought for the hundredth time. The only reason she had done so was because she wanted the chance to try with drama therapy to help the bereaved children from the fishing village, she reminded herself.

They were on their way to Revika and the car was crossing a bridge that spanned a wide stretch of sea between the mainland and an island where the fishing village was situated. Although it was early afternoon the sun was already sinking behind the mountains and the sky was streaked with hues of gold and pink that made the highest peaks look as though they were on fire.

But the stunning views out of the window did not lessen Mina's awareness of Aksel's firm thigh pressed up against her. The scent of his aftershave evoked memories of him making love to her, when she had breathed in the intoxicating male fragrance of his naked body. It was a relief when they arrived in the fishing village, but her relief was short-lived when she saw the hordes of press photographers and television crews waiting outside the community hall to snap pictures of the prince and the woman who they speculated might become his princess.

As they stepped out of the car Aksel slid his arm

around her waist. For a moment she was glad of his moral support but she quickly realised that his actions were for the benefit of the press. When he looked deeply into her eyes she knew it was just an act, and as soon as they walked into the community hall she pulled away from him, silently calling herself a fool for wishing that his tender smile had been real.

They were greeted by the headmistress of the school where most of the children affected by the tragedy were pupils. 'The children are pleased that you have come to spend time with them again,' Ella Holmberg said to Aksel. 'They look forward to your visits.' Noticing Mina's look of surprise, she explained, 'Prince Aksel has come to Revika every week since the fishing fleet was destroyed in the storm. Many of the children whose fathers drowned are suffering from nightmares and struggling to cope with their grief. I haven't mentioned that you are a therapist,' she told Mina. 'I've simply said that you are a friend of Prince Aksel.'

The first thing that struck Mina as she walked into the community hall was the silence. There were more than thirty children present, and many of the fishermen's widows. Their sadness was tangible and would take months and years to heal, but Mina hoped that drama therapy might help the children to voice their feelings.

To her amazement, the minute Aksel stepped into the room and greeted the children he changed from the cold and remote prince she had seen at the palace and revealed a gentler side to his nature that reminded her of the man she had met in London. In order to assess the best way to help the children, Mina knew she must first win their trust, and she was pleasantly surprised when Aksel joined in the games she organised.

By the end of the afternoon the hall was no longer silent

but filled with the sound of chattering voices, and even tentative laughter. Mina sat on the floor with the children grouped around her. 'In the next game, we are going to pretend that we are actors on a stage,' she told them. 'Instead of speaking, we need to show the audience what emotions we are feeling. For instance, how would we show that we are happy?'

'We would laugh, and dance,' suggested a little girl.

'Okay, let me see you being happy.' Mina gave the children a few minutes of acting time. 'How would we show that we are feeling angry?'

'We would have a grumpy face,' said a boy, 'and stamp our feet.'

The mood in the hall changed subtly as the children expressed anger. Many of them stamped loudly on the wooden floor and the sound was deafening, but Mina encouraged them to continue. 'It's okay to be angry,' she told them. 'Sometimes we lock our feelings inside us instead of letting those feelings out.'

On the other side of the room, Aksel felt a peculiar tightness in his throat as he listened to Mina talking to the children. She seemed to understand the helpless fury that was part of grief, just as he understood what it felt like to lock emotions deep inside. He found her depth of compassion touching, but it was part of her job, he told himself.

At the end of the session the headmistress came over to speak to Mina. 'The children are having fun for the first time since the tragedy. You've achieved so much with them after just one visit.'

'I would love to spend more time with them,' Mina said softly. 'I believe that drama therapy sessions over a few months would be very beneficial in helping to unlock their emotions.'

She glanced across the room at Aksel and wondered what feelings he kept hidden behind his enigmatic façade. He was chatting to a widow of one of the fishermen. The woman was cradling a tiny baby and she held the infant out to Aksel. To Mina's shock, he seemed for a split second to recoil from the baby. His face twisted in an expression of intense pain and although she had no idea why he had reacted so strangely she instinctively wanted to help him and hurried across the room to stand beside him.

'What a beautiful baby,' she said to the child's mother. The baby was dressed in blue. 'Would you mind if I held your son?'

The woman smiled and placed the baby in Mina's arms. She was conscious that Aksel released his breath on a ragged sigh, and, shooting him a glance, she noticed beads of sweat on his brow. She supposed that the prospect of holding a tiny baby would be nerve-racking for a man who had no experience of children—but his extreme reaction puzzled her.

The moment passed, Aksel turned to talk to another parent and Mina handed the baby back to his mother and walked back to rejoin Ella Holmberg, but she was still curious about why Aksel had seemed almost afraid to hold the baby.

Ella followed Mina's gaze to him. 'The prince is gorgeous, isn't he? Plenty of women would like to catch him, but until you came along he seemed to be a confirmed bachelor. It was rumoured that he was in love with a Russian woman years ago, but I assume that he was advised against marrying her. Prince Aksel's mother was Russian, and she was as unpopular with the Storvhalian people as Aksel's father.'

Mina's stomach lurched at the idea that Aksel had loved a woman but had been unable to marry her. Had he

come to the Globe Theatre in London to see three perfor-
mances of *Romeo and Juliet* because the story about the
young lovers whose families disapproved of their union
had deep personal meaning for him? She wondered if he
was still in love with the woman from his past. Was that
why he had never married?

'That seemed to go well,' Aksel said to Mina later,
when they were waiting in the lobby for the car to collect
them. 'You made a breakthrough with the children today.'
His expression tightened. 'Watching you with them was
really quite touching,' he drawled. 'You seemed to em-
pathise with them, but I suppose that was part of your
training to be a drama therapist.'

Aksel was struggling to contain the raw emotions that
he had kept buried for the past eight years. Shockingly,
he found himself wanting to tell Mina about Finn. But
how could he trust her? He was still undecided about
whether she had tipped off the press that she had slept
with him at his hotel in London. *Helvete*, it was possible
she had betrayed him just as his mother and Karena had
done, he reminded himself angrily.

He looked into her deep green eyes and the ache in his
chest intensified. 'Who is the real Mina Hart?' he asked
her savagely. 'You acted like you cared about the children, but maybe your kindness this afternoon *was* all an
act? After all, why should you care about them? You have
a talent for making people believe in you, and today you
played the role of compassionate therapist brilliantly. The
journalist who was reporting on your visit is convinced
that you are a modern-day Mother Teresa.'

For a few seconds Mina was too stunned to speak. 'Of
course, I *wasn't* acting. Why shouldn't I care about the
children? Anyone with a shred of humanity would want
to help them deal with their terrible loss.' Her temper

simmered at Aksel's unjust accusation. 'How dare you suggest that I was playing to the press? You're the one who thinks your damn image is so important.'

Tears stung her eyes and she dashed them away impatiently with the back of her hand. 'The person you saw today is the real Mina Hart. But who are you, Aksel? I don't mean the prince—I'm curious about the real flesh-and-blood man. Why do you hide your emotions from everyone? And what the hell happened when you were invited to hold the baby? There was a look on your face—' She broke off when his jaw tensed. 'That little baby was so sweet, but you looked horrified at the prospect of holding him. Don't you want a child one day?' She stared at his rigid face, wondering if she had pushed him too far, but she was desperate to unlock his secrets. 'How do you feel about fatherhood?'

'It is my duty to provide an heir to the throne,' he said stiffly.

'Oh, for heaven's sake!' She did not try to hide her exasperation. 'You can't bring a child into the world simply because you need an heir. I'm curious to know if you would like to have a child.'

He swung away from her as if he could not bear to look at her. *'Damn your accursed curiosity!'* he said angrily.

Mina swallowed. She had glimpsed the tormented expression in his eyes that she had seen at the cabin when she had asked him about the drawing of the baby that had fallen out of his sketch book. 'Aksel...what's wrong?' she said softly. She put her hand on his arm, but he shrugged her off.

Aksel closed his eyes and pictured Finn's angelic face on that fateful morning. How could the loss of his son hurt so much after all this time? he wondered bleakly.

He lifted his lashes and met Mina's startled gaze. 'If you want the truth, I find the idea of having a child unbearable.'

Unbearable! It was a strange word for him to have used. Mina wanted to ask him what he meant, but he strode across the lobby and opened the door.

'The car is here,' he said harshly.

He said nothing more on the journey back to Jonja and his body language warned Mina not to ask him any further questions. It was a relief when they arrived at the palace and she could escape the prickling atmosphere inside the car.

As they walked into the palace Aksel was met by several of his government ministers all requesting his urgent attention. On his way into his office he glanced back over his shoulder at Mina.

'I'm going to be busy for the rest of the afternoon. This evening we will attend a charity dinner, which has been organised by Storvhal's top businesses to raise funds for the families in Revika affected by the tragedy.'

'I don't want to go.' A note of panic crept into Mina's voice. 'I can't spend an evening in the full glare of the public and the press pretending that we are a blissfully happy couple.' She hated knowing that they would be fooling people with their so-called romance.

'Tickets for the event sold out when it was announced that you will be attending with me,' he told her. 'You can't disappoint the guests who have donated a lot of money to the disaster fund to meet you.'

Frustration surged through her. 'That's blatant emotional blackmail...' Her voice trailed away helplessly as he disappeared into his office. Benedict Lindburg, Aksel's personal assistant, noticed Mina's stricken expression.

'It's easy to understand why he's known by his staff as the Ice Prince, isn't it?' he murmured.

'That's the problem—I don't think anyone does understand him.'

The PA looked at her curiously. 'Do *you*?'

'No.' Mina bit her lip. 'But I wish I did,' she said huskily.

Half an hour before they were due to leave for the charity dinner, Mina was a mass of nerves at the prospect of facing the press who Aksel had warned her would be present. Earlier, she had decided to tell him that she would not continue with the pretence that she might be his future princess. But she had changed her mind after she had met his grandmother.

Despite being ninety and in poor health, Princess Eldrun was still a formidable lady. She had studied Mina with surprisingly shrewd eyes, before inviting her to sit down on one of the uncomfortable hard-backed chairs in the princess's suite of rooms at the palace.

'My grandson informs me that you are a therapist helping the bereaved children from the fishing community whose fathers drowned.'

'I hope, through drama therapy, to be able to help the children express their emotions and deal with their grief.'

The princess pursed her lips. 'I believe too much emphasis is put on emotions nowadays. I come from an era when it was frowned upon to speak about personal matters. Unfortunately my son Geir's private life was anything but private and his indiscretions were public knowledge. I was determined that my grandson would not follow in his father's footsteps. I taught Aksel that, for a prince, duty and responsibility are more important than personal feelings.'

'What about love?' Mina asked, picturing Aksel as a little boy growing up with his austere grandmother. 'Isn't that important too?'

Princess Eldrun gave her a haughty stare. 'Falling in love is a luxury that is not usually afforded to the descendants of the Royal House of Thoresen.' She looked over at Aksel, who was standing by the window. 'However, my grandson has informed me that he loves you.'

Mina quickly quashed the little flutter inside her, reminding herself that Aksel was pretending to be in love with her so that his grandmother did not think he was turning into a playboy like his father.

'And are you in love with Aksel?' the elderly dowager asked imperiously.

Mina hesitated. She could not bring herself to lie to the princess, but she realised with a jolt of shock that she did not have to. Like Juliet, she had fallen in love at first sight. She glanced at Aksel and her heart lurched when she found him watching her. His hard features were expressionless, but for a second she glimpsed something in his eyes that she could not define. Telling herself that it must have just been a trick of the light, she smiled at his grandmother.

'Yes, I love him,' she replied, praying that the princess believed her and Aksel did not.

Now, as she prepared to spend the evening pretending that she and Aksel were involved in a royal romance, Mina's heart felt heavy with the knowledge that, for her, it was not a charade. What if he guessed her true feelings and felt sorry for her? The thought was too much for her pride to bear. Tonight she was going to give the performance of a lifetime, she told her reflection. Somehow she must convince the press and the Storvhalian people that she was in love with the prince, and at the same time show Aksel that she understood they were playing a game, and that when she smiled at him it was for the cameras and he meant nothing to her.

A knock on the door made her jump, and her breath left her in a rush when she opened it and met Aksel's ice-blue gaze. His superbly tailored black dinner suit was a perfect foil for his blond hair. He combined effortless elegance with a potent masculinity that evoked an ache of sexual longing in the pit of Mina's stomach. That feeling intensified when he swept his eyes over her, from her hair tied in a chignon, down to the figure-hugging evening gown that a maid had delivered to her room.

'I'm glad the dress fits you,' he said brusquely.

Desperate to break her intense awareness of him, she said brightly, 'It's lucky that I'm the same dress size as your sister. I assume the dress belongs to her?'

Aksel did not enlighten her that he had ordered the jade-coloured silk evening gown from Storvhal's top fashion-design house to match the colour of Mina's eyes. 'I've brought you something to wear with it,' he said instead, taking a slim velvet box from his pocket.

Mina gasped when he opened the lid to reveal an exquisite diamond and emerald necklace.

'People believe that our relationship is serious and will expect you to wear jewels from the royal collection,' he told her when he saw her doubtful expression.

She caught her lower lip with her teeth as she turned around, and a little shiver ran through her when his hands brushed her bare shoulders as he fastened the necklace around her throat. Her eyes met his in the mirror and her panicky feeling returned.

'I'm not sure I can do this—face the press and all the guests at the party.' She fiddled with her hearing aids.

'When I'm in a crowd and lots of people are talking I sometimes feel disorientated.'

'I will be by your side for the whole evening,' Aksel assured her. Mina's vulnerability about her hearing impairment was at odds with the public image she projected of a confident, articulate young woman. Once again he found himself wondering—who was the real Mina Hart? She looked stunning in the low-cut evening gown and he wished they were back at the London hotel and he could forget that he was a prince and spend the evening making love to her.

As ever, duty took precedence over his personal desires, but he could not resist pressing his lips against hers in a hard, unsatisfactorily brief kiss that drew a startled gasp from her and did not go any way towards assuaging the fire in his belly.

'Don't bother,' he told her as she went to reapply a coat of lip gloss to her lips. 'You look convincingly lovestruck for your audience.'

For a second her eyes darkened with hurt, but she shrugged and picked up her purse. 'Let's get on with the performance,' she said coolly, and swept regally out of the door.

The fund-raising dinner was being held at the most exclusive hotel in Jonja. The limousine drew up outside the front entrance and Mina was almost blinded by the glare of flashbulbs as dozens of press photographers surged forwards, all trying to capture pictures of the woman who had captured the heart of the prince.

A large crowd of people had gathered in the street, curious to catch a glimpse of their possible future princess. 'Are you ready?' Aksel frowned as he glanced at her tense face. She took a deep breath, and he noticed that her hand shook slightly as she checked that her hearing aids were in place. Her nervousness surprised him. After all, she was a professional actor and was used to being the focus of attention.

A cheer went up from the crowd when the chauffeur opened the car door and Aksel emerged and turned to offer his hand to Mina as she stepped onto the pavement. For a second she seemed to hesitate, as if she was steeling herself, but then she flashed him a bright smile that somehow failed to reach her eyes.

'Wave,' he murmured as they walked up the steps of the hotel.

Feeling a fraud, Mina lifted her hand and waved, and the crowd gave another loud cheer. 'I can't believe so many people have come out on a freezing night,' she muttered. 'Clearly your subjects are keen for their prince to marry, but it feels wrong to be tricking people into thinking I might be your future bride when we both know that I'll be leaving Storvhal soon and we will never see each other again.'

There was no chance for Aksel to reply as they entered the hotel and were greeted by the head of the fund-raising committee, but during the five-course dinner he could not dismiss Mina's comment. He glanced at her sitting beside him. She was playing the part of his possible future fiancée so well that everyone in the room was convinced she would be Storvhal's new princess. *Helvete*, every time she leaned close to him and gave him a sensual smile that heated his blood he had to remind himself that she was pretending to be in love with him. Her performance was faultless, yet he was becoming increasingly certain that it *was* a performance and the woman on show tonight was not the real Mina Hart.

'Can you explain how drama therapy could help the

children who have been affected by the fishing-fleet disaster?' one of the guests sitting at the table asked Mina.

'When we experience a traumatic event such as a bereavement we can feel overwhelmed by our emotions and try to block them out. But when we watch a film or play, or read a book, we are able to feel strong emotions because we are emotionally distanced from the story.' She leaned forwards, and her voice rang with sincerity. For the first time all evening Aksel sensed that the real Mina was speaking. 'Drama provides a safety net where we can explore strong emotions,' she continued. 'As a drama therapist I hope to use drama in a therapeutic way and help the children of Revika to make sense of the terrible tragedy that has touched their lives.'

A nerve flickered in Aksel's jaw. How could he have doubted her compassion? he wondered. Her determination to try to help the bereaved children shone in her eyes. There was no reason for her to take an interest in a remote fishing village, but it was clear that the plight of the children who had lost their fathers affected her deeply. It was impossible that Mina was faking the emotion he could hear in her voice. It struck him forcibly that she was honest and trustworthy, but his view of all women had been warped by the fact that his mother and Karena had betrayed him. He had believed that Mina had betrayed him and spoken to the press in London, but as he looked at her lovely face he saw that she was beautiful inside, and he knew he had misjudged her.

The rest of the evening was purgatory for Aksel. For a man who had shut off his emotions, the acrid jealousy scalding his insides as he watched Mina expertly work the room and charm the guests was an unwelcome shock. With superhuman effort he forced himself to concentrate on his conversation with a company director who had donated a substantial sum of money to the Revika disaster fund for the privilege of sitting at the prince's table, but Aksel's gaze was drawn to the dance floor where Mina was dancing with Benedict Lindburg.

His personal assistant was simply doing his job, Aksel reminded himself. Benedict understood that protocol demanded the prince must mingle with the guests and make polite conversation, but Mina had looked wistful as she watched some of the guests dancing, and Ben had smoothly stepped in and asked her if she would like to dance.

Aksel frowned as he watched Benedict place his hand on Mina's waist to guide her around the dance floor. In normal circumstances he liked Ben, but right now Aksel was seriously tempted to connect his fist with the younger man's face. The circumstances were anything but normal, he acknowledged grimly. Since he had met Mina his well-ordered life had been spinning out of control.

His mind replayed the scene earlier today when he had taken her to meet his grandmother. He had been fully aware that Mina had not meant it when she had told Princess Eldrun she loved him. But hearing her say the words had evoked a yearning inside him. It was ironic that in his entire life only two women had ever told him they loved him—and they had both been lying. Karena had deliberately fooled him into believing she cared for him, while Mina had gone along with the pretence of the royal romance at his request.

He scanned the dance floor, hoping to catch her eye, but she wasn't looking at him because she was too busy laughing with Ben.

'Excuse me,' Aksel said firmly to the company director before he strode across the dance floor.

'Sir?' Benedict immediately released Mina and stepped back so that Aksel could take his place. The PA could not hide his surprise. 'Sir, the head of the National Bank of Storvhal is waiting to speak to you.'

'Invite him to dinner at the palace next week,' Aksel growled.

He stared into Mina's green eyes and felt a primitive surge of possessiveness as he swept her into his arms. Desire heated his blood when she melted against him. He did not know if her soft smile was real or part of the pretence that they were romantically involved. The lines were blurring and the only thing he was certain of was that he had never ached for any woman the way he ached to make love to Mina.

'Ben,' he called after his PA. 'Send for the car. Miss Hart and I are leaving the party early.'

'But...' Benedict met the prince's hard stare and decided not to protest. 'Right away, sir.'

'Aksel, is something wrong?' Mina's stiletto heels tapped on the marble floor as she followed Aksel into the palace and tried to keep up with his long stride. He did not answer her as he mounted the stairs at a pace that left her breathless. At the top of the staircase he caught hold of her arm and swept her along the corridor, past her bedroom and into the royal bedchamber.

Mina had never been into his suite of rooms before and her eyes were instantly drawn to the enormous four-poster bed covered in ornate gold silk drapes. The royal coat of arms hung above the bed, and all around the walls were portraits of previous princes of Storvhal. From the moment Aksel opened his eyes every morning and looked at his illustrious ancestors he must be reminded that the weight of responsibility for ruling Storvhal sat on his shoulders, she thought wryly.

She was shocked by the fierce glitter in his eyes as he tugged his tie loose and ran his hand through his hair. As far as she could tell the charity dinner had gone well, but Aksel was clearly wound up about something.

'What's the matter?' she said softly.

'I'll tell you what's the matter!' He crossed the room in two strides and halted in front of her. *'You!'* The word exploded from him.

Mina stared at him in confusion. 'What have I done?'

'I don't know.' Aksel seized her shoulders and stared down at her, a nerve jumping in his jaw. 'I don't know what you have done to me,' he said roughly. 'You've bewitched me with your big green eyes and made me feel things that I didn't know I was capable of feeling—things I sure as hell don't want to feel.'

He was on a knife-edge, Mina realised. She did not pretend to understand the violent emotions she sensed were churning inside him, but her tender heart longed to ease his torment and, with no other thought in her mind, she cupped his stubble-rough jaw in her hands and pulled his head down so that she could place her mouth over his.

He groaned and clamped his arms around her, pulling her hard against him so that she felt his powerful erection nudge her thigh.

'Desire was my father's downfall. I vowed that I would never be weak like him and allow my need for a woman to make a fool of me.' He slid his hand down to her bottom and spread his fingers over her silk dress. 'But I need you, Mina.' There was anger in his voice, frustration with himself. 'I want you more than I knew it was possible to want a woman.'

CHAPTER TEN

A SHUDDER RACKED Aksel's body. He could not control his hunger for Mina and it scared him because he had always believed he was stronger than his father.

He needed to make her understand how it was for him. That all he wanted was her body and nothing else—not her beautiful smile, or the tender expression he glimpsed in her eyes sometimes, and not her compassionate heart— he definitely did not want her heart.

'You are not your father, Aksel,' she said gently. 'The people of Storvhal admire and respect you. They think you are a good monarch—as I do. But I want to know the man, not the prince. I want you to make love to me,' she whispered against his mouth, and her husky plea destroyed the last dregs of Aksel's resolve.

Wordlessly he spun her round and ran the zip of her dress down her spine. The strapless silk gown slithered to the floor. She wasn't wearing a bra and Aksel's breath hissed between his teeth as he turned her back to face him and feasted his hungry gaze on her firm breasts and dusky pink nipples that were already puckering in anticipation of his touch.

'You are exquisite,' he said hoarsely. 'At the dinner tonight I was imagining you like this—naked except for the diamonds and emeralds glittering against your

creamy skin. But the truth is you don't need any adorn-
ment, angel. You're beautiful inside and out, and I...'
his voice shook '...I want to hold you in my arms and
make you mine.'

The flames leaping in the hearth were reflected in
his eyes, turning ice to fire. 'Will you give yourself to
me, Mina?'

Her soft smile stole his breath. 'I have always been
yours.' She lifted her hands and unfastened the necklace,
dropping the glittering gems onto the bedside table at the
same time as she stepped out of the silk dress that was
pooled at her feet. 'I don't need diamonds or expensive
gowns. I just need you, Aksel.'

He reached for her then and drew her against him,
threading his fingers into her hair as he claimed her
mouth. His kiss was everything she had hoped for, everything she had dreamed of since the night at the hotel in
London. They had been strangers then, but now her body
recognised his, and anticipation licked through her veins
as he stripped out of his clothes. In the firelight he was
a powerful, golden-skinned Viking, so hugely aroused
that the thought of him driving his swollen shaft inside
her made Mina feel weak with desire.

He laid her on the bed and removed the final fragile barrier of her underwear before he knelt above her
and bent his head to kiss her mouth, her throat and the
slopes of her breasts. The husky sound she made when
he flicked his tongue across her nipples made Aksel's gut
twist with desire and a curious tenderness that he had
never felt before. Satisfying his own needs took second
place to wanting to give her pleasure.

He moved lower down her body, trailing his lips across
her stomach and the soft skin of her inner thighs before he
gently parted her with his fingers and pressed his mouth

to her feminine heart to bestow an intensely intimate caress that drew a gasp of startled delight from Mina.

Aksel was taking her closer and closer to ecstasy, but as Mina twisted her hips beneath the relentless on-slaught of his tongue she wanted to give him the same mind-blowing pleasure he was giving her. She wanted to crack his iron control and show him that making love was about two people giving themselves totally and ut-terly to each other.

He moved over her, but instead of allowing him to pen-etrate her she pushed him onto his back and smiled at his obvious surprise. 'It's my turn to give, and your turn to take,' she told him softly, before she wriggled down the bed, following the fuzz of blond hairs that adorned his stomach and thighs with her mouth.

'Mina…' Aksel tensed when he realised her intention and curled his fingers into her hair to draw her head away from his throbbing arousal. But he was too late, she was already leaning over him, and the feel of her drawing him into the moist cavern of her mouth dragged a harsh groan from his throat. The pleasure was beyond anything he had ever known. He had never allowed any women to caress him with such devastating intimacy, and he had always held part of himself back because he could not bear to be weak like his father. The Prince of Storvhal must never lose control.

But his body did not care that he was a prince who had been schooled since childhood to shoulder his royal responsibilities. His body shook uncontrollably as Mina ran her tongue over the sensitive tip of his erection. He gripped the sheet beneath him and gritted his teeth as he fought against the tide that threatened to overwhelm him.

'Enough, angel,' he muttered, tugging her hair until she lifted her head. His hand shook as he donned a protective sheath. His usual finesse had deserted him and he dragged her beneath him, his shoulder muscles bunching as he held himself above her. He watched her green eyes darken as he pushed her legs wide to receive him, and at the moment he entered her and their two bodies became one she smiled and whispered his name, and Aksel was aware of an ache inside him that even the exquisite pleasure of sexual release could not assuage.

As Aksel drove into her with strong, demanding strokes Mina knew that her body had been made for him. She arched her hips to meet each devastating thrust, until she was teetering on the edge, and her muscles clenched in wave after rapturous wave of pleasure. At the moment she climaxed Aksel gave a husky groan and buried his face in the pillows while shudders wracked his big frame.

His few seconds of vulnerability touched Mina's heart. Her passion was spent and in its sweet aftermath she felt a fierce tenderness as she cupped his face in her hands and gently kissed his mouth.

'I don't believe you are empty inside,' she whispered.

He rolled away from her and stared up at the ornate bed drapes decorated with the royal coat of arms.

'Don't look for things in me that aren't there,' Aksel warned. 'I made love to you selfishly for my own pleasure and to satisfy my needs.'

Mina shook her head. 'That isn't true, although I think you want it to be the truth,' she said intuitively. 'I think something happened that made you lock your emotions inside you.' She hesitated. 'Are you still in love with the woman in Russia who you had hoped to marry?'

'Karena?' He gave a harsh laugh, 'God, no—my youthful infatuation with her ended when I discovered the truth about her. How do you know about Karena, anyway?'

'I don't know much. Ella Holmberg told me you had been in love with a Russian woman but couldn't marry her because the Storvhalian people would not have approved.'

Aksel sat up and raked a hand through his hair. Mina missed the warmth of his body and sensed that he was drawing away from her mentally as well as physically. She was convinced that the key to unlocking him was in his past.

Wrapping the silk sheet around her, she moved across the bed so that she could see his face. She was still wearing her hearing aids, but earlier, concentrating on numerous conversations with guests at the party had been tiring, and she found it easier to read his lips.

'What did you mean when you said you discovered the truth about Karena?' she asked curiously

For a moment she thought he wasn't going to answer, but then he exhaled heavily.

'You cannot underestimate how badly my father damaged the monarchy during his reign. As you know, it wasn't just his many affairs that caused unrest.

'My father married my mother because her family owned a mining company which had discovered huge gold reserves in Storvhal's mountains,' Aksel explained. 'Instead of sharing the discovery with his government ministers, my father made a secret deal, which allowed the Russian company to extract the gold in return for a cut of the profits. He abused his position as ruling monarch and when the Storvhalian people found out that he was stripping the country's assets they were naturally horrified.

'I did not know the full extent of my father's treachery until after his death. My mother had inherited the mining company and she hoped to win my support to continue extracting the gold. I was in a difficult position. My mother was disliked in Storvhal, and by my grandmother, but she was still my mother. I often visited her at her home in Russia, and that's where I met Karena.'

He gave a cynical laugh. 'I was a young man burdened by the responsibilities of being a prince and perhaps it was no surprise that I fell madly in love with the beautiful Russian model my mother introduced me to. It was certainly what my mother had intended,' he said harshly. 'She hoped that if I married Karena it would strengthen my ties with Russia.

'But my grandmother and Harald Petersen were afraid that the Storvhalian people would not accept another Russian princess and tried to dissuade me from marrying Karena. Harald went as far as to have Karena spied on by government agents. I did not approve of his methods,' Aksel said grimly. 'But it soon became clear that Karena had duped me and pretended to be in love with me because my mother had sold her the idea that if I married her she would enjoy a life of wealth and glamour as a princess.'

'You were betrayed by Karena and your mother,' Mina said softly. 'You were hurt by the two women you loved and it's no wonder you shut off your emotions.' Aksel must have yearned for love when he had been a child growing up at the palace with his strict grandmother, she mused. She did not think Princess Eldrun had been unkind, but she had told Mina that she had taught her grandson to put his duties as a prince before his personal feelings.

His hard face showed no emotion and she despaired that she would ever reach the man behind the mask. 'After you had learned the truth about Karena, did you end your relationship with her?'

He nodded. 'I returned to Storvhal and did not expect to see her again.'

Aksel stared into Mina's deep green eyes and wondered what the hell was happening to him. He *never* talked about his past, but it was as if floodgates in his mind had burst open, and he wanted, needed, to let the secrets he had kept hidden for so long spill out of him.

'Eight months after I broke up with Karena I went to see her in Russia.'

Mina looked at him intently. 'Were you still in love with her?'

'No.' Aksel's chest felt as if it were being crushed in a vice. He drew a shuddering breath and dropped his head into his hands. 'Karena had contacted me out of the blue to tell me she had given birth to my child. She told me I had a son.'

'*A son...!*' Mina could hear the shock in her voice. 'You have a child? Where is he?' Her heart hammered against her ribs as she tried to absorb Aksel's startling revelation. 'Does he live with Karena in Russia?'

Aksel lifted his head from his hands, and Mina caught her breath at the expression of raw pain in his eyes. 'Finn is on the mountains, beneath the stars,' he said huskily. 'I took him to the Sami reindeer-herders because they are the most trustworthy people I know. They buried him according to their traditions, and they tend to his grave when I can't get up to the cabin.'

'*His grave...*' Mina swallowed hard. 'Oh, Aksel, I'm so sorry.' Driven by an instinctive need to comfort him, she put her arms around his broad shoulders and hugged him fiercely. A memory flashed into her mind. 'The sketch of the baby at the cabin, that was a picture of Finn, wasn't it?' she said softly. 'What happened to him?'

'There is no medical explanation of why Finn died.

He was a victim of sudden infant death syndrome—
sometimes known as cot death.' Aksel took a deep breath
and inhaled Mina's delicate perfume. There was something touchingly protective about the way she had her
arms wrapped around him and it was not difficult to tell
her the secrets he had never told anyone else.

'I'll start at the beginning,' he said gruffly. 'When
I broke up with Karena I discovered that she had been
cheating on me with a Russian businessman. She assumed the baby she was carrying was his, but when the
child was born her boyfriend insisted on a DNA test,
which proved he wasn't the father. Karena knew the only
other person it could be was me, and another DNA test
showed that the baby was mine.

'But even without the test I would have recognised
that Finn was my son.' Aksel's face softened. 'He was
so beautiful, Mina. I'd never seen such a tiny human
being. He was perfect, and when I held him in my arms
I promised him I would be the best father that any little
boy could have.'

Tears clogged Mina's throat at the thought of Aksel,
whose own father had more or less abandoned him when
he had been a child, promising to be a good father to his
baby son. 'You loved Finn?' she said gently.

'More than I have ever loved anyone.' Aksel's voice
cracked with emotion. 'I asked Karena to marry me. She
was the mother of my child,' he said when Mina looked
shocked. 'I knew the marriage might not be popular in
Storvhal, but Finn was my son. More importantly, I hoped
we could put aside our differences for the sake of our son
and give him a happy childhood. Karena agreed because
she liked the idea of being a princess, but she wasn't interested in Finn. She had kept her pregnancy a secret in
case it harmed her modelling career, and once the baby

was born she went to nightclubs and parties every night.'
Aksel's expression hardened. 'One night she wanted to go
out as usual and was annoyed because it was the nanny's
night off. I was leading a double life, spending the week
in Storvhal carrying out my royal duties and returning
to Russia to see Finn at weekends. I was tired that night,
but I was still happy to look after my son. But he was
restless and cried constantly. In desperation I moved his
crib into my bedroom and when he finally settled I must
have fallen into a deep sleep.

'The next morning I was surprised that Finn hadn't
woken for his next feed and I checked the crib.' Aksel's
throat felt as if it had been scraped with sandpaper. 'At
first I thought he was asleep. But he was paler than normal, and when I touched his cheek it was cold.' His throat
moved convulsively. 'That was when I realised that I had
lost my precious boy.'

Mina blinked back her tears. She had heard pain in
Aksel's voice but his face revealed no emotion. 'Have
you ever cried for Finn?' she whispered.

His expression did not change. 'Princes don't cry.'

'Did your grandmother teach you that?'

He shrugged. 'I blame myself for Finn's death,' he
said harshly.

'*Why?* You've told me that there is often no medical
explanation for sudden infant death syndrome.'

'If I hadn't been tired and slept so deeply I might have
realised something was wrong and been able to save him.'

Mina held him tighter and rocked him as if she were
comforting a child. 'I don't believe there was anything
you could have done. Finn's death was a terrible tragedy. But because you feel guilty I bet you haven't talked
about what happened, not even to your close friends or
your grandmother.'

'No one apart from Karena, my chief advisor and the Sami herders knows about Finn. You are the only person I've told.'

'You mean…?' She broke off and stared at him. 'Don't the people of Storvhal know that you had a son?'

'Harald Petersen thought if news got out that I had fathered an illegitimate child it would prove to the Storvhalian people that I was an immoral and degenerate prince like my father. There had already been one civil uprising in the country, and to maintain peace and order I agreed with Harald to keep Finn's brief life a secret. It suited Karena because she went back to her Russian oligarch who didn't want to be reminded that she'd had a child with another man.'

Mina cupped his face in her hands and looked into his eyes. 'Oh, Aksel, don't you see? You feel empty inside because you have never been able to grieve openly for Finn. You've carried the secret that you had a son who died, and it's not surprising you blocked out your emotions that were too painful to cope with.' She hesitated. 'I want to help you to deal with the painful experiences in your past. There are various kinds of psychotherapy—'

'I don't need therapy,' he interrupted her. 'I realise you mean well, Mina, but no amount of talking about the past can change what happened or bring my son back.'

'No, but it might help you in the future to love again like you loved Finn.'

'I don't want to love. I managed for most of my life without it.' He moved suddenly, taking her by surprise as he pushed her flat on her back and rolled on top of her so that his muscular body pressed her into the mattress.

'It's a fallacy that sex can only be good if emotions are involved. I can't pretend to feel emotions that don't exist for me, but I can give you pleasure when I make love to you.'

He lowered his head and captured her mouth in a hungry kiss that rekindled the fire in Mina's belly.

'This is what I want from you, angel,' Aksel said roughly. 'Your beautiful body and your sweet sensuality, that makes my gut ache.'

Mina's breathing quickened as he ripped the sheet away from her and, after sheathing himself, ran his hand possessively down her body to push her thighs apart. His erection pressed against her moist opening and her muscles quivered as he eased forwards until he was inside her.

She wondered how he would react if she told him she loved him. With horror, probably, she thought sadly. Aksel did not trust emotions and believed he was better off without love, which meant that her feelings for him must remain a secret.

Mina was not surprised when she woke up and found herself alone in Aksel's bed, but her heart sank when she turned her head and saw he had gone. She had hoped that the night of the charity dinner the week before, when the prince had so uncharacteristically opened up to her, would be the start of a new chapter in their relationship. She had hoped that Aksel was beginning to let her into his heart, but he had got up before she had opened her eyes every morning of the past week. She sighed as she looked at the empty space on the pillow beside her.

When they made love every night it was more than just good sex. Much more. He was a demanding and passionate lover, but he was tender and gentle too, and made love to her with such exquisite care that her eyes would fill with tears and he would kiss them from her cheeks and hold her so close to his heart that she felt its erratic beat thudding through his big chest. The Viking prince had a softer side to him, but in the morning she sensed that he regretted what he regarded as his weakness and resented her for undermining his iron self-control.

The situation could not continue, she acknowledged. Every day she remained in Storvhal she became more deeply immersed in the pretence that she was romantically involved with Aksel, furthering the media speculation that a royal betrothal was imminent. The press interest was so frenzied that she'd had to stop going to the village of Revika to visit the children affected by the fishing-fleet disaster, and instead the families came to the palace so that she could continue the drama therapy sessions.

The drama sessions with the children had cemented her decision to retire from acting and become a full-time drama therapist. She hoped it would even be possible for her to work with the children of Revika again after she had finished performing in *Romeo and Juliet* in New York. But first she would have to break the news to her father of her decision to leave his theatre company.

Mina sighed. Joshua was immensely proud of the Hart acting dynasty and he had been disappointed when his older daughter Darcey had turned her back on a promising stage career to train as a speech therapist. Darcey handled their temperamental, perfectionist father better than she did, Mina acknowledged. Looking back at her childhood, she realised that she had always tried to win Joshua's approval because after she had lost her hearing she'd been afraid he would love her less than her brother and sisters. She had spent her life trying to please him, and, if she was honest with herself, she dreaded Joshua being disappointed with her when she told him she was going to leave acting.

It was amazing how parents could influence their children even when they were adults, she mused. Aksel believed he must repair the damage his father had caused to the monarchy of Storvhal, and in his efforts to prove that he was not a playboy like Prince Geir he carried the tragic secret that he had fathered a son who had died as a baby. He had been unable to mourn for Finn and his grief was frozen inside him. Mina had hoped that, having confided in her once, Aksel would feel that he could talk to her about the past, but he had never mentioned his son again and any attempts she made to bring up the subject were met with an icy rebuttal.

The sound of the coffee percolator from the next room told her that Aksel must still be in the royal suite. Usually he ate breakfast early and had already left for a meeting with his government ministers by the time she got up. Hoping to catch him before he left, Mina jumped out of bed and did not bother to pull on her robe before she opened the door between the bedroom and adjoining sitting room.

He was seated at the table, a coffee cup in one hand and a newspaper in the other. He was suave and sophisticated in his impeccably tailored suit, and with his hair swept back from his brow to reveal his chiselled features he looked remote and unapproachable—very different from the sexy Viking who had made love to her with such breathtaking dedication last night, Mina thought ruefully.

She suddenly realised that Aksel was not alone and his chief advisor was in the room. To her astonishment Harald Petersen dropped onto one knee when he saw her and said in a distinctly shaken voice, 'Madam.'

As the elderly advisor stood up and walked out of the suite she glanced at Aksel for an explanation. 'What was all that about?' Her eyes widened when she saw that the front page of the newspaper had three photographs of her wearing different wedding dresses. Closer scrutiny revealed that a photo of her head had been superimposed on the pictures of the dresses, and the accompanying article discussed what style of wedding dress the Prince of Storvhal's bride might wear if there was a royal wedding.

Mina dropped the newspaper onto the table. 'Aksel, this has got to stop,' she said firmly. 'The press are convinced that we are going to get married, and we must end the pretence of our romance. It isn't fair to mislead the Storvhalian people or your grandmother any longer.'

'I agree.' He stood up and walked over to the window to watch the snow that was drifting down silently from a steel-grey sky.

'Well...good.' Mina had not expected him to agree so readily. Perhaps he had grown tired of her and was looking for an excuse for her to leave Storvhal, she thought bleakly. Her stomach hollowed with the thought that there really was no reason for her to stay. She was staring heartbreak in the face and she was scared that all the acting skills in the world would not be enough to get her through saying goodbye to Aksel without making a complete fool of herself.

'It's time to end the pretence,' Aksel murmured as if he was speaking to himself. He swung round to face her, and his mouth twisted in a strange expression as he ran his eyes over her auburn hair tumbling around her bare shoulders and the skimpy slip of peach satin that purported to be a nightgown.

Desire ripped through him, and for a few crazy seconds he almost gave in to the temptation to carry Mina back to bed and make love to her as he longed to do every morning when he woke and watched her sleeping beside him. All week he had managed to resist, reminding himself that it was his duty to be available to his ministers during working hours. He would not be held to ransom by his desire for Mina, Aksel vowed. He would not allow his weakness for a woman to deter him from his responsibilities as monarch as his father had done.

'The reason Harald knelt before you is because, by tradition, only the wife or intended bride of the prince can sleep in the royal bedchamber,' he told her.

Mina paled as his words sank in. 'We can't allow your chief minister to think I am going to be your bride. I have to leave Storvhal.' She could not hide the tremor in her voice. 'I've received a message from my father to say that *Romeo and Juliet* will open on Broadway a week early, and rehearsals are to begin in New York next week. It's the ideal opportunity to make a statement to the press that the pressure of my career has led to us deciding to end our romance.'

Aksel's brooding silence played with Mina's nerves. 'There is an alternative,' he said at last.

She shrugged helplessly. 'I can't see one.'

'We could make the story of our royal romance real—and get married.'

She fiddled with her hearing aids, convinced she had misheard him. 'Did you say…?'

He walked towards her, his face revealing no expression, while Mina was sure he must notice the pulse of tension beating on her temple.

'Will you marry me, Mina?'

Her surge of joy was swiftly extinguished by a dousing of reality. Aksel hadn't smiled, and surely a man hoping to persuade a woman to marry him would smile?

'Why?' she asked cautiously.

He shrugged. 'There are a number of reasons why I believe we could have a successful marriage. It is evident from the press reports that you are popular with Storvhalian people. They admire your work with the children in Revika. I also think you would like to continue to help the children,' he said intuitively. 'You could combine being a princess with a career as a drama therapist, and I believe you could be happy living in Storvhal.' He glanced away, almost as if he wanted to avoid making eye contact with her. 'It is also true that I have shared things with you about myself that I have not told anyone else,' he said curtly.

He meant his baby son. Mina's heart clenched and she reached up and touched his cheek to turn his face towards her. 'I swear I will never tell anyone about Finn…but I truly believe you should tell the Storvhalian people about him. I don't think they would judge you or compare you in any way to your father. You are a good prince, and everyone knows it. You need to be able to grieve properly for your son and lay the past to rest, and only then can your life move forwards.'

Something flared in his eyes, and Mina held her breath, willing his icy control to melt. But then his lashes swept down and his expression was guarded when he looked at her again.

'You haven't given me an answer.'

'My answer is no,' she said gently, ignoring the voice inside her head that was clamouring to accept his offer. He had said he believed they could have a successful marriage and perhaps that meant he was willing to build on their relationship, but it wasn't enough for her. 'You listed several reasons why we should get married, but you didn't mention the *only* reason why I would agree to be your wife.'

He watched her broodingly but made no attempt to close the physical space between them. Mina told herself she was relieved, knowing that if he pulled her into his arms and kissed her she would find it impossible to resist him. But perversely, part of her wished he would take advantage of the sexual chemistry they both felt. When he made love to her she could pretend that he cared for her. But there must be no more pretence, she told herself firmly.

'Is it so important that you hear me say I love you?' he demanded tautly. 'Would your answer be different if I uttered three meaningless words?'

His cynicism killed the last of Mina's hope. With a flash of insight she realised that if she married him she would for ever be trying to please him and earn his love, as she had done with her father throughout her childhood. She remembered how desperately she had sought Joshua's praise, and how a careless criticism from him had crushed her spirit. She deserved better than to spend her life scrutinising every word and action of Aksel's in the vain hope that he might one day reveal he had fallen in love with her.

'I would only want you to say those words if they *weren't* meaningless,' she told him honestly. She walked towards the bedroom. Her heart felt as if it were being ripped from her chest but her pride refused to let her break down in front of him. 'If you'll excuse me, I need to pack and phone the airport to book a flight home.'

CHAPTER ELEVEN

BENEDICT LINDBURG ENTERED the prince's office and found Aksel standing by the fireplace, staring at the flames leaping in the hearth. 'I've arranged the press conference as you requested, sir.'

'Thank you, Ben.' Aksel's stern features lightened briefly with a ghost of a smile. 'I'll be with you in a moment.'

The PA departed, leaving the prince alone with his chief advisor. 'You mean to go ahead and make a statement, then?' Harald said tensely. 'For the good of the country and the monarchy I urge you to reconsider, sir.'

Aksel shook his head. The people of Storvhal have the right to know the truth, and my son deserves to have his short life made public. Mina's words flashed into his mind. *You need to be able to grieve properly for your son.*

'I intend to commission a memorial for Finn, which will be placed in the palace gardens.' So often he had imagined his son running across the lawn in summertime and playing hide-and-seek in the arboretum. The gardens were open to the public, and he wanted visitors to pause for a moment and think of a baby boy whose time on earth had been cut tragically short.

The conference room was packed with journalists who were clearly curious to learn why they had been called to the palace. Aksel strode onto the dais, and as he looked around at the sea of faces and camera lenses he had never felt so alone in his life. His throat ached with the effort of holding back his emotions as he prepared to tell the world about Finn. He opened his mouth to speak, but no words emerged.

Dear God! He lifted his gaze to a ceremonial sword belonging to one of his ancestors, which was hanging on the wall. The ornate handle was decorated with precious jewels including a stunning green emerald that glittered more brightly than the other gems. Aksel thought of Mina's dark green eyes and a sense of calm came over him. She'd been right when she had said he could not look to the future until he had dealt with his past. Until he'd met her, he had not cared what the future held, but now he no longer wanted to be trapped in the darkness.

He took a deep breath and looked around at the journalists. 'Eight years ago, I had a son, but he died when he was six weeks and four days old. His name was Finn... and I loved him.'

Yellow taxis were bumper to bumper all the way along Forty-Second Street, and car horns blared as Mina darted through the traffic. She stumbled onto the pavement and collided with a mountain of a man who put his arms out to catch her.

'After watching you cross the road with complete disregard for your safety, I think I'd better warn your understudy that there is a very good chance she will be playing the role of Juliet when the play opens tomorrow night.'

Mina looked up at her father. 'I've got things on my mind, and I wasn't concentrating,' she admitted.

'I've noticed,' Joshua said drily. 'You've seemed distracted during rehearsals. But I suppose it's to be expected that you're nervous about making your debut on Broadway.'

Of course her father would assume that the only thing she could be thinking about was the play, Mina thought as she followed Joshua into the theatre. He strode into his office without giving her another glance and she sensed that he had already forgotten about her. His criticism hurt, especially as she had tried hard during rehearsals to hide her misery. It seemed that she could never please her father, she thought bitterly. He hadn't commented when she had told him she was giving up acting to pursue a career as a drama therapist, but she sensed he was disappointed with her.

Joshua looked surprised when she followed him into his office. 'As a matter of fact, I'm not worried about the first night,' she told him. Her frustration bubbled over. 'Can't you see I'm upset?' Heartbroken was nearer to the truth, she acknowledged bleakly. 'You must have seen the media reports that my relationship with Prince Aksel is over.' She bit her lip. 'I understand how important the theatre is to you, but sometimes, Dad, I wonder if you care about me at all.'

Joshua's bushy eyebrows knitted together. 'Of course I care about you,' he said gruffly.

'Do you?' Mina hugged her arms around her body. She could tell her father was shocked by her outburst, but this conversation was long overdue. 'Ever since I lost my hearing I've felt that you pushed me away,' she said huskily. 'It seems like nothing I do is good enough for you.' She swallowed. 'When I became deaf, I was scared that you didn't love me as much as Darcey and Vicky and Tom. You are proud of your other children, but you've never once told me that you are proud of me.'

Joshua did not respond. Mina was sure he would insist

that he had not treated her differently from her brother and sisters, but to her shock he sank down onto a chair and sighed heavily. 'I didn't mean to make you feel that I loved you less than the others, but I…well, the truth is…' For a moment Joshua Hart, the great Shakespearean actor, struggled to speak. 'I have always felt guilty that you lost your hearing, and I thought you must blame me.'

'Why would I blame you?' she asked, stunned by her father's confession. 'It wasn't your fault that I had meningitis.'

'Don't you remember I was looking after you the night you became ill because your mother was performing in a play?' Joshua said. 'You were running a slight temperature, and I gave you some medication and intended to check on you later, but I became immersed in learning my lines. By the time your mother came home and checked on you, she realised that you were seriously ill and called an ambulance.

'If it wasn't for your mother's quick actions, you could have died,' he said thickly. 'If I had called a doctor sooner, you might not have lost your hearing. I watched you struggle to cope with your deafness and I felt eaten up with guilt and sadness that I had let you down. The specialist said that we should treat you the same as we had when you could hear and not make an issue out of your hearing impairment, but when you cried because you had been teased by the other children at school it broke my heart. I think I distanced myself from you so that you did not have to cope with my emotions on top of everything else, but I didn't realise that you thought I loved you less than your siblings.'

Mina brushed a tear from her cheek. She was astounded by her father's revelation. 'I never blamed you, Dad. I was just unlucky to fall ill, and I don't suppose the outcome would have been any different if you had called a doctor earlier. Meningitis is a horrible illness that can develop very quickly. I had no idea that you felt guilty. I thought you didn't love me because I am deaf.'

'I'm sorry I didn't show how incredibly proud I am of you,' Joshua said deeply. 'You are a brilliant actress, and I know you will be a wonderful drama therapist.' He stood up and opened his arms, and Mina flew across the room and hugged him.

'Oh, Dad, I wish I had told you how I felt years ago.' She had been afraid that her father would admit he did not love her, Mina realised. Her fear of rejection and her father's feeling of guilt had created a tension between them, but she hoped that from now on they would be more open with each other.

'What happened between you and your prince?' Joshua asked. 'He has been in the news again today. Haven't you seen the headlines?' He picked up the newspaper from his desk and handed it to Mina.

Her heart missed a beat as she stared at the picture of Aksel on the front page. He looked as handsome and remote as he had done the last time she had seen him, when she had turned down his marriage proposal and he had walked out of the royal suite without saying another word.

Benedict had accompanied her to the airport. The usually chatty PA had been strangely subdued and had called to her as she was about to walk through to the departure lounge. 'I was hoping that you might be able to understand him,' he said accusingly.

Mina had struggled to speak through her tears. 'Look after him, Ben,' she'd choked, and hurried off before she changed her mind and asked him to drive her back to the palace.

The newspaper headline proclaimed: *'Prince Faces Further Heartbreak!'*

Mina quickly read the paragraphs beneath Aksel's photo.

> *Prince Aksel of Storvhal has made the shocking revelation that he fathered a child eight years ago. Tragically his son died when he was six weeks old. The announcement has caused a storm of public interest in Storvhal and comes a few days after the announcement that his relationship with English actress Mina Hart has ended.*
>
> *The Prince issued a statement saying he was deeply saddened by the break-up and took full responsibility for Miss Hart's decision not to marry him. He went on to say he would always regret that he could not be the man Miss Hart deserved.*

'Why did you decide not to marry him?' Joshua Hart said gently. 'Don't you love him?'

'I love Aksel with all my heart, and that's why I turned him down.' Her voice shook. 'He doesn't love me, you see.'

Her father studied the newspaper article. 'Are you sure he doesn't? It seems to me that he has laid his heart on the line. Why would Aksel think that he can't be the man you deserve?'

'I didn't know he felt like that,' Mina whispered. She looked at the photograph of Aksel being mobbed by journalists who were no doubt demanding to know more about the child he had fathered. His hard-boned face showed no emotion, but there was a bleak expression in his eyes that tore on Mina's heart. He must find talking about his son desperately painful, especially as he was facing the press alone.

He had been alone all his life, she thought sadly. Brought up by his grandmother who had taught him to put duty before personal happiness, he had been rejected by both his parents and Karena, the woman he had fallen in love with soon after he had been thrust into the role of Prince of Storvhal and a life of responsibility.

It was little wonder that Aksel found it hard to open up and talk about his feelings. Perhaps he did not love her, but she hadn't stayed in Storvhal and asked him outright how he felt about her because she had been afraid that he might reject her, just as she had been afraid to confront her father and risk Joshua's rejection.

Swallowing the tears that threatened to choke her, she turned to her father. 'I've been such a coward. I have to go to Storvhal right away.' She looked at Joshua uncertainly. 'But what about the opening night of the play?'

He squeezed her arm. 'I'd better go and tell your understudy to prepare for the biggest role of her life,' he murmured.

The tall white turrets of the royal palace were barely visible through the snow storm. Winter was tightening its grip on Storvhal and by early afternoon the daylight was already fading, yet Mina found the dramatic landscape of snow and ice strangely beautiful. The car drove past a park, and the sight of children building a snowman was a poignant reminder that even as a young prince Aksel had not been free to enjoy simple childhood pleasures and he had never played in the snow or built a snowman.

Benedict Lindburg met her in the palace entrance hall. 'The prince is in his office. I didn't tell him you were coming,' he told Mina.

Taking a deep breath, she opened the office door. Aksel was sitting behind his desk and had a pile of paperwork in front of him. The light from the lamp highlighted his sharp cheekbones and the hard planes of his face. He looked thinner, she noted, and her heart ached for him.

He frowned as he glanced across the room to see who had walked in without knocking. When he saw Mina his shoulders tensed and his expression became shuttered.

'Mina! I assumed you were in New York preparing for the opening performance of *Romeo and Juliet* this evening.' Although his tone was coolly detached his ice-blue eyes watched her guardedly. He picked up a pencil from the desk and unconsciously twirled it between his finger and thumb. 'Why are you here?'

As she walked towards his desk she hoped he could not tell that her heart was banging against her ribs. But then she reminded herself that she was through with being a coward and hiding how she felt.

'My father has released me from my contract with his theatre company and I've handed the role of Juliet over to another actress.'

Aksel looked shocked. 'Why would you turn down the chance to star on Broadway? Surely it's the opportunity of a lifetime that every actor aspires to?'

'I have different aspirations,' she said steadily. 'I hope to make a career as a drama therapist, but more importantly, I've changed my mind about marrying you—and if your offer is still open I would like to be your wife.'

The pencil between his fingers snapped in half and the lead tip flew across the desk.

'Why the change of heart?' he demanded. 'I thought you needed to hear a declaration of my feelings before you would accept my proposal.' Aksel's jaw tensed. 'I have to warn you that my feelings haven't changed.'

For a second her courage nearly deserted her, but for some reason she remembered the snowman in the park and her resolve strengthened.

'Nor have mine,' she said huskily. 'I fell in love with you the moment we met.'

'Mina, don't!' He jerked to his feet and strode around the desk. 'I don't want you to say things like that.' He raked his hair back from his brow and she noticed that his hand shook. The tiny indication that he felt vulnerable moved Mina unbearably.

'That's too bad, because I refuse to keep quiet about my feelings for you any longer.' She lifted her hand to his jaw and felt the familiar abrasion of blond stubble against her palm. 'I love you, Aksel. I know you can't say the words, and maybe you never will, but I don't believe you are empty inside. You were hurt, and you're still hurting now, especially since you have spoken publicly about your son.

'I can't imagine how painful it must have been for you to lose Finn,' she said gently. 'I hope that being able to talk about him will help to heal the pain in your heart, and I want to be beside you, to support you and to love you with all my heart.'

For a moment he gave no reaction. His skin was drawn so tightly across his cheekbones that his face looked like a mask, but as she stared at the rigid line of his jaw Mina suddenly realised that he was far from calm and in control of his emotions. His eyes glittered fiercely, and she froze as she watched a tear cling to his lashes and slide down his cheek. 'Aksel—don't,' she whispered, shaken by the raw pain she saw in his eyes.

'Oh, God!—Mina.' His arms closed around her and

held her so tightly that the air was forced from her lungs. 'I love you so much it terrifies me.'

His voice was ragged and she could hardly hear him, but she watched his lips move and her heart felt as though it were about to explode.

'I couldn't bear to lose you. It would be like losing Finn all over again,' he said hoarsely. 'I convinced myself that I would be better off not to love you. I thought that if I denied how I felt about you the feelings would go away.' He rubbed his cheek against hers, and Mina felt a trickle of moisture on his skin.

'I didn't want to love you,' he whispered. 'But when you left I felt like someone had cut my heart out, and I had to face the truth—that I will love you until I die, and without you my life is empty and meaningless.'

He drew back a fraction and looked down at her. 'I planned to wait until *Romeo and Juliet* had finished its run on Broadway, and then come and find you and try to persuade you to give me another chance.' He brushed away the tears on her cheeks with his thumb pads. 'Does the thought of me loving you make you cry, angel?'

'Yes, because I know how hard it is for you to speak about your feelings,' she said softly. 'You were taught to put your duties as a prince before your personal happiness.'

'The night in London and the time we spent together when you came to Storvhal were the happiest times of my life. I have never met anyone as caring and compassionate as you, but I told myself I could not trust you because it made it easier to deny my feelings for you.' Aksel's throat moved convulsively. 'You were right when you guessed that I had buried my grief about Finn, but you gave me the guts to face up to the past and tell the Storvhalian people about my son as I should have done years ago.'

He dropped his arms from her and walked around his desk to take something out of a drawer. Mina caught her breath when he came back and opened the small box in his hand. The solitaire diamond ring glistened like a tear drop, like the bright stars that watched over the mountain where his baby son rested.

'Will you marry me, my love, and be my princess? Will you walk with me all the days of our lives and lie with me all the nights, so that I can love you and cherish you with all my heart for ever?'

She gave an inarticulate cry and flung her arms around his neck. 'Yes—oh, yes—on one condition.'

Aksel searched her face and felt that he could drown in her deep green eyes. 'What condition, angel?'

'That, as soon as our children are old enough, we will teach them to build a snowman.'

He understood, and he smiled as he slid the diamond onto her finger. 'We'll also tell them how much we love them every day. Out of curiosity, how many children were you thinking we should have?'

'Four or five—I'd like a big family.'

'In that case—' he swept her into his arms and carried her out of his office, heading purposefully towards the stairs that led to the royal bedchamber '—we'd better start practising making all those babies.'

Aksel glanced over the bannister at his PA, who was hovering in the hall. 'Ben, I'd like you to draft an announcement of the imminent marriage of the Prince of Storvhal to Miss Mina Hart, who is the love of his life.'

Benedict Lindburg bowed and surreptitiously punched the air. 'I'll do it immediately, sir.'

On Christmas Eve the bells of Jonja's cathedral rang out in joyful celebration of the marriage of the Prince of

Storvhal and his beautiful bride. Despite the freezing temperature, a vast crowd lined the streets to watch the candle-lit procession of the prince and princess as they travelled by horse-drawn carriage to the palace where they hosted a feast for five hundred guests, before they left by helicopter for a secret honeymoon destination.

Mina wore her white velvet wedding dress for the short flight to the cabin in the mountains. She carried a bouquet of white roses and dark green ivy, and wore a wreath of white rosebuds in her hair.

'Have I told you how beautiful you look, my princess?' Aksel murmured as he lifted her into his arms and carried her into the cabin. 'You took my breath away when you stood beside me at the altar and we made our vows.'

'To love and to cherish, till death do us part,' Mina said softly. 'I meant the words with all my heart, and I will love you for ever.'

Aksel kissed her tenderly, but as always their passion quickly built and he strode into the bedroom and laid her on the bed. 'You could have chosen to spend our honeymoon at a luxury hotel anywhere in the world,' he said as he stripped out of his suit and began to unlace the front of Mina's dress. 'Why did you want to come here to this remote place?'

'It's the one place where we can be completely alone.' Mina caught her breath as he tugged the bodice of her wedding gown down and knelt over her to anoint her dusky pink nipples with his lips.

He smiled. 'Just the two of us—what could be more perfect?'

'Well…' She took his hand and placed it on her stomach. 'Actually—there's three of us.'

She held her breath as emotion blazed in his eyes, sadness for the child he had lost that turned to fierce joy as the meaning of her words sank in.

'Oh, my love.' Aksel's voice cracked as he bent his head and kissed her still-flat stomach where his child lay. 'As I said—what could be more perfect?'

* * * * *